CW01337121

The Book of
Lost Enchantments

Editors: Rosie McCaffrey, Jennifer Bottum, Ty Powers
Proofreader: Katherine Waghorn
Formatter: Susan Veach
Cover Design: Rena Violet
Page Art: Irina Beliakova, Jessica Dodge & Francesca Scillia

Published by Wizard Supply Co VT
Newbury, Vermont USA
ISBN:
Paperback: 978-1-965409-00-8
Hardcover: 978-1-965409-01-5
Ebook : 978-1-965409-02-2
The Book of Lost Enchantments Copyright © 2024 by Jessica Dodge
All Rights Reserved

For permissions, inquiries, or bulk purchase information, please
contact:
Theforgottenwitch@gmail.com

This book is a work of fiction. All the names, characters, businesses, events, and incidents in this book are either the product of the author's imagination or used in a fictitious manner. Any resemblance to actual persons, living or dead, or actual events is purely coincidental and a work of the author's imagination.

Dear Magical Reader,

As we reach the end of the Triquetra Chronicles, I want to thank you from the bottom of my heart for joining me on this journey. Writing Freya's, Artemas's, and Mary's stories has been a labor of love, and your support has meant the world to me.

The books in this series—*The Forgotten Witch, Misplaced Magic*, and *The Book of Lost Enchantments*—can be read in any order. Now that the series is complete, you might find new connections and hidden gems with each re-read. While these stories stand alone, they weave together the tales of three interconnected families, enriching the experience whether you read them solo or as a series.

Thank you for embracing these characters and their worlds. Your readership and enthusiasm have brought them to life in ways I could only dream of.

Warmest wishes,

Jessica Dodge

TABLE OF CONTENTS

Chapter One

SNOWFLAKES AND CINNAMON ROLLS

In the quiet moments before Nora Cameron's life took an irreversible turn, destiny stepped out of the shadows, and fate held its breath.

As the clock struck six in the evening, the sun had long ago dipped below the horizon, hidden behind the silhouette of the mountains—a familiar sight during early December in Vermont. Outside the bakery window, the snow fell gently, illuminated by the warm glow of the outdoor light above the bakery's entrance.

Nora was putting the last batch of cinnamon rolls in the refrigerator for tomorrow morning when her phone buzzed, alerting her that it was time to close up shop and head home. She tucked her phone back into her pocket and threw the dirty linens into a basket near the back door below a large framed photograph. Her mother and father stared back at her with big grand smiles, holding a gigantic wooden spoon with the words Belwether Bakery engraved into the wood. The spoon had been a gift from the chamber of commerce for being the oldest business in town.

Belwether Bakery had been in her mother's family for four generations, and her parents planned to pass it on to Nora when they retired next year. It had weighed heavily on her thoughts for months now. Even though Nora loved baking, it wasn't her passion like it was her mother's. She didn't want to take over the bakery; she wanted to follow her own dream, but she was unsure of just what that was. She thought that maybe going back for a master's program in the fall would help her figure it out. However, if Nora didn't take over the bakery, it would mean no retirement for her parents and, even worse, the eventual closure of a place that had been in her family for generations—her concerns had kept her in limbo for many years. She didn't want to upset the balance, but she knew that she would never be happy if she stayed for the wrong reasons.

Moments like these made her wish she wasn't an only child so the burden wouldn't rest solely on her shoulders. Her guilt was why she had been avoiding the conversation with her parents for such a long time now. She knew she couldn't continue stalling if she wanted to start college in the fall, so she needed to have the talk with them sooner rather than later.

She looked up at the old cuckoo clock, which looked like a little gingerbread house. Its jittery hands, shaped like dabs of white icing, read 6:41. Time to head home. She quickly wiped down the counters and checked to make sure all the ovens were off, then flipped off the old tin lights as she grabbed her jacket and headed out the back door of the small bakery.

Her Volvo station wagon was parked under one of only three streetlamps in town, and the light cascaded down onto it, illuminating the snow that was now steadily falling. The car was covered in a four-inch blanket of fluffy snow, and she used the sleeve of her jacket to brush it off, just enough to open the door. Popping her head into the car, she started it, then grabbed for her snow brush. However, it wasn't in the backseat of the car where she always kept it.

"Crap," she muttered under her breath. She must have left it in her parents' car yesterday after she had cleaned it off for them. Resigning herself to the fact that she would be dusting off the entire car with her arm, she stretched her jacket sleeve over her hand and began the frigid job.

She had almost completed it when her phone rang in her pocket. She stopped, dusting the snow from her sleeves, and pulled her phone out. She looked down to see Eve's name flash across the screen. Eve had been her closest friend since they were five years old, their bond unbreakable through the years. Nora figured that Eve was likely calling to catch up and arrange a dinner or lunch date, knowing they were overdue for some quality time together. And, of course, Nora suspected Eve was eager to share details about the new guy she had started dating a few weeks back.

"Hey, what's up?" Nora said in a tired voice.

"You sound beat. You okay?" Eve asked.

"Yeah, just a long day, and I am out cleaning off the car. I think I might be frozen to my core now. Winter came on quick this year," she said as she got into the car and warmed her hands in front of the heaters.

"You're telling me. I got two crash claims just this morning."

Eve worked for the local insurance company, and winter was always a busy time for them with car accidents and house fires.

"Hey, I was hoping we could get together tomorrow for lunch. Think you can break away for an hour?" Eve asked.

"Sure, as long as we can do it around one. I can't leave during the lunch rush; Mom would kill me," Nora told her as she watched the windshield wipers glide back and forth across the window, sliding the newly fallen snow as they went.

"Of course. I'll see you tomorrow, Rae's at one. Wait until I tell you about what Ryan and I did last weekend," Eve said with a giddy little laugh before hanging up.

Nora smiled as she tossed her phone onto the seat next to her. *I might consider myself psychic if it weren't for Eve's predictability,* she thought. She sat there for a moment, watching the snow fall, attempting to thaw her fingers that had turned into popsicles in the chilly air. She pulled out of the small parking lot and headed north toward her apartment.

The roads were snow covered, and even with all-wheel drive, the car was slipping and sliding all over. The town crews hadn't started their second round of plowing yet, and the roads were awful.

Nora's heart pounded in her chest as she gripped the steering wheel, her knuckles white with tension, as she slowly crawled the nine miles to her place. When she finally pulled in, her neck was so tight that she could barely turn her head. She hated driving in snowy weather; it always caused her anxiety to flare and left her on edge. She would much rather walk or ride the bus; however, living in rural Vermont left both options out. She parked, shut off the engine, grabbed her phone and bag off the front seat, and made her way into her tiny apartment.

Nora rented the small space from her parents. It was a quaint, converted maple sugaring shack that sat at the bottom of her parents' long winding driveway. They had transformed it into a tiny house for her grandmother to live in when she could no longer stay by herself but wanted to maintain her independence. Her grandmother had always been fiercely independent and had refused to be put in a nursing home. Nora shared a lot of things in common with her, but fierce independence was not one of them. Nora always seemed to be relying on others in some way or another. Her grandmother had struck out on her own in her twenties and volunteered to be a medic nurse in the Second World War. She had picked up and moved countries, and after the war was over, she continued to travel and explore the world, whereas Nora had barely made it out of New England.

Gram had passed away while Nora was away at college, and the burden of regret lingered with her to this day. She was supposed to come home for their monthly family dinner that weekend but opted to stay on campus instead and attend a party thrown by a guy she had a crush on. Her parents called the next day to tell her that Gram had died of a stroke the night before. They had been close, and even though Gram was nearing ninety years old, the news of her death came as a shock to Nora. She still couldn't forgive herself for not coming home that weekend.

Two months after her gram's death, Nora graduated and settled into the sugar shack as a pit stop before finding her own place. The decision was more than just practical; it was a way for her to reconnect with the memory of her grandmother, a way to feel close to her once again. That had been nearly five years ago now, a fact that sent a pang of anxiety through her, knotting her stomach.

The idea that she was still living off her parents at the age of twenty-nine made her feel less than confident about the trajectory of her life. All her other friends were married, starting families, or well on their way to established careers. Nora had seen those things come and pass her by, so close that she almost had that life once. However, those times were gone and now she had no man, no real home of her own, not even a career she had worked hard for and could be proud of. She might as well be a damn high schooler again. She didn't even want to think about what her grandmother would say if she knew she hadn't pushed forward to find her dreams and just fell in step with the plans her mother had laid out for her.

She trudged into her apartment, snow clinging to her, along with a heavy cloud of self-pity. Pushing aside a stack of books, she set her bag down on the table but then glanced back at the book on top, a new Barbara Davis novel she had just gotten. She wanted to dive into its pages, but she was beat, so she turned away and walked over to the fridge.

She pulled out half an apple pie and a container of whipped cream, then snatched a fork from the counter and headed to the couch to watch a little television. They had started their Christmas countdown before Halloween this year, and Nora had put off watching it in protest, until now. It wasn't just the premature start of the Christmas season that bothered her, but also the idea of watching people fall in love. Love was not something she was particularly keen on these days. She had been in a serious relationship with a guy named Sam a few years back, but it had ended quite badly. So badly, in fact, that even after two years, she still had no interest in getting back into the dating world.

Pulling herself from the depressing line of thought, she decided that tonight the boycott on the television stations would end as she flipped on a movie. She thought a little light-hearted Christmas rom-com was just the thing to dull her mind.

Pulling a fluffy fleece blanket off the couch, she wrapped it around herself and sat with the pie resting in her lap, adding a very generous amount of whipped cream to the top of it. Yup, that's where her life was at the moment—television movies and pie straight out of the tin.

As much as she had wanted the rom-com to distract her from her own life, it only reflected just how lonely she actually was, leaving her feeling empty despite a stomach full of apple pie. With only a fork full of pie left and the end of the movie playing mindlessly in the background, she closed her eyes and fell asleep, dreaming of what her life might be like if it were a television movie. Yet, what lay ahead was far from a rom-com happy ending.

Chapter Two

HOROSCOPES AND
PIE CRUMBS

The next morning, Nora woke up slumped over on the couch, her head resting in the empty pie tin among the crumbs, as her phone's alarm blared. She fumbled to pick it up from the couch and stopped the noisy alarm, then tossed the phone back down, resting her head back against the sofa.

After sitting there a long while, still half asleep, she finally stood up and wandered into the kitchen. She turned on the coffee pot and settled down at the table, switching her phone back on. It was her morning ritual to check her email, scroll through Instagram for a few minutes, and then read her daily horoscope while she waited for her coffee to brew.

She found six new emails, three announcing online sales,

two bills, and lastly, a message from her doctor's office reminding her she needed to schedule her yearly physical. It was hard for her to admit, but even after two years, she still hoped there might be an email from Sam. Spurred on by the rom-com she had watched last night, the hope was fleeting, not based in reality at all. Trying to push away the unwanted thoughts of him she tapped on her horoscope app and delved into her daily prediction, hoping it might tell her she would be winning the lottery today.

"Capricorn, things may not go as planned today but keep heart that the universe is always moving you in the right direction. Stay your course and new opportunities will arise," she read aloud. "Well, that seems like a nice way to say you're about to have a shit day. Perfect!" she muttered to herself as she got up and poured a cup of coffee.

She felt like her sign did not fit her personality at all. Capricorns were supposed to be strong-willed and fiercely driven by their career goals, and here she was at twenty-nine, still grappling with the question of what career path to pursue. The idea of becoming a therapist had crossed her mind, but she quickly dismissed it, realizing she didn't have her own life sorted out enough to offer advice to others. Nursing had been appealing once, inspired by her grandmother's legacy, but her mother had steered her toward business instead, hoping it would help her one day when she took over the bakery. So, that's what she had majored in, even though it hadn't sparked the least bit of passion in her. Nothing had ever felt like quite the right fit for her.

The clock on the stove read eight thirty. *Shit*, she had less than a half hour to get ready and hit the road. She took her coffee into her bedroom and peeled off yesterday's clothes. Moving aside her notebooks, she rooted through the stacks of clothes sitting on top of her dresser and opted for a pair of her favorite jeans, a cream-colored thermal shirt, and an oversized evergreen cable-knit sweater that hung loose on her petite frame.

The night spent sleeping on the couch had left her feeling extra groggy. She had puttered around, and now there was no time for a shower. Instead, she quickly washed her face, applied a quick bit of mascara overtop her blue eyes, and ran her fingers through her long auburn hair. As her fingers traveled halfway down her long wavy locks, they encountered the last bite of apple pie she hadn't finished before falling asleep the night before.

"Crap," she cursed as she attempted to rinse out the crystallized sugar from her hair in the sink.

After spending about five minutes picking out pieces of pie crust and bits of apple, she quickly inspected herself in the mirror. Despite her attempts at cleaning herself up, she still looked like she had pulled an all-nighter.

Dashing into the kitchen she pulled on her boots and jacket, then grabbed her coffee, keys, and bag from the table and headed out the door in a rush.

It had snowed most of the night, leaving the world looking like something straight out of a Christmas card. Nora loved the first heavy snowfall of the year; it was always so magical how the world transformed from a mix of grays and browns to a beautiful fantasy world of shimmery white. A *snow globe day*, she could hear her grandmother say in the back of her mind as she always had on mornings like these, and it brought a smile to her face.

She brushed the snow off the railing that led from the house down the walkway to the parking area. To her surprise, not only had her small walkway been shoveled and her driveway plowed but her car had been cleared off as well.

"Thank you, Dad!" she said as she jumped in and started her car. She had almost forgotten that it had snowed last night, and if he hadn't helped her out, she would have been more than just a few minutes late. Even though the gesture was sweet and much appreciated on a morning like this, Nora couldn't help but feel like it was just another thing that made her feel less like an adult. Her father still cleaned off her car and shoveled her driveway. These were tasks she would have taken care of herself if she were living on her own. She tried to push away the angst and be grateful for the help, but as she pulled out of the driveway, her stomach stayed knotted up.

It didn't take long before Mother Nature distracted her from her thoughts though. The drive to the bakery was magical on mornings like this. The snow had coated every inch of the trees and shrubs, painting the world in a glittery white. The evergreen boughs weighed down with snow almost touched the ground, and the morning sun lit the crystals in the air like tiny specks of magic. The roads had been plowed but still sported a thin layer of snow, and the only visible pavement was from the tire tracks from the morning traffic.

"Under a snowy vale, there lies a hush so deep, in winter's grip, the world's asleep," she muttered to herself as she drove.

Nora enjoyed creating poems or songs as a kind of outlet she often turned to when alone. It had been a suggestion from a friend after her grandmother's death, a way to process her feelings. It seemed like a good fit as she had always enjoyed writing and had kept journals since she was a child. She had taken the suggestion and to this day still practiced it as a way to deal with emotions. However, inspiration often struck at the most inconvenient moments, like when she was driving in her car, so she would mutter them aloud, releasing them into the universe, trusting they would return to her when she had a pen and paper in hand.

It was nine on the dot when she pulled into her parking spot.

When she entered the bakery, her mother tossed her an apron and motioned for her to wash her hands and get to work. Nora poked her head around the corner and looked into the front of the shop. The bakery was packed with people, and it looked like they had already sold out of the cinnamon rolls and scones she had pre-made the night before.

"Why's it so busy?" she asked her father as she took off her jacket and tied the apron around her waist.

"Unexpected holiday tour bus. I guess this place made it on the list of most quaint hometown bakeries to visit during the holidays on some online blog," her father told her as he loaded the oven with a tray of ginger cookies.

Nora always loved the smell of the bakery this time of year. The cinnamon, ginger, and allspice mixed with the sweet undertones of sugar and dough made it feel like the holidays. She began mixing up another batch of cinnamon rolls when her mother came back to grab a tray of scones to refill the cases out front.

"Mom, do you want me to take over out there?" Nora asked, seeing the stress creasing her mother's face.

"No, I'm fine. Just help your father," she yelled back as she walked out of the room.

Nora looked over at her father. "I don't get why she doesn't want my help. She could take a break and let me help once in a while."

"You know your mother, and 'break' is not a word in her vocabulary," her father said, trying to ease the tension. He was the peacemaker in the family and Nora's biggest supporter.

Her mother and she had never been particularly close in the past. It wasn't that they had a bad relationship or even a strained one; they simply didn't have much in common. They were like oil and water, always coexisting but never quite getting close enough to understand one another. Nora was a daydreamer like her father, always with her head in the clouds overthinking while her mother's feet were planted firmly on the ground.

"You know, you could always just go out there and help," her father said, giving her a wink.

Nora gave him a nod and a smile as she untied her apron and headed toward the front of the shop. Just as she was about to enter, she heard a familiar voice, and it stopped her in her tracks. It was her high school science teacher, Mrs. Conroy. Nora rested herself against the wall next to the door to eavesdrop. She knew if she stepped out, she would be stuck there talking to her for an hour.

"Cynthia, hi. The bakery looks so festive this year."

"Thank you, Marg, what can I get you?" her mother said in the sweet cheery voice she saved for the customers.

There was a long pause, and Nora imagined Mrs. Conroy's stout frame peering over all the goodies tucked away behind the glass cases in the front of the shop.

"I think I'll take a half dozen of the ginger snaps and two scones." She heard her mother bagging up the cookies and scones when the dreaded question came.

"How is Nora doing these days?"

"Good, she is getting ready to take this place over."

Nora swallowed hard at her mom's reply, knowing she was about to break those plans and guilt began to bubble up.

"I heard she was engaged to some boy from the city."

Nora's heart sank into her stomach at the mention of Sam, and the guilt she had felt just a moment ago turned into a building anxiety.

"Oh, sadly, it didn't work out between them. That will be $15.65," her mother said, in a tone a little less sweet, as if to tell Mrs. Conroy to mind her own business.

She smiled at her mom's sharp retort, which left Mrs. Conroy speechless. After Nora and Sam's relationship ended, her mother had told her she had been married once before, something she had kept from Nora until then. Her mother's experiences mirrored Nora's in some ways, and they found common ground in their shared heartbreak and betrayal. It was a strange twist of fate that the turmoil of Nora's relationship with Sam had brought her closer to her mother, perhaps the only silver lining behind the whole ordeal.

The sound of the chimes over the front door let Nora know it was safe to step out from her hiding spot, and she appeared in the doorway overlooking the cash register where her mother stood.

"Thanks for not getting into the details with her," Nora said.

"Oh, Nora, of course. I wouldn't do that to you. I'm sorry you had to hear that."

"No, it's fine. Why don't you go and have a coffee with Dad out back, and I will take over here," she told her, scooting her aside and forcing her toward the door.

"Okay, but please make sure you use the new wax paper and not the tongs for the peanut butter cookies, they will fall apart if you don't."

"I got this, go," Nora said, rolling her eyes as her mother walked into the back of the bakery.

After that, the morning flew by. The tour bus departed, and there was only a brief lull before the lunch crowd arrived. Nora rejoined her father in the back so they could catch up with the demand. Nora was putting a tray of peanut butter cookies in the oven when her phone buzzed in her back pocket. She shut the oven door, then pulled out her phone. She had received a text message from Eve that read, *Everything okay? You're never late.*

"Crap," she muttered to herself and quickly texted her back.

Sorry. The shop has been crazy busy this morning. I hate to do this, but I have to cancel. I can't leave while it's so busy. Let's reschedule. Pizza at my place tomorrow? She hit Send and watched as the little blue check mark appeared, letting her know it had gone through. If Nora were being honest with herself, she hadn't really wanted to go to lunch with Eve today anyway. After the mistake of watching the Christmas rom-com last night, her heart was feeling rather tender, and she wasn't sure she could take listening to Eve talk about how nice her new boyfriend was.

She tucked the phone back into her pocket and went back to rolling out the dough for one of her mother's famous apple crisp pies.

Nora spent the rest of the day lost in contemplation, wrestling with the stark contrasts between herself, her mother, and her grandmother. Both her mother and Gram were pillars of strength and independence. Growing up under their influence, she had thought she would inherit at least a fraction of their confidence and drive. After all, shouldn't those qualities have been ingrained in her, passed down through her genes, or nurtured by their example? Despite her best efforts to mirror them, she always found herself gripped by fear and anxiety whenever she tried to step out of her comfort zone. Each attempt to forge her own path seemed to end in disappointment or disaster, and Sam was the perfect example of that. So, instead of stepping up to the plate and pushing forward, she had let her mother steer her direction straight into taking over the bakery.

Lost in her own thoughts while she made and froze cookie dough, it had grown dark outside. Her parents had long ago closed up shop and headed home, but it wasn't until Nora received a ping on her phone that she realized just how late it was. Her screen showed 8:15 p.m. She had gotten so lost in thought that time had slipped away from her.

She set the last batch of dough in the freezer and washed her hands before checking everything was prepped and ready for the next day. Untying her apron, she slung it on the hook before replacing it with her jacket and winter hat. She glanced around the room one final time to make sure that everything was turned off before she walked over to switch off the lights and lock up. There was a sticky note attached to the light that read, *Make sure you let your car heat up before you take off. Drive safe on your way home, love Dad.* Nora rolled her eyes as she crumpled the note before tossing it into the trash.

When she opened the back door to leave, she was surprised to see it snowing heavily again. The forecast hadn't predicted any incoming weather. But that was Vermont, and the weather was unpredictable at best. She zipped up her jacket and pushed against the wind to get to her car. Forgetting to grab her snow brush from her parents' backseat, she found herself cleaning off her car with her sleeve once again.

After completing the chilly task, she settled into her car, patiently awaiting the warmth of the heater to defrost her windows. As she watched the heat slowly dissolve the frost on her windshield, her thoughts circled back to her grandmother.

As Nora watched the snowflakes pirouette in the wintry breeze, she couldn't help but think about the tales her gram had spun about her winters spent in Scotland. According to her, Vermont held a special allure that reminded her of Scotland, especially in the early winter months. It was one of the reasons she and Nora's grandfather had decided to settle here. It had made him feel more at home even though he was an ocean away from where he had grown up.

Nora's childhood had been peppered with bedtime stories infused with the magic of her grandmother's Scottish adventures.

She often described it as a land of enchantment and wonder, painting a picture straight out of a fairy tale. Her grandmother's time spent there had been some of the happiest of her life, as it was the place where she met and fell in love with Nora's grandfather. Her grandmother had always expressed her desire for Nora to visit Scotland one day and experience her roots, but Nora hadn't even managed to make it to Florida on spring break with her friends back in college.

Tonight the sky glimmered with the same snowy enchantment her grandmother had often spoken of, and it caused a shiver to chase down her spine. It was as if she could feel her gram's presence, and she glanced around the car. Finding nothing but frost-bitten windows, she laughed away the feeling, then put the car in drive and pulled out onto the road.

The snow came down in a thick white haze, and even with the windshield wipers on the fastest setting, she struggled to see more than a few feet in front of her. Her hands tightened on the steering wheel, knuckles turning white with tension, and she leaned forward as if it might give her a better vantage point. Coming around a bend in the road, the back of the car slid to the side, and she slowed down. The roads, still unplowed, were like a slip-n-slide and were a challenge even with studded winter tires.

Nora clenched her jaw as a set of oncoming lights appeared in the distance. The roads were heavily covered in snow, and the falling snowflakes made it almost impossible to see where the road actually was. As the oncoming car passed, she moved over to give it space, and her tires sank into the road's shoulder. She felt the car pull to the right, and her heart leapt into her throat. Trying to counter the pull, she cranked the steering wheel in the opposite direction, but it was no use. The car's back end began to fishtail, and she lost control.

Fear gripped her as the car spun out of control and careened off the road, descending down an embankment and toward a frozen lake. The sequence of events unfolded so rapidly that by the time her head struck the steering wheel, knocking her unconscious, she wasn't even aware that the car had broken through the thin ice of the lake. The vehicle vanished into the icy depths, its headlights piercing the murky darkness until they dimmed and extinguished, leaving no sign that Nora had ever even been there.

Chapter Three

VOICE IN THE DARKNESS

She woke with a jolt into total darkness. She spun around, trying to get her bearings, when a man emerged from the murky black abyss that surrounded her. He was in his early thirties, dressed in a style reminiscent of the nineteen forties, with slicked-back dark hair and eyes the color of a crystal blue sky. For a moment she thought she knew him but couldn't place where from. As she searched her mind, trying to remember his face, her head began to feel swimmy, and she became aware of a cold that was seeping into her very core.

Still confused, she sat there, staring at him. He said nothing but offered her a kind smile and extended his hand for her to take, but she hesitated, still trying to place him.

"Go. You must take his hand and go," a voice rang out, cutting through the darkness. It was her grandmother's voice.

Nora's heart raced at the sound of it, and she frantically looked for her, but there was nothing other than the man and the ever-consuming darkness. He bent forward, extending his hand closer to her this time, concern growing in his eyes.

"Nora, my sweet dove, *go!*" Her grandmother's voice echoed once again, this time growing in intensity.

The change in tone sent a shock of fear racing through Nora, and she reached up and took the man's hand. As their palms met, a bright blue glow ignited at their touch, moving up her arm and into her chest. When it reached her center, it felt like a bomb exploding, sending a shockwave of energy surging through her. She wanted to scream, to cry out in pain, but before she could even open her mouth, she passed out.

Distant voices echoed in Nora's head as her vision pulled in and out of the darkness. As her vision came back, she could make out the headlights of a car cutting through the heavily falling snow. The muted voices quickly turned into deafening shouts and within seconds she felt a cold so harsh it was like fire on her skin. A fear, deep and primal, coursed through her, and her heart raced in confusion.

"Oh, thank God. She's alive," she heard a woman's voice say as she tried to sit up.

Her head pounded, and she felt like she might throw up from the pain.

"Whoa there, take it slow," a man's voice said.

Nora looked up, expecting to see the same man whose hand she took. But standing over her was an older gentleman in his sixties with concern etched across his face. A woman similar in age stood beside him, holding onto his arm for balance as her feet sank into the deep snow.

Still feeling disoriented, Nora slowly sat up and looked

around. The headlights of their car cut through the darkness illuminating her surroundings, and she began to recognize where she was. Long Pond.

All of a sudden everything came rushing back. She had been in a car accident. Her heart raced faster, and she began to breathe heavily.

"You just stay put. We called an ambulance, and they should be here any minute," the old woman said as she wrapped a jacket around Nora's wet, shivering body.

Nora looked over her shoulder at the lake and saw a large break in the ice. Had her car gone into the water? Then she began to look around for the man but there were no signs of anyone else there.

"Where is the man who pulled me out?" Nora asked, confused, her eyes still scanning her surroundings for him.

The woman looked at her husband with concern in her eyes and then back down at Nora.

"What man, dear? There was no one here when we arrived but you."

"Are you sure? Did you pull me out then?" Nora asked, looking up at the old man.

"Quite sure. No, I didn't. When we came around the corner, my wife saw you lying there on the edge of the lake. For the life of me, I don't know how she did with the snow coming down so heavily. I could barely see a foot in front of my face," he told her.

"It was the glow," his wife said. "There was a blue glow that caught my attention and then I saw you."

At the mention of a blue glow, Nora's mind raced back to the moment she took the man's hand and the blue light that had ignited at their touch, followed by a pain like nothing she had ever felt before.

"It must have been the headlights of your car before they shut down," the man said.

"Then how did I get out of the car?" Nora asked, her thoughts circling back to the man again. Maybe he had left once he helped her out of the water, or was her mind playing tricks on her? She did hit her head hard enough to be knocked out.

"You didn't swim out?" he asked her.

She was about to tell him no when their conversation was cut short by distant sounds of sirens. In the distance, the red lights of the ambulance could be seen dancing across the snowflakes.

"Oh, thank God," the woman said, with relief in her voice.

After that, everything blurred into a whirlwind, from the ride to the hospital, the battery of tests and X-rays, to finally being picked up by her parents, who were in a total panic when they arrived. Despite her parent's worries, she had only suffered a minor concussion and was told it was nothing short of a miracle that she had survived the frigid water. The whole event was still so foggy in her mind, only bits and pieces coming to the surface. She didn't recall crashing into the lake or swimming out of the frigid water to the shoreline, but she did vividly remember the face of the man she had seen after being knocked out.

At first, when she awoke in the snow, she thought he had been real, but now she wasn't sure. No one else had seen him. Had he just merely been a result of hitting her head? Or was he something more, a guardian angel perhaps?

The following day, when her car was pulled from the frozen lake, all the windows were intact, and the doors were mysteriously still shut. She had left the bakery at 8:30 that night and hadn't been discovered until after 10:20. No one could figure out how she had gotten out of the vehicle or how she had managed to survive the freezing temperatures once she had.

While her mother insisted it must have been a miracle, Nora was beginning to think something different. The more she thought about this stranger, the more his face seemed like a memory, someone she had met before, a long time ago. None of it made any sense, but whoever he was, he had played a role in getting her out of the car. She hadn't shared this detail or the fact she heard her grandmother's voice with anyone, not even her parents, but she was certain they both had played a role in saving her life that night.

Her parents had insisted she stay with them for the next forty-eight hours while she recovered from the concussion. She had tried to resist at first, but her father had quickly told her that there would be no point arguing with her mother about this, so she gave in and stayed.

As she lay on her old twin mattress in her childhood bedroom, staring up at the familiar ceiling, her grandmother's words echoed in her mind. "Nora, my sweet dove, go." However, those words held a different meaning to her now. Having come so close to losing her life, she realized how much she had put off actually living it. The thought left her with a panicked feeling, and she grabbed her notebook and pen off the nightstand. Channeling her emotions, she began to write down the beginning of a poem, but her head ached so bad that she barely got two words on paper before giving up.

Setting the notebook aside, she grabbed the pill container off her nightstand, popped two ibuprofen in her mouth, and chased them down with a sip of water. Just as she was setting her glass down, her phone buzzed. Eve had messaged, asking if she was okay and wanting to know if she needed anything.

I'm fine. Just a bump on the head. No need to come over. My parents are waiting on me like a queen lol. Rain check on the pizza party?

Nora hit Send and then laid back on the bed. She could have called Eve to come over and keep her company; she was bored out of her mind just sitting around her old room. But she wasn't in the mood to be cheered up or treated like some invalid. So, she just lay there, looking around the room until her eyes settled on her old closet, still filled with all her high school clothes. Feeling her headache begin to subside, she sat up and got to her feet.

She walked over and began thumbing her way through her old prom dresses and an array of hideous sweaters from the nineties until she reached the very back. There, tucked away and resting in the shadows, was a small cluster of her grandmother's clothing. Shocked to see them, she felt a wave of sadness wash over her as she remembered the day they had cleared out all her grandmother's belongings from the sugar shack. She had thought her mother had donated everything to Goodwill, but apparently, that wasn't the case.

Nestled against the back wall were her grandmother's cherished possessions: a cream-colored cable-knit sweater, a long smock dress adorned with a cheerful rose pattern, a silky black-and-white polka-dot blouse, and her beloved wool peacoat. Her grandmother had worn these items frequently, and many of Nora's memories were tied to these very clothes.

Nora carefully removed them from the closet and laid them out on the bed. First, she picked up the sweater and pulled it on over her T-shirt. It still carried her grandmother's scent, a sweet blend of wild roses and honey. As she looked at herself in the mirror, she didn't see her current reflection; instead, she saw twelve-year-old Nora, bundled up in an oversized sweater, eagerly begging her gram to tell her another story before bed.

Tears welled in her eyes and cascaded down her face at the memory. She wished so badly that she could just sit and talk with her one more time. To ask for advice, to hear one more of her stories, to get one more hug. With a heavy heart, she peeled off the sweater, as the wool had grown itchy, and set it back on the bed alongside the others.

Next, she picked up the black-and-white polka-dot blouse and slipped it on. Its silky fabric, cold to the touch, was a harsh contrast to the warmth of the wool sweater. She dried her eyes and let out a slight giggle when she caught her reflection in the mirror. Her grandmother, ever the classy lady, could pull off this style like no other, while Nora felt like she had just stepped out from selling tickets at the circus. Thinking the jacket might just pull the outfit together more, she threw it on and looked at her reflection once more.

She felt out of place in her grandmother's clothing, like a child playing dress-up. It mirrored her life in a way, where nothing ever seemed to fit quite right. Here she was, having just narrowly escaped death, yet she still had no clue what she wanted or where she was headed. Going back to college was a start but she still felt like that was just a shot in the dark, hoping it would lead her in the right direction.

People often talk about near-death experiences and how they say their life flashed before their eyes, how they clearly knew their life's purpose after the event. But all Nora had experienced was seeing some guy she didn't even know and hearing her grandmother's voice urging her to go. It seemed even near death her life lacked direction. She just wished that if she knew where her passion lay, it would make this whole thing a lot easier, but nothing seemed to spark inspiration in her.

"Gram, if you're up there, give me a sign. Point me in the right direction. I need direction," she said, looking up at the old plaster ceiling.

With a heavy sigh, releasing the hope of some miraculous answer, Nora began to remove her grandmother's clothes. Tossing the jacket onto the bed, she peeled off the blouse and was about to toss it back onto the pile when something caught her eye in the mirror.

Nora spun around and retrieved the jacket, flipping open one of its sides to reveal a pocket on the inside panel. A sliver of blue had caught her eye, and she hesitantly reached into the pocket to retrieve whatever it was. She pulled out a royal blue envelope from the silk-lined pocket. Turning it over in her hands, she found her name scrolled across the front in her grandmother's neat cursive writing.

Time seemed to stand still as Nora held the envelope in her hands, her heart pounding in her chest. With a mix of anticipation and trepidation, she carefully tore open the seal, revealing a graduation card inside. Tears welled up in Nora's eyes as she gazed at the front of the card, where a golden retriever adorned in a cap and gown smiled back at her. The words *Congrats, Grad!* scrolled across the top in puffy gold letters. Taking a deep breath, Nora opened the card, and a smaller envelope fell into her lap, revealing the card's handwritten note.

Nora,

I am so proud of you, dove. Now, before you decide your direction, go discover your roots.

Love, Gram.

Tears streamed down Nora's cheeks as she read the heartfelt words penned in blue ink. With trembling hands, she reached for the smaller envelope, feeling a mix of emotions coursing through her. Opening it, she pulled out a solitary plane voucher, its dates open-ended and its destination: Scotland.

Chapter Four

THE ALBUM

Three days after the accident, Nora visited her doctor for a follow-up appointment and received a clean bill of health. Despite her mother's insistence that she stay at the house for one more night, Nora assured her she would be fine and asked to be dropped off at the sugar shack. This granted her some much-needed alone time. Nora hadn't mentioned finding the card to her parents; she needed time to process everything. She had prayed for direction, and her grandmother had pointed her directly at Scotland. She wasn't sure how she felt about it. On the one hand, she wanted to go, to break away from her predictable routine, and on the other, she was scared.

She mulled the idea over in her head as she entered the kitchen and placed her bag on the table. Her stomach rumbled with hunger as if it realized where she was. Surveying the contents of the fridge, she discovered a few containers of spoiled takeout and a half-empty gallon of milk. Disappointed, she shut the door and turned her attention to the freezer, where she found a frozen pizza. Her mother had spoiled her these past few days with her home-cooked meals and now the frozen food looked less appealing.

She preheated the oven and walked over to the window that looked out in the direction of the lake. It had started to snow again, and the flakes floated softly down on the frozen air, coating the ground in a thin layer. A chill chased down her spine, and she absent-mindedly touched the bruise on her forehead. The image of the man she had seen in her dream state during the accident kept flashing back to her. She still could not place him, but she thought she knew his face. The oven beeped and pulled her from her thoughts.

She walked over and stuck the pizza in the oven then grabbed her notebook and pen off the table and wrote down everything she could remember about the accident.

As she wrote, anxiety built in her stomach, and she closed her eyes, trying to quell the feeling. Ever since the accident she had been having panic attacks. She had always been an anxious person, but this was a different kind of anxiety, one that she hadn't dealt with before. It started low in her belly and worked its way up, causing her heart to race uncontrollably. With each heartbeat, the energy built inside her until panic took over. Her mother had said it was completely normal to experience panic attacks and anxiety after a traumatic event. She was probably right, but Nora felt like there was something else there, as it felt eerily similar to the sensation she got when she had taken the man's hand in her vision.

The one thing that seemed to soothe her was writing. So, she sat at her kitchen table and channeled her emotions onto the crisp white paper in lines and verses. There was something therapeutic about the pen gliding across the paper as her thoughts poured from her. She continued to write until her forearm began to ache, and she set the pen down.

Getting up, she pulled the pizza from the oven and let it cool on the counter, then walked into her bedroom. A thought had occurred to her while writing about the man's appearance. He looked like he was dressed in the style of the nineteen thirties or forties, and it dawned on her where she might have seen him before.

She opened the closet door, reached behind a stack of shoes and old hiking gear, and retrieved a cardboard box. Bringing it over to the bed, she sat down, dusted off its top, and carefully opened it. Many of her grandmother's belongings had been removed from the sugar shack after her passing, but Nora had held onto this small box of keepsakes.

There was an array of things inside—an old felted wool beret, a brooch with a bird on it that her gram was never without, a miniature of the Eiffel Tower her grandparents had gotten on their honeymoon, a small handful of framed photographs of her grandparents and father when he was a child, and a photo album with her name, Edith, embossed at the bottom of the puffy blue leather cover.

Nora pulled the album from the box and switched on the lamp on the bedside table. She rested against her pillow and started flipping through the album. It had been years since she last explored its pages. After her grandmother's passing, it was the one thing she had requested to keep, as it held many fond memories for her. The loss had been so fresh and painful at the time that she couldn't bring herself to look through it. Instead, she had placed it into the box with the other items and tucked it away in her closet, not giving it much thought, until now.

Nora paused for a moment to run her fingers over her grandmother's name, sunken into its cool leather cover. Nostalgia washed over her, and she pushed down the sadness before it bubbled over. As she flipped open the album, a plume of dust burst into the air and rained down around her. Her grandmother had used the album as a storybook at bedtime when Nora was a child, telling her the tales behind each photograph. Nora had loved it and the way her grandmother lit up every time she told her the stories inside its pages.

The first page was her grandmother's high school graduation photo. A beautiful younger version of her looked back through black-and-white eyes. The next page held a mixture of pictures, one featuring her standing in front of a car with her high school sweetheart, another capturing her sunbathing on a rocky beach in Maine, and one showing her walking down the streets of New York City with her best friend Barbara. Nora couldn't help but smile at the sheer joy her grandmother radiated in every photograph. With her wide infectious smile, it was as if a radiant halo of happiness surrounded her.

Tucked within the album were postcards, one showcasing the bustling streets of Edinburgh while another captured the serene beauty of a place named Letterfearn. Numerous snapshots showed her grandmother amidst the diverse landscapes of Scotland—from the winding cobblestone streets and towering buildings in the city to the rugged countryside adorned with fields of heather and grazing sheep with the sea in the background. There were also images of her serving as a medic nurse during World War II, tending to wounded soldiers and standing guard over stretchers. A large photograph dominated the next page. Her grandmother stood proudly on the steps of a military hospital in her nurse's uniform, flanked by her fellow nurses.

Nora continued to flip through the album until she landed on the page she was searching for. There, standing next to her grandmother, was a man with his leg bandaged, leaning on a crutch, while her grandmother offered support on the other side, helping to hold him up. It was the very same man she had seen in her vision after the accident, but why? Why would this man be whom she saw in the face of death? It didn't make any sense. Had she pulled his face from the recesses of her mind because this album had been a comfort to her in childhood, and she had remembered him? She recalled what her grandmother had told her about the man. He had been the first patient she treated during World War II and said he had a story to tell, like the ones in the movies.

Her grandmother had pursued a nursing education, and when the call for nurses went out, she knew she needed to volunteer and aid in the fight. Stationed in Scotland as a medic nurse during the winter of 1943, right in the heart of World War II, she had been sent to assist the Craigleith Military Hospital. It marked her first time leaving the United States, and she had fallen in love with Scotland the moment her feet touched the ground. However, her idealism had left her unprepared for the trauma she would face.

By November 1943, the hospital had reached nearly full capacity, and many wounded soldiers couldn't make it home for the holidays. This left her and only four other nurses to care for the men during the holiday season.

One particular Scottish soldier had captivated her with his story of survival. He was an avid reader and had carried a small book with him into battle. His infantry came under attack, and he was struck by two bullets, one to his left leg and one to the chest, right above his heart. The only thing that had saved him was the tiny red book, a novel he had kept in the breast pocket of his uniform. The force of the gunshots had blown him backward, and he suffered a severe head injury, making it impossible for him to read. When he found his way into her unit, Nora's grandmother took pity on him and helped him finish the book that saved his life, reading around the bullet holes in each page.

Why would she dream up this man that her grandmother helped back in World War II? She peeled back the clear film holding the picture in the album and removed the photograph. On the back in her grandmother's neat cursive writing was the name Colin MacDonald.

She turned it back over and looked at the man again, remembering his kind eyes and gentle smile as he helped her in her vision. Her grandmother had insisted that she take his hand as if she knew he could save her. The hair on the back of her neck rose, and she felt a strange energy course through her. She slid the photo back into the album and began to close it when another picture caught her eye.

There was a yellowed photo of her grandmother, in her twenties, standing on a street in Edinburgh, with Edinburgh Castle perched in the background atop Castle Rock. She stood holding a book in one hand and a bottle of wine in the other, as snow fell around her like glittering sparks of magic. This particular photo had always held a special allure for Nora, even when she was a child. Gazing at it, she could almost transport herself to that very moment, feeling the enchantment that was captured within the old grainy film.

Nora looked back into the box full of her grandmother's

memories and pulled out the framed wedding photograph of her grandparents. Sadly, Nora never had the chance to get to know her grandfather, as he had passed away when she was just a baby. Even though she had heard stories of him her whole life, he was merely a face in framed photos. She noticed her grandmother lacked the spark in her eyes that she had in the album's photos. Engraved at the bottom of the frame was their wedding date, March 25, 1944. Wondering if the trauma she had seen during the war had stripped her grandmother of that spark, Nora tucked the frame back into the box but kept out the album and the brooch.

As she set the album aside and placed the box back into her closet, a thought sprang to the forefront of her mind. What if she decided to go to Scotland and turn the album into a guide for her trip, a personal quest to locate each of the places in her grand-mother's photos? Perhaps even recreate a few. Picking the album back up, she flipped through its pages again until she found the picture of her grandmother standing in front of Edinburgh Castle. Carefully peeling back the clear plastic holding it in place, she took a photo with her phone. This would be the first picture she would recreate upon arriving in Edinburgh.

After all these years hidden in her gram's jacket pocket, the plane ticket voucher was the first step to embarking on the trip Nora's grandmother had planned for her, and the photo album idea was the perfect way to pay tribute. Nora walked to her dresser mirror and pulled down a plaid scarf hanging from its side. A gift from her grandmother on her twentieth birthday, it had been wrapped in a small box with a note that read *Your family tartan*. Nora often wore it during the holidays, its plaid looking quite festive, a mix of green, red, and blue. But now it held a deeper significance for her, and she knew it needed to accompany the album on the trip.

She pulled her suitcase out of her closet and laid it on her bed. It had once been black, but it looked more like a charcoal gray with all the layers of dust that clung to it from never being used. Unzipping it sent a plume of dust flying into the air, causing her to sneeze several times.

"Tell me you don't travel without telling me you don't travel," she joked out loud to herself.

She carefully pinned the brooch to her scarf, then tucked it snugly away in an inner pocket. As she placed the cherished photo album in the center of the suitcase, the realization hit her—this was it. She was committed.

She returned to the kitchen, retrieved her bag, and pulled out the blue envelope containing the ticket voucher. With trembling hands, she dialed the number listed on the back and endured nearly an hour on hold as the airline searched for available flights. Finally, she received confirmation: in just two days, she would be boarding a plane bound for Scotland.

Chapter Five

RESERVATIONS

Nora was seated at her kitchen table, busy making Airbnb reservations and booking guided tours of Edinburgh, when a knock at the door interrupted her. She wasn't surprised to find her parents standing there when she answered.

"Hi, honey," her father greeted her, giving her a side hug as he entered the house. "Your mom and I thought you might need a little dinner, so we picked you up some homemade cheddar and broccoli soup from Rae's on our way home."

"You guys didn't need to do that," Nora said, taking the soup container from her father and placing it on the counter next to the half-eaten frozen pizza from earlier. Her mother glanced at the pizza, wrinkling her nose in disapproval, and then she noticed Nora's laptop on the table.

"What is this all about?" her mother asked, stepping over to the table and pointing at the open reservation page for the room Nora had booked in the city.

She hadn't planned on telling them until tomorrow, giving her mother little time to shame her into backing out. "I was going to call and tell you guys, but seeing you're here," she began, bracing herself for her mother's reaction.

Her mother crossed her arms, a clear indication of her displeasure and readiness for an argument. Nora cleared her throat nervously. "The other day when I was going through my old things in my closet at the house, I found Gram's clothes that you kept."

There was a brief softening in her mother's eyes before guilt clouded them as she glanced at her father. Nora wondered if he had known she had kept some of his mother's things; judging by his expression, he hadn't.

"In the inside pocket of her old wool peacoat, I found an envelope with my name on it. It was a graduation card, and inside was an open-ended plane voucher to Scotland," Nora explained.

"You're kidding," her father said in surprise.

Nora shook her head and walked over to her bag, pulling the card out. She handed it to her father, whose eyes brimmed with tears as he opened it and read it.

"That must have been what she had Carol doing that was such a big secret the month before she passed," her mother said.

"Finding it after the accident felt like a sign, so I booked the next flight out. I leave in two days," Nora added quickly, sensing her mother's disapproval brewing.

Silence filled the room, the air heavy with unspoken tension.

"You can't just up and go to Scotland right now. It's one of the busiest times of the year for the bakery!" her mother snapped, her hands now firmly planted on her hips.

"I know, but I feel like if I don't do it now, then I won't ever do it," Nora replied, trying to keep her voice steady despite her rising frustration.

"This kind of flighty, impulsive thinking makes me worry about how serious you truly are about taking over the bakery," her mother continued, her tone sharp and disapproving.

Nora felt her anger bubbling up inside her. Not once had her mother ever asked if taking over the bakery was what she wanted to do. She had always just assumed Nora would happily follow in her footsteps. She was on the verge of saying something she might regret when her father intervened.

"I think it's a great idea. You deserve a little break after everything, and I'm sure we can handle the shop without you for a few days," he said, giving Nora a reassuring wink.

He was so much like her gram with his kind heart and ever-optimistic outlook. Nora felt lucky to have him there to counterbalance her mother's sharpness.

Cynthia shot her husband a look before relenting. "How long will you be gone?"

"Eight days. I'll be back well before Christmas," Nora replied.

"Where are you flying out of?" her father asked.

"Boston, but I bought a ticket to ride the bus down, so you guys don't need to drive me," Nora explained.

"I'm pretty sure you won't have a new car by then, so why don't you let your father at least take you to the bus station?" her mother insisted.

Nora nodded in agreement. "That would be great."

"It's settled then. Bruce, we better be off. I still have to cook dinner," her mother said to her father before briskly turning toward the door. She obviously wasn't happy about the situation, but Nora knew she couldn't stop her; she was a full-grown adult, after all.

Her father walked over, planted a kiss on her head, and whispered, "I'm proud of you, pumpkin. I think this is going to be good for you. Gram always knew best." Nora looked up at his tall lanky frame and into his crystal blue eyes, which resembled her own, and smiled.

"Thanks, Dad," she whispered back.

She watched as their headlights cut through the falling snow and up the long, winding driveway to the house that sat on the hillside overlooking the sugar shack. A jolt of excitement raced through her as she turned back to her computer and began searching for a place to book in Letterfearn.

The next two days flew by with preparations, and Nora had not slept much the night before her trip. Her excitement and apprehensions had kept her tossing and turning.

It seemed as soon as she had finally fallen asleep, her alarm had woken her up, its cheery ringtone breaking into the pleasant dream she was having about a handsome stranger on an airplane, just when it was about to get good.

She shut off her alarm, rolled out of bed, and began getting ready. Her father was due to arrive in a little under an hour and her stomach was in knots of worry as she double-checked her lists and made sure she had packed everything she would need. Once she was satisfied that she had remembered everything, she jumped in the shower, then quickly got dressed.

She lugged her bags into the kitchen and made herself a cup of coffee and a slice of toast as she looked over her itinerary for what must have been the hundredth time.

Her father pulled into the driveway at exactly 7:45 a.m. He was punctual, and she knew he would arrive before their set time to leave, so she had a cup of hot coffee waiting for him when he came in.

"Good morning. You all set to go?" he asked as he kicked the snow from his boots before entering the main living area.

"All set," she said in a tone that was less than enthusiastic.

"Well, that doesn't sound like someone who's about to go on the adventure of a lifetime. What's wrong?" he asked.

"I don't know. I'm just not sure I'm cut out for solo travel."

"Listen, you're going to be fine. I think it's high time you go and do something adventurous," he said in a comforting tone. "I know what will make you feel better. Look what your mother made you," he said, holding up a tiny brown paper bag from the bakery.

Nora took it from him and peeked inside. At the bottom was a lemon poppy seed muffin with lemon drizzle icing, her absolute favorite. She looked up and smiled.

"I thought maybe she would come by and say goodbye this morning."

"She wanted to, but she had to go to the shop a little early to make up for me not being there for a few hours. The muffin is her way of saying she loves you and that she hopes you have a fun time."

Nora highly doubted that last part. She wasn't entirely convinced of her mother's seeming acceptance of her trip. She knew her mother loved her, but she also understood her tendency to become stubborn when things didn't go her way and figured her absence this morning was more out of spite than anything else.

"Let's get going. We don't want to be late for that bus," her father said, bringing her back to the present. Nora smiled, grabbed her muffin, and followed him out the door with her bag in tow.

Chapter Six

THE TURBULENCE OF COURAGE

The ride to the bus station went by far too quickly and by the time they arrived, Nora's nerves had reached a new high.

Her father handed her bag to the driver as Nora pulled up her electronic ticket on her phone for him to scan.

"Have a wonderful time, honey. Remember, we are only a phone call away," her father said as he pulled her into a hug. She hugged him back, then boarded the bus, waving to him as she walked to her seat.

The inside of the bus was hot, and she took off her jacket before sitting down. With her queasy stomach, she knew from past experiences to avoid sitting at the back of the bus. As she looked around, she noticed the worn-out seats covered in years of stains and emitting an unpleasant mix of odors reminiscent of sour milk and stinky feet. She prayed her stomach would hold out for the three-hour trip, but with her nerves taking up residence there, she wasn't very confident.

Putting in her earbuds, she rested her head back on the seat, listening to an audiobook she had started a few weeks ago but hadn't had a chance to finish. It helped pass the time and before she knew it, they were pulling into Boston International Airport.

As soon as the large gray airport came into view, her heart sank back down into her stomach. Was she actually doing this? She swallowed hard as she began gathering her things to depart the bus.

The airport was a chaotic tangle of people rushing from one gate to the next. Nora's stomach flipped as she followed the signs that led her down a long corridor to the security point. Once she was through, she found her gate and sat down in one of the cold plastic chairs that faced the large windows overlooking the tarmac. Snow began to fall softly from the thick cloud cover overhead and she almost wished a snowstorm would roll in and force the flight to be canceled. It would give her an excuse not to go ahead with the trip without looking like she chickened out. But there would be no such luck today as the loudspeakers announced boarding in ten minutes.

She broke out in a cold sweat as the unfamiliar energy she had been experiencing since the crash raced inside her rapidly, causing the room to spin. Dropping her face into her hands, she rested her elbows on her knees and began taking in long, deep breaths, trying to calm herself.

"You okay?" an older woman next to her asked, seeing the panic taking over her.

"I'm just a little anxious about flying. It's my first overseas flight," she told the woman as she peeked up from her hands. "I'm not sure I'm gonna be able to do it," she confessed, tucking her phone into her pocket and standing up as though she had made her mind up to leave.

"Oh, don't you worry, you're going to be just fine. Everyone gets the jitters their first time on a long flight. Where are you headed?" the old woman said, trying to talk her down from the edge of the panic attack.

"Scotland, on a kinda spur-of-the-moment adventure. How about you?" Nora asked, feeling her anxiousness subsiding a bit as she talked.

"Oh, how fun. I'm headed over to visit my sister in Bristol." Nora smiled at the woman, who seemed pleased with herself for helping her calm down. She was about to ask if she was also traveling alone when a woman's voice in a thick Boston accent announced over the loudspeaker that the flight would now begin boarding.

"Come on, let's go up together," the old woman suggested as she stood and grabbed her bags.

Pulling her phone back out of her pocket, Nora and the woman headed to the gate where a long line was forming. She pulled up the scan code for what must have been the twentieth time before she got to the flight attendant. She thought her nerves had calmed down, but she was wrong. They came racing back to the surface in just the few steps she had taken toward the gate.

As Nora presented her phone for the attendant to scan and boarded the plane, her heart thundered in her ears, drowning out the lively chatter of fellow passengers. Swallowing down the mounting panic, the fear of traveling alone to another country gripped her chest like a vice.

"You've got this," the old lady said as she walked by, patting her shoulder and giving her just enough encouragement not to turn and make a run for the terminal doors.

Navigating through the jumble of passengers stowing luggage and settling into their seats, Nora found her seat three rows from the back on the aisle. It wasn't the most ideal spot as she would have rather had a window seat, but at least it was close to the bathroom—a small comfort, knowing how uneasy her stomach had been feeling.

As she settled in, she pulled the book she had been reading, *The Last of the Moon Girls*, out of her bag, thinking it might help distract her from the lingering panic that was still coursing through her. However, she gave up quickly after reading the first sentence of chapter six four times. There was just too much going on in her head to concentrate on the words on the page. Instead, she found herself looking around at her fellow passengers. This particular flight was mostly made up of people of retirement age. A handful of middle-aged women in the front looked to be on a business trip, and one teenager traveling alone. Seated beside her was a woman in her late forties with her teenage daughter. They were engaged in a lively conversation about the places they would visit in London, punctuated by the girl's giggles at her mother's whispered remarks.

Nora's thoughts turned to her own mother as she watched the two. She hadn't wanted to admit it, but she was a little hurt that her mother hadn't come to say goodbye this morning. However, she wasn't completely surprised either. She knew her mother didn't actually approve of the trip. She was very pragmatic and would have never rushed off on some trip without a year's worth of planning. In fact, Nora couldn't remember a time when she and her father had even gone on vacation. The bakery was all she did. It was her blood and bones, her life, so much so that Nora had sometimes wondered if her mother loved it more than she loved her.

She had really known only the hard-working side of her mother growing up. She was work-driven, and even on the days they closed the bakery, she would be in the kitchen experimenting with new recipes or reading cookbooks. There was no doubt in Nora's mind that it was her mother's true passion, and she envied her in a way. She longed to find something in her own life that ignited a sense of purpose like that. Glancing down at the book in her lap, Nora thought about her love of reading. While it was undoubtedly a passion of hers, she doubted it could ever become a career. Instead, she saw it as a means of escaping from the realities of her own life.

Once they were in flight, Nora ordered a drink, hoping it would help curb the anxiety still floating around inside her. However, she quickly regretted the choice, as twenty minutes later the plane hit turbulence, and the booze began doing acrobatics in her stomach. It had taken almost the rest of the flight to Heathrow before her stomach had finally settled down and her nerves had burned themselves out.

As she waited to board her next flight, she pulled up the itinerary on her phone, along with the map of Edinburgh Airport she had screenshot. She had mapped out the route from where the planes departed to the bus terminal. However, the idea of trying to figure her way around the public transportation was nerve-wracking and she wished she had just scheduled a car to pick her up.

She spent her time on the short flight from London to Edinburgh writing lists of places she wanted to visit that were not on the planned schedule. Like the military hospital where her grandparents had met and the spot on the Royal Mile where she could recreate the photo of her grandmother. Nora had a fondness for lists. They helped organize her thoughts and provided some semblance of control, which she otherwise felt she didn't have. She created little boxes next to each item and checked them off when they were complete, which gave her a sense of accomplishment. It was amazing how such a seemingly small thing could help calm her down.

By the time they landed in Edinburgh, she had quelled her anxieties almost completely, replacing them with excitement now that her feet were about to touch down on Scottish soil.

After collecting her luggage and navigating through customs, she made her way to the signs marked "Transportation" and followed them down to the bus terminal. It was buzzing with activity, travelers scurrying to catch their rides into the city or farther out into the countryside. Nora found the queue for her bus and waited alongside a group of Chinese tourists who were also headed into the city's center.

When the bus finally arrived, Nora felt a surge of excitement course through her, replacing the anxiety she had been feeling all day. She climbed aboard and found a seat by the window this time, not wanting to miss out on seeing the city.

Her pulse quickened as they pulled out of the terminal and the city unfolded before her like a grand tapestry, its streets alive with the hustle and bustle of everyday life. The bus navigated its way through the labyrinth of streets, and Nora marveled at how old some of the buildings were, providing a glimpse back in time.

As they passed by Princes Street, with its bustling thoroughfare lined with shops and cafes, the towering spire of the Scott Monument caught her eye. Its dark Gothic steeple pierced the gray sky and reminded her of the tower the evil queen had kept Sleeping Beauty in.

As they turned onto North Bridge, Nora's breath caught in her throat at the panoramic view of the city spread out before her. To the east, the rugged peaks of Arthur's Seat rose majestically against the horizon, while to the west, the silhouettes of Edinburgh Castle and the Old Town skyline cast long shadows across the landscape.

When the bus finally made its stop at the head of Cockburn Street, she grabbed her bags and departed. Stepping onto the cobbled street, she stood entranced as she looked out over the lively cityscape surrounding her. The ancient stone buildings with their rich gray stone stood tall with a sort of Gothic magic to them, transporting her to another time. They sat snugly side by side, like giants shoulder to shoulder, with a mixture of times past and a splash of modern development. At the bottom of each building was a wide variety of shops, each adorned with twinkle lights and wreaths hung on almost every storefront window, giving them the warm, inviting charm of the holiday season. The sounds of laughter, along with the aroma of nutmeg, coriander, and allspice drifted out of a pub, accompanied by a lively jig being played on a fiddle. She took in a deep breath, filling her lungs and her soul with the magic that hung in the air around her. The view seemed to ignite something deep within her and at that moment all the fear and panic from the day slipped away, replaced with an all-encompassing awe of her surroundings.

She pulled out her phone and snapped a picture, sending it to Eve and her parents with a simple note: *I've arrived!* Depositing the phone back into her pocket, she stared out into the bustling city once again.

As she stood amidst the rich history that surrounded her in every direction, she thought about the spark of magic her grandmother got in her eyes whenever she spoke about her time in

Scotland. Now, surrounded by the very essence of that enchanting place, Nora could clearly grasp the allure, as if the city itself whispered stories on the cold wind. Touching the notebook tucked into the side of her bag, she smiled. She couldn't wait to write them down in verse.

Chapter Seven

FULL SCOTTISH BREAKFAST

Nora walked up three flights of stairs to the small flat she had rented in the large flagstone building adjacent to the nearby hotel, which had been out of her price range. Upon entering the giant blue door, she found a quaint apartment with high ceilings, large windows, and modest furnishings. The main living space was a large room with a small galley kitchen that opened into a living area featuring an impressive old fireplace, now modernized with an inlay gas unit. To the left, a small hallway led to two rooms: a tiny bedroom and a bathroom. The entire place was painted white, accented with colorful furniture, including a large mustard-yellow armchair near the window.

After Nora unpacked her things, her initial excitement fizzled out. Despite her plans to explore the city for a bite to eat, the weariness from the long day of travel began to weigh heavily on her. Before she knew it, she found herself dozing off in the armchair overlooking the street below.

She woke up just as the sun was breaking into a new day. Its rays cast streaks of golden light into the living room and across the chair she had fallen asleep in. She stood and arched her back, trying to rid herself of the stiffness from sleeping in the chair.

She walked over to the large windows overlooking the street below. The sun was just lifting its head above the horizon. Glancing down at her watch, she was surprised to see it was 8:26 a.m. She had slept almost fourteen hours straight. She never slept that much, but the travel, time zone change, and fighting her anxiety all day must have done a number on her.

She walked into the small kitchen, brewed herself a cup of coffee, and returned to the window overlooking the street. The morning rush was in full swing, and people darted about, bundled in their winter attire.

Nora reached for her carry-on, retrieving her small notebook and pen. People-watching had always been a soothing pastime for her, a way to ease her mind and stave off overthinking. It also often sparked inspiration for new poems or short stories. Selecting someone from the bustling street below, she would watch for a few minutes, then put pen to paper and write down what struck her about them.

As she scanned the streets, her eyes fell upon a small group of teenagers gathered near a signpost below her rental. Their laughter and lively chatter filled the air. Among them were two boys and three girls. One of the girls seemed standoffish, positioned on the outskirts of the circle as the other two girls engaged in flirtatious banter with the boys.

Letting her pen glide over the paper, she whipped up a funny little poem.

Oh, how I wish I was not shy. I could flash my boobs and get the guy. But that's not me. I'm meek and mild, but how I wish I was more wild.

She read her words back to herself and giggled. Nora knew she was no Emily Dickinson or Elizabeth Barrett Browning, but that was perfectly fine by her. Her poems weren't meant to be serious. She wrote more like Doctor Seuss or Shel Silverstein, whimsical and fun. And anyway, she wrote for herself, not to share with the world.

Looking back to the street, her attention shifted to a mother struggling with a small child who wanted to look in a shop window adorned with toys and Christmas decor. She pulled on the boy's gloved hand, urging him to hurry along. The boy protested, putting up a good fight until eventually his mother won and hurried him up the street and out of view.

Shiny toys and blinking lights, attract the eyes of little tikes. They look in wonder, their eyes grow wide, and beg and plead to go inside. But Mother has no time for games, there are more important things she claims. With tears and screams, they're pulled away, with promises to come back, another day.

As Nora finished writing the last words, she realized that she was drawing from her own experiences. There was never a moment for play as her mother was always consumed by work. Nora often wondered if her mother's habit of overworking was just her way of keeping her mind busy so that the demons of her past didn't surface. It was always easier to keep yourself busy rather than to deal with the hurt. She knew this firsthand from her experience with Sam. When she was a child, she hadn't understood, thinking her mother had loved the bakery more than her own daughter. But now, as an adult, she understood that loss and grief made people go inward. In a way, it might have been her way of protecting Nora from the sadness she carried.

Shaking herself out of her spiraling thoughts, she scanned the street again until her eyes landed on a man holding out a map while his wife pointed down at different spots on it. He looked up and briefly surveyed his surroundings before burying his nose back into the map.

Nora was about to begin to pen down a line when it reminded her that she had a scheduled tour booked for the afternoon. She pulled her phone out of her back pocket to double-check the exact time. The instructions said to meet at Mercat Cross, a historic monument near St. Giles' Cathedral at twelve o'clock. She checked her phone's map to see where she was in respect to the meeting location. It looked close and as long as she gave herself enough time she could easily walk there.

She drank the last sip of her coffee, tucked her notebook back into her bag, and went to get herself ready for the day. Dressing warmly in a long-sleeved shirt with a heavy wool sweater, she opted for the warm boots she had worn on the plane instead of the cute leather ones she had packed in her bag. If she was going to be on a walking tour of the city, she damn well wanted to be warm and comfortable.

Women from Boston came to the bakery in Vermont all the time in the winter dressed in leggings and tall leather boots with long oversized sweaters. Of course, they looked stylish, but they also looked like human popsicles. The older she got, the more comfort and warmth won over fashion. *Probably another reason I haven't had a date in two years*, she thought.

Her stomach grumbled as she combed her hair. It had been

more than eighteen hours since she had eaten, and all of a sudden it was catching up with her. She began to get lightheaded, and for a moment she had to sit down to steady herself. She never went this long without eating. She stood back up and grabbed a bottle of water from the tiny refrigerator. It helped fill the giant void she felt in her belly just enough to get her back up and going again. She glanced at the clock above the stove. There was still a little over an hour before she had to meet the tour guide, so she decided to venture out into the streets to find a place to get a bite to eat.

Grabbing her winter hat, a pair of wool mittens, and her down-filled jacket, she headed out the door into the chilly December air. A breeze blew down the street, and the cold bit into her jeans causing her to shiver and raise the collar of her jacket.

The rush of the morning crowd had begun to peter out, and the streets became more relaxed. As she walked down the uneven cobblestones, she continued to take in the stunning architecture of the city. The buildings alternated between gray and tan-colored sandstone, sitting snugly next to each other as if fused together by time itself. There in the long string of conjoined buildings was a turret that sat neatly above a shop that sold touristy goods and trinkets. Painted in the bright blue of the Scottish flag, the shop stood out with its crisp white shutters and a black entryway. Out front a crowd gathered around racks sporting T-shirts and hats with the word Scotland written across them in bright bold letters. Her eyes wandered past the shop and down the street where the buildings weaved along the curving road. Their ornate chimneys filled the cold gray sky with tiny puffs of white smoke creating a light smog that hung just above the rooftops. The sounds of a bagpipe carried on the wind skirted their way through the streets, bringing with them the smell of freshly roasted coffee.

She followed her nose to a small cafe that sat tucked between a clothing boutique and a tiny antique shop. A sign in its window read Mel's Breakfast and Lunch served daily. *Bingo!* she thought as she opened the bright red door. A gust of warm air with the rich aromas of coffee and savory spices greeted her as she stepped in from the cold. The cafe was small with a long counter that housed several stools, a window booth, and four tables that ran the length of the room.

Nora chose a small table that sat two by the window and pulled out a chair.

After peeling off her mittens and hat, she pulled out a menu from between a salt and pepper shaker set that sat in the center of the table. The menu included foods she had never heard of, such as Lorne sausage, black pudding, haggis, and tattie scones, along with what she thought were unusual breakfast choices like fried mushrooms, tomatoes, and baked beans. She was relieved to see eggs and bacon on the menu, as well as toast.

Within a few minutes, a waitress came walking over to her with a notepad in one hand and a coffee decanter in the other.

"Hi there, what can I get for you?" she said in her thick Scottish accent as she flipped over a coffee cup and filled it up.

"Hmm, I'm not quite sure," she said, looking down at the menu as her stomach let out a loud groan as if to say, *Hurry up and fill me.*

"Sounds to me like you're in need of a full Scottish breakfast," the waitress said with a bit of a giggle.

Nora turned a light shade of red and gave the woman an awkward smile.

"What's a full Scottish breakfast?"

"Well, you got your Lorne sausage, black pudding, tattie scones, baked beans, fried eggs, and bacon, along with mushrooms, tomatoes, and toast. You can also add haggis if you would like."

"Oh, I don't know if I'm that hungry. How about we skip the black pudding, baked beans, and haggis," she told the girl.

"You got it. It'll be right out," the waitress told her as she pulled the pen from her ear and scribbled on the notepad before walking back into the kitchen.

Nora looked out the window, watching people walk by as she sipped her coffee. It started to snow, and the scene looked like something she had seen on one of her grandmother's postcards. She thought about the tales her gram had told her when she was a child. Fantastical stories of magic here in this same city. She had always told Nora that it wasn't until she came to Scotland that her life truly began. Nora clung to this idea, hoping the same fate would await her, that her life might finally begin to take shape with a little help from that good old Scottish magic her grand-mother spoke of.

She was only going to be in the city for a few days before she ventured into the Highlands for the remainder of her trip. Nora had chosen to visit the village of Letterfearn, from one of the post-cards in the album. As far as she could tell, it was the only spot in the Highlands her grandmother had documented going to. It was quite far north, near the Isle of Skye, and the thought she was ven-turing there alone made her a bit nervous, to say the least. But she was doing her best to get excited. She had rented a cabin on the lake, or loch as they called it here, for the week. It looked like the ideal spot to hunker down and get in some relaxation and reading.

Nora picked up a paper on the empty table next to her and began reading the local news. She was halfway into an article about a lunar eclipse that was going to take place in the northern part of the country within the next few days when the waitress came back over. The plate was piled so high with food it looked as if it could have served an army.

"Here ya go," she said, setting the enormous plate of food down in front of her.

"Wow, that's a lot of food."

"I bet you get at least half that in you," the waitress joked. "Just let me know if you need anything else," she said as she walked over to a group of people who had just come in.

Nora had no idea where to begin. There was what looked like a sausage patty, fried eggs, bacon, some sort of flatbread, and a load of grilled mushrooms and tomatoes. The first thing she went for was the bacon, then the eggs. She was unsure about the other things on her plate, but she figured, when in Scotland! She forked a heap of the mushrooms and tomatoes. They were surprisingly tasty, and she ate almost all of them. She moved on to the potato flatbread, which she loved with its crispy edges and salty taste. By the time she was done sampling everything, she had almost cleared her plate. She was used to having muffins or scones for breakfast at the bakery, not a three-course meal. She was so stuffed she was worried her pants button might pop off and ricochet across the room.

She looked down at her phone. It was almost time to meet the tour guide, and she had about a four-minute walk to the monument, according to Google Maps. She paid her bill, bundled herself back up, and headed out into the cold, windy street toward the next adventure on her list.

Chapter Eight

HEART OF THE CITY

As Nora strolled down Cockburn Street and onto the Royal Mile, an unfamiliar sensation stirred within her. Initially, it felt like the onset of panic but soon morphed into something resembling the pull of a magnet, urging her forward. The closer she got to the monument, the stronger the sensation became until her entire body thrummed with it, resonating like a tuning fork that had just been struck. Snow spun up on the wind, whirling around her in a tiny vortex. Then, as quickly as it had come on, the feeling disappeared, as if whatever unseen force had drawn her toward that section of the street had completed its task and receded into the shadows.

The cold, dense air began to shift, and the snow continued falling softly from the thick, overcast sky. Nora pulled her hat down over her ears and approached the monument. It had a large stone base and high above, on one pillar, sat a unicorn. St. Giles' Cathedral towered over it on its left with its grand architecture. The street and the buildings almost seemed to meld together with their matching rich gray stones.

Nora spotted an older woman standing on the right side of the statue, holding a small sign that said Beckon Rock Tours. Excitement bubbled in her chest at the sight. This tour was a chance for her to get to know the city where her grandmother had lived back in 1943. A chance to immerse herself in its history, to uncover its stories that lingered in its Gothic alleyways and corners, and to forge a connection with her grandmother's past.

"Hello, I'm Nora Cameron. I am part of your twelve o'clock tour," she told the old woman as she walked up to her.

The woman looked to be about her parents' age, with her silver-white hair peeking out from under a knit cap.

"Yes, Ms. Cameron. My name is Mairi. We are just waiting for a few others that will be joining us," she said, her accent gracefully flowing from her as she pulled out a folded guide map from her pocket and handed it to Nora.

"Try and stick with the group, but if you wander off, this should help get you back on track."

"Thank you," Nora said as she took the map and tucked it into her jacket pocket.

Slowly people began to gather for the tour: a handful of Japanese tourists with large cameras around their necks, a Swiss couple with maps at the ready, and an American family of four— mother, father, and two sons. Once everyone had arrived, Mairi took charge, leading them up the Royal Mile. The first and most obvious landmark she highlighted was the cathedral and monument where they had met. Nora gazed at the massive windows adorned with beautiful stained glass and the ornate spires that lined the edges of the roof and steeple. Pulling out her phone, she zoomed in, attempting to capture the beauty of the cathedral's windows along with the sharp and powerful lines of its structure.

Opposite the cathedral stood the Dugald Stewart Building; its modern architecture and boxy shape sat in stark contrast to the centuries-old buildings surrounding it. It reminded Nora of the buildings in Boston. Finding it less than interesting, she turned away, deciding not to take a photo. Instead, she walked over to Mairi who was trying to gather the group's attention so that they could continue on.

Just a few steps up the cobbled street, Mairi stopped, pointing down rather than up toward the towering medieval buildings.

"Here we have the iconic Heart of Midlothian. It marks the spot of the Old Tolbooth, a building used for many things over the years, the city prison being the most noted. In 1736, a mob stormed the Tolbooth to rescue a group of prisoners who were scheduled to be executed for their involvement in the Porteous Riots. The building was demolished in 1817, and the memorial was built in its place in 1886," she told the group as they all looked down at the different colored granite bricks set into the cobblestone in the shape of a heart, with a circle in its center.

Nora had just snapped a photo with her phone when all of a sudden Mairi opened her mouth and spat on the heart. The group looked up at her, eyes wide and full of shock.

"For luck," she chuckled, then waved her hand down at it, as if saying, *Your turn.* "As an act of defiance against the horrible things that happened on this very site, to ward off the evil and bring in the luck," she told them, giving a nod of her head.

The first to spit on the heart were the two teenage boys, along with the rest of their family. Then the Japanese tourists and the

Swiss couple, leaving Nora last. It felt weird to spit on something out in public around so many people, but Mairi didn't seem to want to move on with the tour until everyone had their go. Nora looked down and spit, aiming directly at the center of the heart's circle. Mairi nodded in approval and continued on.

"Well, that was kinda weird," the mother of the American family said to Nora as they fell in step next to one another. "My name's Lesley, by the way."

"Nora, nice to meet you. That definitely wouldn't fly back at home," Nora said, and the woman chuckled and nodded her head in agreement.

They walked next to each other until the group slowed and came to a stop in front of a building reminiscent of a small castle. It housed a large turret on one end, complete with a balcony that looked straight out of a princess movie. The rest of the building broke away into sharp angles, giving its sturdy stone facade and its large chimneys a rather masculine feel.

"This here is the Writers' Museum. It's dedicated to celebrating the lives and works of three of Scotland's most famous literary figures: Sir Walter Scott, Robert Burns, and Robert Louis Stevenson. I suggest you have a look inside before you leave the city. It's something not to be missed," she said, waving her gloved hand at the elegant yet hard-edged building. The group marveled at the exquisite specimen as they all snapped photos and craned their heads up toward its spire that rested on the top of the corbelled corner.

Once everyone had their fill of the museum, they moved on, up the street, edging closer to Edinburgh Castle atop Castle Rock.

"Are any of you believers in the supernatural? Well, Edinburgh has a haunting history with witches. Back in the sixteenth and seventeenth centuries, the city was a center for witch hunts, and many unfortunate individuals faced persecution here. One eerie reminder of this time is the Witches' Well, located near the base of Edinburgh Castle," she said, pointing up the hill toward the grand castle emerging from the rocks. Its large bordering walls perched below the sturdy gray fortress seemed to be made of the very rock it sat upon. It was regal and daunting, commanding attention as it stood sentinel over the city, a stone guardian over-looking the people of Edinburgh.

"It's a memorial dedicated to the hundreds of women and men who were executed during the trials. There are bound to be some spirits wandering these streets from Edinburgh's marked past, don't you think?"

Nora shuddered at the thought of the lives lost in the hysteria, their blood once staining the very ground she walked upon. The grim thought cast a dark shadow over her mind. She tucked her hands inside her pockets, feeling suddenly exposed in the chilly air. As she glanced up the hill toward the well one last time, a sudden gust of frigid wind whipped down the street, blowing past her with such fury it stung her cheeks and tangled her hair.

"See," Mairi said, lifting her hands into the air as the wind blew past the group and smiling as if her point had just been made. She moved forward and guided them up the street and then stopped in front of a large stark-gray building.

"This here is the National Library of Scotland. It was built—"

Suddenly a loud thunderous noise cut Mairi off and stopped everyone in their tracks. Surprised, the group looked around in a panic for the source of the sound.

"Oh, nothing to worry about. It's only the One o'Clock Gun. Every day since 1861, except Sundays, a gun is fired from the castle at exactly one p.m. It was used to help ships synchronize their clocks. Now it's more of a tradition. You get used to it after a time, but it does tend to scare the tourists the first time they hear it," she chuckled.

Everyone let out a small laugh of relief. After all the talk of witches and ghosts that wander the old Gothic streets, the group was a bit on edge. As they began walking up the sloping street, Nora caught sight of a building she recognized. She stopped, pulled out her cell phone, and opened up the picture she had taken of her grandmother's photo. Looking back up, she saw the very place her grandmother had stood back in 1943. The building to the left matched the one in the photo, and looming above it in the background was the castle.

All of a sudden that feeling came rushing back over Nora, and her body hummed with electricity. This was her chance to recreate the image. She remembered seeing a small wine and spirits store a few shops back where she could get a bottle of wine for the photo. She looked ahead at the group walking up the street, then looked back over her shoulder toward the shop. Her rational and organized mind did something she normally wouldn't do. She broke away from her schedule and threw caution to the wind.

"I'll catch back up," she muttered to herself as she darted off in the opposite direction.

Chapter Nine

THE BOOKSHOP

Nora quickly made her way down the bustling street and into the wine and spirits shop. Despite the time of day, the store was surprisingly crowded. Weaving through the clusters of people, Nora finally found the large wine section at the back of the shop. The amount of choice was overwhelming.

The overcrowded space made her feel a bit claustrophobic, and she began regretting stepping foot inside. At this point she didn't care what type of wine it was; she just needed a bottle to hold for the photo. She hastily grabbed a bottle of red from a center display set up like a Christmas tree and walked back to the front of the shop to pay.

The crowded space had her on edge, and she tapped her foot impatiently as she stood in line. Glancing out the window onto the street, she watched a strong gust of wind pick up, causing tiny whirl-winds of snow to spiral into the air. *Like the energy rising in my chest,* she thought.

After paying for the wine, Nora stepped back out into the cold chill of the wintry air that hung heavy upon the city and began walking back to the spot where her grandmother had stood in the photograph. Recreating the image required more than just the wine bottle though; she needed a small red book as well. Scanning her surroundings for a bookstore or a gift shop, she found nothing. She hadn't noticed any bookshops on her way to the monument either. *Perhaps there'll be one ahead where the group was walking,* she thought. The wine sloshed around in the bottle as she increased her pace to a light jog to catch back up.

As she approached them, the soft, warm glow of twinkle lights caught her eye, and she turned to her right and found a small book-shop nestled between two towering buildings across the street from where she stood. Its large teal door, weathered with age, showcased a wreath crafted from holly and evergreen boughs. Flanking the door were two sizable windows with tiny panes bathed in the warm glow of Christmas lights.

Nora looked around, certain she had stood in this very spot when she recognized the building from her grandmother's photo. Yet, as far as she could remember, there had been no bookshop. She pulled out her phone and snapped a photo, then stepped forward and crossed the street, feeling that strange pull from earlier come rushing back. A wave of excitement shot through her as she turned the old ornate brass knob, wondering what she might find.

As soon as the door cracked open, another gust of wind blew so forcefully past her that the door burst all the way open, causing her to stumble as she entered. If she hadn't known better, she would have thought it had purposely pushed her in.

The door had brushed against a set of chimes hanging above it, their loud tinkle alerting the clerk to her presence. The aroma of old books and leather-bound covers greeted Nora as she stepped into the cozy shop. Mahogany bookshelves, worn with time, stretched from floor to ceiling, holding rows upon rows of what looked to be old antique books. A small book display sat on the top of a long counter, a little farther into the shop. As she drew closer, she made out that it was an array of old books on Yule and the winter solstice.

Boasting high ceilings with a second-story loft overlooking the ground floor, the shop felt like a step back in time; every detail, from the vintage light fixtures to the antique cash register, transported her to the forties. Nora could have spent her entire trip in this shop, looking through all the old books. She could picture herself getting lost in all the magical tales that surrounded her. Just the thought of it filled her with an energy that made her feel more alive than she had in years. A smile spread across her face as she took it all in.

"Hello, may I help you?" a scratchy voice said from behind a stack of books resting on a long counter that spanned one-half of the back wall. A short woman with salt-and-pepper hair and the thickest glasses Nora had ever seen stepped out from behind the counter with a cane and an inviting smile. Nora had been so swept up in the sheer beauty of the shop that she had almost forgotten what she had come in to get.

"Hello, this might sound a little odd, but I'm looking for a small red book."

"Do you know the title?" the woman asked, with a raise of a snowy white eyebrow.

"To be honest, any red book will do. It's for a photograph I need to recreate," she told the woman, feeling a bit awkward asking for a book solely for the color of its cover.

"Aye, I see. Looking for a Christmas book, then, I take it? 'Tis the time of year," she said as she walked over toward a large spiral staircase that wound its way to the second story, filled with even more books than the first. "I know just the section. You follow me," she told her, waving her forward to follow her up the staircase.

The wrought iron stairs, a masterpiece in their own right, featured curved bars that formed exquisite tulip-shaped fixtures supporting the railing, which the woman held onto as she climbed. She struggled, pulling herself up one step at a time. Upon reaching the top, she paused for a moment, resting on her cane to catch her breath.

"Oh my, I'm not as young as I think I am," she joked as she began walking again, leading them toward the back corner of the loft.

"Here we are. I think you might find what you are looking for here. Just remember, sometimes the best books are where you least expect them." She winked and then headed back to the stairs.

Odd thing to say, Nora thought as she began scouring the shelves for a small red book to recreate the photo. Several books with red spines caught her eye, but each one she pulled out revealed a different colored cover—brown, burgundy, green, but not red. Moving to the next case, she encountered the same thing—lots of red-spined books with mismatched covers.

How strange, she mused. She couldn't recall coming across many old books where the spine color differed from the color on the cover. Perhaps it had been more common than she thought.

About to return to the first bookshelf, figuring the burgundy-covered book would be the closest match she might find to red, something caught Nora's eye. Between the bookshelf and the wall was a flash of red. She took a few steps back and took another look. Snugly wedged between the wall and the weathered bookshelf was a tiny red book.

Setting the wine bottle down, she attempted to fish it out of the crack. Extending her arm into the narrow gap, she tried to reach it, but her arm was too big, and her fingertips just barely grazed the edge of the book's spine.

Pulling her arm back out, she spun around, scanning the room for something to fish it out with, but nothing caught her eye. On a second pass, her gaze landed on a small silver sword with a leather-wrapped hilt resting above the window—an unexpected touch of medieval King Arthur decor—and just what she needed. Glancing down over the railing, she saw the woman engrossed in sorting a large stack of books.

Seizing the opportunity, she grabbed a small stepladder, typically used for reaching books on the top shelves, and positioned it beneath the window. Climbing up with silent prayers that it wouldn't creak and alert the woman, she reached for the sword. To her surprise, it was much heavier than anticipated, nearly causing her to lose her footing as she carefully removed it from the wall.

Descending each step carefully, she made it down without a sound. She quickly made her way over to the book and slid the sword below it. With a gentle maneuver, it slipped between the pages. Like rescuing a bird with broken wings, she lifted the book up and out of the gap.

It was made of dark red leather and embossed with tiny golden leaves around its edges. The resemblance to the one her grandmother held in the photo was uncanny, and if she hadn't known better, she would have thought it was the very same book. Its beauty captivated her, pulling her in. She was just about to open it when the old woman yelled up, startling her.

"You finding everything okay, miss?" she called out from below.

"Yes, thank you."

Grabbing the sword, she quickly returned it to its place on the wall and slid the ladder back into position. Nora glanced down at the tiny red book, a smile playing across her lips. She retrieved her wine bottle and descended the stairs.

Upon reaching the bottom, she walked up to the counter, her eyes searching behind the stack of books for the woman.

"I think I found what I was looking for," she said, handing the book over to her as she popped out from behind a teetering stack.

"This book? Interesting. I would have guessed another for you, but the books know best," she said with a curious smile.

"How much?" Nora asked, pulling out some money from her jacket pocket, hoping it would be within her price range. All the books in the shop appeared to be antiques, and if it happened to be a rare book, there was a chance she wouldn't have enough money to buy it.

"No charge, my dear," she said, waving her hand in front of herself in a stopping gesture.

"No, I should pay for it," Nora insisted.

"I am the guardian of these books, and I can gift them as I choose. And today, I choose you," the woman told her, taking her hand and placing the book into it.

It was at that moment that Nora noticed something in the old woman's eyes that she hadn't seen before. Behind her thick spectacles, the elderly woman seemed to possess two different colored eyes, one blue as the sky itself and the other as rich as newly turned soil. She couldn't help but stare at them for longer than she probably should have. Finally breaking from her awkward gaze, Nora thanked the woman and carefully tucked the book into her jacket pocket.

As she walked over to the door leading out into the street, she paused, turning back and looking at the shop one final time. She wished she could have spent the rest of her day there getting lost in the books, but she had a task to check off her list.

She stepped out into the crisp, cool air, only taking a few steps away from the shop before she had the urge to turn back around. Glancing over her shoulder, she realized there was no sign or name adorning the windows or the door of the bookshop. *Peculiar*, she thought. This place must have been a long-standing staple of the street, one that all the locals were sure to have known about, but only the luckiest of tourists stumbled upon it, much like she had. The more she looked at it, the more the old bookshop almost seemed to glow—not from the enchanting Christmas lights that surrounded it, but as if the old gray stones themselves had an almost blue hue that surrounded each of them. A shiver ran down her spine as she stared at it, the air around her tingling with an eerie chill.

Brushing aside the idea, she decided it must have been the snow, combined with the setting sunlight, causing the odd effect. With a mental shrug, she turned back around and continued up the street.

When she arrived back at the spot where she would recreate the photo, everything was perfect—the snow, the light, and, most importantly, the book. Nora was going to be able to stage the image almost perfectly. Locating the exact spot on the street where her grandmother had stood, she spotted the tour group just ahead and ran to catch back up.

"Hey, could I get you to take a photo of me?" Nora asked Lesley, the mother from the American family.

"Of course," she said, taking the phone from Nora's hand.

Posing just as her grandmother had, the wine bottle held high in one hand and the little red book in her other, tucked up next to her heart.

"Beautiful," Lesley said with a kind smile as she snapped the shot, then handed Nora back her phone.

"Thank you. I'm trying to recreate a few photos that my grandmother took here in the forties."

"What a fun idea. I love that!" She smiled at Nora and moved back to stand beside her husband, weaving her arm through his. The sight made Nora's heart sink a little, and in that moment, she was reminded of just how alone she truly was here.

"And this here is our last stop, Royal Mile Whiskies, a great little shop for something to warm you up on your way home today." Mairi laughed, pointing to a quaint whisky shop with large windows trimmed in gold and filled with bottles of different shapes and sizes. Its polished black doors and trim stood out in contrast to the large gray building it sat snugly below, giving it a dark masculine feel. The rich aroma of aged spirits wafted through the crisp air, igniting a lively discussion within the group about which distilleries they had booked tours with while in the country.

Distracted by her thoughts, Nora stepped away from the group to inspect the photo Lesley had taken. She was surprised to find it was almost identical to the cherished image of her grandmother. She smiled, knowing how much she would have loved it.

As the tour ended and the group began to disperse, Nora made her way over to Mairi to thank her before bidding farewell to Lesley. She left the group behind with a sense of anticipation stirring within her. She navigated her way back to her rental, eager to put her feet up, uncork the wine, and delve into the mysterious little book she had stumbled upon at the enchanting little bookstore.

Chapter Ten

BROKEN BELLS

As Nora made her way back to her rental, the alluring scent of freshly baked bread captured her attention. It came from a small bakery across the street. Sporting a black-and-white striped awning and the name Mimi's in large gold letters above its door, it called to her. Deciding to pick up a baguette to accompany the wine and a few scones for tomorrow's breakfast, she crossed the street.

As she stepped inside the quaint little shop, the smells transported her straight back to Vermont, causing a very brief bout of homesickness to course through her. It faded quickly when she saw the bakery's impressive holiday displays.

The shop was decked out in its full Christmas attire, with fresh garland wrapped in lights hung around the borders of the room and beautiful homemade gingerbread houses sitting along the counter like a little snowy village. Three displays of sugar cookies with intricate icing work, along with thumbprint jam cookies and gemmed fruitcakes dazzled Nora as she browsed the selections. The entire bakery could have come straight out of the North Pole with its festive cheer. Nora took mental notes on how to improve the displays at Belwether Bakery back home.

Walking up to the long counter, she looked down into the display cases with their rounded glass fronts. Large trays and pedestal plates filled the inside of the cases, each with a crisp black-and-white nameplate of things she had never heard of—empire biscuits, Scottish macaroons, Ecclefechan tarts, and millionaire's shortbread, to name a few. Getting lost in the wide variety of sweets, she had almost forgotten what she had walked in for.

"Hello, can I get something for you?" a lanky teenage girl behind the counter asked.

"Hi, yes. Can you give me four of those amazing-looking gingerbread cookies, two scones, and a rosemary baguette?" She was unable to stop herself from indulging a little. Heck, that was one of the best things about being on vacation—calories didn't count!

"You got it," the girl said as she went about grabbing the items Nora had asked for and wrapping them up.

After paying and preparing to leave, Nora had the idea to capture a photo of the festive bakery to send to her parents and Eve. Just as she turned around and pulled out her phone, a set of large decorative Christmas bells hanging above the door suddenly came crashing down, landing mere feet away from her. The unexpected crash startled both Nora and the girl behind the counter so badly they simultaneously screamed as the bells let off a clang that reverberated off the tile floor.

"Oh my God, are you okay?" the girl asked, coming out from behind the counter to inspect the damage.

Adrenaline surged through Nora as she stood frozen, staring down at the large ornament broken at her feet. The metallic taste of fear lingered on her tongue while the hair on her arms prickled with the remnants of the close call.

"I'm fine," she said after a moment, "but it looks like your bells have seen better days."

The bells, crafted from cheap tin and bearing the weight of the garland and giant bow, had hit the tile floor from a considerable height, causing them to crack down their centers.

"I'm just glad you didn't get hurt. If you'd left just a few seconds later, it might be you on the floor," the girl said as she dragged the broken decoration out of the doorway and back behind the counter.

Nora smiled at the girl and reassured her again that she was fine before heading out of the bakery and back into the quickly fading day. Her heart had not stilled from the scare and was still pounding in her chest as she walked up the street toward her rental.

The dimming light had triggered the streetlamps and Christmas lights throughout the city to come on, and the sight stilled her racing heart. The city around her transformed as the snow still fell softly, picking up the glow of the twinkle lights around her and making them look as if they were sparks of magic floating in the air. The collecting snow gave the streets a thin layer of slush that made the walk a bit slippery.

Glancing at her phone, she was surprised to find that it was only three forty in the afternoon. Fatigue was starting to set in, a combination of the early sunset and lingering jet lag. While she was accustomed to the shorter days of winter in Vermont, the darkness setting in even earlier in Scotland was playing tricks on her internal clock, urging her to head home and crawl into bed.

Once she arrived back at her rental, she set the bottle of wine on the counter and went to look for a bottle opener. Three drawers and two cupboards later, she found one tucked behind a set of wineglasses. Once she uncorked the bottle, she poured herself a glass of wine, broke off a large hunk of bread, and headed into the living room to relax. She picked up her notebook and pen, ready to write down the events of her day, but nothing came out. She was too tired but didn't want to give in to sleep just yet. If she did, it would mean a three a.m. wake-up call from her internal alarm clock.

Instead, she got up, walked over to her jacket resting on the kitchen counter and pulled the small red book from her pocket. Returning to the overstuffed chair by the window, she flipped on a lamp and set her glass of wine on the side table.

Running her fingers across the gold-embossed vine that wound its way around the entire cover, she admired the small book's elegance. Oddly, there was no title or author's name on the cover, just the intricate design and a small dent in the upper right-hand corner, where it had taken an impact, leaving its almost perfect cover damaged. Intrigued, she turned the book over to check the spine, but it, too, was devoid of any text. She opened the book only to find a marbled first page followed by nothing but emptiness. Fanning through the rest of the book, all she discovered were more blank pages. It wasn't a book at all; it was a journal.

"I do believe this is a sign, Nora Cameron, to write down your thoughts from the day," she told herself as she got up and grabbed the pen off the table.

She flipped the book open again, but this time, instead of blank pages, there was page after page of print. Her heart sank as she quickly closed the book and looked around the room in alarm, as if someone had just played a trick on her. What had just happened? She could have sworn those pages were blank.

"What the hell?" she muttered to herself as she frantically flipped through the book again. "Maybe I should go to bed. This time change is messing with me."

Instead of following her own advice, she turned to the first page. Still no title, author's name, or publisher information. The thick paper held a font likely imprinted by an antique press, its elegant script featuring slanting text and a graceful transition from thick to thin letters. It smelled of old paper and aged ink, and Nora spotted a darkened stain, reminiscent of a cigarette burn, in the same spot on almost every single page. It wasn't enough to block out the text, but the book was certainly worn as if it had been read many times.

"**It was a cold December night when my heart broke. Shattering into a thousand tiny shards like a smashed Christmas bobble upon a marble floor.**" she read aloud. Captured by this first line she rested back into the chair and continued to read.

Chapter Eleven

THE LITTLE RED BOOK

The tale began with my solo voyage from my home in Edinburgh to my beloved Grandmother Mary's cottage in Oban in the winter of 1667. The journey was a long and solitary venture, with only the rhythmic clatter of hooves and the creaking of the carriage to keep me company. As I watched the snowy landscape unfold outside the carriage window, my apprehensions, along with the cold, began to tighten my neck, growing worse with every hoofbeat upon the frozen unforgiving ground.

I loved my grandmother dearly, but this was not a social visit. I was to attend a Christmas ball hosted by Duke Campbell of Argyll in an attempt to procure a husband. Despite my grandmother not being of noble birth, she had once saved the duke's wife and newborn son during childbirth. In gratitude, he had treated her kindly ever since, extending invitations to all his gatherings. However, this was the first time my grandmother had accepted one of his invitations, doing so as a favor to my mother.

My mother, harboring hopes that my grandmother might succeed where she had not, sent me on the journey with the expectation of her finding me a suitable match at the ball. At the age of twenty, I was certain my marital status bore the weight of my mother's disappointment, and my grandmother, ever the diplomat, accepted the responsibility of helping to find me a suitor. My mother claimed that I thwarted every well-to-do man she sent my way, and she wasn't entirely mistaken. I had no desire to become someone's wife, paraded around at social gatherings like a possession upon some man's arm. I knew it was unavoidable, but I longed for more time. Perhaps another year or two to explore my passion for writing would give me solace before submitting to the expectation of being someone's wife. Yet, my time had been stretched to its limits, and there were no more extensions to be granted. Nevertheless, I would do my duty and play my part while I was here, solely to please my grandmother, who had always been more than kind and loving to me.

I had only just arrived in Oban at my grandmother's cottage long enough to warm myself by her fire and indulge in a slice of her home-made bread with berry jam and a hot cup of tea when one of the duke's carriages pulled up to her quaint home to take us away to the grand castle in Inverary. Festivities were planned two days prior to the ball, and the duke had requested our presence. A raw mixture of excitement and dread floated around inside me as we climbed in and ventured on. The ride took almost an entire day, given the condition of the roads, and my back pained me to be sitting in another carriage again so quickly. Although short in comparison to the trek from Edinburgh to Oban, the ride was still frigid. Even in the duke's finest carriage, the frost seemed to be working its way in, nipping at our fingertips and noses. My grandmother began coughing and pulled her cape tighter around her frail frame. Just as I began to fear she would not be able to endure much more of the cold that had permeated inside the carriage, the hoofbeats slowed, and the castle finally came into view.

We had arrived just before the sun had begun to set, and the world outside was a cold wintry white. The castle grounds had been festooned with every fancy frill and bauble for the festive season. Giant wreaths and evergreen garlands hung above every window and doorway, along with clusters of holly and ivy serving as fine decorative touches on each of the fence posts. Crimson flags waved in the cold winter breeze from the turrets, and above the main doors, a strip of red fabric adorned with the Campbell clan crest hung neatly on display. The grandeur of the castle laid out before me was both impressive and a little daunting. Yet, as I gazed upon it, I couldn't help shake the feeling that I was a mere speck in its vast shadow, questioning my presence here at all.

For the three-day event, the duke had graciously offered us a guest cottage on the castle grounds. The carriage came to a stop in front of the cottage, a humble stone house with smoke gracefully billowing from its chimney. Eagerly, we stepped out of the frigid carriage and hurried inside, escaping the cold. The footman followed, carrying our bags into the cozy space. The cottage welcomed us with warmth from a generous fire blazing in its sizable hearth. After warming up near the fire, we unpacked our modest belongings in preparation for dinner in the castle's main hall.

Despite my grandmother's age, she still had the strength to pull my corset strings so tight that I could scarcely breathe, ensuring I looked every bit a lady, a role I despised. After pinning up my hair and smoothing out my modest dress made of dark burgundy wool, I realized it lacked the luster that would likely embellish the other women at the dinner. Nonetheless, it was one of the finest dresses I owned, and I wore it well.

Any flicker of excitement I had felt during the ride from Oban to the castle quickly faded with the familiar sound of the horse's heavy hoofbeats outside the cottage. Doubt crept in, and I questioned my suitability to grace this grand hall among such well-to-do guests. I felt like an imposter, lacking a significant social standing. Nerves churned in my stomach, and my corset seemed to constrict even further as I held my breath, the coachman's knock on the door intensifying my nervous belly.

The carriage took us the brief distance from the cottage to the main entrance of the castle, where a line of carriages had gathered, delivering the duke's guests who had journeyed in for the event. Following suit, we disembarked from the carriage and passed through the grand doors that were opened by two finely dressed men.

While I had stood on the edges of lawns and gazed upon the grounds of many castles from afar in my childhood, the reality of Inverary Castle's exterior surpassed my youthful dreams. My heart quickened as we entered, and a nervous energy surged through me, a vibration that I feared was visible to any who might cast a glance in my direction. Sensing my unease, my grandmother gently squeezed my gloved hand, offering me reassurance that all would be well.

"Be at ease, my child. You appear as if you're a frightened rabbit," she whispered as we ventured further into the grand castle. A soft, nervous laugh escaped my lips, and I surveyed the well-dressed attendees streaming down a long hallway, making me acutely aware of the lackluster quality of my own attire.

The castle's interior exceeded the grandeur of its exterior. Large decorative bells, holly, and paper ornaments adorned the ceiling. Evergreen garlands, trimmed with holly berries, gracefully wound their way up the banisters of the two grand staircases that led to the second floor.

We were ushered into the grand hall by a tall handsome man who directed us to our table setting. I picked nervously at a small thread that had come loose from my dress, making it all the more evident that I was out of place. Social gatherings, especially those of such grandeur, were not my forte. I loathed the forced conversations and the way men eyed me as though I were some prize to be won. I would have much rather been sitting by the fire reading or writing a book of my own.

My mother often remarked that my pretty looks and fine figure granted me the choice of any man within my social standing. Yet here within the walls of the castle, these men were well above those standings, and I questioned whether this held true. Perhaps, in this setting, I would seem an easy target — a woman of lower class, eager for the attention of a man from a higher rank.

Despite these thoughts, I had no aspirations to be anyone's wife. Nevertheless, the responsibility to marry well had fallen upon me after my father's passing, to help sustain the family, and thus, I found myself in the duke's home.

"Where is the duchess and her son?" I whispered to Gran, curious to lay eyes upon the boy she had saved. There were whispers he was obstinate yet known for his kindness.

"I do not see them," Gran said as she scanned the room, her eyes searching from one person to the next.

We were seated toward the end of the grand table and presented with mugs of mead as servants brought out trays laden with roasted meats and fowl adorned by colorful root vegetables. White bread was served, its delicate richness contrasting with the coarse brown bread I was accustomed to. A sizable meat pie was placed before me, and a slice was served onto my plate. The tender venison, potatoes, and carrots infused with a medley of spices were quite a treat, and I quietly savored each bite as I listened to the men's lively conversations.

My ears caught fragments of conversations drifting from one end of the table to the other. They spoke of a hunt to be hosted by the duke within the coming days. Soon the discussions shifted to politics and the delicate dance of power between our beloved Scotland and the ever-watchful eye of England. While the men continued their talks, my thoughts meandered, weaving through the fabric of their words like threads in a tapestry. I wondered what it would be like to be a wife who must endure talks of these matters regularly.

The dreadful thought made me yearn to leave, to escape. The tightness of my corset, combined with a full belly and the shallow breaths I had been taking all night, left me faint. Unable to endure the constriction any longer, I excused myself, feeling that I might be ill, much to my grandmother's disappointment.

As I walked toward the door that would free me from the grand hall and the uneasy evening, a large set of brass bells, accompanied by a giant string of garland, suddenly came crashing down, landing at my feet.

Nora stopped reading, her blood running cold as she read the last sentence over again. Hadn't that been nearly the same thing that had happened to her at the bakery this afternoon? *What are the chances?* she thought as she turned the page and began to read again.

Gasps of surprise filled the room as men rushed to my aid. I reassured the men I was fine when the duke stepped up and looked me over. I tried to reassure him, but he was visibly upset and demanded to know who had hung the decorations as he scanned the edges of the room where his servants stood. No one stepped forward except my grandmother, who quickly escorted me out of the hall, thanking the duke on our way out before returning to the cottage.

"That was surely a sign," she remarked when we entered the cottage, her superstitious tendencies coming to the forefront.

"Yes, a sign they need better help. Now, if you would please help me out of this so that I can properly breathe again," I quipped, prompting her to scoff as she untied my corset. Exhausted from the long day, I changed out of my formal attire and dressed for bed, but Gran remained awake. Even in my deep slumber, she woke me several times as she moved about the cottage's kitchen late into the night.

The next morning greeted me with soft golden rays of light filtering through the window, accompanied by the inviting aroma of freshly baked bread drifting from the tiny kitchen of the cottage. I followed my nose to discover a beautiful loaf of bread that my grandmother had baked, alongside a steaming pot of tea. *It must have been what she was doing in the kitchen so late last night,* I thought.

"Good morning," she greeted me, seated in a rocking chair near the crackling fireplace, embroidering as she rocked. She looked spry for someone who had gotten very little sleep the night before.

"The sun has finally made an appearance, I see," I remarked, glancing out the window toward the castle. The world outside had been blanketed with a fresh layer of white snow overnight, sparkling under the morning sun.

"I think I might go explore the grounds," I told her as I poured myself a cup of tea.

"I think that is a wonderful idea. Just make sure you're dressed for the weather. It's quite cold despite the sun," she advised as she set her embroidery aside and walked over to refill her own teacup.

After eating my fill of bread with butter, I bundled up to combat the cold and fetched my overcoat. As I put it on, I accidentally popped one of the top buttons. Unwilling to stay indoors while my grandmother mended it, I tucked the button into my pocket and ventured into the wintry wonderland with only half of my coat properly secured.

It turned out to be a regrettable decision, as misfortune struck as soon as I stepped outside. A large clump of snow tumbled from the roof, landing squarely down the back of my neck. At that very moment, I should have known it was destined to be an unpleasant day.

Nora's eyes were growing weary as she neared the end of the page, and she set the book down. Almost nodding off, she decided it was time for bed. She needed a decent night's sleep. Rising from the chair, she stretched and glanced back at the book, its crimson cover standing out in stark contrast against the dimly lit room. There was something peculiar about the book beyond its lack of title or author—it felt strangely familiar, as if it echoed a story she remembered from her childhood.

Walking down the narrow hallway, Nora opened the door to the bedroom. An unexpected gust of cold air greeted her, sending a shiver down her spine. Puzzled, she scanned the room for the source, checking each of the large windows to ensure they were firmly shut. Looking down at the street below, she saw it was quiet, the snow still falling softly. The buildings appeared sleepy under the blanket of night, their façades illuminated by the gentle glow of the old ornate metal lamp posts lining the street. It reminded her of a scene from Dickens's *A Christmas Carol*.

Turning back around, Nora felt another shiver chase through her as the chill began to work its way into her clothes. Maybe there was no heat in the room, and with the door left closed all day, it grew cold. This seemed like the most likely case as she couldn't find a radiator or any heat vents. Grabbing her bag, she stripped off her clothes, quickly replacing them with a cozy pair of red flannel pajamas before diving under the covers.

Despite the warmth and comfort of the inviting bed, sleep would not come. Wide awake and staring into the darkness, she lay there for what felt like an eternity. Her mind wandered to the little red book. She couldn't help but think about how odd it was that she had narrowly avoided being struck by a set of Christmas bells, much like the character in the book. It wasn't just the strange coincidence that unsettled her; the story within the book felt oddly familiar, as if she had heard the tale before, even though she knew she hadn't. Her grandmother had mentioned that her grandfather's ancestors were from Oban; maybe that connection was the

source of this weird feeling. Whatever it was, the story tugged at something deep within her, filling her with a mix of unease and eagerness to continue reading. However, that would have to wait; she needed to sleep.

Just as she was on the verge of surrendering to restlessness, sleep's gentle embrace finally claimed her, and she drifted off into the realm of dreams.

Chapter Twelve

THE CHRISTMAS MARKET

Nora stirred, awakened by the morning sun filtering through the curtains, casting its warm glow over the bed where she lay cocooned in blankets. At first, she was hesitant to expose herself to the chill in the room, but she eventually mustered the courage to emerge from beneath the covers. To her surprise, the cold had dissipated entirely. Instead, the room felt almost too warm with the sun's rays beating through the curtains with some intensity. Blinking against the brightness, Nora stole a glance out the window, noticing the sun's high position in the sky. Alarmed, she looked at her watch: 11:05 a.m.—the day had slipped away unnoticed as she slept.

"Damn it. I missed the cutlery and spirits tour," she announced to the empty room as she got out of bed. This had been the only other tour she had booked for the trip—a walking tour exploring the best bars and restaurants in the city. Her stomach turned, fueled by the awareness that she was now off schedule, with no clear idea of how to salvage the day.

Chiding herself for not setting an alarm, Nora sighed and made her way into the kitchen. The idea of not having a set plan for the day made her a little anxious. It was her last full day in the city before she ventured out into the Highlands to the village of Letterfearn tomorrow, and now her plans were completely up in smoke.

She set a pot of coffee brewing and watched it impatiently while it slowly dripped into the pot. As the rich aroma filled the air, she leaned against the counter, still mulling over the unexpected turn of events. There was nothing she could do to change the missed tour, but she decided to make a new plan, determined not to let this blip spoil her entire day.

She walked over to the large window that faced the Royal Mile and looked out into the bustling street. It had snowed again overnight, and although the city was blanketed in white, the bright mid-morning sun was beginning to melt it. The edge of the roof dripped, and the sun cast tiny prisms of color against the kitchen walls with each drop of melting snow. Following their rainbow trails across the room, her eyes landed on the little red book resting on the side table.

Stepping forward, she picked it up. She still couldn't shake the eerie coincidence that had unfolded—the near miss with Christmas bells echoing a scene from the very book she held in her hands. A shiver ran down her spine as she thought about the uncanny parallels between fiction and reality. It was odd: it read like a journal but was printed and bound like a book. And what about the book appearing as blank pages at first, only to transform into printed text in her hands, adding another layer of mystery to the whole situation. *Maybe it is one of those illusion books with heat-activated ink,* she thought. Still, that didn't explain the strange coincidence with the Christmas bells. Perhaps it was just that—a bizarre coincidence.

Interrupting her stream of thought, the coffee pot's beep signaled that her much-needed caffeine was ready. Setting the book aside, Nora went back into the kitchen.

Pouring the steaming coffee into her mug, she couldn't resist the temptation of the gingerbread men peeking out from the bakery bag. She plucked one out and without hesitation, dipped its foot into the coffee and then promptly bit it off. The sweet taste of sugar and spices provided a welcome distraction as she washed it down with a sip of the hot coffee.

Nora, still nibbling on the cookie, strolled back into the bedroom and retrieved her grandmother's photo album from its snug spot in her bag. Carrying it into the kitchen, she felt a spark of serendipity. If this album was to be her travel guide, now was the perfect moment to let its pages unfold the map of her next adventure. This was her chance to be a little spontaneous and go off course.

Flipping through the pages of memories, she paused at a photo capturing her gram in front of a Christmas tree in the hospital ward, hand raised up toward the top of the tree, and a radiant smile gracing her face.

Nora paused for a moment, staring down at the photo, and then it came to her. The Christmas Market was something on her list to do anyway and now that the tour was out, it was the perfect activity for the day. Swiftly grabbing her phone, she mapped out the location of this year's market while finishing off her gingerbread man.

Eager and a tad proud of herself, she hurried to prepare for the day, ready to embark on the new and unexpected adventure her grandmother's memories were unfolding for her.

After a good shower and some clean clothes, she was ready to go. Grabbing her bag and her jacket she walked out the door of her rental. As she prepared to leave the building, Nora reached to zip up her coat. However, just before she could secure it, the zipper jammed halfway up, leaving half her chest exposed to the wintery air. She tugged at it and tried to free the fabric from its grasp.

"Good thing I opted for layers today," she muttered to herself as she gave up on trying to free the stubborn zipper.

Despite the sun casting its full glow, the temperature lingered just above freezing as Nora stepped out into the frigid morning. Emerging from under the awning, she checked her phone, pulling up Google Maps to pinpoint her destination. Just as she was about to step out onto the street, a large clump of snow slipped from the awning, landing squarely down into the open gap of her jacket.

"Shit," she said as she let out a small scream, the cold snow sliding down her back. She began jumping up and down while pulling at the bottom of her jacket to release the snow. People stared at her like she was a crazy person but at that very moment, she couldn't care less. All she wanted was the icy snow out of her shirt. As hard as she tried, it was no use as the snow melted quickly at the touch of her warm bare skin and left her with goosebumps from head to toe.

Quickly, Nora made her way down Princes Street, her breath visible in the crisp air. The unexpected snow shower had left her chilled, and she was eager to find the market and a hot cup of cocoa.

Extending across the large gateway into the market, a festive red and white banner proudly announced Edinburgh Christmas Market in gold-trimmed letters. She found herself taken aback by the sheer size of the space. It unfolded before her like a festive labyrinth, not just a multitude of vendors but also an assortment of fair rides. Twinkle lights brightened every stall, and small Christmas trees nestled in pots were scattered along the thoroughfare. The air seemed to crackle and spark with Christmas magic, and she felt like a wide-eyed child as she looked around in wonder.

Amidst the lively hum of voices, the distant sound of a bagpipe wafted from the far end, complemented by cheerful tunes of traditional Christmas music echoing from a nearby merry-go-round. The smell of mulled wine and hot chocolate filled the air where she stood.

Turning around, she found a small stall painted in pine green with a vinyl banner that said Coffee and Cocoa in bold red letters and lit with twinkling fairy lights. A tall woman, slightly older than Nora, stood behind the counter, taking orders. She joined the line behind a middle-aged couple dressed in business attire. The man whispered something to the woman, who chuckled and playfully nudged him. Watching their flirtatious exchange, Nora guessed they were newly dating and out on a lunch date.

The sun ducked behind a cloud as a pang of loneliness settled in her stomach while she watched the couple pay for their cocoa and disappear into the bustling crowd. As much as she hated to admit it, she missed the kind of companionship she once had with Sam. *It would've been nice to have someone to share this experience with, exploring Scotland together.* Then her thoughts drifted to her grandmother, who had ventured to Scotland alone. She didn't need anyone with her to find the magic of this place; she had discovered it on her own with her adventurous spirit.

Nora needed to channel her grandmother's drive and zest for life by embracing this adventure. Now was her time to truly immerse herself in the magic of the moment.

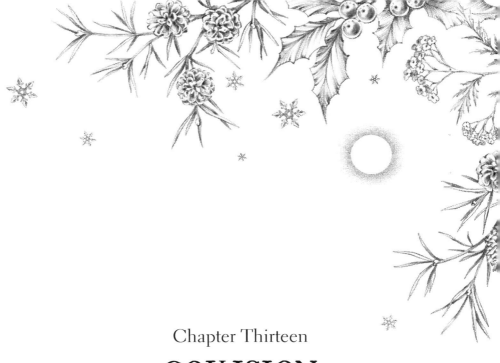

Chapter Thirteen

COLLISION

After ordering a cup of cocoa, Nora continued wandering the pathways through the sea of vendors with a new determination to step outside her comfort zone.

The countless vendor stalls formed a bustling row, accompanied by hundreds of people strolling through, enjoying the spirited atmosphere of the market. Ahead, a fiddler played a lively jig while the sweet smells of Christmas—ginger, allspice, and cinnamon—filled the air from a nearby tent selling an array of baked goods.

Traveling down a long row of vendors, Nora sipped at her cocoa and perused a few stalls that caught her eye. A jeweler displayed hammered silver and gold necklaces, a small booth offered homemade herbal tea blends, and a vintage music tent showcased old records and memorabilia. Her eyes lit up when she spotted an Oasis pin, and she knew she had to have it. The band had been a favorite of hers in high school, and she remembered attending one of their concerts with her friends as a last hurrah together during their senior year.

After purchasing the pin and securing it to her jacket, she tossed her empty cup into a bin and made her way down toward the end of the row. The smell of fresh popcorn and spicy-rich foods hit her nose, and her stomach began to groan. That lone gingerbread man she had eaten earlier was having a hard time combating her hunger. She followed the savory aroma of meat mixed with tangy spices over to a vendor's tent to her right with a sign that read Meat Pies.

Doing her best to be adventurous, she got in line. This was not normally something she would have gone for, but she reminded herself that stepping out of her comfort zone was the only way to experience a truly authentic life. *Something as small as trying a meat pie counts*, she thought as she stepped over to the menu.

The only meat pies she had ever eaten were turkey ones her mother cooked after Thanksgiving. These pies looked very different from that. They were small square individual sizes with brown flaky crusts and slits carved into their tops to show off what was inside. She had a variety of pies to choose from—minced, lamb, beef, pork, and venison, and it took her a moment to decide.

"Can I help ya?" a portly man behind the table asked as she stepped forward.

"Yes, could I get a venison pie?" she asked. She had eaten venison before but never in pie form.

He nodded and turned to face a large pair of warmers, pulling a pie from the smaller of the two and putting it in a to-go box. Then he uncovered a Crock-Pot and generously added a dollop of what appeared to be mashed potatoes on top of the pie, completing the savory dish.

"That'll be seven pounds," he said, handing her the pie along with a white plastic fork.

Nora paid the man and then retreated back to the thoroughfare, stabbing her fork into the pie and pulling out a morsel of carrot and a small piece of meat. *Here goes nothing*, she thought, taking a tentative bite. The flavors of rosemary and thyme danced on her tongue, accompanied by a subtle hint of what she guessed was red wine. The meat was tender and melted in her mouth while the buttery crust provided just the right balance of texture. To her surprise, it was quite delicious. *See, trying new things isn't that bad*, she thought as she chewed her bite and looked around.

Navigating through the bustling market felt like playing a game of pinball, bouncing off people's shoulders as she moved through the busy rows. Trying to protect her pie while struggling amid the crowd, Nora finally found an empty spot near a vendor tent and tucked herself away to eat the rest of her pie in peace.

Emerging from her hideaway after a few minutes, she was just about to toss the final bit of pie in the trash when the damn cannon went off again. She turned abruptly toward the sound and unexpectedly crashed into someone. She had collided with a man walking in the opposite direction, and the last morsel of the pie tragically landed squarely on his chest.

"Oh my God, I am so sorry," she sputtered, her cheeks blooming with embarrassment. Quickly she stepped back to inspect the person she had just run into. Her eyes met a man who looked to be around her age. He had a thick head of dark blond hair, a light five o'clock shadow, and his green eyes were full of utter annoyance. He was handsome, yet the furrowed brows and irritated expression indicated he was far from pleased. Nora's heart leaped into her throat, and the once-enjoyable meat pie now felt like a heavy brick in her stomach as she braced for the aftermath of the collision.

He looked down at his chest and then up at her, his eyes narrowing with disgust.

"Stupid bloody Americans. Why can't you just stay in your own country?" he spat, brushing off a piece of crust and carrot from his jacket.

Momentarily stunned by his rude response, Nora stood there as he briskly walked away. *Who the hell did he think he was? What a complete ass*, she thought as she picked up the to-go box from the ground and tossed it into a nearby bin. She watched him as he pushed through the crowd, his arrogance apparent in every step he took as he faded from view. She had never been talked to so rudely.

She took a few deep breaths, attempting to calm herself, but his words kept echoing in her head, surfacing the question that had been buried in her mind since her arrival: Why was she here? Yes, she wanted to honor her grandmother's final wish, but deep down she had wished this journey might lead her to discover her own true calling. Now Nora couldn't help but wonder if maybe she should have stayed in America. Maybe she was chasing after something that didn't exist. Perhaps it was time to stop fighting against the tide and embrace the familiar, to accept her fate and take over the bakery like her mother had always expected. But even as she entertained the idea, a small voice inside her whispered that there was still so much more out there waiting for her, if only she had the courage to reach out and seize it.

As her mind raced, the sky darkened with a thick layer of clouds, and large snowflakes gently descended as she began walking through the market stalls again. Trying desperately to pull the heavy thoughts from her mind and focus on the present, she began searching for something she could buy as a memento. In spite of the array of enchanting crafts, nothing caught her eye.

As hard as she tried to enjoy herself, the run-in with the rude man sent her into a downward spiral that she just couldn't pull herself out of. She eventually gave up looking and decided to head back to her rental. There was no point—she was locked in this mood and the only thing that was going to pull her out of it was a tall glass of wine.

She turned on her heels and began walking back toward the front of the market when a vendor tent pulled her attention. The small stall was tended by an old gentleman, his back hunched with age and his hair as white as the snow itself. He sold small hand-painted ceramic Christmas baubles adorned in a Celtic folk art style with rich, earthy tones. The ornaments hung off display stands around the stall, enchanting the space with the spirit of the holiday season.

Nora explored the tent, spinning a few bulbs as she inspected them from every angle. One caught her eye—a small ornament, no bigger than a tangerine, in a deep royal blue. White foxes painted against the blue backdrop ran through fallen leaves toward a small Celtic knot with three points connected by a circle. It reminded Nora of the old blue-and-white china plates her grandmother used for special dinners during her childhood.

Unable to resist, she slid the ornament off the hook, turning it in her hands. The cold ceramic quickly warmed to her touch, and after a moment, it almost felt as if it were growing hot. Walking over to the man, she held it out in front of her.

"Hello, how much for this?" she asked.

"Why, hello. Let me see," he said, pulling down a pair of wire-rimmed glasses from his head of thick white hair and placing them on the bridge of his nose. He inspected the ornament. "Oh, this is one of my favorites. I painted it years ago. I'm glad it's finally found its owner," he said as he wrapped it in tissue paper and then tucked it safely in a bag. "For you, my dear, it's free. I do believe it's meant for you." He handed her the bag.

A peculiar feeling settled in her gut. His words were almost the same as what the woman at the bookstore had said to her just yesterday. What a bizarre coincidence.

She looked at him and smiled, even though a creeping feeling was working its way through her.

"Thank you, that's very kind, but I would like to pay you for the hard work you put into making it."

"No need. I am just happy it's finally found its purpose," he said to her with a sparkle in his eye.

Not wanting to offend the man and ready to be done with the market, she thanked him and took the bag, then headed back onto the main thoroughfare toward the exit.

Approaching the gateway that led back onto the street, Nora spotted a tall Christmas tree to her right. Adorned with thousands of sparkling twinkle lights, it was the perfect tree to recreate the photo of her grams, even if it was outdoors.

Walking over, she spotted an older woman nearby enjoying a large, frosted sugar cookie.

"Excuse me," Nora asked hesitantly, "would you mind taking a photo of me?"

The woman smiled warmly. "Of course, dear."

Posing gracefully, Nora lifted one hand toward the tree's top, just as her grandmother had in the photo, and forced a smile even though her heart wasn't truly in it.

Taking her phone back, Nora thanked the woman and made her way out of the gates onto the bustling street. Glancing back at the tree, she found it almost entirely obscured by the throng of people wandering through the market, only its tip peeking above the crowd. An odd sensation stirred within her, the same energy she'd felt near the monument yesterday. She rubbed her arms, attributing the feeling to a mere chill, but deep down, she sensed it was something far more mysterious in the Scottish air around her.

Chapter Fourteen

THE COLLISION OF WORLDS

I t was a quarter past two when Nora returned to her rental, and the sun was dipping into the sky behind the towering buildings in the city. Her plans to stop at a restaurant on the way back had been halted as the temperature plummeted. It had grown bitterly cold since she left the market, and all she wanted to do was turn on the gas fireplace in the apartment and warm herself by it.

She figured there must be half a dozen pizza places in the city that delivered, and right about now, pizza sounded like just the cure for the day she'd had.

Entering the rental, she set her bags on the small kitchen table and quickly made her way over to the fireplace to turn it on. After flipping on a few switches, the fire came to life.

The flames flickered, dancing around the faux logs behind

the glass. She stood before it, the warmth seeping in through her cold-stiffened jeans and dispelling the chill. Soaking up its warmth, she searched for a pizza place on her phone. Deciding on a large pizza with bacon, feta, and extra olives, she placed her order, then strolled over to her bag and extracted her journal. She began jotting down her thoughts about the day.

As she began recounting her day, something struck her. The morning's events eerily mirrored the incident described in the last page of the little red book she had read the night before. Just like the woman who had broken a button off her jacket, preventing it from fastening properly, Nora's zipper had gotten stuck, and they had both found themselves caught off guard by the snow cascading from the roof down their backs. How had she missed the likeness between the two events? In that frantic moment, her primary concern had been removing the snow and finding a hot drink to warm herself up, leaving little room for contemplation. It wasn't until now that the similarities dawned on her.

Her gaze shifted to the book resting on the side table. There was something very odd about it, beyond the absence of a title or author. It seemed to radiate a magnetic energy, much like the pull of the moon on the ocean. She found herself irresistibly drawn to it, but such a notion seemed absurd, didn't it? After all, it was just an old book, and besides, didn't all good stories pull you in?

Setting her journal aside, she approached the little red book. As she picked it up, a mixture of intrigue and trepidation flooded her senses. Uncertain about whether she genuinely wanted to delve into its pages once again, she hesitated, leaning forward as if to return it to the table. However, she knew that curiosity would eventually get the better of her, so she gave in and dragged the overstuffed chair in front of the fireplace, took a seat, and hesitantly opened the book.

She searched for the last page she had read the night before. When her fingers finally traced the familiar spot, she settled back against the chair, throwing her legs up over the armrest. Her feet dangled in front of the warm glow of the fire as she began to read, once again giving into the allure of the mysterious little red book.

As I explored the castle grounds, I came upon two men carving figures from ice outside what I assumed to be the ballroom windows that faced the east. The duke had spared no expense preparing for the ball, making it a lavish event to be talked about well into the coming year.

The cold had quickly worked its way into my shoes, and I could feel the frosty chill nipping at my toes. I ventured back to the small cottage and found my grandmother just as I had left her, sipping tea by the fire and embroidering.

"How was your walk?" she asked, looking up from her work.

"Beautiful, but cold. The grounds are beautiful."

"Indeed, they are," she said, pulling the needle up and through the fabric.

"Gran, was last night the first time you've seen the duke since you saved his wife and son during childbirth?" I asked, a question that had preoccupied my mind during my walk earlier.

"No, my dear," Gran replied, her eyes reflecting a distant memory. "I tended to the duchess many times over the years, but it has been some time since we have seen each other."

"How long has it been?"

"Let me think. Their son, James, had to have been around fifteen the last time I was here, so right around five years, give or take," she said, continuing to work her needle.

"James is my age?" I inquired, a bit surprised.

"Yes, born at the start of the year during a horrible ice storm."

I sat there for a moment, digesting this new information. I had thought the duke's son to be much older than myself. Hoping that Gran would continue with her story, I sat silent for a long moment. However, instead of continuing she focused her attention back to her embroidery.

"What is it that you are working on?" I asked as I walked over and peered down at the small piece of fabric in her hands.

"A stomacher for your ball gown," she said as she pulled the needle through the rich emerald-green velvet.

It was a beautiful Celtic knot woven through the fabric with golden thread.

"What does the knot signify? It's beautiful."

"I'm glad you like it. This is the trinity knot, the ancient symbol for life, death, and rebirth. It can also be used as a powerful protection charm and to bring you a bit of luck," she told me.

There had always been whispers throughout the village that Gran was a witch, and in moments like these, those whispers felt more like truth.

"It should look quite fetching under the gown the duke sent over," she told me.

"Gown?" I scanned the room but found nothing.

"It's on your bed. One of his servants brought it by while you were out."

I hurriedly entered my room to discover, resting upon my bed, a sizable box adorned with a rich blue silk ribbon tied in a bow. I eagerly untied it, letting the ribbon fall to its sides as I lifted the lid of the box. Nestled within was the deepest red velvet gown my eyes had ever seen — its hue so deep, it resembled the most opulent garnet. I lifted the gown from its nest and laid it upon the bed, studying it with a sense of awe. Never before had I possessed such a lavish gown. Dresses such as these were customarily reserved for those fortunate enough to hail from nobility. Even though my mother married well and was considered part of the gentry, a dress such as this was well beyond our means.

"It's quite lovely," Gran said as she stepped up beside me to look down on the exquisite gown.

"It is that. But why did he gift it to me?" I inquired.

"I assume it has something to do with the incident at supper last night with the bells. His way of apologizing? And it looks to be just your size."

"But how was it made so quickly?" I asked. I had a petite frame and most dresses needed to be tailored to my size, but this one looked as if it would fit perfectly.

"An old dress of the duchess's or his sister's, perhaps?"

A smile I could not contain washed over my face as I stared down at the gown.

"We have been invited to dine with the duke and duchess this afternoon, so clean yourself up," she said.

A carriage arrived to escort us to the castle, although it was but a short walk. The wintry chill prompted us to accept the offer graciously. Upon our arrival, we were directed to a modest dining room, much more intimate than the grand hall from the night before. The duke, seated at the head of the table, rose as we entered. We bowed our heads and curtsied before taking our seats at the far end.

"Mary, I am delighted that after so many years, you have finally graced us with your presence," he warmly expressed.

"Thank you, Your Grace, for extending your invitation to my granddaughter Cora as well," she replied, dipping her head.

"I wanted to express my gratitude, my lord, for the remarkable dress you bestowed upon me," I added, straightening my back.

"Oh, it's my pleasure. I thought it was the least I could do after last night's events," he responded, looking a bit embarrassed. He glanced toward the door. "My wife and son will be joining us shortly," he informed us. A few moments later, the door opened revealing a woman in a stunning day dress crafted from rich moss-green silk. She was slender with brown hair streaked with strands of silver that was neatly pulled back into a low bun. She had been absent at last night's dinner, but I could not blame her as it was nothing more than a group of men bragging and boasting about one another.

We all rose as she approached the table, resuming our seats only after she and the duke had taken theirs.

"Mary, it is truly wonderful of you to come. It has been ages," the duchess remarked, smoothing out her dress.

"It has, my lady," my grandmother agreed, offering the duchess her most genuine smile. "This is my granddaughter, Cora."

"My lady," I said, bowing my head.

"So very nice to meet you, Cora. Have you traveled far to join us?" the duchess asked.

"Yes, I have come from Edinburgh, my lady."

"I was just there myself last week meeting with an old friend. Wonderful place," the duke said, glancing over toward the door and then over to the bracket clock resting on the mantel over the large fireplace at the back of the room.

"Do you have any interests?" the duchess inquired, her gaze shifting back to the doorway where the duke was still looking.

"I do. I have a great fondness for reading and writing," I replied, feeling a sense of relief to be among individuals who would surely appreciate my literacy, unlike my mother, who often insisted that a woman's place wasn't among the pages of a book.

"How delightful. What sorts of books capture your interest?" the duchess asked.

Catching Gran's encouraging smile and subtle nod, I continued, "I enjoy a wide range, but I particularly enjoy books by Robert Greene, Thomas Nashe, and of course plays by William Shakespeare."

The duchess smiled warmly, nodding approvingly. "Our son shares a similar passion for reading. 'Nose in a book and head in the clouds,' as I always say."

"Speaking of our son, I apologize for his absence. That boy is never punctual. I don't understand how he expects to oversee and manage affairs here when he can't even manage to join us for meals on time," the duke said, casting another glance toward the doorway.

The duchess was about to make a remark when servants began to emerge from a side door with large trays laden with roasted vegetables, bread, and a generous cut of venison. As they began to set them upon the table, I saw the duke's gaze lingering on the empty seat beside his wife, a mix of disappointment and anger etched on his face.

The tantalizing aromas drifting into the room caused my stomach to protest audibly, and I cursed myself for not having a morsel of bread before we left.

The meal stretched on, prolonged as the duke and duchess waited in vain for their son to join us. The tension of his absence hung heavy in the air as my corset hung heavy against my full stomach. Eventually, they gave in to the fact that their son would not be gracing us with his presence, a fact that left me wanting as I was eager to meet him. The duke pushed aside his plate and stood from his seat at the table.

"I have something special to show you before you retire for the evening," he announced, pushing in his chair. He guided us out of the dining room and into the grand hall. As we entered, a gasp escaped my lips, for there stood a majestic evergreen tree in the center of the room, reaching nearly to the twenty-foot ceiling. I had never witnessed a tree indoors before, and its grandeur sent a wave of warmth through me.

A man atop a ladder secured a large red bow to the tree's pinnacle, its long ends cascading down almost to the floor. Two women delicately hung a string of dried fruits on the branches — apples, oranges, and cranberries standing out against the dark forest green.

"Last year, I spent a considerable amount of time in Strasbourg. They have a delightful tradition of bringing a fir tree into their homes for the festive season, adorning it with dried fruits and baubles. I was so fond of it that I wanted to bring the tradition back here for this year's Christmas ball," the duke explained.

"Delightful, isn't it?" the duchess inquired.

"It is indeed," my grandmother agreed, with a strange kind of knowing smile upon her lips.

A servant approached with a large tray of gingerbread, and each of us indulged in the seasonal treat. Captivated by the grand tree and the transformation of the great hall, I held onto mine, intending to savor it during the short carriage ride back to the cottage.

"Now, you will just have to wait to see the rest of it tomorrow night," the duke declared, walking back into the hallway and closing the doors.

"I look forward to seeing you both tomorrow evening for the ball," he added, waving us toward the door. We bowed and expressed our gratitude before making our way down the entryway to the grand front doors. As I exited, I turned back for one last glimpse of the castle adorned in its Christmas charm, a newfound excitement bubbling within me for the upcoming ball.

Just as I stepped through the door, I collided with a gentleman entering, my gingerbread landing squarely on the center of his chest. Looking up, I encountered the gaze of a handsome man around my age, with chestnut hair and eyes as green as the tree in the great hall. My heart raced as our eyes met.

"Peasant, watch your step," he scolded, brushing the crumbs off his chest before storming into the castle. He blew past the duke's guards and down the hallway that led to the dining room, leaving a trail of arrogance in his wake.

Nora stopped reading, a realization hitting her like a shockwave. Was she going crazy, or was that almost the same thing that she had experienced at the market with the obnoxiously rude man? What the hell was going on? One event could be dismissed as nothing. Two, a coincidence, maybe. But three? Now that formed a pattern.

A sense of unease crept over her as she stood up, set the book down, and began to pace the room. She walked to the window and looked down onto the street below as the snow began to fall heavily once again, swirling about on the wind, echoing the chaos she felt in her head.

The events in the book seemed to align too closely with the unfolding of her own day. She shook her head, trying to dispel the thought. The idea of a book predicting her future was absurd. After all, weren't there arrogant men back then as well? It wasn't so much a coincidence as it was a testament to the fact that things hadn't changed much with the opposite sex over the past four hundred years.

All the same, before she left the city tomorrow, she planned to go back to the bookstore and question the woman about the odd little book. While she might not have the answers to the strange coincidences that had subsequently unfolded since she bought it, Nora hoped the woman could at least tell her the title and author, offering a little more information that she might be able to google.

Nora looked back down at the book, every rational cell in her body telling her to close it and turn on a TV show until her pizza arrived. But the little irrational voice in the back of her mind urged her to keep reading, just in case there was something she might want to avoid tomorrow.

Chapter Fifteen

THE BALL

I immersed myself in a bath filled with lavender-infused water, attempting to wash away the grime accumulated over the past few days. No matter how vigorously I scrubbed, I couldn't wash away the disgust that lingered in my mind from yesterday's encounter with the intolerable man at the castle.

Throughout the night, I tossed and turned, still put off by his rude behavior. I chided myself for allowing him to stir my emotions in such a way, my heart pounding at the mere memory of his rudeness. Who did he think he was, calling me a peasant? I might not have been born a noble, but I was far from a peasant. Did I stand out so much from the other guests at the castle that he deemed me to be of the lower class? The thought sat heavy in my mind, stirring up a wave of unease.

I loathed the fact that he had managed to burrow under my skin, occupying even a sliver of space in my thoughts, and I hoped he would not be present at the ball tonight. As I sat with a sour expression upon my face, my mind should have been focusing on the importance of tonight for my family. My mother's hopes rested upon me finding a suitor of considerable financial standing, one who could provide for not only me but her as well.

I had always dreamt of marrying for love, much like Shakespeare's Lysander and Hermia from *Midsummer Night's Dream*, whose love was true. My mother, however, would scoff at such romantic notions. *Marriage is a duty*, she'd say, *and if you're one of the fortunate ones, love may follow*. Despite her grim perspective, I had always chosen to believe otherwise. Admittedly, though, as I found myself mere hours away from meeting a potential suitor, her words echoed in my mind.

Attempting to calm myself, I sank under the water, unwilling to part with its soothing warmth. Upon emerging, I found Gran standing there, offering a cloth for me to dry off.

"You best be getting out. It will be hours until that hair of yours is dried, and we will need time to tame it," she advised as I stepped out of the tub into the chill of the room.

Swiftly donning my chemise, I settled in front of the fire while Gran skillfully brushed out my long dark wavy hair. It brought me back to my childhood when I would visit, and she would gently brush and braid my hair into a crown that wrapped its way around my head. She would tuck small sprigs of lavender and rosemary in and around the braid, and I could still remember the sweet earthy aromas lingering from the mere memory.

In contrast to my mother's harsh tugs and complaints about my wavy locks, Gran had always seen the beauty in them, saying the goddess had blessed me with hair as beautiful as the ocean's waves. I cherished her deeply, not only for the countless acts of kindness she had shown me over the years but also for loving me for every ounce of the person I was, not wishing me to be anyone other than myself.

"Remember, your mother is expecting you to find a husband, which means you need to be poised and gracious. If I don't send you home with a decent suitor, she may never speak to me again," she remarked with a wispy little laugh.

The notion of finding a suitable match sent my heart into a whirlwind of apprehension again. What truly defined a man as suitable? His title, his looks, or perhaps his temperament? I did not know. Through my father's work, I often found myself in the company of gentlemen and even engaged in light flirtations at social gatherings. However, the thought of any of them as potential husbands had never crossed my mind.

"How shall I know if he is a suitable match?" I asked, turning in my seat to look at her.

"You will encounter many gentlemen this evening, all vying for your attention with their charm and wit. Some may possess striking looks, others wealth or titles. Allow the butterflies in your stomach to be your guide. Should you feel them stir, focus on that feeling and heed its meaning. Let your intuition be your compass, my dear," she advised. Her soothing words brought a sense of peace, quieting my anxious heart and calming my breath.

Why were women subjected to the ritual of being beautified and paraded around like some possession to be purchased? We should be free to find love, not chosen by a man for a mutually beneficial arrangement. It was absolutely dreadful. Despite my distaste for being paraded around the ballroom as if I were for sale, a small spark of excitement flickered within me. I had never attended a royal ball after all, and I thought of the scene from The Faerie Queene, where knights and ladies danced amidst enchanting courts, a world of allegory and chivalry that seemed far removed from the harsh realities of my own time.

Despite Gran's spryness for her age, her hands no longer moved as swiftly as they once had, and it took a considerable amount of time for her to fashion my hair. A comfortable silence fell between us as she secured a roll of horsehair at the crown of my head and skillfully pinned my hair up and around it, allowing a few strands to dangle gracefully around my face. She had woven one strand into a long braid and artfully tucked it around the pouf to give it a graceful touch. The remaining strands were fashioned into ringlets using a set of hot iron tongs that she skillfully wrapped the hair around.

"Can I ask you a question?" I said, breaking the silence that had settled over the room as Gran worked.

"Of course, my child," she replied, her gentle voice inviting the conversation.

"When you wedded Granda, were you already in love? Or did it bloom over time?" I inquired, curious if Mother's words were true.

"Your granda and I hailed from the same small village and had known each other for years. Our match, arranged by our fathers, began as a friendship but gradually blossomed into love," Gran recounted, her voice tinged with reminiscence.

I sat there, wondering if I might be fortunate enough to fall in love over time, with whomever I wed, like Gran had. I had my doubts, as my mother had never shown a sliver of love toward my father. Their relationship seemed to be based solely on duty and a mutual understanding of the expectations of marriage. Love was not part of that equation for them.

"Fear not, my dove. I shall see to it that whoever you choose is a match blessed by love," Gran assured me, her voice carrying a soothing melody of reassurance.

By the time she had finished, it was nearly five o'clock, and we had little time to complete the preparations. I had anticipated the moment all day, yearning to slip into the heavy velvet dress, to feel its weight upon me. However, as I stepped into it and pulled my arms through its thick velvet sleeves, excitement was not the feeling that overcame me. Instead the weight of my duties to my family snuffed out that small spark of excitement I had felt moments ago.

"Come, come. Let me help fashion this stomacher into place before we lace you up." Gran took a small needle and thread and secured the tiny triangle of fabric into the bustline of the gown, leaving the trinity knot resting snugly between my breasts.

"It's exquisite," I told her as I looked down at the sparkly gold threads.

"And so are you, my dear. It matches you perfectly, and let's hope it brings you some good luck tonight in meeting a suitor," she joked, her laugh breaking away into a cough.

I smiled weakly. She looked at me, her kind blue eyes seeing through the surface to the trepidation I was hiding underneath. Rolling up her sleeve, she removed a silver bracelet from her wrist and placed it upon mine.

"What is this?" I asked, looking down. The bracelet had a beautiful Celtic knot that wove its way around the cuff.

"This was a gift from your granda many moons ago. I want you to wear it tonight as a symbol that love may arise from familiar or unexpected places," Gran said, her voice laden with hope.

I smiled as I spun it on my wrist, admiring its beauty.

After I assisted Gran with her evening attire, the clock indicated quarter to seven, and a carriage arrived at the cottage door. Draping our capes on, we ventured out into the brisk night air. As we drew closer to the castle, my nerves rose within my chest, leaving my palms sweaty and my heart racing.

The castle grounds were bustling with people and carriages, all eagerly awaiting their turn to make a grand entrance into the opulent castle. My stomach turned as our carriage came to a halt outside the imposing castle doors. The footman swung open the door, gesturing us toward the grand entrance.

Once we were inside the castle, a gentleman presented Gran and I, then guided us with a gracious nod toward the great hall. Along the hallway leading to the ballroom, a cacophony of voices intermingled with the strains of music poured forth from the room.

As I entered the great hall, it felt as if everyone's eyes had fallen upon me. My dark red gown stood out amidst a sea of greens, golds, and blues.

"You look stunning in that gown, my dear," a voice said from behind me. I turned to see the duke standing in the doorway.

"Thank you, Your Grace," I said, taking a deep curtsy as my gran followed suit beside me.

"Enjoy the ball," he said as he whisked past us and into the crowd.

The other guests quickly returned to their lively dances, revelry, and the clinking of glasses, all set to the sprightly tune played on a fiddle. The dance floor was a flood of Campbell clan kilts with a smattering of several different clans weaving in and out as they danced. The hall's grandeur surpassed even that of the previous day. Rows of flickering candles adorned the tables and delicate white paper ornaments were suspended from the ceiling, like snowflakes frozen in mid-air.

However, it was the tree that once again captured my attention. Fully decorated now, it stood trimmed with dried fruit, bows, and delicate glass ornaments, undoubtedly an extravagant expense. Intrigued by the concept of an indoor tree, I couldn't resist gravitating toward it for a closer look.

"Gran, I'm going to have another look at the tree."

She smiled and waved me off, then went to find a seat near the edge of the room.

Approaching the tree, I was taken aback by its immense size. I had only seen it from a distance yesterday, but now its true grandeur became apparent up close, dwarfing even the tallest of men in the room. Standing beside it, I felt as if I were a tiny doll in its shadow. As I gazed upward in awe, a voice rang out from behind me.

"Odd, isn't it?" a man said.

I turned to find a gentleman in his forties, wearing a kilt, its tartan that of the Stewart clan. He had a pompous air about him with his sharp nose and beady little eyes. His gaze, however, seemed more fixated on me than on the impressive tree he spoke of.

"I find it delightful," I said, turning away from the man and back toward the tree, which was much more pleasing to look at.

"Delightfully distasteful if you ask me," he said back.

"It just so happens, I didn't ask you," I retorted, knowing better but not being able to stop myself. He scoffed at me and then disappeared into the bustling crowd.

"I'd much prefer the company of this tree than that man," I mused to myself.

Remaining close to the tree, silently wishing that no one would approach to claim a space on it. Alas, it seemed I had unwittingly attracted the attention of nearly every gentleman present as they formed a line, each awaiting his turn. Blasted red dress, I thought as I smiled my most charming smile at each one.

Thankfully there was a set number of dances on the card, or I might have been dancing into the wee hours of the morning.

The first to claim a spot was a tall, well-dressed man of my age, with dark hair and deep brown eyes. Although he was quite handsome, any charm he held quickly vanished as he spoke solely of himself, showing no interest in learning anything about me. The following partner was a shorter man in his thirties, not the most striking figure at the ball, but his humor proved infectious. I quite enjoyed myself, yet he was not someone I could see myself wedding.

The succession of suitors that followed presented a variety of short-comings. Some were too old, too handsome, not handsome enough, not of high enough intelligence, or they simply carried an air of arrogance that I could not bear. It became increasingly apparent that none of these men would make a suitable match, leaving me with the realization that I might disappoint both my grandmother and mother with my lack of interest in any of these prospective suitors. I had left the last space on my card empty just in case I found someone of interest during the night, but that moment seemed less likely, now the night was coming to an end.

Seeking refuge by the grand tree once again, I gave my weary feet a much-needed break and tried to evade any potential suitors asking for a final dance. Tucking myself at the back edge of the tree, I marveled at the glass baubles suspended from the evergreen boughs. Among them, one in particular caught my eye—a deep blue reminiscent of the sky's color as day melded into night. In striking contrast, delicate foxes were painted in bright white, their forms outlined in gold. Tiny red holly berries nestled within clusters of leaves adorned the scene around the foxes. Enchanted, I couldn't resist reaching up to touch the beautifully crafted ornament.

"Beautiful, isn't it?" a man's voice said, startling me as I pulled my hand back down to my side.

To my surprise, the duke stood beside me, a kind smile on his face that reassured me there was nothing to fear. Nevertheless, a flush of embarrassment colored my cheeks at being caught in the act of reaching out to touch one of his expensive ornaments.

"It is very beautiful," I told him, stepping back from the tree and giving him a curtsy.

"Did you notice that each one has a different kind of animal on it?" he said, taking one down off the tree and turning it in his hands. "This one is my favorite. I feel a kinship with the stag. It has always been my favorite of all woodland creatures."

I smiled at him as he placed the bauble back onto the tree. He had such a kind manner about him. Nothing like I had pictured a duke to be.

"I admire that you have taken on a tradition from another land and brought it back here to share with us all. I think it's wonderful," I told him.

"It is. I do hope that it catches on someday," he said, looking up at the grand tree. He reached out and took down the bauble with the foxes on it. "My Christmas gift to you. May it be the first ornament you hang on your own tree one day."

"Thank you, my lord," I said, taking it from his hands and giving him another bow.

"You are more than welcome, my dear."

He offered a slight nod and then departed back onto the dance floor, blending into the whirlwind of people engaged in the final dance of the night. Glancing down at the exquisite bauble in my hand, a surge of excitement filled me. It was now the most splendid possession that I owned. Cradling it carefully, I observed the last dance unfold.

A thankful sigh escaped my lips, realizing that I had managed to escape the final dance invitation. The night was finally drawing to a close. My feet throbbed with soreness, and the tightness of my corset added an ache to my chest.

I turned to look at the tree one final time before heading back into the throng of guests in search of my gran. Walking to the edge of the room, I scanned the far wall through bobbed heads that danced around like a moving wall, blocking my view. Just as I was about to cut across the floor, a man came bursting through the dancers and ran directly into my shoulder as he pushed by. I stepped backward, almost falling over my dress that was pooled at my feet, and at that moment I lost grip of the bauble. I watched in horror as it fell to the ground, landing on the thick hem of my skirt. Thankfully it had saved the tiny thing from shattering, but as I bent down to grab it, I noticed a large crack running down its center.

Tears welled in my eyes as the once-pristine beauty of the bauble now stood blemished beyond repair. My gaze lifted to see who had so rudely jostled me without even a word of apology. In that moment, he turned back, his eyes brightened at the sight of me, then dimmed as he recognized me, and I him. It was the same insufferable man from yesterday, the one I had hoped to avoid throughout the evening.

I shot him a look which he returned before turning around abruptly and stomping off into the crowd of people.

"What insolence," I said aloud as I watched him walk away.

An older woman to my right stepped up next to me and whispered in my ear, "The young lord is excessively indulged and tiresomely self-important, if you ask me."

My jaw dropped. That was the duke's son, the very son that my gran had saved during childbirth? The boy who had been granted a second chance at life.

Chapter Sixteen
THE LITTLE BLUE BAUBLE

Nora reread the passage describing a small blue ornament adorned with foxes. Her eyes shifted toward the bag from the market resting on the small kitchen table. A sense of disbelief crept in. *No, it can't be*, she thought as she stood up and walked over to the bag. Lifting the ornament from its snug little resting place amidst the sea of tissue paper, she turned it in her hands, inspecting it. It was identical to the one described in the book with one difference— this one lay in perfect condition without a crack down its center.

"This shit keeps getting weirder and weirder," she muttered to herself after placing it back into the bag.

A knock at the door startled her. The pizza! After giving the driver a nice tip, she went back into the living room with the box and landed back into the chair. The pizza only temporarily pulled the book from her mind. Once she had eaten three slices, her full belly left her feeling sleepy.

She had had enough of this crazy day, plus her eyes were dry and growing heavier by the minute. Before she fell asleep in the damn chair again, she put the pizza away, set the book on the side table, went into the bedroom, and crawled into bed. This would be her last night in the rental before her trip to Letterfearn in the Highlands tomorrow. She was excited and a little bit nervous about heading north into the more secluded part of the country. Before she even had the time to mull over plans for the next day or the odd events that seemed to be seeping out of the book's pages and into reality, sleep overtook her.

The next morning, Nora packed her belongings and conducted a final sweep of the rental. Before tucking the photo album into her bag, she flipped through it, snapping pictures with her phone of places she wanted to see before leaving the city. Satisfied, she consulted her itinerary, checking her bus departure times. It was going to be tight, but if she hurried, she could squeeze in a few more places from the album and visit the bookstore before catching her bus to Letterfearn. Leaving a small tip for the cleaner, she headed out the door, ready to get some answers about her mysterious little book.

Her bags bounced along the cobblestone streets of the Royal Mile as she towed them behind her. The playful tag on her luggage, proudly announcing her status as a Hogwarts alumnus, swung back and forth as she made her way up the street. She reached into the white paper bag from the charming bakery she had visited the other day, pulling out a scone. Disappointingly, the scone proved stale, prompting her to toss it in the first rubbish bin she came across. She opted instead for another gingerbread man, pulling one from the bag and biting off its tiny shoe.

Nearing the bookstore, Nora paused at a street vendor to purchase a cup of coffee. With a busy schedule ahead, she knew she was going to need the pick-me-up. Not only that, but she needed something to wash down the remnants of the two-day-old gingerbread man. It was then she saw a place from the album she had missed the first day she had walked on the Royal Mile. An old church-style building fronted with a statue of a man named Adam Smith stood before her. She pulled out her phone and tried to capture a photo that looked like her grandmother's, then tucked her phone away and kept moving down the street.

She passed the little wine and spirits shop where she had bought the bottle of wine and began scanning the street for the bookshop. Nora knew the bookstore was just a few shops up the street from the liquor store, but she couldn't find it. Confusion overtook her as she approached the top of the street without spotting the quaint little store. Turning back, she slowed her pace, scanning every inch of the street in search of the elusive bookshop. Could it be in the opposite direction of the wine shop? *My jet lag was pretty severe that day*, she thought as she peered down the other end of the street. Dismissing the idea, she remembered taking a photo when she stepped out of the shop—she should be able to spot the bookstore in that image.

She pulled her phone from her back pocket again and scrolled to the picture. She was definitely standing in the right spot as there was a little candle shop across the street from where she stood in the picture and where she was standing in the present. But there was no bookshop, just a small bar and a clothing boutique. Scrutinizing the photo, she saw the bookshop's teal door right on the edge of the picture next to the pub, but when she looked in front of her there was nothing there but a brick wall between the bar and boutique.

"What the hell?" she said as she looked around completely puzzled. Her head was spinning as a dizzying array of questions played in her mind like the triangle in a Magic 8 Ball, bobbing in and out.

What was going on? A whole bookshop doesn't just up and disappear. There had to be a logical explanation. Maybe she was on the wrong side of the street and wasn't getting the correct angle. She walked across to have a look, but there was still no bookshop in sight. Completely perplexed, she stood for a long time looking back and forth between the photo and the street before her, hoping beyond hope she wasn't imagining things. Was she going mad? Had the stress of the trip and the fact she had put off telling her parents about not wanting to take over the bakery made her crack?

She glanced back down at her phone and noticed she only had a few minutes to get to Edinburgh Bus Station. She pulled up Google Maps and began walking the route toward the station as snow started to fall softly, landing on her phone screen, and melting away into tiny droplets of water that obscured her view. She was wiping them off when she caught a glimpse in the reflection of her phone of a couple standing in front of a large storefront window.

Nora looked up to see one of the grandest wreaths she had ever seen. A couple posed for a photo, sharing a kiss within the wreath's center. A pang of longing swept over her, and in that moment, she missed Sam. She shook her head, blinking away tears that threatened to spill forth. She hated herself for still missing him, even after how badly things had ended between them. His final words still echoed in her head. *I need a partner with a clear vision for the future, someone who knows who they are and what they want.* Even now after two years, those words stung, mostly because she knew they were true.

In that moment she realized his words had made her retreat

inward, building a wall around her heart for safety's sake. After the breakup, she had always chosen the safe, easy way, and maybe that was part of her problem. Look at her now, though. She had pushed herself to take this solo trip to Scotland, marking the first genuinely daring and exciting thing she had done since their relationship had ended. She was trying to change, to break out and become her own person, to find what made her tick and she was proud of that.

Nora reflected on her reluctance to take over the bakery. Maybe her subconscious was rebelling against the safety and predictability that path would take. The more she thought about it, the more the mysterious little red book and the disappearing bookstore seemed like her mind's way of injecting a bit of excitement into her life. As she came up to Edinburgh Bus Station, the idea made sense to her.

The bus station stood apart from the other buildings with its sleek modern look. The atmosphere buzzed with anticipation, a symphony of departure announcements and hurried footsteps matched with the rhythmic clatter of train wheels from Waverley Station next door, creating a mosaic of sounds. Travelers lugging backpacks and dragging suitcases weaved through the vibrant tapestry. A distinct scent of freshly roasted coffee combined with a hint of train exhaust clung to the air. Ready to head to the next stop on her adventure, Nora found her way through the organized chaos to Bus 19, to Kyle of Lochalsh.

She weaved through the people and walked the long row of buses to where hers was boarding. Handing her bags over to a man packing them below the bus, she got in line. The bus was nearly full when Nora boarded, and luckily she managed to secure a seat close to the front, knowing it was going to be close to a six-hour ride. Past experiences had taught her that her stomach preferred this location on a bus. The memory of her sixth-grade field trip to Montreal flashed in her mind, a lesson learned the hard way. Back then, thinking she was cool sitting in the back, she ended up vomiting all over Tommy Hood, her unfortunate seatmate. Nora cringed at the recollection; it had taken her ages to live down that embarrassing mishap.

As the bus began its journey, Nora watched the ancient city faded from view and the vast countryside expanded before her. They soon ventured onto a large bridge with huge white steel cables, fanning out like sun rays drawn by a child, spanned across a large body of gray water that mimicked the sky at that very moment. The farther they drove on the M90, the wider and more rigid the landscape began to look. She watched as the sun crept in and out of the thick gray clouds, as if it were trying to escape its confines and race the bus, keeping steady pace beside it.

Nora retrieved her notebook. The couple kissing in the wreath's center and the resurfacing emotions about Sam had her feeling a bit raw. She knew writing them down in verse might help them escape her mind, so she began to pour her emotions out onto the page. It was the third verse she wrote that stopped her in her tracks: A *heart not broken but drowned instead. In depths of sorrow, lost and misled.* Nora realized the extent to which Sam still held a piece of her heart, a piece she had freely given away and never reclaimed. She knew she needed to let him go, mend the missing pieces of her, and move forward with her life. But these things were easier said than done.

She decided to write a list of all the things she enjoyed doing that did not include the attention of a man. The list began with the obvious things, such as reading and writing, then moved on to things like gardening, crocheting, ice skating, and hiking. She surprised herself by filling out almost two full pages before her stomach let out a groan of hunger. Unzipping her shoulder bag, she rooted around for the last gingerbread cookie. She had been so caught up in finding the bookshop that she had neglected to eat breakfast. The lone gingerbread man would have to tide her over for the four remaining hours she would be on the bus. Things weren't looking in her favor, but she would survive.

After finishing the gingerbread man and jotting down more thoughts in her notebook, Nora found herself playing the mental game of "Guess Their Job" with the couple ahead of her. The man, middle-aged with clean-cut hair and a freshly shaved face, was dressed in a North Face jacket and a pair of well-worn Salomon hiking boots. Judging by his polished appearance and high-end yet not overly flashy hiking gear, Nora figured he was in middle management, possibly in corporate finance. The woman, noticeably younger, had freshly bleached hair and sported new hiking boots and a rain slicker she had forgotten to remove the tags from. Nora guessed she was probably his secretary who was trying to impress him but had absolutely no hiking experience whatsoever.

Eventually, Nora decided to rest her head and attempt to sleep. All this thinking about Sam had her mind still spinning, and she figured a quick nap might do the trick of washing him free of her thoughts. She managed to doze off for a few hours until a sudden kick to the back of her seat jolted her awake.

Waiting for her eyes to adjust, she turned around and peered through the crack between the two seats to see who had so rudely interrupted her nap. There, seated next to a petite woman in her fifties, was the arrogant man from the Christmas Market.

Chapter Seventeen
SASSENACH

As she peeked through the crack, Nora's eyes met his, and she quickly turned around, her mouth going dry at the sight of him.

"You," she heard him say in a disgusted tone of voice.

She had had enough of this guy's attitude. What had she done to him anyway, other than get a bit of meat pie on his chest?

Nora pulled every ounce of courage she had and popped her head up over the seat and said, "Yes, it's me. Is there a problem?"

"If by 'problem' you mean that my country has been infiltrated with Americans coming over here to go on Outlander tours, then yes, there is a problem," he said in a smug voice. The woman beside him looked over and gave him a scowl, then slowly pulled her jacket over a shirt that said Sassenach.

"I'll have you know that I am not here for an Outlander tour. I'm here to experience my roots."

"Let me guess. You took a DNA test and found out you're two percent Scottish, so you decided to fly over to Scotland to try to figure out where this fits into your life. Maybe meet a rugged Scotsman and fall in love, yadda yadda yadda," he said in such a condescending tone she wanted to reach over the seat and slap him across the face. Instead, she just turned back around and crossed her arms.

"Nailed it, didn't I?" she heard him say.

Nora peeked her head back up to face him again.

"Why on God's green earth would I want to fall in love with a Scotsman? From what I can see, they are arrogant dickheads," she said in such a forceful tone she surprised herself. This guy really got under her skin. She turned back around to face the front of the bus again but not before she saw the woman beside him give her a thumbs-up.

That had shut him up but had also sent her head spinning. Half of what he said sounded like her life story, and she hated how it sounded coming out of his mouth. She spent the rest of the bus ride ruminating on what that meant but came to no conclusion other than she loathed him.

The driver announced their arrival at Kyle of Lochalsh, a small coastal town that reminded her of a little place she visited in Maine each summer as a child. They drove through the small town center, where only a few shops sat, before pulling into the bus stop. Soon the passengers were filing off the bus.

Nora stood up, slinging her bag over her shoulder as she stepped into the aisle, coincidentally at the same time as the man behind her. They collided once again, and her bag dropped onto the floor. Her forgetfulness stung as she realized she hadn't zipped it back up after eating the gingerbread man. To her dismay, the glass ornament from the market leaped out of the bag and landed on the bus floor. She hesitated for a moment, not wanting to look down and find it smashed into tiny pieces. Fortunately, the carpeted floor had kept it from shattering, but a long crack now marred its length. Frustrated, she shot the man a sharp look as she realized that her ornament now matched the one in the book.

"Excuse you!" Nora said, squinting her eyes in frustration.

"Maybe you should start watching where you are going. If I remember correctly, it was you who ran in front of me at the market as well," he said in an arrogant voice that was like nails on a chalkboard.

"Your age must be showing because your memory seems to be warped," Nora said as she gingerly tucked the ornament back in her bag and zipped it up before stomping off the bus, leaving him behind. Her breath caught in her throat as she looked out over the port. To her right, a vast loch stretched out framed by dusty blue mountains painted with snow in the distance.

A large bridge emerged through a thin layer of fog that clung to its massive pylons, while small boats dotted the cold gray water. The wind began to blow, rippling the once-calm waters that reflected the heavy overcast sky like a mirror. Nora found something calming, almost hypnotic, to the movement of the tiny ripples across the loch. She smiled, and just then, a stray sunbeam broke free from the clouds, casting a warm yellow glow over the loch.

Pulling herself away from the view, she swiftly retrieved her bags and headed up the street, making a conscious effort to put as much distance as possible between herself and the man from the market.

Scanning her surroundings, she was happy to find he had

disappeared after departing the bus. She began walking up the street toward the center of town. All the houses seemed to be painted white and made of rugged stone, the kind that could withstand the harsh winds that came off the loch during the winter months. Her bag in tow, she made her way onto a small sidewalk that wound its way up the street. Finding a bench under an awning for a local hardware store called JJ's, she pulled her phone out of her pocket and googled a car service in the area. She found a company called Car Hire and dialed them up.

While she waited for her ride to arrive, she stopped at a small cafe nearby for some hot coffee and a restroom. She had decided not to use the facilities on the bus after an older man had spent nearly an hour in there. However, as soon as she opened the cafe door, she heard a familiar voice. There he was, like a bad penny and ordering an Americano of all things. Before the door even opened the entire way, she turned around and walked in the opposite direction down the street. The coffee and bathroom would just have to wait.

She made her way back to JJ's and sat on the cold wooden bench as she waited for her ride to show up. She pulled out her cell phone and looked over the photos she had taken during the tour on the Royal Mile. It was the first time she had gone back and looked at them since that day. A warmth came over her as she scanned through them, realizing these were the memories she would one day add to an album like her grandmother's. She landed on the photo she had recreated with the wine bottle and the book. There was something there she hadn't noticed on the first inspection of the photo after Lesley had taken it. She zoomed in on the little red book. There, hovering just around its edges, was a bright blue glow. She zoomed back out, looking for the source of the reflection, but she couldn't find it. Was it a trick of the light, or perhaps her flash had been on? She was just about to zoom back in on it when a small navy blue car pulled up and parked next to her, its engine idling as the driver hopped out and popped the trunk.

"You Ms. Cameron?" he asked, his accent much richer and thicker than the ones she had become used to in Edinburgh.

"That's me," she said, walking over and shoving her suitcase and bag into the trunk. She hopped into the backseat, glad to escape the bitter cold. Northern Scotland felt more like the arctic tundra with the bitter wind blowing off the sea.

"Where can I take ya?" the driver inquired.

"I need to get to Letterfearn. Forty-one Lochland, rental on the north end of the loch."

"Aye, I know the place. I've taken loads of people to that cottage," he assured her, pulling onto the snow-covered road that would lead her to the next destination on her adventure.

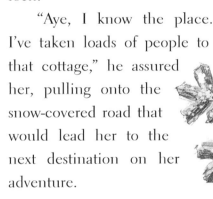

Chapter Eighteen
LETTERFEARN

Five minutes into the car ride, Nora was still trying to shake off the unpleasant encounter with the annoying man on the bus. She couldn't fathom why, out of all the buses, she had to end up on one with him. *What an unfortunate coincidence,* she thought. His arrogant tone and complete rudeness had left her seething. While she had dealt with her fair share of unpleasant customers at the bakery, nothing compared to the confrontations she had with that man in the past two days.

Swallowing hard, she tried to quell her anxiousness over the whole situation. She refused to let that awful man ruin her beautiful ride to Letterfearn. As she bit back her annoyance, the sky grew an even darker shade of gray, and freezing rain began pelting the windshield of the car.

However, the landscape became so increasingly beautiful that her mind could think of little else. She was in complete awe of her surroundings. The world around her transformed into the land that fairy tales were made of. Towering mountains surrounded her in every direction, their majestic presence creating a breathtaking scene as the loch peeked in and out of view while they drove. Nora's eyes lit up as she spotted a familiar landmark up ahead: Eilean Donan Castle, a sight she'd seen in travel guides and photos on Instagram. The grand old stone castle stood proudly on its tiny island, connected by an ornately arched stone bridge. A thin blanket of snow covered the ground around it, making the gray stone of the castle stand out in harsh contrast to the deep blue of the loch behind it. A delicate pattern of frost climbed the base of the castle walls, adding to its fairy-tale quality, as if kissed by the ice queen herself.

Nora remembered a little bit about the place from a travel pamphlet she had picked up at the airport. It was one of Scotland's most iconic castles, steeped in history and known for its role in the Jacobite rebellions. The breathtaking scene tempted Nora to ask the driver to stop, but weariness from her travels and a pressing need for a bathroom held her back. Instead, she quickly pulled out her phone and snapped a photo as they drove by.

The driver continued down the A87, a narrow roadway lined with fieldstone walls and scattered with old stone houses on either side. They were now deep into the Scottish countryside. Its sloped valleys and rolling hills that led to towering mountains overlooking everything below reminded her of Vermont. No wonder so many Scots had settled in Vermont in the eighteenth century. It must have felt like home to them.

Under the thin layer of snow, Nora could discern rusty oranges and dark greens of the fading fall foliage, shrouded in winter's frosty grip.

The next road they turned onto was so narrow it resembled more of a bike path than an actual road, and a wave of concern washed over her as she wondered what would happen if they encountered another car. Fortunately, the driver navigated the narrow road with ease, as though he knew every twist and turn like the back of his hand. Nora figured he must have grown up around here and trusted that his familiarity with the roads would guide them safely through the winding path.

"Are you from around these parts?" Nora inquired.

"Aye, I was born just a few miles down the road. Lived here my whole life," he said.

"What is the best place to explore that's not in a travel guide?" she asked.

"Aye, there are lots of beautiful places around here but one of my personal favorites is Tobar Mhoire."

"What is Tobar Mhoire?" she asked, leaning toward the front seat, intrigued.

"It's a magical well named after the Virgin Mary. A place of peace. It is said that the well's waters have healing powers and that if you bring an offering to it and make a wish, it will come true. However, I've been wishin' to win the lottery for years, and it hasn't happened," he chuckled.

"Can you tell me how to get there?"

"You just give me a call, and I'll take ya there. It's not in walking distance of where you are staying," he said with a smile.

"That would be wonderful, thank you," she said, flashing him a smile in the rearview mirror.

"Aye, we're almost there," he announced as he turned onto a stone bridge that took them onto an even smaller one-lane road marked Old Military Road.

"That's the River Shiel," the driver announced as he pointed out the side window to the cold dark river that wound its way through the landscape like a serpent. "It's an off-put of the loch."

"It's beautiful but looks very cold," Nora said, looking out at its icy banks.

"Indeed, but quite nice in the summers."

"I can believe that. It's absolutely beautiful up this way."

"That it is," he said, flashing a proud smile at her in the rear-view mirror.

Clusters of fir trees gathered on one side of the road, ascending the mountainside, while the loch dominated the entire right-side view from the car. The icy waters nestled in the valley, embraced by the surrounding mountains, sent a strange tingle creeping up her spine and a flurry of nerves fluttering in her belly. A sudden flashback to the night she went into the frozen lake at home came rushing back. Her body shivered at the memory of the cold, so piercing it felt like fire against her skin. Her shoulders curved inward involuntarily, and she crossed her arms, rubbing them as if trying to ward off the nonexistent chill.

Things had been so busy after the accident with preparing for the trip that she hadn't had much time to process it all. Now, as they drove on the edge of the loch, her muscles tightened, and she dug her fingernails into the cloth back seats, waiting for the car to slip on a patch of ice and veer off into the water. As her nerves built, so did the weather, going from calm overcast to a thick white haze of snow.

Nora twisted the edge of her jacket in her hands and tried to focus on anything but the water. She turned away from the loch and pulled all of her attention to the other side of the road where ancient stone houses dotted the landscape. Sloping hills covered in fir trees made for their backdrop, with small stone walls bordering each of the neighboring properties. Her fingers loosened their grip on her jacket, and her shoulders began to relax as she focused on the scenery.

Soon the snow slowed along with her anxiety, and she turned her attention back toward the water. The same types of stone houses sat on the loch's shores, their presence seemingly absorbed in the reflection of the loch's mirror-like waters. Along its shores, Nora noticed a handful of rusty tin buildings and what she assumed were boathouses.

These houses appeared older than buildings in Edinburgh — much older. Some had been painted white over their old flag-stones and were adorned with typical nautical blue shutters and teal doors, while others retained their dark gray fieldstone, weathered with age, likely witnessing more history than she could even fathom.

The anxiety she had felt just moments ago had all but faded away, and a new feeling washed over her as she gazed out over the Scottish landscape. It felt like the mountains held ancient memories that traveled on the wind down to the rocky shore of the loch. She had never felt a connection to a place until that very moment, as if something deep within her was stirring, something awakened by this magical place.

As they rounded another bend in the road, a small cluster of houses came into view. Just a few more feet down the road, four newer cabins perched atop a tiny embankment overlooking the water. Sitting in a long row, each had a small deck out front that faced the loch even though it was impossibly cold to sit out and enjoy the view this time of year. Tiny puffs of white smoke billowed from their chimneys, and the snow sat snug upon their roofs. *How charming*, she thought, a smile edging up the corners of her mouth.

"This is you," the driver said as he pulled up in front of the tiny group of cabins.

"Oh, yes," she said, still feeling in a daze of calm. "Thank you so much for the lift. How much do I owe you?" she asked, getting her bags together before opening the door to the cold.

"That'll be forty quid."

"I'm sorry, I never asked your name?" she said, handing him fifty quid.

"Stuart, Miss. Thanks."

"Thank you so much for the ride, Stuart. I'm Nora. Do you have a card so I can call you when I need a lift to that well?" she asked.

"Aye," he said, pulling a card from his visor and handing it to her.

"Thanks, Stuart," she said. As she opened the door, a gust of wind almost slammed it shut again.

After removing her bags from the car, she waved Stuart off and made her way up a small flight of steps to a walkway that led down to the cabins. She pulled out her phone to retrieve the Airbnb reservation instructions.

"Cabin 5, last cabin on the walk, pin code 1667," she read as she walked the long pathway to her quaint little bungalow. She counted the cabins as she went, but there were only four on the walk. She looked down a short set of stairs that led to an old stone cottage that sat snugly in a cove close to the water. It was much, much older than the newer tiny house-style cabins on the walkway. The number five was nailed to a post at the bottom of the steps. Even though she had thought she would be in one of the newer tiny cabins, she was thrilled with the more secluded spot of the small cottage.

Basking in the absolute beauty of her surroundings, she didn't notice a man standing in front of the door to her cottage until she came right up on him. Confused, she watched as he punched a code into the keypad.

"Um, excuse me, but I think you're at the wrong cabin. I'm number five," she said.

The man stopped and stood still as stone for what felt like an age before he spoke.

"No?" was all he said as he spun around.

And there, standing in front of her rental, was the asshole from the market.

Chapter Nineteen
A BITTER CHILL

The wind chased down through the mountains and across the loch's icy waters, bringing with it a bitter chill. Seeing the man from the market standing in front of the cabin was a complete shock to Nora, and the sting of the icy cold wind felt like a slap across the face from the universe itself.

"What are you doing here?" she asked, setting her bags down and placing both hands on her hips in a defensive stance.

"Me? What are *you* doing here? This is my rental," he said in his irritatingly arrogant tone.

"No, you're mistaken. This here is *my* cottage. See," she said, holding her phone out to show him the reservation.

He looked down at her phone, a look of confusion creasing his brow as he took out his own phone.

"Can't be. Look," he said, holding his phone out to show her the exact same reservation instructions: Cabin 5, last cabin on the walk, pin code 1667.

"I don't understand," she said, confused, as she looked back down at her own phone. "It's obviously some kind of mistake."

Just then a small black wiry dog came skulking out from the edge of the cabin, stopping in its tracks when it saw the two of them. Nora was taken aback by the dog's mismatched eyes—one blue, one brown—as it turned to glance in her direction. After a moment, it shifted its attention toward the man and emitted a low growl followed by a series of sharp barks. The dog stood firm, its hackles raised, refusing to look away from him. Nora couldn't help but recall the saying about dogs sensing evil as she watched the man take a step back.

"Yours?" he asked in an annoyed tone.

"No, not mine," she snapped back.

He lifted his foot in a defensive stance, and Nora busted out in protest, "You better not even think about it."

"If he comes for my ankles, I have no problem booting him into the loch like a football."

"Asshole," Nora said under her breath as the little dog looked at her and darted off into the brush behind the cabin, leaving her to deal with the man by herself. The man watched the dog disappear and then turned back to the door.

"I'm sure there is another cabin around here somewhere. Maybe you should go find it," he said, punching in the code to the door, opening it, and then abruptly slamming it in her face.

Nora stood stunned, her face turning red as the anger boiled up inside her. She had had enough of this jerk, and there was no way she was going to let him take her cabin. She punched in the code and walked in behind him.

"Bloody hell, you're like a magpie at a picnic," he said as she stormed in.

"What the hell does that even mean?" she asked, parking her suitcase against the wall.

She was about to give him a piece of her mind when the sight of the inside of the cottage temporarily silenced her. It looked nothing like the images online, which had been of the newer cabins only. If not for the annoying asshole standing in the center of it all, the cottage's next-level rustic charm would have been a welcome sight.

"Well, I'm not going anywhere. This is my cabin," she said, trying to sound as resolute as she could.

"Listen, love, I have just as much right to this cabin as you, so why don't you bugger off and find some other person to annoy," he said, falling back onto the leather sofa and kicking his feet up onto the small wooden coffee table in front of it.

"Yeah, not likely," she told him as she pulled out her phone and dialed the number on the Airbnb page.

"Hello," a woman's voice answered on the other line after one ring.

"Hi, my name is Nora Cameron. I am staying in cabin number five in Letterfearn."

"Aye, yes. Hello, Nora, how are you finding everything?" the woman asked in an overly cheery tone.

"There is a bit of a problem here. It seems that you might have double-booked the place as there is a strange man sitting on my sofa."

"Oh, goodness me, I am so sorry. Give me a minute, please, so I can look this up."

Nora could hear the woman tapping away at keys and cursing under her breath before she picked the phone back up.

"I am so sorry. I'm not sure how this happened. We have never had any issues like this before. Looks like you have had your reservation a bit longer than Mr. Grant. He only booked it two days ago. May I speak with him?" she asked in a sheepish tone.

Nora felt bad for the woman since she had no idea what she was in for. She walked over to the sofa and held out her phone.

"Someone would like to speak to you, Mr. Grant."

He raised his eyebrow at her at the mention of his surname and snatched the phone out of her hands.

"Yes, hello?"

Nora watched with a satisfied expression as the news was relayed to him. She noticed his mouth turning even more downward than before, something she thought impossible. He stuck his free hand into the pocket of his corduroy pants like a sulky child and looked down at his brown leather shoes.

"Yes, I understand. These things happen. I will find somewhere else to stay. Please don't worry," he said, in a tone that was soft and much more forgiving than she had expected.

She flashed him a cocky smile, gloating over her victory as he hung up the phone. He shot her a scathing look as he righted himself on the sofa.

Standing up, he tossed the phone at Nora. "Bravo, you win," he said through gritted teeth as he gathered his belongings and walked to the door. "Always coming in second to the American, it seems," he muttered before walking through the doorway and slamming the door so hard that the little sign that read *At the loch, every hour is happy hour* flew off and landed on the floor at Nora's feet.

She stood stunned and a bit confused. What just happened? There was no way she thought he was going to leave that easily. She had prepared herself for an all-out fight to the death over who got to stay, but as soon as he talked to the woman on the phone it was as if he had turned into a completely different person. This left her head spinning and she walked over to the window, pulling the curtains to the side and peering up the stairs toward the other cabins.

He was on the steps with his cell phone pressed to his ear, talking in a very loud and agitated voice.

"Tell Tom I said, 'fuck off,' then. I'm skipping Letterfearn and moving on to the next destination on the list. I want to get this nightmare over with as soon as possible. I'll be catching the next bus out of here, and if he doesn't like it, he can fire me." He stopped talking and turned around as if he felt Nora's eyes watching him. She ducked back behind the curtain, her heart jumping up into her throat. She waited a few minutes before daring to peek back out the window. The stairs and walkway were empty, and she let out a sigh of relief.

Thank God he had not put up a fight because she wasn't sure if she even had it in her today. She was exhausted, hadn't eaten anything other than a gingerbread man, and had been holding an overly stretched bladder for almost six hours.

With that thought, Nora raced into the little side bathroom next to the door and emerged a minute later feeling at least a bit better. Now, she needed something to eat. The Airbnb reservations had a number for a local shop that would deliver groceries. She made a list and called the market's number, placing an order for some essentials for the week.

While she waited, Nora explored the rest of the cottage. The downstairs was one large room aside from the small bathroom. The kitchen looked recently updated with new appliances and a large kitchen island, but she could see its old charm peeking through. The island not only provided a spacious work surface but also served as the dining area since there was no table and chairs—just four bar stools lined along the long side of it.

Past the kitchen, the room expanded into a sizable sitting area with a wall full of windows overlooking the loch. A long brown leather sofa sat against the windows, facing the kitchen. To its left was a large, very old stone fireplace flanked by floor-to-ceiling bookcases filled with books. This sent a wave of excitement through her. *I guess there was no need for the four books I packed with this collection sitting at my fingertips,* she thought. She walked over and surveyed the titles. Most of the books were old, with titles she had never heard of, but her eyes stumbled upon a few classics she recognized. A book of Robert Burns's poems, which she figured every home in Scotland would have, *A Christmas Carol* by Dickens, *Animal Farm* by Orwell, and a small group of Jane Austen books. She noticed a few travel and guidebooks on Scotland and the Highlands, and the rest were obscure authors she had never heard of but was excited to explore over the few days. It was just what she had envisioned for her relaxing week away in Scotland.

A cluster of logs was set in the fireplace, ready to light, and next to it sat an iron circle full of split firewood. *This is the perfect place to sit, relax, and read,* Nora thought, smiling to herself as she continued to explore the cottage.

A steep set of stairs led to a small simple bedroom on the second floor. A queen-sized bed took up most of the space, alongside a nightstand with a beautiful stained-glass lamp and a small dresser to the right. A nautical blue-and-white striped overstuffed armchair sat next to the only window that looked out over the loch.

Nora walked back downstairs and over to the fireplace. The cottage was a bit chilly, so she decided to start a fire. Grabbing a box of matches off the mantel, she knelt in front of the old stone hearth and struck a match, placing it under the kindling. It fizzled out before igniting anything. She tried again, and then again, her frustration mounting with each failed attempt. She had used all but two matches, and if she didn't get this lit, she was looking at a very cold night ahead.

"Come on, fire, light," she said as she pulled both matches out of the box. Her fingers tingled as she doubled them up and struck them against the side of the matchbox together. There was a hiss and then a pop of blue light before it mellowed into a soft yellow flame. Setting the twin flames in a small notch between two logs, the small twigs caught fire below and then spread to the large branches above. She watched as the flames devoured the nest of twigs and branches before setting the larger logs aglow.

Once she was sure the fire would stay lit, she brought her luggage into the kitchen. She took out her journal, notebook, travel guide, and her grandmother's photo album, placing them on the coffee table in front of the large sofa.

She uncapped her pen, opened her notebook, and began describing her journey to Letterfearn. She wanted to make sure she got it all out before she had forgotten any of the little details. As she wrote, that familiar energy surged through her once more. It was the same sensation she'd felt that first day on the Royal Mile, the same inexplicable pull that had drawn her into the bookshop. She couldn't place what it was, possibly the excitement of new adventures, or maybe it was just being in Scotland itself that did it. She wondered if this was the feeling of magic her grandmother had always described when talking about this place.

She wrote for a few minutes, put her notebook aside, and walked over to the large windows facing the loch. The thermometer on the outside deck read -3°C, and although she had no idea

what that equated to in Fahrenheit, she assumed it was somewhere in the single digits.

A shiver ran down her spine, and an uneasy feeling settled
over her like a heavy cloak. The twilight and the icy loch brought
back memories of the night of the car accident, reminding her of
how close she'd come to death. The thoughts of her own demise
left her throat dry, and she pushed down the morbid thoughts,
trying to quell the anxiety bubbling in her belly.

The flurries turned into a thick haze of snow now, and it
seemed to be sticking quite rapidly to everything around it.
Through the snowy haze, something in the loch's center caught
her eye. The water churned in large swirling waves as if something beneath was stirring.

She stood transfixed, straining her eyes to see what was in the
middle of the loch disturbing the water. She held her breath and
watched as a dark shape began to emerge from the loch's center.
The heavy snowfall made it almost impossible to determine what
the shape was, but whatever it was, it was quite large. She leaned
closer to the window, trying to get a better look. The cold snaked
its way through the old windowpanes and caused her to shiver.
Her heart began to race as she saw what looked to be a large head
atop a long neck crane in her direction. She held her breath as
the hairs on the back of her neck rose, when all of a sudden, there
was a knock on the door.

Chapter Twenty

THE STORM

Her eyes glued to the spot in the loch where she was certain she had just seen something emerge; Nora's mind spun with tales of loch monsters when the knocking came again. Breaking from her own thoughts enough to remember that she had ordered food, Nora grabbed her wallet out of her bag and went to the door.

Standing there with two large bags of groceries was Stuart.

"Hello again, Miss," he said with a smile.

"Stuart, I wasn't expecting you. Come in out of the snow," Nora insisted as the snow rapidly clung to his hat and beard.

He stepped inside and knocked off his boots before handing her the two bags.

"I do most of the deliveries in the area, people and food

alike," he chuckled. "Quite the squall out there, good thing you ordered when you did, or I wouldn't have been able to get it to you. Unusual weather," he told her as he took off his hat and brushed the snow off.

"It looks like it's really coming down. Are the roads bad?" Nora inquired, her thoughts drifting to Mr. Grant. Despite his rudeness, she couldn't shake a slight worry for his safety out in this awful weather. She didn't like him, but she also didn't want anything to happen to him just because she had won the battle over the Airbnb. The last thing she needed was an unfortunate mishap weighing on her conscience.

"Aye, they're not good."

"By any chance did you see a little black dog around here when you drove in?" she asked, worrying about the dog out in this kind of weather.

"No, but I couldn't see much because of the snow."

Nora nodded and smiled. "Here, you better get back on the road and get home before they get any worse," she said, handing him a tip.

"I think that is a good idea. The missus doesn't like me out in this kind of weather, but it's close to Christmas, and I can use the extra money."

"Thanks for coming back out here," she said, holding up the bags.

"My pleasure. Now, you make sure you don't go wandering outside during the storm. Tourists go missing all the time in these parts. They wander off into the snow and get turned around, either wind up in the icy waters of the loch or lost up in the mountains."

Nora looked back over her shoulder toward the loch, and the uneasy feeling came rushing back. "I plan on staying right next to that fire and reading," she assured him as she turned back around.

"That's a good lass. Stay in and stay warm by that fire," he said, putting his old paper-boy hat back on and turning to the door.

"Drive safe," Nora said as he exited, the wind blowing so fiercely that it cut her words off.

As she shut the door, the uneasy feeling spread through her like a chill that arrives with the first frost. She walked over to the fire and stood with her back to the flames, trying to chase the feeling away. As the heat of the fire cut through her jeans, she gazed out the window toward the loch. It was night now and with the thick snowfall and only a sliver of the moon peeking out from behind the clouds, the loch looked like a portal into another world, eerily shrouded in a ghostly white veil. She crossed her arms, rubbing them as she tried to tamp down the nervous feeling surging through her like a storm.

What had she seen in the water before Stuart had shown up?

She loved watching *The Why Files* on YouTube and it had become her Friday night ritual, complete with a cider and a pizza from Rae's. The host delved into various mysteries, especially cryptids, like bigfoot and mothman, aiming to uncover the truth and debunk many of the popular hoaxes. One episode covered Champ, the so-called lake monster in Lake Champlain in Burlington, Vermont. Scientists and historians had concluded it was just a giant lake sturgeon. *The mysterious thing in the water was probably something similar*, she thought, *like a floating log or chunk of ice, not a loch monster*. With the weather conditions and the heavy snow, it surely had to have been a trick of the light. There was always an explanation for these types of things, one being she hadn't eaten all day. Then again, she was in Scotland, home to the most famous loch monster of all time, Nessie.

Walking over to the bags of food sitting on the island, Nora unpacked the order and tucked things away in the cupboards and refrigerator, leaving out a frozen pizza. While she waited for the oven to preheat, she thought about the little red book and wondered if perhaps the main character or the story had seen a dragon or some other mythical creature. No, she had concluded that all the coincidences in the book were just a figment of her imagination, her mind's way of bringing some excitement into her life. But were they? Something gnawed at her, a tiny bit of doubt that was about to win the argument as she walked over and took the tiny red book out of her bag.

Turning the book over in her hands and running her fingers across the smooth leather surface, Nora noticed something on its cover that she had missed. There in the gilded gold pattern that bordered the book was the same Celtic knot that was on the ornament. She pulled the ornament from her bag and held it up to the book. The knotted triangle within a circle was identical to the one in the book, even down to the crack running down its center. There were too many coincidences for this to be something she had made up in her head.

She set the ornament back into her bag and took the book over to the sofa. Hesitating, she wasn't sure if she really wanted to keep reading. What if the main character got hurt or died? Would the same fate await her? Maybe if she didn't read it, those things wouldn't happen. What if reading it brought those events to life? If the book was foretelling the future, however, didn't that mean it had answers? What if it actually helped her prepare for what came next? These were all good theories, but in the end she decided she would rather know her fate, so she opened the book and began to read.

I cradled the fractured ornament in my hands as I watched the duke's son storm off. His father also watched from the doorway with a look of disgust staining his once joyful demeanor. How had such an ill-mannered person come from such kind and gentle parents, I pondered as my gran and I waited for our carriage to arrive.

"That rude man who ran into me yesterday was the duke's son," I whispered to her.

"Yes, I know," she said, surprising me.

"You knew that was him? Why didn't you tell me? What a dreadful man."

"Remember, dove, we don't always know the inner workings of someone's mind. There is almost always a reason for behavior such as his."

"You are much more forgiving than I."

"What is that you have there?" she asked me, noticing the small blue bauble in my hands.

"The duke gifted it to me. For my first Yule tree, he said," I told her with a smile that soon faded as I looked down upon the crack that ran its length.

"The duke is a kind man."

"It's too bad we cannot say the same for his son," I said as our carriage pulled up and escorted us back to the cottage.

As my gran helped me out of my gown and took the pins down out of my hair, I apologized for not finding a proper suitor. The whole plan was for me to secure a suitable husband, and I had failed. Even though I had not intended to find one, a wave of guilt washed over me. It had been my duty, yet I had not taken it seriously and now the opportunity had passed. My mother pinned her hopes on my finding a man who could provide for us both. Father's savings were dwindling rapidly, and within a year, there would be nothing left to sustain us.

"Oh, no, no. Do not fret. Tomorrow we shall see how many come knocking upon the door for a promenade around the grounds," she said with a smile. "Now, you go and rest. It's been a very long day."

I lay in my bed trying to sleep, but I kept replaying the moment the duke's son had run into me, causing me to drop the ornament. The look he had in his eye when he first realized what he had done and the way his expression changed when he noticed it was me. It was strange, as if he had some personal slight against me. But why? It didn't make sense; he didn't even know me.

Not able to sleep, I got up and walked quietly toward the kitchen to make a cup of tea when I heard Gran's soft low voice, whispering a melodic kind of chant I'd never heard before.

I crept to the edge of the door and peered in. She sat in front of the fire, tossing what looked like dried flowers and stalks of weeds into the flames. The fire greedily devoured them and the room filled with an aromatic smoke as the flowers and herbs burned to cinders on the logs. The flames reflected in Gran's eyes, dancing and moving about, and for a moment I swear her eyes looked as if they were completely white, devoid of their natural color.

Once she had tossed the last of the stalks into the fire, she braided what looked to be a lock of her gray hair, tucking a small piece of paper into the braid before tossing that into the fire as well. The hair hissed as it hit the flames and let out an unpleasant smell, and for a moment the smoke looked as if it turned a glowing shade of blue.

I stood still as stone, and for the first time, I understood. The signs had always been there, the dried herbs, strange symbols, and whispered charms, but I was too young to comprehend what they meant. Now I knew the whispers were true: Gran was a witch.

Chapter Twenty-One

UNINVITED GUEST

T here was a sudden knock on the door, and Nora jumped, sending her crashing back to reality. Startled, she lost her grip on the book, and it fell to the floor. She stopped and waited, listening for another knock, but none came.

Must have been the wind from the storm, she thought. As she bent down to retrieve the book, she saw a shadowy figure skirt past the window next to the door and around toward the side of the house where she was sitting. Could it be Stuart? No, he had left some time ago now and wouldn't have ventured back out in the awful weather. Her heart jumped into her throat. She hadn't even considered asking about crime in the area. Horrible scenarios she had seen in scary movies flooded her mind. No, she was not going to let her fears get the best of her. Maybe someone had gone off the road and just needed help, but why would they be skulking around to the backside of the house? The knock came again, louder and more rapidly this time, on the window facing the loch. The sound bounced off the glass and reverberated through the cottage, sending fear racing down her spine with each sharp knock.

She quickly got to her feet and ran to the kitchen in search of some sort of weapon. She pulled out three drawers before finding a knife that looked so dull she doubted it would even cut an apple, but at least it was something. She gripped its base, her knuckles turning white with the pressure.

The outside porch light did nothing but cast a warm glow upon the falling snow that was now coming down so heavily it obscured everything in a hazy white veil. She crouched behind the kitchen island, lifting her head just high enough to peek through the window that faced the loch. Her eyes were glued to the window, but the light from the lamp behind her caused a mirror-like effect. All she could see was the reflection of the room staring back at her.

The rapping came again, this time from the other large window facing the loch. Her heart was pounding so hard in her chest that all she could hear was her own blood pumping rapidly through her veins. She bit her upper lip, knowing that whoever was out there was watching her, but she was blinded by the window's reflection and the snowy shield that fell beyond it. Her palms were sweaty around the knife's base as she crouched, still as stone, staring at the window.

Again the low, reverberating rap of knuckles upon glass echoed through the room. Each strike caused her stomach to clench in fear. In that moment Nora realized how utterly alone she was. She needed to call 999; there was undoubtedly someone attempting to break in, or at the very least, scare the living daylights out of her. She reached into her jeans pocket, only to find her phone missing. Scanning the room, she spotted it resting on the coffee table in front of the couch, positioned just in front of the windows. Glancing behind her at the door, she was relieved to see that the bolt lock was engaged. All she needed to do was gather her courage, sprint into the living room, grab her phone, and call for help, but as soon as she attempted to move, her feet felt like lead weights.

Still clutching the knife in her right hand, she finally propelled herself into the living room. Just as she was inches away from her phone, the knocking came again—louder, more like pounding this time. She looked up toward the mirror-like reflection of the glass. She could make out the silhouette of a man standing only feet away. A startled scream escaped her lips as she grabbed her phone. She had just begun to dial when a familiar voice cut through the glass.

"Christ sake, let me in. It's bloody freezing out here!" She stopped. She knew that voice. In fact, it was a voice she had wished never to hear again.

She stepped forward just as he cupped his hands to the window and peered in, revealing his face. It was the annoying man she couldn't seem to shake. He stared back at her and motioned toward the door, then vanished into the snow. Within a moment he was knocking at the front door.

Nora walked over and peeked out the window near the entrance, and he shot her an irritated look.

"Really? It's absolutely freezing out here. Please open the door," he said in a tone that was a mix of attitude and desperation.

She hesitated for a moment. Was it wise to let him inside? Here she was, a woman alone in a remote area of a foreign country, and he wasn't exactly giving off the warmest of vibes. But leaving him out in the blizzard was not an option; he might freeze. With a sigh, she unlocked the door and swung it open.

The wind blew snow into the tiny cottage, smattering Nora's arms and face with snowflakes that melted almost instantly, leaving her speckled in icy water.

He stepped in and shut the door behind him. He was covered in snow, and his cheeks and nose were the shade of ripe tomatoes. Dusting the snow from his bag, he set it on the small wooden stool by the door as he kicked the snow from his boots and looked up at Nora.

"Whoa, there," he said, taking a small step back.

Nora had forgotten that she was still gripping the dull kitchen knife in her hands as if she were Norman Bates.

"I know we didn't get off on the right foot before, but no need for weapons," he said, lifting his hands above his head in a fake surrender.

Nora rolled her eyes and walked toward the kitchen, tossing the knife onto the counter.

"What are you doing back here? You scared the shit out of me."

"Sorry, I knocked on the door a few times, but you didn't hear me, so I went over to the window. I figured I would be able to get your attention there. I didn't mean to scare you, I swear," he said in a sincere tone.

"That still doesn't explain why you are here in my rental again," Nora said, leaning against the island and crossing her arms.

He stood there, an awkward expression falling across his face. In that moment, for the first time, she saw something other than arrogance—there was a hint of vulnerability in his eyes, and he let down his guard slightly.

"Ha, funny story," he said, taking off his flat cap and dusting clumps of snow off his shoulders. "I'm a writer, a journalist, actually. I was sent into the Highlands on assignment and when this double-booking thing happened, I just decided to head to my next location, but this blasted storm came, and all the outgoing buses stopped. I tried bribing a few cabbies to take me over to Aviemore, but no one would do it for fifty quid," he said, running his fingers through his dark blond hair and stepping off the welcome mat and a bit closer to where Nora stood. "By the time I gave up and tried to get a room at one of the local hotels, they were all booked along with the four bed-and-breakfasts."

There was a long drawn-out pause as if he were waiting for her to say something, but when she didn't, he went on. "I know this is really awkward, and we got off on the wrong foot, but could I please just crash on the sofa tonight? I will be out of here before you even wake up tomorrow. I'm sorry for being such an ass. I swear I'm not as bad as you think I am."

Nora stared at him; she wasn't sure she believed him. Was this change in demeanor due to his desperation or because he had actually felt bad about his behavior when they first met?

"How do I know you're not some crazy psychopath? For all I know this could be your game," she replied in a tone snarkier than she intended, but something about him just set her on edge.

"Oh, you got me. I find desperate American women and follow them all the way into the Highlands during the bloody coldest time of the year. Then wait for a snowstorm to roll in so I can beg to sleep on their sofa and then what? Murder you in the middle of the night? Believe me, I don't have the energy for all that. Plus, I wasn't the one wielding a knife around," he spat back.

The sharpness of his voice and the fact he called her desperate made her blood pressure rise, and she could feel her cheeks turning red. There was that cocky man she remembered, not far below the shiny new surface.

He stepped forward and pulled a wallet from his jacket pocket. Opening it, he handed her a card. Nora took it tentatively and looked down. It was an ID badge for the magazine, *Tartan and Thistle*. There was a picture of him with the words *Alistair Grant, staff reporter* in bold font above a barcode.

"See, I promise I'm not some psycho killer."

She looked up at him and then back down at his name on the card: Alistair Grant. She wasn't sure she trusted him, and she definitely didn't like him, but she knew she couldn't turn him away. Plus, where would he go? In this kind of weather, he could freeze or wander off into the lake, and she didn't want that on her conscience. Stuart had said that people went missing around these parts all the time in weather like this. She let the slack out of her shoulders and looked back up at him.

"Okay, Alistair. You can stay the night on one condition: you feed the fire throughout the night so I can get some proper sleep," she said with a smug smile and a raise of her eyebrow, handing his wallet back.

A look of annoyance shot across his face, and he cracked his lips as if he was about to retort. However, he must have thought better of it because he just shook his head in compliance and walked past her into the living room. She knew she held all the cards, and she decided she was going to milk it for all it was worth. Judging by the expression on his face, he knew it too.

She watched him wander over to the bookcase, and an awkward silence fell over the room. Nora wasn't sure what to say or do next. She didn't feel like engaging in conversation or remaining in the tense atmosphere any longer, so she decided to head upstairs and read in bed.

Nora walked over to the coffee table and retrieved her notebook and the little red book before heading toward the upstairs.

Alistair was now looking through the books on the shelves to the right side of the fireplace.

"Did you look at these?" he asked as she began walking away.

"Yeah, I looked through them but didn't really recognize many of them."

"Not surprising. They are all quite old and rare. Don't you think it a bit strange that they would keep them in a holiday cottage? They must be worth money," he said, pulling one off the shelf and dusting its edges off.

"Maybe they don't know or don't care."

"Or maybe they're just sodding idiots," he echoed back absentmindedly in his snarky tone as he returned the book and continued to scan the shelves.

"Well, good night." It was only a little after seven, but she really didn't feel like entertaining him anymore. This made him stop, and he shifted his gaze back toward her.

"What's your name?" he asked.

"Nora."

"Thank you for letting me stay here, Nora. I really appreciate it," he said, giving her just a hint of a smile.

"You're welcome," she said, taken aback by his genuine sincerity.

Ascending the staircase, she stole a glance back at him. His usual arrogance had lifted momentarily, revealing a side of him she hadn't noticed before. For the first time since their paths had crossed, she saw a glimmer of vulnerability beneath his callous exterior. *He's rather handsome when stripped of his defensive facade,* she thought. She quickened her steps, trying to escape her own wandering thoughts. She knew better than to even think about walking down that road.

As she stepped into the bedroom, the floorboards creaked

beneath her feet, and she pulled the door shut. She checked the door for a lock, just in case he happened to be an actual psycho. She turned it and walked over to the dresser.

She slipped into her cozy PJs and grabbed her notebook and pen before sliding beneath the covers. The upstairs, with its chilly drafts, prompted her to tug the blankets up to her chin. She turned on the table lamp and the room lit with a soft glow, and she settled in to write, but her thoughts wandered incessantly back to Alistair.

She scolded herself for succumbing so easily to a charming smile and a simple thank you. No, he had been an outright ass, she had to remind herself. Just because she thought he was handsome and didn't want him to freeze to death in the storm didn't mean anything. His kindness, she reasoned, was merely a result of having no other choice. Tomorrow, when the storm broke, he would depart, and she could put this internal conflict to rest.

Staring down at the blank page, she realized she didn't trust herself to write a poem about him, as the only lines that were coming to mind were lustful ones. Writing them down might solidify her feelings, and she couldn't have that. Instead, she set aside her journal and retrieved the little red book, turning to the next chapter, titled "Death and Magic."

Chapter Twenty-Two

DEATH AND MAGIC

Resting on Gran's lap was a very old and tattered-looking book. The edges of its leather cover peeked out from behind the yellowed paper, and she repeated the words once again in the same rhythmic cadence, like an ancient chant. As if searching for something, she ran her fingers along the lines of script in its pages, and her singing stopped, leading to a fit of coughing.

My heart pounded inside my chest so loudly I feared she might hear. I stepped back into the shadows of the room, watching as she continued the charm reminiscent of the old pagan ways. What was she doing, and why did she dare do it here on the duke's property? Though the witch trials had died down, the threat still lingered, and if she were caught in such an act, we could both face dire consequences, even in these supposedly quieter times.

I recalled a whispered conversation I had overheard between my mother and Aunt Beth last winter. Beth had returned from a visit to Gran's with some of her tonics, expressing concern that Gran was becoming careless in her old age. She mentioned that Gran had her books and herbs openly displayed in the house instead of in her altar room where they should have been hidden away. At the time, I thought it was merely Beth worrying about the possibility someone might think Gran's practices were witchcraft, but now different thoughts were emerging about that conversation.

Beth had also shown Mother a small silver hair clip that Gran had given to her, claiming it would help attract suitors after the tragic loss of her husband. Beth, accustomed to the comforts of high society, had quickly spent what little her husband had left her. She believed she needed another well-to-do man to maintain that lifestyle and had been on the search for a new husband directly after the appropriate mourning time was over. Not more than a week after she began wearing the clip, two influential men were courting her. I had dismissed it as a coincidence, but now I couldn't help but wonder if Gran had charmed the hair clip.

This brought me straight to the thought of the stomacher Gran had embroidered for me. As she sewed it onto the dress, she expressed her hope that it would bring me luck in finding a suitor. I wondered if that was the reason my dance card had filled so quickly. Had it all been due to a spell she had placed on the stomacher, intending to aid me in finding a husband?

My head spun as whispered words wove threads that connected to tales and stories about Gran being a witch. There had been talk of her miraculous deeds: saving livestock, crops, and even people from ailments that should have claimed their lives. Then came the whispers of her narrowly escaping death herself when she was young, after one of her close friends, Freya, had been hanged as a witch. I hadn't wanted to believe it, but now there was no hiding the fact. I tucked myself back into bed, rested my heavy head on the cold rigid pillow, and willed myself to sleep. *Perhaps by morning, it will all be just a bad dream, conjured from too much dancing and a tired mind,* I thought as my eyes grew heavy, and sleep finally overtook me.

The cold woke me the next morning, seeping its way into my blankets and pulling me from the realm of dreams. I rose from bed and slung my cape over my shoulders to ward off the chill. *The fire must have gone out in the middle of the night,* I thought as I pulled the curtain aside and glanced toward the kitchen. It was then that reality pierced through the foggy haze of my morning thoughts, and I recalled the events of the prior night. Not the ball, but Gran sitting by the fire, weaving some sort of spell with her herbs and song. My skin prickled with fear as I ventured into the kitchen.

To my horror, Gran was lying face down on the cold wooden floor in a pool of vomit. She was cold to the touch, and for a fleeting moment, I feared the worst. I rested my head on her chest; to my relief, there was a very slow and very light beating. I attempted to get behind her and pull her toward the bed, but I was only able to move her a few feet. In a state of panic, I grabbed blankets and a pillow, creating a makeshift bed for her on the floor.

"Gran, wake up!" I yelled, trying to rouse her, but she didn't move.

I hastily grabbed my cape and donned my boots and hurried out the door, leaving them only partially fastened. The frigid cold sliced at the exposed skin on my ankles as I briskly traversed the snow. As the chilly air cut through my lungs, I had to gasp for breath. The castle wasn't too far from the cottage, but the snow and my hastily chosen attire hindered my progress.

With each freezing step, my mind raced, fearing that if the cold hadn't roused me, it might have been too late for Gran. Though only a few minutes passed, it felt like an eternity by the time I approached the grand front doors of the castle. A surprised footman opened them for me as I sprinted up, clad in my nightwear, my cape wrapped tightly around me. I swiftly recounted the situation to one of the servants, who promptly sprinted up the lengthy hallway. I doubled over, gasping for breath as the cold air continued to sting my lungs.

In a matter of moments, the duke appeared, and I straightened myself, bowing respectfully as he approached. I tried to maintain whatever semblance of dignity I could muster, even though I stood before him in nothing more than my undergarments and a cape.

"What has happened?" he inquired, his voice filled with genuine concern as he assessed my distressed state.

"Gran has fallen ill, my lord. She lies unresponsive on the cottage floor, and I couldn't manage to lift her into bed. I fear something grave is amiss," I explained, my words tinged with fear as I fought back tears.

"Gwen, go and fetch Arthur and Henry, send them to Thistle Cottage right away, and wake my son as well," he ordered in a tone I had not heard him use before. "Come, let us go to her," he continued, taking his coat from Gwen and leading the way toward the front doors. He signaled to a tall man outside, who promptly disappeared and returned with a small carriage.

We entered the carriage in silence, not exchanging a word during the short trip to the cottage. Honestly, I hadn't anticipated the duke himself coming. I had assumed he would send for a doctor, forgetting the deep bond he and my grandmother shared. The duke felt a debt to Gran for saving his son and wife's lives years ago and from the look of it, he intended to honor that debt.

When we entered the cottage, Gran remained in the same spot where I had left her, swathed in blankets, cold and unresponsive on the floor. The duke knelt beside her, lowering himself to her side and bringing his ear near her mouth.

"She is breathing, but barely. Has she been feeling unwell lately?" he asked, looking up with concern in his eyes. I thought back to the prior day and how she had been having fits of coughing when she spoke. Before I could reply, a small group of men entered the house.

"Lift her gently, and let's get her back to the castle," he instructed the men.

They delicately raised Gran as if she weighed little more than a twig and carried her out to a much larger carriage.

"Go get yourself dressed. My men will transport her to the castle and place her in a guest room until a doctor can properly assess her condition."

I hurried into the back room and changed into a simple green wool skirt, forgoing the tightening of my corset. I quickly threw on a matching bodice and pinned up my hair. Meeting the duke back in the kitchen, we both felt the discomfort of being alone in each other's presence and hastily made our way back into the cold morning air toward the waiting carriage.

Upon our return to the castle, the men had already settled Gran into a room, where she lay comfortably in a large bed with a warm fire crackling in the nearby fireplace.

"The doctor has been summoned, my lord," Gwen, the duchess's lady's maid, informed us as we entered the room.

"Thank you, Gwen. Tea?" the duke requested, his gaze filled with compassion as he looked down at Gran. "You never answered my question. Had she been ill?" he asked, turning back to me.

"Nothing more than a light cough, my lord."

He took a deep breath and looked back at Gran lying motionless in the large bed.

"Why don't you try talking to her? Perhaps you can reach her somehow, even in her forced slumber," he suggested. "Gwen will bring you tea and something to eat," he said before turning and leaving the room.

As I sat beside Gran on the bed, holding her hand, I pondered how everything had unfolded so swiftly. What transpired last night? Had the spell she was weaving gone awry? A sinking feeling gripped my heart, settling in my stomach as I realized I hadn't considered the spellbook before ushering everyone into the cottage. If anyone laid eyes on it, they would undoubtedly brand Gran a witch.

My mind raced, retracing my steps. No, the book hadn't been in the kitchen. I would have noticed. Gran must have stowed it away before falling ill. Beads of sweat formed at my hairline as I contemplated the book resting in the cottage, unattended. What if someone went back to gather her belongings and stumbled upon it?

That could not happen. Leaning forward, I kissed Gran's head, resolving to return and locate the book. Just as I turned to leave, the duke entered the room, accompanied by an older gentleman.

"Cora, this is Martin McDougal, our physician," the duke introduced as they approached the bedside.

"Can you provide more details about her illness?" the doctor inquired.

"Other than a slight cough the past few days she seemed perfectly well until I discovered her this morning. She was lying on the floor, surrounded by vomit, and she felt very cold," I conveyed.

The physician leaned in, conducting a thorough examination. He listened to her chest, then lifted her eyelids and peered into her mouth.

"What did the vomit look like?" he continued, still scrutinizing her.

"I'm not entirely certain; the room was still dim," I replied.

"Was it dark or light in color?" he pressed.

Taking a moment to recollect, I remembered it distinctly against the aged wood floors, even in the low light.

"It was dark, notably darker than the wood floor," I affirmed.

He turned and exchanged a look with the duke.

"Her eyes are showing an unnatural dilation, and judging by the appearance of her mouth, I suspect she ingested some form of toxin, possibly belladonna," the physician explained, pointing out her lips, which had turned a dark shade of blue within moments.

"Are you suggesting she was poisoned?" I questioned, fear welling within me. Why would anyone want to poison Gran? Then my heart stopped. Had she accidentally poisoned herself during the spell? Thinking back on what I had witnessed last night, I remembered one of the plants Gran held having small black berries on it. She must have known what they were; why would she willingly consume them? At that moment, I knew I needed to return to the cottage, locate the book, and find the spell she had been weaving last night.

Chapter Twenty-Three

THE CAILLEACH

Nora stared down at the last page of the chapter and let out a sigh of relief. Nothing in the book mirrored the events of her day. She had been going back and forth on whether she believed the book was somehow linked to her own life. The shadow effects of the two must have just been her mind conjuring up some adventure or even just pure coincidence.

She was about to set the book on the side table when the smell of fresh Italian spices wafted up the stairs and into her room. Her stomach let out a groan, and it dawned on her that she had never cooked the pizza. She had left it thawing on the counter. With Alistair's unexpected arrival and the awkwardness that had filled the space, she had quickly retreated to her room without even thinking about it, but apparently, he had found it.

The smell filled her with a sudden hunger that left her stomach cramping from too many hours of neglect. She followed the scent down the stairs, where she found Alistair pulling the pizza out of the oven.

"Hey, hope you don't mind, but you had left this out, and I figured I better cook it, or it would have gone to waste," he told her as she walked toward him.

"I'm glad you did. I had completely forgotten to eat until the smell forced my stomach to remember," she said with a slight smile before pulling out one of the bar stools and sitting down across from where he stood.

She watched as he cut the pizza into slices, pulled two plates from a cupboard, set a slice on one, and handed it to her.

"Thanks."

"Don't thank me. It's your pizza; I just put it in the oven," he said, with a sharp edge to his tone as he served himself a slice and then walked over to the stool beside hers.

They sat in an awkward silence as they began to eat. Nora had no idea what to talk about, and she wasn't even sure she wanted to talk. After all, their previous interactions had been more than unpleasant. She wasn't sure she should risk breaking the unspoken truths they had going.

"Have you been to Letterfearn before?" Nora asked, finally breaking down, not able to take the silence any longer.

"No, not really. I have been to Kyle and a few other towns near here on assignment though. You?"

"No, it's actually the first time I have ever been outside the US. Letterfearn was a place my grandmother talked about often when I was a child, so I decided to come see it for myself," she said, pulling a piece of pepperoni off her pizza and eating it before taking a large bite.

"Really? Your first time out of the States at your age?"

Nora stopped chewing; those last words stung, and she had to bite back a retort. They were finally having a normal conversation, and she didn't want to rile things up even though his comment had been more than a little rude. She swallowed her bite along with her pride and said nothing.

He must have known that he had struck a chord because he quickly came back with, "I've never been to the US. What state are you from?"

"Vermont," Nora said, finishing off her slice and reaching across the island to grab another piece. "You said you are a journalist on assignment. What are you writing about?" she asked, changing the subject and bringing the conversation back around to him.

"Yeah, I am writing an article about the top ten Outlander travel destinations," he said in a disgusted tone of voice.

"Oh, is that so?" Nora said, trying to stifle a giggle as she thought back to his comment on the bus about her being on some Outlander tour. "Is that why you are so jaded toward all the sassenachs out there?"

"Well, you're not wrong on that account," he said. A slight laugh escaped his lips as he chewed a bit of crust.

"Is *Tartan and Thistle* a travel magazine?"

"No, this is a special article I got stuck with for the Christmas edition. That bloody show has destroyed the Highlands in my opinion. You can't even grab a bite to eat without some American tourist asking you if you're related to any Frasers."

"Oh, come on. I'm sure tourism helps these little towns."

"Tourism may boost these towns, but Airbnb and sublets drive up prices so much that locals can't afford to stay. It's pushing them out of their own bloody villages," he said, his tone tinged with frustration.

Nora swallowed hard but chose to say nothing. The subject was obviously a sore spot with him. He grabbed another slice and headed over to the sofa.

Nora spun around on her stool to face him as he sat down and kicked his feet up onto the coffee table. Something about the way he lounged there, feet on the table, one hand resting behind his head, filled the room with the same arrogant demeanor he had sported when they first met. She had definitely struck a chord.

"Why do you really hate Americans so much?" Nora asked, finishing the last of her slice and walking over to one of the chairs that faced the sofa.

His eyes dimmed as he looked at her. He reached over and grabbed a book resting on the table next to his feet.

"Have a look at this," he said, abruptly changing the subject. He seemed as good at diverting questions as she was. He pulled his feet off the table and stood, handing the book to her.

Nora ran her hand over the old cloth-covered hardback. There was no title on the cover, but the spine announced that it was a compilation of Highland folklore tales, *The Legends of Highland Lore*. Upon opening it, the smell of old paper and mold greeted her, and she carefully turned its frail pages. The book was quite old, published in eighteen twenty-five by a printer in Edinburgh. Nora carefully skimmed through the pages, finding beautiful block prints at the start of each new story.

"That is a first edition and quite a rare find. Worth thousands," Alistair said as he watched her carefully fan through its pages.

"How do you know that?" she questioned him.

"My grandfather was a rare book dealer," he snapped back, as if she had offended him by merely questioning him.

"It's very beautiful."

"Like I said before, don't you think it odd that they would have all of these rare old books in a holiday property?"

"It is odd," Nora said absently, still preoccupied with the beauty of the book. She stopped on a page three-quarters of the way through and paused. At the start of a new story, there was a block print of an old woman, with one light-colored eye and one dark, with a small scar above her left eye. She bore a striking resemblance to the old woman from the bookstore. The chapter was titled "The Cailleach."

Suddenly the same surge of energy she had been experiencing since arriving in Scotland came rushing back, racing out from her core to the tips of her fingers and the bottoms of her feet. She felt her face flush, and her heartbeat rattled so rapidly in her chest she thought it might explode within her.

"Are you alright?" Alistair asked, his brow furrowed as he looked at her.

"Yeah, I'm fine. Just tired. I think I'll head back up to bed. Do you mind if I take this with me?" she asked, holding out the book.

"Go for it. I have my own stack," he said, pointing at a small pile of books resting on the edge of the coffee table.

"Thanks for cooking that pizza," she said as she walked up the stairs.

"Goodnight, Nora," she heard him say as she stepped out of sight. Her name on his lips sent a shiver through her, a sensation that she loved and hated at the same time. It was just like her to be getting butterflies from some guy who was a complete jerk. Why was it that women tended to like the bad boys, the ones with attitude and angst, she wondered. Just then Sam sprung to the forefront of her mind. She had thought he was one of the nice guys, not some bad boy with attitude, but it turned out he was just as bad, if not worse. At least with a bad boy you knew what you signed up for. Taking a deep breath, she pushed any lingering thoughts about him out of her mind and crawled back into bed. She flipped back to "The Cailleach" and began reading.

Deep in the Highlands of Scotland, there exists a mythical figure known as the Cailleach. She is an ancient deity deeply woven into the fabric of Celtic folklore. Legend has it that she sculpted the landscape, dropping immense boulders from her apron pockets to create mountains, while her staff carved valleys as she traveled the land.

Referred to as the winter hag or queen of witches, she is often portrayed as an elderly woman with one eye reflecting the color of the sky and the other mirroring the hue of the earth. Her dominion extends over the winter season, reigning from Samhain to Beltane. As winter unfolds, the Cailleach's powers intensify, veiling the land in frost until the spring arrives, marking the moment when she engages in a symbolic battle with her sister, Bride—the goddess of spring—and succumbs to the forces of renewal.

In Celtic mythology, she is both a destructive and a regenerative force, signaling the end of one cycle and the beginning of another. She has been known to transform into a hare or stag to disguise herself. With the ability to call upon all creatures to aid her, she has reign over everything from the wild fox to the mythical beasts that roam the land.

She is wise, seeing through any veil held to deceive her. Like the trinity knot, she signifies life, death, rebirth, and the perpetual cycles of nature. Tradition shows that people often leave offerings to appease her, hoping for a mild and manageable winter ahead. The Scottish Cailleach stands as a powerful link between mythology and the natural world in the hearts of the Scottish people, with countless stories and legends exploring her enduring presence, some of which you will discover within these pages.

Chapter Twenty-Four
SHADOW BENEATH THE ICE

A cold so harsh that it rivaled death's embrace woke Nora. The darkness encircling her was filled with the crushing sound of complete silence, and it took a moment for Nora's eyes to adjust. In the pitch-black surroundings, she could barely make out murky silhouettes of trees and small shrubs around her. A cold breeze blew past her, bringing with it the scent of evergreens. The daze of sleep had worn off, replaced by fear. Had she fallen asleep while reading and sleepwalked? The cold seeped into her scant clothing, and as her feet stumbled, she discovered she was standing in a foot of snow. An eerie scream of an animal shattered the deafening silence, causing her to quickly turn around. All she could discern in the darkness was a break in the trees up ahead.

Beyond all better judgment, she walked toward the clearing, drawn by the mysterious sound. Had it been a fox or perhaps a screech of an owl? The closer she got to the opening in the tree line, the more aware she became that she was entering some sort of open field. By the time she broke the edge of the clearing, her feet were so numb she could scarcely feel them. The sound of the animal called out again with its long, loud screech—*an owl*, she thought—as she mindlessly followed its call.

Not until she had made it halfway into the large field did she hear the sound again, this time low and guttural, breaking her trance and sending a shock of fear racing through her. Definitely not an owl. Then came an even more terrifying sound—the ominous cracking of ice below her feet.

In the split second it took her to realize she was not standing in a field but on a frozen loch, she found herself in the icy cold water, plunging deep below its surface. The shock hit her like a bolt of lightning.

The loch's freezing water tightened around every muscle in her body, making it impossible to fight its deathly grip. She tried to kick to the surface, but her legs and arms felt like lead weights, and as much as she tried, she could not get them to work. The cold and darkness quickly consumed her, as if they had been perched below, waiting for her to descend into their depths. It took only a moment for her to succumb, and as her lungs burned and began to give in to their watery end, she felt movement beneath her.

Something skimmed the bottoms of her feet, then her middle, and she felt as if she was being lifted upward. Unable to move, Nora watched as the ice broke apart, and her body emerged above the water's surface. Gasping for air, she was carried toward the bank of the loch and gently slid onto the snowy shore. Confused and disoriented, Nora glanced back toward the water, searching for what had saved her, but the only thing she saw were large ripples where something had been.

Fear coursed through her as the numbness from the cold spread. She tried to get onto her feet but her legs remained stubbornly frozen and unresponsive.

"Help!" she screamed, her voice cracking with desperation. She cried out again and again, but her calls were unanswered. Her cold wet body had no fight left in it, and she slumped forward, falling limp on the frigid ground by the loch's edge. *Stay awake,* she begged herself, but gradually the cold claimed her, and she surrendered to its icy embrace. Right before she faded into the abyss, she saw a giant creature emerge from the water. Its long neck craned downward as its gentle, luminous green eyes locked on hers, as if it were waiting for her, waiting to guide her into the next realm.

Nora woke with her heart racing and sweat dripping from her hairline. She looked around surprised to see she was snug in bed, in the upstairs of the rental. Despite the bed and the cozy blankets she was wrapped in, she felt an inexplicable chill, as if she had just emerged from the frigid waters of her dream. She pulled the quilt up to her chin and glanced at the clock on the wall—it was only five in the morning.

Despite her efforts, she couldn't coax herself back to sleep. Not willing to risk waking Alistair downstairs, she decided to give him time to pack his bags and leave before venturing down, and that might take several more hours. Picking up her phone off the nightstand, she went to check her email and read her daily horoscope, but service was essentially nonexistent, so she gave up. Setting the phone back on the nightstand, she looked over at the old dresser where her bag lay open, the Christmas bauble from the market peeking out from its safe resting spot. She still couldn't believe all the crazy coincidences that had happened since she bought the little red book.

Reaching to the nightstand, she pulled it out from the stack. She wanted to know what happened to Cora's grandmother. Had she survived, or had she met the same ill fate as her own grandmother? The bond between them felt like another echo from the pages into Nora's own reality, deepening her investment in the story. Flipping on the lamp, she pulled her hair up into a ponytail, arranged the pillows against the bed frame, and flipped to where she had left off.

I hurried back to the cottage, feverishly searching through Gran's belongings for her book. It didn't take long before I discovered it tucked discreetly beneath her pillow. The book was large and thick, its deep brown leather cover embossed with symbols unfamiliar to me. Its weathered cover and fragile pages suggested it might be centuries old. The scent of countless herbs lingered on it, a testament to years of spells cast in its presence.

My heart raced at the realization that the book had been left in a place where it could have easily been discovered. Seated on the bed, I cradled it in my hands for a long while. Opening it felt like entering a realm of uncertainty, and I feared I might uncover dreadful spells for unholy purposes that would make me see Gran in a different light. However, as I held it, a soothing energy seemed to emanate from within the book, as if the power contained within was reaching out to me, reassuring me, coaxing me to open the book and explore its contents.

With care, I turned the aged pages, inspecting each one meticulously. There were spells ranging from charms for love and protection to ensuring fruitful harvests and gentle winters. There were incantations to summon rain and to halt it. Spells to aid in childbirth and to deal with husbands too eager to spread their seed. As I delved deeper, the incantations darkened, spanning from bringing one back from death to the summoning of spirits from beyond. The next page I turned was marked with a raven feather delicately tucked within. It marked a spell titled "Realm of Sleep."

~A handful of dried hops, calendula flowers, and dried valerian. One single belladonna berry, dried — any more, and it will cause death to those who ingest it. Boil the blossoms in water for tea and burn the stalks over an open flame while repeating:

As my mind fights the pull of night, the dream realm calls from beyond twilight. With the aid of earth, water, and fire, bring me the sleep I truly desire. To sleep as deeply as the dead, then awake with the sun, within my bed.~

Gran was trying to craft a sleep remedy for herself. That must have been why she was up so late when I saw her, I thought as I gazed down at the spell inscribed in deep black onyx ink. The doctor's diagnosis was correct — it was belladonna poisoning. It appeared she had been too frail to handle the potent ingredients in the potion. I urgently scanned the book for an antidote or incantation to counteract the effects of the berries' toxins. The book was quite thick, and it seemed it would take ages to find what I was looking for, if there even was such a spell.

To my relief, after what must have been an hour, I stumbled upon a spell that could counter the one she had cast upon herself. It was titled "To Dispel Magic from a Spell Gone Awry." The instructions called for rowanberries from a tree near the shores of Loch Ness, boiled in water drawn from a copper bowl at Tobar Mhoire in Letterfearn. However, before the water was collected, the Ansuz rune was to be drawn at the head of the well while saying, "Wisdom from this water's well, counteract, reverse this spell." The tonic was meant to be consumed along with the ingredients of the spell that caused harm. Below, a small note indicated that the counter-spell must be done within three days of the original enchantment, or it would prove ineffective.

I closed the book, carefully wrapped it in Gran's wool shawl, and tucked it into her bag nestled beneath her belongings. Standing there for a fleeting moment, I contemplated how I would explain this situation to the duke. I realized I needed his assistance in acquiring the necessary items to counteract the spell, but I could not tell him how I obtained the information.

Upon my return to the castle, I discovered Gwen gently applying a cold, wet cloth to Gran's forehead as she lay in her enchanted slumber. The sight of her stillness struck my heart with heaviness; she appeared ashen, and dark sunken circles that matched the blue hue of her lips enveloped her eyes.

"Oh, Miss, come. I shall leave you two to be alone," Gwen declared, standing up and gesturing for me to take her place beside Gran's bedside.

Seated there, tenderly dabbing the cool cloth on her forehead, my mind still raced to find a way to explain the situation to the duke. Revealing the truth would only jeopardize Gran's safety, potentially branding us both as witches. I needed to leverage his debt to her for saving his wife and son. I aimed to convince him that Gran required an ancient remedy known to all wise women — one she had taught me how to make. Just as I solidified my plan, he entered the room, accompanied by the duchess.

"How is she?" the duchess inquired. She shielded her mouth and nose with a cloth in fear that Gran might be contagious.

"She remains unchanged, my lady," I replied before turning my attention back to Gran.

"I'm sorry, Cora, but the doctor believes she's too old and frail to fight," the duke expressed, his tone tinged with regret.

"Your Grace, I have been searching my mind for a remedy that might aid her in the battle she is facing. I believe I know just the one, an ancient remedy she has used to save countless others, but I'll need your assistance to obtain the required ingredients," I implored.

"If it holds any chance of helping, we are willing to assist in any way we can," he assured me.

"The remedy calls for rowanberries from Loch Ness and water from Tobar Mhoire in Letterfearn," I told him, hoping my fabricated tale would hold under his scrutiny.

"Gwen, go fetch my son," the duke commanded, his hand resting on my shoulder. "I will do whatever I can to save her. You have my word."

My heart sank at the duke's words. I had not expected him to send his son on such an errand. I had thought it would have been one of the men who had come to Gran's aid at the cottage instead. Dreading the interaction that lay ahead, I turned my attention back to Gran and willed myself to stand tall and not show any weakness in his presence. Within a few minutes, I heard sharp footsteps echoing on the flagstone floors, rapping down the hallway and into the room.

"Father, Mother, you called for me," a voice spoke. I resisted the urge to turn around, recognizing the familiar tone. It was their son, the same insolent man who had been so disrespectful to me in our previous encounters.

"James, I am sending you to Tobar Mhoire in Letterfearn for water. You must also gather rowanberries to bring back with you for the remedy," the duke commanded.

"But Father, I was planning on leaving for Edinburgh in the morning. Why not send Arthur or Henry?" he protested.

"Because you owe this woman your life, and it is time to repay the debt. You can postpone your departure a few days," the duke said in a booming voice that echoed off the stone walls.

As they exchanged words, a sense of unease gripped me. The spell specified the need for berries from a particular rowan tree and water collected in a copper bowl from the well in a very particular way. I couldn't merely delegate these tasks without arousing suspicions. I needed to be part of this journey. The prospect of traveling with this man dismayed me, but if it meant saving Gran, I would endure a hundred days in his company.

"I will go as well, my lord," I interjected, abruptly interrupting their conversation.

"Cora, my dear, no, I think it best if you stay here with your gran. She needs your strength beside her."

"But, my lord, I must go," I protested. I had not anticipated his resistance, and my mind was in a frantic rush to devise reasons why I must go along without revealing the truth. This was not merely a trip to gather ingredients for a medicine; this was the working of a spell, and things must be performed and gathered in a specific way, or the spell would not take. However, I could not tell this to the duke.

"I fear if you leave with James that you may return to an empty bed. The doctor does not believe she is much longer for this world," he told me.

I stood for a long moment unsure of what to say to sway him. What he didn't know was without the items needed for the spell, Gran's death was all but certain. Before I was able to gather my thoughts and plead my case to the duke, James interrupted.

"It's a three-day ride there and back, and all you'll do is slow me down." His tone dripped with condescension. I watched as the duke shot him an unhappy look, then turned back to me. "What James is saying is true. He can get there and back much quicker on horseback than if you were to go with him in a carriage," the duke explained.

"My lord, with the utmost respect, Lord Campbell lacks the knowledge to harvest the berries in a manner that preserves their potency. If done incorrectly, the medicine made with them will be ineffective. It's a skill Gran has been teaching me for as long as I can remember. This is what she has been preparing me for," I said, meeting both their gazes.

The duke sat in silence for a moment, contemplating my words.

"And are you sure this cannot be taught to James now?" he finally asked.

"No, my lord. It took many lessons before Gran was satisfied with my technique."

"Well, if that be the case, then there really isn't much choice in the matter. James, you will take Ms. Douglas with you," he conceded.

"No. I will not be escorting some maid across the land," James retorted.

"You have no say in this matter and will do as I say. Cora, go pack your bags. James will pick you up within the hour," the duke ordered, cutting off his son's objections.

Bending forward, I planted a kiss on Gran's forehead.

"I will pull you from this spell, but I need you to stay strong, to stay alive," I whispered softly in her ear before hastily making my way out of the bedroom, through the castle, and toward the cottage.

Chapter Twenty-Five

THE FIRST PART OF
THE JOURNEY

I hastened back to the cottage, keenly aware of the urgency. I needed to pack swiftly for the journey, ensuring I had all the necessary items, including Gran's book carefully concealed among my belongings.

As I retrieved the book from its hiding spot at the bottom of Gran's bag, I was drawn to open it against my better judgment. Despite its pull, I resisted, knowing I didn't have much time left before the duke's son arrived. I quickly gathered the remnants of herbs around the hearth, bits and pieces that were left from Gran's conjuring. I would need them when we returned with the water and berries for the countering spell. I swept what I could find into a small pouch and tucked it into my bag. I made sure to leave nothing behind that might force us to turn back.

I had just finished securing the last of my belongings when the rhythmic beating of the horse's hooves echoed on the frozen ground outside the cottage. A knock followed, and the footman stood ready to take my satchel and guide me to the waiting carriage as I opened the door. Stepping into the carriage, I found James seated across from me, arms crossed, and his gaze fixed on the window, paying me no attention.

"My Lord Campbell," I said upon entering. Without acknowledging my presence in any way, he said nothing, and I felt like a mere ghost as I sat down across from him.

Silence surrounded us like a heavy cloak as we traveled the bumpy, snow-covered road. The discomfort of the journey was matched only by the awkward silence within the carriage. He sat with his arms crossed, peering out the small window with an irritated expression etched on his face.

How could he be so perturbed by the mission to save the woman's life who had helped save his and his mother's lives all those years ago? It wasn't as if she were some destitute peasant he was helping. Gran had been his mother's trusted midwife for years. She had crafted countless remedies upon request for illnesses and other ailments for his family. The more I thought of it, the more my blood boiled; it was painfully obvious that he seemed indifferent to whether she lived or died. The woman at the ball was right: he was certainly tiresomely self-important, with not a care for anyone but himself.

I seethed at the thought. As my anger grew, so did the snowstorm outside. Out the carriage window, the sky darkened even further as the sun began to set, and the world appeared shrouded in a white veil. The inside of the carriage grew colder, and I watched as James pulled his scarf higher up around his neck. Frost licked the small window leaving veins of ice that looked like delicate lace creeping out from the window's edges. The wind began to howl, and the carriage slowed.

"Will the storm be a problem for the carriage?" I asked.

"Of course, as these carriages are not built to travel in weather like this. Must I remind you that if I were on this mission alone, it would be on horseback and much faster. We will be lucky to make it there and back in a week at this pace," he scoffed.

A sinking sensation crept over me at his words. *It can't take a week,* I thought. We only had three days for Gran to take the antidote for the spell, or it would not work. At that moment I began to doubt myself, wondering if I should have just told James how to procure the water and berries.

"Is there anything we can do to quicken this trip? The doctor said that she may not even live three more days."

"Then you should have stayed with her," he snapped.

Anger rose in me, and I coiled back but did not strike him with the harsh words dashing through my head. Instead, I pushed them down, crossing my arms and digging my fingernails into the fabric of the mittens on my hands. A large gust of wind thrashed the carriage as the sky continued to dim, and my icy demeanor added a new depth of cold to the inside of the carriage.

After traveling for a short while longer, the carriage came to a stop. The footman opened the door to inform us that we needed to find shelter before nightfall. The snow had become unmanageable to ride in, and he feared that the carriage would not be able to push on much farther. I knew that with the storm raging, we could not continue on, but I worried that stopping so soon for the night would set us back too far. We only had a limited amount of time, and the clock was ticking, but the weather was beyond my control.

"One of my father's tenants lives just up the road, another half mile or so. They have a barn for the horses and will let us bed down for the night," James explained.

As the carriage resumed its journey, the chill from the open door left me shivering, so I wrapped my arms tightly around myself, trying to warm up.

"Here," James said, unfolding a wool blanket that sat next to him. He leaned forward and handed it to me. I was taken aback by the small gesture of kindness, and I hesitated for a moment before wrapping it around my shoulders.

"Thank you," I said, offering him my most genuine smile but he turned away from me, his gaze fixated on the window once again.

Within minutes, the carriage stopped again, and James stepped out. Peering through the window, I saw a large man approaching with a lantern. James reached out and shook the man's hand.

"Do you and Addie have room to host us for the night? We couldn't go on much farther in this weather," James asked the man.

"We?" the man questioned, looking toward the carriage.

"My father has sent me on a mission with the healer's granddaughter. We need to go to Letterfearn, then to Loch Ness, in search of medicine," James yelled over the biting wind.

"Of course. You know you are always welcome," the man said, patting him on the shoulder.

James motioned for me to join him, and I stepped out of the carriage into the raging storm. We quickly followed the man into the humble house while the footman took the horses and carriage into the large barn.

"This is Malcolm Turner and his wife, Addie," James said as a woman with long red hair stepped out from another room to greet us.

"Good day, it is a pleasure to make your acquaintance. I am Cora," I said, as James had neglected to introduce us.

"It is a pleasure to make your acquaintance," Addie said just as a little girl with bright red curls came rushing into the room.

"James, James!" she called out, wrapping herself around his legs.

"Well, hello there, Alice," James responded, lifting the little girl up and twirling her around in the air. She squealed in delight. "And this is Alice. She is a rabbit."

I watched as he lovingly set her down, genuine warmth gracing his smile, and for a moment I barely recognized the man before me. Below the callous exterior, there seemed to be a softer side to the duke's son.

"I'm not a rabbit. I'm a girl!" she laughed, jumping down and running away to the other room.

Addie and Malcolm watched the banter between James and their daughter, smiling as if it were a regular occurrence.

"I just made some stew and fresh bread. Come, come," Addie invited us.

I stripped off my cape, coated in a layer of snow, and set it on a peg next to the door. James followed suit, and I followed him into the modest kitchen where we sat on opposite sides of a large oak table. James had not glanced in my direction once since we entered the house, and I wondered if Malcolm and Addie perceived the unease between us.

Addie gathered the food and began to serve us as Malcolm added logs to the fire. Alice played with a carved wooden rabbit and a small cloth doll on the floor near the hearth.

"Come, Alice, time for dinner," her mother called, and the child dropped her toys, joining us at the table.

As we ate, I listened to Malcolm and James talk about the poor crops from the past harvest season, expressing concern that there might not be enough food to last the winter if spring came late as it had the previous year. My thoughts drifted back to the spellbook in my bag and how there were spells to shorten the winter and fatten the harvest. If only they knew that with the proper herbs and incantations, they might never have to worry about such things again.

This brought up something I had not thought of until now: if Gran had all this power at her fingertips, why did she live such a modest life? Why didn't she have an abundance of food and the finest things?

"It's the hardships that shape us," Addie remarked to James, almost as if the universe had responded to the question simultaneously.

After dinner, I assisted Addie in tidying up and washing the dinnerware while the men enjoyed a dram of whisky by the fire.

"Malcolm says you and James are searching for medicine. May I ask who for? Is the duke or duchess unwell?"

"No, they are in good health. It is for my gran, the duchess's old midwife," I told her as she handed me a plate to dry. "She took ill this morning, and the doctor believes she won't make it much longer in her condition." My stomach sank as the words left my lips and urgency filled me with a nervous energy once again.

"Oh dear, I'm so sorry. Well, you have the right man for the job. James will certainly do what he can to help your gran."

I wasn't sure if that was truly the case. He seemed indifferent to the whole situation while Addie talked about him as if he were a kind and caring man. I had not previously witnessed this gentler aspect of him, but it was not the first I had heard of it, either. This left me wondering once again why he seemed to have such a grievance against me.

"Yes, thank you so much for letting us stay the night here," I said, hoping that my face did not betray me and show my true feelings about James.

"Of course. We love James. He is like a son to us," she said, glancing at him with a fond smile.

"May I ask how you know Lord Campbell?" I inquired, feeling a bit nosey and wanting to know more about who this man truly was.

"The duke and Malcolm are close. Malcolm's father was the master of horses years ago at the castle, and they grew up riding together. When it came time for James to learn how to ride, the duke tasked Malcolm with the job. For almost eight years, James came to our house every week for lessons in the backfield," she said, looking over at him with fondness in her eyes.

"You have known him since he was a child then?" I deduced, speaking aloud my thoughts.

"Yes, we love him like one of our own, and he has been like a brother to Alice ever since she was born."

I stood staring at the two men seated by the fireplace. I could see it now: James looked at Malcolm with the same regard and affection that a son does for his father. The admiration seemed to go both ways.

"He is a wonderful young man and will be a right and just duke someday, just like his father," Addie remarked with pride. After finishing up in the kitchen, we moved into the sitting room where the men and Alice were gathered around the fire.

"I'll fetch you some blankets," Addie said, disappearing into another room. She returned moments later with two blankets and two pillows and created makeshift beds on opposite sides of the fireplace.

"Here ya go," she said, offering a warm smile. "Come now, Alice, let's get you to bed. We best be letting James get some rest." She took the little girl's hand, leading her into the other room. Malcolm nodded in farewell and followed them.

James waved to Alice as she hung over her mother's shoulder, and I glimpsed that softer side of him once again. As soon as they had left the room, he bedded down for the night, facing in the opposite direction without a single word. He had paid me no mind the entire night, acting as if I were not even there, as he did now. If it were not for Malcolm's and Addie's kindness, I think he might have sent me to sleep in the barn with the footman and the horses. I remained perplexed as to why he harbored such disdain for me.

As I pulled the blanket up around me, the chill between us seemed to deepen the cold in the room. I prayed for sleep to come, willing the night to be over so that we could continue on our mission. Gran's gaunt face kept flashing into my thoughts, the blue hue of her lips, as if death were perched at her bedside, just waiting to—

A loud crashing sound interrupted Nora mid-sentence. With a start, her heart lodged itself into her throat, and she sat bolt upright. Another crash echoed up the stairs. She jumped up. Grabbing her phone off the nightstand, she set the book aside before racing out of the room and toward the noise.

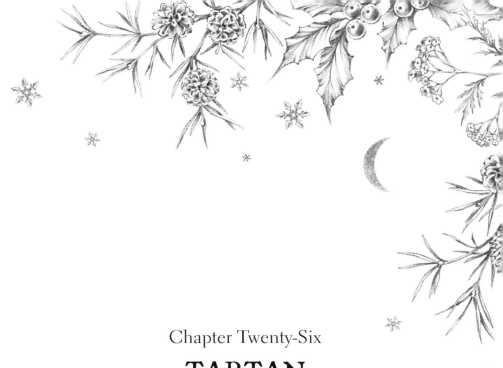

Chapter Twenty-Six
TARTAN

Nora came racing down the stairs to see the cause of the loud crash. Alistair was bent over next to the stove picking up a cast-iron pot and pan from off the kitchen floor. The smell of fried eggs and burnt toast wafted up to greet her as she descended the final step.

"Sorry, did I wake you?" he asked as he scrambled to tuck the pans back into the cupboard they had fallen out from.

At the sight of him, she quickly ran her fingers through her tangled locks, a subconscious attempt to appear a bit more presentable. Glancing down at her pajamas, she wished she had gotten dressed before she started reading this morning. She had hoped to avoid him and had even entertained the notion that he might have left and the sound she heard had been the door slamming behind him. She wasn't that lucky. Apparently, he had no intention of departing anytime soon, by the look of things.

"No, I've been up reading," she replied as she made her way over to the pot that was full to the top with fresh coffee. "What's all the fuss down here anyways?" she asked as she poured herself a large mug.

"I have good news and bad news. What do you want first?"

"Bad," she said, bracing herself. She wanted to rip it off like a Band-Aid.

"Okay. Bad news is the storm isn't over."

Nora looked out the windows toward the loch and saw that it was still heavily snowing outside.

"Because of this freak storm, there are no outbound buses until tomorrow," he said, flipping the eggs and then attending to the lightly burnt toast.

"I see. And the good news?" she said in a slightly snarky tone.

"I am making you breakfast."

"Oh, I get it. You are buttering me up because you have no place to go, and you want me to let you stay here another night," Nora said, taking a long drawn-out sip of her coffee.

An awkward silence fell over the room as he buttered the toast. Piling a plate with eggs, he placed the toast to the side and handed it to her.

"That obvious?" he asked, turning around and pouring himself a cup of tea.

"Just a bit," she said with a smirk. "But it might be working," she added after taking a bite of food. He turned around and gave her a slight smile.

"Listen, I know we got off on the wrong foot, and I acknowledge I've been an arse."

"Maybe just a little. Remember not all of us *Outlander* fans are annoying."

"Oh, I know. It's mostly just the American ones," he joked, but there was something in his tone that didn't convince her he was kidding.

She rolled her eyes as he walked around the island. He pulled out a barstool and sat next to her.

"Does that mean you aren't going to be able to get your story to the magazine in time?" Nora asked, chewing through a bite of egg.

"To be honest, I really don't give a shit. I wasn't even supposed to be on this article anyway. I had been assigned a story about Sir Robert Brigton, a politician who had been tied to a human trafficking ring. I was about to be sent over to Myanmar to investigate but I was taken off the story last minute."

"What did you do?" Nora interrupted, wishing immediately that she hadn't asked the question from the look that washed across his face.

"Nothing. The magazine owner's niece from California decided she wanted to play investigative journalist and asked him to send her undercover with a couple of bodyguards instead. He took me off the story and replaced me with her, a twenty-something Valley girl," he said in a bitter tone as he chewed his toast a little harder than he needed to. "I had been working on this story for months, but he just hands her all my notes, and off she goes."

It was then that Nora understood the resentment he had against American women. Looking at him, she sensed hurt and disappointment just below the surface, and she couldn't blame him for feeling that way.

"I'm sorry," was all she could come up with to say. It didn't feel like enough, but then again, they didn't know each other that well. Plus, she didn't want to overstep her bounds by asking him anything else about the situation now that they were starting to get along.

"Thanks, it is what it is. So, what do you do when you're not traveling to the Highlands?" he asked, quickly changing the subject.

"I work at my family's bakery. My parents are retiring and handing me the reins this spring," she told him.

"Must be nice. Get handed a business and not have to work your way up the corporate ladder," he said in that same bitter tone.

"Well, it's not all it's cracked up to be, especially if you have no interest in running it," she snapped back.

"You have no idea how lucky you are. Try coming from a home with a single mum who didn't have a pot to piss in after my dad abandoned her. I never got a thing handed to me. I had to work hard for all of it. And anyway, if you don't wanna take it over, why are you doing it?" he asked. His words stung as she realized that her story seemed insignificant compared to his.

"Because it's been in my family for generations, and if I don't take it over, their legacy dies. It's a lot of pressure," she retorted, even though she had felt like he had already won this argument. The uneasy ache of guilt and fear over the situation began to work its way to the surface. She did not want to talk about this anymore, especially with him. Nora set down her fork, unable to finish her breakfast now that her stomach had turned with the unpleasant conversation about the bakery.

"Spoiled Americans," she heard him say under his breath as he walked over to the window and looked out toward the loch. She swallowed hard, then bit her tongue. She wanted to give it right back to him, but she chose instead to end the irritating banter and change the subject.

"I saw something in the loch yesterday just before you arrived," Nora said, looking toward the center of the watery expanse and remembering the dream that had put her in a cold sweat this morning.

"Really. What?" he asked condescendingly.

Nora froze. She had wanted to change the subject, but why had she changed it to this? His tone made her regret her choice almost immediately.

"Not sure. Something large moving out in the center," she said, stumbling over her words.

"It was snowing pretty heavy. How could you have even seen the center of the loch?" he said in a snarky tone as he looked toward the water.

"I don't know."

"What do you think it was? The Loch Ness Monster or maybe a Laidly Worm?" He laughed at her. Her cheeks reddened. She was not going to let him get under her skin, and she knew she had seen something in the loch that night even if he thought she was crazy.

"What is a Laidly Worm?" Nora asked, looking away from the loch and back at him.

"A water spirit, like a giant water dragon. Just a bunch of non-sense made up by parents long ago to keep their kids away from the lochs. That folklore book you took up to bed last night has a chapter on them."

"I guess I didn't get that far yet."

Nora thought about the folklore volume resting on her night-stand and then about the little red book. She yearned to get away from Alistair and back to reading. She wanted to know what happened next, but she felt rude just taking off up to her bedroom when Alistair had cooked her breakfast. If they were going to be stuck together for another day, they were going to need to try to get along.

"Well, I guess I should probably get some writing done. Do you mind if I stay another night? I promise to stay out of your way," he said, turning around and facing her.

God, every time he looked her directly in the eyes, her heart went racing up into her throat. Why was it that her body and her mind couldn't be on the same page about this guy? She had to remind herself that nothing good ever came of a chance meeting like this. Sam was the prime example, and she wasn't about to make the same mistake twice.

"Of course. I can't send you off packing in this snow, can I?"

"Well, you could, but I might freeze and die. Then who would load the fire for you in the middle of the night?" he joked, as the softer side of him showed through his callous exterior once again.

"You're right, I hadn't thought of that," Nora joked back as the tone in the conversation lightened a bit.

As Nora walked back into the kitchen to pour herself another cup of coffee, the lights began to flicker. They dulled, then came back to life a few times before they went out completely.

"No, no, no," Alistair said, walking back into the kitchen and flipping open his laptop. "Shit," he said, looking at the black screen. "Wonderful. My dumb arse should have plugged it in last night. Now I don't have enough battery to even turn it on."

Nora pulled her phone out of the pocket of her plaid PJs and looked at it. Crap, she hadn't charged her phone last night, either, and it was also just about dead, sitting at two percent. She slid it back into her pocket and looked back to Alistair.

He stood for a long minute looking down at his computer and then out toward the loch. "Maybe we should take a look around outside and see if we can spot the downed power line. If we find it and call the power company, they might be able to get the power on faster," he suggested.

"That's not a bad idea. Let me get changed," she said.

She headed upstairs, pulled on a pair of jeans and an old UVM sweatshirt, then rooted around in her bag for her mittens and winter hat. Unzipping a pocket, she pulled out the scarf her grandmother had bought for her twentieth birthday and wrapped it around her neck, using the brooch to secure it.

As she descended the stairs, Alistair was at the door, pulling on his boots.

"Are you sure you are going to be warm enough?" Nora asked, watching him zip up a jacket that looked more about style than warmth.

"It's what I got," he told her, zipping it all the way to the top.

"I think there is a jacket in the closet by the bathroom," she told him, walking over and opening the closet door. Inside hung a large army-green parka. She grabbed it and walked it back over to him. "I think you better wear this. I don't want to have to carry you back after you freeze to death."

He didn't say anything but took the jacket and put it over the one he had on.

"That scarf. Is it your family tartan?" he asked.

"Yes, a gift from my grandmother. My grandfather was from here; he was a Cameron."

"That's not a Cameron clan tartan, you know?"

"Yes, it is. My grandmother specifically told me this was my grandfather's tartan when she gave it to me," Nora argued back, feeling a bit annoyed at all the questions about her scarf as she started sweltering in all her layers.

"Well, that's not the Cameron clan tartan. It's the MacDonalds."

"What? No. You must be mistaken."

"I'm not. I know this tartan quite well as it's my best mate's."

Nora was confused. Why had her grandmother told her that this was her family tartan if it hadn't been? Maybe she didn't know what the Cameron tartan looked like or had gotten it confused with another. A lot of the tartans looked similar in color but with different plaid patterns.

"Does the Cameron tartan look like this one?" she asked.

"No, not at all. The Cameron clan's is red," Alistair stated matter-of-factly.

Suddenly the man from the photo album, standing beside her gram in the hospital, the same man she had seen when she had come so close to death in the car accident, rushed into Nora's mind, like an old film reel flickering back to life.

The name Colin MacDonald had been written on the back of the photo. MacDonald. Nora's head spun with confusion as she began to mull over all the stories her grandmother had told her about her time in Scotland, about her grandfather.

The inconsistencies in her grandmother's stories about Scotland and her grandfather began to nag at Nora's mind. Despite the fondness with which her grandmother had always spoken of their time in Scotland, she rarely mentioned her grandfather outside of those war stories. It was as if there was a hidden layer to their history that Nora had never noticed before: a duality.

The more Nora thought about it, the more an idea began to form in her mind. Maybe it wasn't just their time in Scotland that was different; maybe her grandmother was talking about a completely different man. Not the grandfather she knew from the photos on the family mantel, but the man she spoke of in her stories, the man in the album, Colin MacDonald.

Chapter Twenty-Seven
LOCKED OUT

"Are you okay?" Alistair asked as Nora stood stunned into silence, her mind reeling over the idea that her grandfather might not be her actual grandfather.

She mulled the question over in her head. Was she okay? She wasn't sure. Her head was a jumble of stories that no longer made sense.

"I'm fine," she said, looking down at the scarf that dangled from her neck.

"Your gran probably just didn't know which tartan was which," Alistair suggested.

She gave him an off-put smile.

"Seriously, what's going on? You look like you've seen a ghost," Alistair insisted.

"Would you know how to look up the name of a doctor who was stationed at Craigleith Military Hospital back in 1943?"

"Yeah, I'm sure I could dig up that information. Why?" Alistair asked, looking confused.

"I'll tell you later. I've got to get out of here before I boil to death in these layers," she said, opening the door and walking out into the cold. A foot or more of snow covered the walkway leading to the road.

"Let me see if there is a shovel around here somewhere," Alistair said, trudging around the corner of the cottage and disappearing into a small overhang with firewood stacked in it.

Nora glanced around, her mind buzzing with a newfound idea. Memories of a bedtime story Gram had shared many times flooded back. It was about a newspaper clipping in the album depicting a colossal machine with disc-shaped wheels—The Bombe Machine was written in bold print underneath it. Gram had told her that her grandfather's assignment had taken him to Bletchley Park in Buckinghamshire, England, where he had worked as a code breaker, interpreting the bomb's results to help break the Enigma codes during World War II. However, her grandfather had to keep the top-secret nature of his work from Gram, and she didn't learn the full extent of his contributions until decades later when the information was declassified.

Thinking back on it now, Nora felt a pang of confusion. Her grandfather had been a medic surgeon for the army, not a code breaker. How could he have been involved with Bletchley Park? Yet, she remembered the story and how Gram's eyes lit up with pride whenever she recounted his efforts to help end the war.

The more she thought about it, the more the pieces didn't quite fit together. Was there something she was missing? Gram had always grown solemn at the end of the story, closing the album and saying something in another language. *What was it?* Nora thought, and then it came to her. "Gus an coinnich sinn a-rithist," she said aloud.

"I wasn't gone that long. You know Gaelic?" Alistair said as he came back around the corner with a shovel.

"I don't. It's just something my grandmother always said at the end of a story she told me when I was little. What does it mean?" Nora asked.

"Until we meet again," he told her as he began to clear the walkway.

Nora's heart sank; nothing made sense.

She looked back at the cottage; she needed answers, but the electricity was still out, so no internet access. Resigned to the fact that her research would have to wait, she followed Alistair up the walkway as he shoveled. The wind had died down, but it was still bitterly cold. Something about the day's chilly embrace stopped her racing mind and calmed her.

She tried to determine if any power lines were down to the left of the cottage, but all seemed fine. She was accustomed to the way snowstorms in Vermont transformed the landscape, but it was different here. The way the snow clung to the trees and mountains off in the distance looked almost like a painting. Perhaps the sky itself made everything feel so enchanting. Even though it was filled with a thick duvet of clouds, it looked much larger than the sky she was used to in the Green Mountains.

"Those there are the Five Sisters of Kintail," Alistair said, as her eyes fixed on the mountains.

She turned and looked at him. "What?" she asked, confused.

"It's what we call those mountains, part of an old legend," he explained, pointing at the rugged blue mountain peaks far off in the distance. "There were Five Sisters of Kintail, but they were so vain they drew the attention of an ancient wizard. To teach them a lesson about vanity, he transformed them into towering peaks, frozen in eternal stone, as a punishment for their pride. Some people think their spirits still whisper on the winds that blow down from the peaks, lending their magic to the land they once roamed."

"Is that in the book too?" Nora inquired with a smile.

"Possibly." He smiled back before turning to work on the stairs so they could get a better look at the lines that ran back to the other cabins.

When Nora turned back around, she caught something moving out of the corner of her eye, a little black shadow. The tiny black dog that had stood up for her the first day she had arrived scampered near the water.

"Here, boy," she called. The dog's nose lifted from the ground and then toward where she stood on the walkway. Trudging through the snow, he made his slow ascent up the hill toward her. Disappearing in and out of view, he had almost made it to her when he lifted his nose to the air and sniffed in Alistair's direction. Once the dog caught sight of him, he turned tail and trotted back down the embankment toward the loch. Poor thing had been out in the storm this whole time alone. Why hadn't he come back to the cabins to find shelter? Maybe the dog didn't like men. She really couldn't blame him. Alistair didn't exactly exude warmth even if he was starting to grow on her a little.

Alistair had missed the entire thing as he shoveled but Nora surmised that he was fine with the dog staying far away, especially after their last encounter.

She watched the dog's lanky little frame walk all the way to the edge of the water where he sat staring out into the distance as if he were waiting for someone to come back. The loch was a mix of open water and was quickly forming ice around the edges on the shallow inlets. As tiny whitecaps formed on the frigid waves, Nora scanned the massive expanse of water from her vantage point on the stairs, unable to see its start or end. It seemed to go on forever. A small boat bobbed in the waves near the shoreline, and she wondered if maybe that was what she had seen last night. Perhaps a trick of the light and the heavy falling snow had made her think it was farther out in the water than it really had been.

As she gazed over the loch, she felt like she was caught within a spell. Her rational mind typically won her inner dialogue, but here in Letterfearn by the loch, she found herself wanting to believe in loch monsters and magical portals into different realms.

"Hello, hello, over here!" came a voice calling out on the wind.

Alistair had shoveled to the top of the stairs, and they were now on the upper walkway that led past the other rentals. Standing under the small overhang of cottage three was an old woman in a nightgown. She waved her hands to draw their attention, even though they could see her quite clearly.

"Oh, my God, what is she doing out here in a nightgown?" Nora asked.

"Do you need help, love?" Alistair asked, shoveling his way over to her cabin.

"Yes, I've locked myself out," the old woman said, her teeth chattering behind her blue lips.

"God, she looks half frozen," Nora whispered as they approached the woman.

Before they had even reached her, Alistair was pulling off his jacket.

"First, let's get you into this," he said, wrapping it around her shoulders. She was a petite woman, and the jacket was so large it nearly went below her knees. Nora took off her hat and handed it to her after she had zipped the coat up.

"Do you remember your passcode?" Nora asked.

"I do, but it's not working. I thought I saw something in the loch and came out to get a better look when the door shut and locked behind me."

"Let me call the lettings agency and see if we can figure this out," Alistair said, taking his phone out of his back pocket. He held it up and turned it from one direction to the other. "Crap, no reception. The storm must be messing with the towers in the area."

Nora looked at him, worry in her eyes. The woman didn't look well.

"How long have you been locked out here?" Nora asked.

"I'm not entirely sure," the woman answered, shivering.

Nora looked down at her bare ankles and feet, which were in nothing but a slim pair of slippers.

"We need to get her somewhere warm quickly," Alistair said. "Do you think you can walk down those stairs?" He pointed to the stairs leading down to their cottage.

The old woman nodded, and he took her arm in his, guiding her slowly. Nora watched him help her down the flight of stairs as the winds and snow fought against their progress. The once arrogant man she had loathed to be around seemed to have a softer side. Maybe he wasn't who she had first thought him to be.

By the time they had gotten her down the stairs, the old woman could barely stand. Alistair stopped at the front door and punched in the code. After a click and a pop, he opened the door and escorted the old woman inside.

"Nora, see if you can find some extra blankets," Alistair said as he helped the woman into one of the armchairs near the fireplace. Once she was seated, he stoked the fire and added a few extra logs to get the temperature up in the room.

"Here," Nora said, draping a thick wool blanket over the old woman's shoulders.

"Let's see if we have water for some tea. That should help warm your insides up," Alistair said, walking over to the sink and turning on the facet. "We're in luck, the cabins must use a gravity-fed well," he announced as he filled up the kettle.

"Are you okay?" Nora asked, seeing the paleness of her skin and the bluish tinge that still clung to her lips. Firelight danced in her eyes, mimicking the ancient battle between fire and ice.

"I'm not entirely sure," she said in a cryptic tone, leaving Nora to wonder if she was alluding to something other than her health.

"Do you need a hospital?" Nora asked, her voice full of concern. "Is there someone we should call, family perhaps?"

"Once I warm up, I should be fine," she told Nora as she leaned forward to warm her hands. "No, I'm afraid it's just me," she clarified. "My son and daughter-in-law were killed in a car accident six months ago. We were estranged at the time, and I have been struggling with whether I should reach out to my granddaughter. I took this trip to try to decide what I need to do."

Nora recognized the sadness in her eyes. Her grandmother used to get the same look after telling the story about her grandfather and the code-breaking machine. It was heartbreak in their eyes, the look of someone who had lost someone they loved.

"I'm so sorry to hear that. I can't imagine how hard that must be," Nora said, trying to be as gentle as possible. "What's your name?"

"Betty Shortbridge, and you, dear?" she asked. The color was beginning to work its way back into her cheeks slowly as the extra logs caught fire and the room began heating up.

"Nora, and that's Alistair." She pointed over her shoulder toward the kitchen.

"Hold on to that one. He's a keeper. Kind and looks to boot," she said with a sly smile.

"Oh, no, we're not a couple. We actually don't even know each other. The cabin got double-booked, and we ended up having to share it due to the snowstorm."

"Seems like Fate just dealt his hand. Now it's up to you to play it well," she said, smiling and winking at Nora.

As Betty's words worked their way under Nora's skin, she looked over her shoulder into the kitchen where Alistair was filling three cups of tea. As much as she tried to ignore it, butterflies had begun to take up residence in her stomach each time she looked at him.

Nora turned and smiled back at Betty as Alistair walked over with the cups of tea.

"Where are you from, Betty?" he asked her as he handed her a cup.

She breathed in the aromatic steam that rose from the tea before she answered. "Northern Wales. As a child I used to take trips into the Highlands with my mother. I have very fond memories of it. I decided that I wanted to come back one last time before I was too old to travel," she explained, blowing on her tea and taking a long drawn-out sip.

Alistair gave Betty a genuine smile as he handed Nora a cup.

"I'm going to use the landline to find out if someone can help us get your cabin unlocked," he told her, then walked over to the corded phone near the hallway closet.

"Are you sure you're feeling okay?" Nora asked, noticing Betty's legs were still shaking.

"Much better. Thank you for helping me. I'm not sure what I would have done if you two hadn't come around when you did."

"I'm glad Alistair suggested we go out to see if we could spot the downed power line," she said, taking a tentative sip of the hot tea. "You said you had stepped out to look at something in the water. What was it?" Nora asked, curious to know what could have drawn Betty out into the raging snowstorm in her nightgown.

"I'm not entirely sure. It was large and was moving along the center of the loch. With the snow coming down so heavily, I could barely make out the shape from inside, so I stepped outside to get a better look. But as soon as the door opened, it was gone."

Nora looked over her shoulder toward the loch. Betty's story sounded eerily similar to what she had seen yesterday. That couldn't be a coincidence.

"I saw it, too, yesterday. What do you think it was?" Nora asked in a whisper.

"At first, I thought it might be a tree floating in the water, but then I saw it move. It glided across the loch and then dipped down under its surface, reemerging in another spot farther up. At that point, I thought it might be a beaver or maybe some kind of large fish, but then the wind blew, and the snow let up for a brief moment. It was then I saw its head break the surface of the water. I knew then it was not a beaver or fish. I believe it's an afanc."

"What's an afanc?"

"A water monster."

"Is that a Scottish folklore creature like the Laidly Worm?"

"Oh, no, it's a Welsh one, but I think they are all the same—creatures left behind by the old gods," she told Nora in a serious tone.

"You really believe in this kind of stuff?"

"I do. I have seen some things that are unexplainable, things that make you believe."

The old woman's words hung heavy in the air, unsettling Nora. The line between reality and lore blurred, leaving her torn between reason and the eerie possibility that these supernatural creatures might be more than just stories. And if they were, she might have one right outside her window.

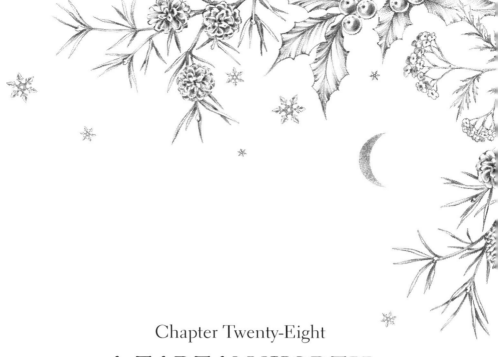

Chapter Twenty-Eight

A TARTAN WORTH
A THOUSAND WORDS

After a long drawn-out silence, Nora felt her heart racing. She hadn't been seeing things; it hadn't been a trick of the light. Something lurked in the loch. Betty had seen it too, and from the sounds of it, she was convinced it was indeed some sort of water spirit.

Looking back over her shoulder at the loch, Nora hoped she might spot the elusive creature once again, but all she could see was the white haze of heavily falling snow. The storm had picked up again, and the temperature continued to drop, frosting the edges of the large windows overlooking the loch.

"Betty, what passcode have you been using?" Alistair called out from the corded phone by the stairs.

"Nineteen fifty-three," Betty called back to him.

He nodded to her and relayed the information to the person on the other end of the phone. After exchanging a few more words, he hung up and rejoined them by the fire.

"So, the reason you couldn't get into your cottage was the passcode you were using was wrong. It should have been nineteen fifty-two. You were off by one," Alistair said in a very gentle way, trying to save her pride as much as possible.

"Oh, dear." A look of sadness washed over her face. "I guess my age is showing. I will leave you two be and head back to my own cabin now," she said, beginning to stand on wobbly legs.

"Whoa, there, why don't you stay and have lunch with us until you've thawed out a bit more," Alistair said, guiding her to sit back down. Nora was taken aback by the kind and gentle way he was treating Betty, almost the complete opposite of how he had treated her when they first met. She was glad for that but also a bit annoyed.

"I'll make us something," Nora announced, heading over to the kitchen. She tried to recall what Stuart had delivered the previous night, hesitating to open the refrigerator without a clear plan. Conserving its cold was important, given the uncertain duration of the power outage. The remnants of Alistair's burnt toast gave Nora an idea. Grilled cheese sandwiches.

Using a box of matches, Nora lit the stove and grabbed the old cast-iron pan. While she waited for it to heat, she buttered the toast and quickly grabbed the cheese from the fridge. As she sliced it, she watched Alistair and Betty engrossed in a conversation about Northern Wales and the King Arthur lore surrounding her town. Betty's eyes sparkled with a mix of wisdom and a touch of mischief, making Nora wonder what other stories she held in the treasure trove of her experiences.

Prompted by something Betty said, Alistair laughed. His

demeanor had done a complete one-eighty in Betty's presence, as if the armor he wore had melted away. He had an undeniable charm to him when he smiled, and the sound of his laughter stirred something deep within Nora, something she had pushed down since things had ended with Sam. She wasn't sure she was ready to reawaken that feeling, but something about Alistair pulled at her, and she realized she may not have a choice in the matter. Her heart and head were yet again battling each other.

She continued to watch them as she cooked, but her mind began to wander back to the photo album and the man named Colin Mac-Donald. Something nagged her, and she needed to look at that photo again, at all of the photos again. She had a feeling that when she did, the puzzle pieces might start fitting together. Her mind returned to a particular photo of her grandmother sitting on a stone wall with a picnic blanket draped over it. She wasn't quite sure why, but she couldn't get the image out of her head. As soon as they got Betty safely back to her rental, she would pull out the album for another look.

"Order up," she announced, walking over with three grilled cheese sandwiches on a tray. "I know it's nothing fancy, but there really isn't anything like a good grilled cheese to warm you up." She handed one plate over to Betty and the other to Alistair before setting the tray down and taking hers over to the sofa.

"Not bad. Just needs a few onions," Alistair said, chewing through a bite.

"Onions?" Nora asked.

"Oh, darling, you Americans eat so bland." Betty laughed.

After they finished lunch and had tea, Betty looked much better, the color returning to her cheeks.

"I think I'm ready to get back to my cabin and crime novel," she said, slowly getting to her feet.

"I'll walk you back and make sure you can get in," Alistair said, getting up and heading toward the door.

Betty gave Nora a warm smile as Alistair helped her into the over-sized jacket. "Thank you both for your kindness."

"Of course. Safe travels back to Wales, and I hope things work out between you and your granddaughter," Nora said as Alistair walked her to the door and out into the storm.

Nora stayed behind, her thoughts returning to the practical matters at hand. She began searching for candles and flashlights in case the power outage lasted through the night. A few decorative candles adorned the mantel above the fire, and she found a flashlight in the closet by the bathroom.

Her breath was visible as she walked up the stairs, the second floor feeling much colder without the furnace running. Rooting around her room, she found nothing useful for lighting but grabbed the photo album. She headed back downstairs and over to the living room, where the large windows offered a bit more light to read by before the evening fully descended.

Settling onto the sofa and opening the photo album, Nora began to thumb through its pages, examining the photos closely. Only a few of the snapshots were in color, and she quickly found the one on her mind. It was a vibrant image of her grandmother bundled in a large wool coat and blowing a kiss to the camera from her seat on an old stone wall, a tartan blanket beneath her. The same tartan print that adorned Nora's scarf. Her stomach flipped. Surely that couldn't be a coincidence.

Then something else caught her eye—the little red book resting next to her grandmother on the blanket. Nora's heart skipped a beat as she leaned in for a closer look, revealing a small dark spot on its cover. Hastily turning to the photo of her grandmother holding the book and the bottle of wine on the Royal Mile, Nora examined the book in her hands. Partially concealed by her ring finger was the unmistakable mark of a bullet hole. Her heart sank, and questions swirled in her mind. Why include the book that saved a Scottish soldier's life in these photos? Why would that soldier give up the miraculous book that had stopped a bullet and saved his life? Unless that very soldier was the one behind the camera taking the photos.

Flipping back to the other picture, Nora carefully peeled back the clear plastic to reveal a date on the backside: December 30, 1943, with a note underneath—*New Year's getaway trip to visit Marjorie.* The pieces of her grandmother's timeline in Scotland seemed to be falling into place, yet the mystery deepened since they didn't add up to what Nora had been told.

Her grandfather hadn't been stationed at Craigleith Military Hospital until January 1944, so this getaway had been with someone else, and she was pretty sure she knew who it was—Colin MacDonald. Just as she was about to flip to the next page and continue her search, Alistair came back in, windblown and covered in a layer of snow.

"Bloody hell, it's gotten colder," he said, kicking off his boots and putting his jacket on the pegboard by the door. "I got her back to her cottage, stoked the fire, and made sure she had matches to light the stove for some tea. I waited until she was settled in and then headed back."

"I'm so glad you suggested we go look for the downed power line. God knows what would have happened to her out there," Nora remarked.

"Me too," he said, walking over to the fireplace. He added more wood to the bed of thick coals. A plume of sparks hovered in the air just above the logs for a brief moment before petering out and floating down as ash.

"Looks like I need to bring more wood in if the power doesn't come back on. Without the oil furnace, this place is going to burn a ton of wood to keep it livable," he said, poking the logs and sending a puff of wood smoke out into the room. "What do ya have there?"

"My grandmother's photo album of her time here in Scotland when she was younger."

Alistair walked over and sat next to her on the sofa, catching her off guard. Betty's presence today seemed to have thawed him a bit more. Surprised by his interest, she tilted the album toward him slightly. He was so close she could smell the fresh air that still clung to his clothing, and she struggled to concentrate on the album in her lap.

"Oh look, it's the spot after the bridge on Old Military Road," Alistair said, pointing down at the picture of her grandmother blowing the kiss.

"What?"

"You must have passed it coming here. I can tell from the break in the stone wall and the mountains off in the distance. It's definitely the spot," Alistair observed.

Nora looked down; he was right. She remembered the spot; it had been where Stuart pointed out the river. How had she not noticed that before? She knew her grandmother must have visited Letterfearn because of the postcard in the album, but now she was curious how many of these pictures were actually taken here. She began flipping the pages, looking for any landmarks she might recognize, when Alistair stopped her.

"No way! Look," he said, pointing at a photo of a loch with rising mountains in the background. Far off to the right sat a small cottage near the water, the very cottage they were sitting in.

Chapter Twenty-Nine
FINDING THE TRUTH

Nora's eyes fixated on the photo. The area no longer looked as it had back in the forties, with a lush green hill sloping down to the cottage. The hill now housed four tiny cabins and a long wooden walkway. The recent development in the area had taken away from its original rustic Highlands charm. The cottage in the photo looked like it had been sitting snugly in that cove, untouched by time for centuries. Alistair had been right; the Airbnb culture had overrun such secluded pristine places like this.

"This is outside a pub in Kyle. I had a dram there before I got the last cab back here yesterday," Alistair said, looking at the photo that showed her grandmother resting against a post outside a building made of stone. A large body of water took up most of the background as the dark stormy sky reflected back into it. Her profile looked out toward the watery horizon, and there was a dark shadow across her face from a large-brimmed hat.

"She was beautiful," Alistair said, looking at it.

"She was," Nora said, flipping the page.

"What year were these taken?"

"Between the fall of nineteen forty-three and the spring of nineteen forty-four. My grandmother was stationed in Scotland during the war."

"Is that why you wanted to find a certain doctor stationed at Craigleith Military Hospital back then?" he asked.

She paused for a moment. His eyes were fixed on hers, and it took everything inside her not to stare back. Instead, she turned her attention back to the album and away from his gaze.

"Yes, I want to know if my grandfather was stationed at the military hospital during the time my grandmother was there. Some things in her timeline are not adding up," Nora said.

"Interesting. What does this have to do with the MacDonald tartan?"

"What do you mean?" Nora asked, closing the album and turning to look at him.

"You asked me to help you look for that doctor after you got all weird when I told you your scarf was the MacDonald tartan, not Cameron," he said, lifting his eyebrows in question.

Crap, she had forgotten that he was an investigative journalist. He was already starting to put the puzzle pieces together. She paused, mulling whether she wanted to share her theory with him. He was a stranger, after all, but that might not be a bad thing. He would have an outsider's perspective on things that Nora might have overlooked. After a drawn-out silence, she decided to let Alistair in on what she thought she had discovered.

"When you told me the scarf was the MacDonald tartan, it

forced me to look at something that had been right in front of my face for a long time. I believe my grandmother held on to a very big secret for many years," Nora explained. Just thinking about it raised her anxiety. She could feel her heart start to race again.

"What kind of secret?"

"I'm not a hundred percent certain, but I don't think she was telling the truth about who my grandfather was," Nora said, running her thumbs on the grooved edges of the album.

Alistair said nothing but pulled his phone out of his pocket and stood up, walking over to the windows overlooking the loch.

"Oh, I have enough service here to pull up a Google page."

Nora spun in her seat and watched him tap away at his phone.

"What was your grandfather's name?" he asked, looking up at her, his eyes reflecting the light of the phone in them.

"Dr. Donald Cameron."

He read silently for a long while, and Nora found herself holding her breath. He went back to tapping away, and Nora stood up and began pacing the room, her heart racing faster with each passing minute. She was trying to quell her anxiety but it was threatening to overtake her with a full-blown panic attack. What if it were true, and her dad had a completely different father than he thought? She was sure he didn't know, and the task of telling him would certainly fall on her. The idea of it made her sick. She wasn't sure she could do that to him along with telling them about the bakery.

Nora walked over to the window to gaze out into the murky darkness. The storm had intensified, and the sound of tiny ice pellets hitting the windows echoed back into the room. Turning away from the tempest and back to her own internal turmoil, she made her way into the kitchen to search for any wine left behind by previous renters, but she came up empty.

"Got something," Alistair finally said, walking over to one of the barstools. "I found this in an old archive from the hospital. Donald H. Cameron was stationed as a surgeon at the Craigleith Military Hospital on January 28, 1944. He was transferred to St. Thomas' Hospital on February 8, 1944. He was stationed there until he was relieved on June 18, 1944."

Nora stopped pacing, her face turning pale as she took in what Alistair was saying. Her grandfather had not been stationed at Craigleith Military Hospital with her grandmother. She had already left for London before he had even stepped foot in the facility.

"Can you see if his name is associated with the code breakers at Bletchley Park in Buckinghamshire?" Nora asked, her palms getting sweaty.

This time it only took but a minute for him to answer. "No, there was no record of him there according to the National Archives."

"Try the name Colin MacDonald," Nora said, beginning to pace again, knowing what came out of his mouth would solidify what she had been thinking this whole time.

"Yes, listen to this. 'Corporal Colin MacDonald played an intricate role in helping decode a series of messages in January 1944 that contained precise information about German defenses, troop movements, and probable allied invasion targets. This information was critical in confirming the Allies' fears about the impending invasion and shaping the strategy for Operation Overlord.'" He paused for a moment before going on.

"'The deciphered messages, along with other intelligence sources, influenced the decision to begin the invasion from Normandy's beaches on June 6, 1944. The success of D-Day consti-tuted a watershed moment in the war, paving the path for Western Europe's liberation from German rule.' Sounds like he was a badass," Alistair said, setting down his phone.

Nora's chest felt like it was being squeezed so tightly that she couldn't take a breath, and her head was beginning to throb. It was true. All the stories had been about Colin MacDonald.

"Are you okay?" he asked as she paced for the tenth time in the past three minutes. "Are you going to tell me what's going on?"

Nora stopped and looked at him. Maybe she needed to talk this out. Maybe Alistair could help her make sense of the jumbled mess in her head. She walked over and sat on the couch, and her foot began incessantly tapping the floor as her nervousness continued to grow. She took in a long, slow breath before she began.

"My grandmother told me bedtime stories from the pictures in this album all through my childhood. I loved them and the way she would light up when she told them to me. But now I think all those years ago, she was trying to give me clues to a secret she had held onto her whole life," she said, the realization dawning on her as she spoke.

"She had been telling me the true story the whole time, except it wasn't until just now that I finally figured it out. All the stories about my grandfather were actually about Colin MacDonald, not Donald Cameron. She knew who my dad's true father really was and kept it secret, leaving behind little breadcrumbs for me to follow all these years. That's why she had been so desperate for me to travel to Scotland. She must have figured that those breadcrumbs would eventually lead me to the truth," Nora said, tears filling her eyes as she realized she had been her grandmother's sole confidant.

"I can understand trying to keep the pregnancy a secret. Children out of wedlock during those times were looked down on, but why not leave the breadcrumbs for your dad to follow?"

"I don't know, but she must have had a reason," she said as the tears broke free to stream down her cheeks and onto her lap, speckling her jeans.

For a moment Alistair just stood still, and it seemed he was unsure of what to do or say. Then he got up, walked to his suitcase resting next to the door, and unzipped the front pocket, pulling out a bottle of whisky.

"I realize drinking won't solve your problems or wash them away, but I do think it helps cut the edge," he said, uncapping the bottle and taking a swig before handing it over to Nora. She cracked a smile as the tears continued to slide down her red cheeks as she grabbed the bottle and took a sip, feeling the whisky's warmth run down her throat and fill her belly. The sensation calmed her and dispelled the tightening in her chest that had threatened to consume her just moments before.

"That's heavy. Are you sure your father doesn't know?"

"I'm sure. He jokes all the time about how he got his ears from his dad, and just last month, he went in to have his carotid artery checked to make sure he didn't have any aneurysms forming. He's done that for years because his father had a genetic condition that had to be monitored his entire adult life. There is no way he knows."

Just saying those words made the tightness in her chest come rushing back. Her dad was turning seventy-three years old this year. Did she really want to break the news to him at that age? Reveal that the man he thought his whole life to be his father wasn't? She didn't know if she could do that to him.

"I honestly don't know what to think right now," Nora confessed as she picked up the photo album, opening it to the picture of her grandmother and Colin MacDonald. She studied it closely, looking at every tiny detail. She saw it then: the spark they both shared in their eyes, his fingers brushing up next to hers, the affectionate way they leaned into each other. She saw what had been hidden in plain sight all those times before—the essence of love enveloping them.

Chapter Thirty

AMBER SPIRITS

The day quickly slipped into evening as they talked, the whisky warming their bellies and loosening any semblance of tension they once had between them. The storm had faded into nothing more than a few light flurries that danced in the air outside the large windows that faced the loch as the sun dipped beyond the horizon.

"Did you grow up in Edinburgh?" Nora asked as she took another swig from the bottle before handing it back to Alistair.

"No, I grew up in Perth, but after my dad left, my mum moved us to a small town called Broxburn, about twelve miles outside the city."

"How old were you when he left?" Nora asked as she positioned herself cross-legged on the couch next to him.

"I was almost nine. He was a right bastard, left us with nothing, and never looked back. We moved to Broxburn, where mum's family was from after that, and lived with my grandparents for a few years until she got back on her feet."

"God, I'm sorry. That couldn't have been easy for either of you."

"I was young and only remember bits and pieces of him, but my mum never got over it. Love can be a curse, especially if it's only one-sided. That's why it's just me and my goldfish," he said, looking down at the bottle in his hand and taking another sip.

"I get that. I kinda stay clear of all that relationship stuff as well," Nora confessed to him.

"No bearded lumberjack back in Vermont then?" he asked.

"Ha! No, definitely not. It's just me."

Her words echoed back in her head, and they sounded lonelier than usual. They sat together on the couch, understanding each other in shared silence. Eventually, Alistair spoke up to ask if she skied. From that point on they got lost in the idle chit-chat that often followed serious conversations. Nearly an hour had passed before they noticed the temperature in the room had dropped and the light had dimmed due to the dying fire.

"I better put some more logs on," Alistair said, standing and making his way over to the old stone fireplace. "You ever think about how much a fireplace like this has seen? All the lives it has helped keep warm and safe from the cold throughout the years?" He gingerly ran his fingers over the old wide field stones that made up its face.

As Nora watched him stoke the fire, a wave of longing swept over her. She wasn't certain if it was that she hadn't been alone with a man for this long in years, the influence of the alcohol, or perhaps a combination of the two. Whatever it was, the distraction had her fully in its grip.

"Did you ever find any candles?" he asked, turning around to face her. He was cast in silhouette, the warm glow of the fire dancing around behind him. This did nothing for her wandering mind, and she had completely missed his question.

"Nora?" he said, breaking her out of her fanciful thoughts.

"Yeah?"

"Did you find any candles while I was walking Betty back?"

"Yes, a few," Nora replied, rising from her seat and crossing the room to the counter by the sink where she had placed four candles and a box of matches. She set the candles on the kitchen island and lit them one by one. The shadows and candlelight waltzed around the room, moving with one another in an ancient dance, bringing back an old charm to the renovated space.

"Are you hungry?" Alistair asked, walking over to her in the kitchen.

"I could eat."

"Do you know what's in the fridge?" he asked before opening it.

"I think I just got the basics: milk, bread, cheese, a few veggies, that kinda stuff."

"Well, let me see what I can whip up."

"Anything is fine with me, as long as it soaks up a bit of this whisky," she joked, but in all seriousness, she did need to sober up. She felt quite tipsy, and the alcohol had kicked her hormones into overdrive. She was worried she might do or say something she would later regret.

Alistair picked up a candle and quickly opened the fridge.

"The power's been out for almost ten hours now, so we better eat some of this before it goes bad," he said as he pulled out a few things, shutting the door with a swift motion. He set a large piece of wrapped salmon on the counter, along with a tub of cream cheese and a small cucumber. Spinning around, he grabbed the bread off the counter behind him, along with a kitchen knife.

He unwrapped the fish, lit the stove, and buttered the bread, crisping it up in the pan that Nora had used for the grilled cheeses earlier. The smell of burning butter and yeast from the bread filled the air, causing Nora's stomach to groan.

After toasting the bread, he assembled a sandwich generously layered with cream cheese, smoked salmon, and crisp cucumber slices—a culinary combination Nora had never encountered. She eyed it skeptically as he handed it to her.

"Aren't you supposed to cook the fish first?" she asked.

"What? Don't tell me you've never indulged in a smoked salmon and cucumber sandwich before?"

"Can't say that I have. Not a huge fan of fish."

"Okay, well, hold that thought because I am about to change your mind."

"To be honest, I don't recall adding salmon to my list for the food delivery."

"That's because you didn't. I bought it. I thought maybe cooking dinner would convince you to let me stay that first night, but you already had the pizza thawing, so I went with that instead."

"Probably a good thing because fish would not have won me over," she laughed.

"I usually make it with dilly cream cheese, but this should be fine," he told her, taking a large satisfying bite.

Nora eyed the sandwich, contemplating her level of hunger. A little voice inside her head nagged her to try something new. Getting outside of her comfort zone to help find her way was the whole idea behind the trip, after all. At that moment, her stomach emitted another audible growl that even Alistair couldn't ignore.

"You better listen to your stomach. It knows best," he joked, taking another bite.

Nora brought the sandwich up to her nose, taking in the medley of scents—the rich, smoky woodiness mixed with the briny scent of the fish and the enticing creaminess of the cheese. To her surprise, the first bite, cautious and small, was delicious, so she took a larger bite.

"See, I told ya," Alistair remarked, raising his eyebrows.

They lingered in the candlelight, savoring their meal. Eventually, they cleaned up and returned to the living room, where a partially emptied whisky bottle awaited. While Alistair set two candles from the kitchen on the coffee table, Nora walked over to the bookcase.

"I read some of that book on Scottish folklore last night. There are some really interesting tales in there. What do you make of all the magical creatures and gods and goddesses of old? Do you think they really existed?" she asked, running her fingers across the old books that lined the shelves.

"That's a hard question to answer. The journalist side of my brain thinks if you searched deep enough, most of those stories stem from some sort of truth. The stories were told so many times that they became twisted and spun into magical tales over the years. Then there is a part of me that believes that deep in the Scottish mountains there is ancient magic still alive. My rational mind always fights the part of me that wants to believe in magic and most of the time wins," he said, taking another sip of whisky.

"I know what you mean," Nora said under her breath, tucking a book back that she had pulled out. She turned around to face Alistair, curious to see his expression as she asked, "What about fate and coincidences? Do you believe in those things?"

Alistair paused, his gaze drifting toward the flickering candlelight. "I'm not entirely sold on fate," he began slowly, his words mingling with the aroma of whisky in the air. "It feels like we carve our own paths in life, but then again, sometimes life throws unexpected curveballs that make you question everything." He paused, taking another sip of whisky, the amber liquid glinting in the dim light.

"My mum used to work as a cleaning lady at The Crossroads Inn in Broxburn when I was a teenager. I was at a bit of a cross-roads myself after finishing uni, not really sure what I wanted to do." A faint sparkle danced in his eyes as he recalled the memory.

"One day, the woman who cleaned with my mum called in sick, and I had to step in and help her because there was a big business conference happening that evening in town. I had just finished tidying the last room on the second floor when I bumped into a man coming out of the stairwell," he said, the memory painting his features with a sense of nostalgia.

"Turns out, it was the owner of *Tartan and Thistle*. We struck up a conversation, and six months later, I was working there. If it hadn't been for that woman calling in sick that day, who knows where I'd be now? I guess one might call that fate or maybe it was just perfect timing."

"I would say that was fate." Nora smiled. "And what about unexplainable coincidences?"

Alistair's eyes met hers, a hint of skepticism in his expression.

"Sure, strange things happen. Maybe the universe has a quirky sense of humor. But are they played like a hand of cards by something bigger than us, like a god? I'm not entirely sold on that," he said as the shadow from the candlelight moved on the wall behind him, like the shadows of the very gods he questioned.

Lost in thought, Nora felt the butterflies return to her stomach as she watched him. She wished she could have blamed the

feeling on too much alcohol, but there was no more denying it—
she was falling for the very man she could barely tolerate only a
few days ago. She was falling for Alistair Grant.

Chapter Thirty-One

A SPARK OF PANIC

The shadows danced around them to the sounds of the crackling logs, making the ancient discussions of fate and coincidence feel like a timeless exchange between two souls.

As Nora pondered Alistair's words, she turned back around, letting her fingers glide over the spines of the books once again. One particular book caught her eye, and she pulled it from the shelf: *The Unfortunate Traveller* by Thomas Nashe. The title sparked a memory; where had she heard it before? Then recognition hit her like a wave—the little red book. It was the same book that Cora had told the duchess about during their dinner at the castle.

She pulled the book from the shelf, turning it in her hands. The serendipity of finding this particular book at this moment wasn't lost on her. As she contemplated fate and its mysteries, the book seemed like a sign, a subtle nod from the universe.

Nora carefully thumbed through its pages, releasing the scent of aged paper and dust into the air. Closing the book, she returned it to its place on the shelf, her mind racing with all the bizarre things that had happened to her in just a few days since she stepped foot in Scotland.

"You know, I do think it's strange that they have all these old rare books here. I wonder what the story is behind them?" Nora mused, turning around to find Alistair looking at her in a way she had not expected. A hint of longing showed in his eyes, for a fleeting moment before he looked away.

"I'm curious too. Why don't we do a bit of digging?" he suggested, pulling his phone back out of his pocket. "Okay, we better do this quick; I only have ten percent of my battery left."

He searched for the cabin rentals on Airbnb and then delved into researching the history of the rental company that owned them. A halo of blue light from his phone lit his face in the dim room, casting him in an ethereal light while he scrolled.

"It's a small family-run business. Husband and wife, it looks. They have bought three parcels of land in the past four years and built tiny holiday cottages on them. One in Inverness, one in Carnach, and this one here in Letterfearn," he said, reading from his phone. He scrolled for a few more minutes until he came upon something interesting.

"Listen to this. The property was purchased through an estate sale. The woman who owned it had no surviving relatives and the estate passed to the Crown under the principle of 'bona vacantia,'" he told her, propping himself up more to read on. "It was built in 1589 and because of its age, it was considered a historical building, and they were only allowed to do minimal renovations to it."

"My God, these books must be the old owner's personal library. I bet she is rolling over in her grave knowing they are in a rental," Nora said.

"These people have no idea what they have. I bet there's twenty thousand pounds worth of antique books here," he said, looking up at the shelves of books.

"Does it say who the original owner was?" Nora inquired.

"I'm sure I can dig it up," Alistair said, tapping away at his phone again. Nora could tell he was in his element when he was in research mode; he had an air of confidence that filled the room. It was no wonder he was a journalist.

"Now, that's weird," he said, his eyes darting back and forth as he read whatever it was on his phone that had sparked his attention.

"What?" Nora asked, her curiosity piqued.

"The woman who owned it was M. MacDonald, it says. No first name that I can find yet. Crap, my battery is almost dead," he said, his eyes moving faster as he read.

Nora's heart plummeted into her stomach at the mention of the name. The chances of finding the rare old book mentioned in the little red book was one thing, but now finding out the cottage was once owned by a MacDonald had Nora's head spinning. What were the chances that this MacDonald was part of the same family as Colin? It was a common name in these parts, but the fact that her grandmother had a picture of the cottage in her album made her think that if they dug a little more, they would probably find out that it was. What was the universe trying to tell her? She had already discovered the secret about her grandfather; what else was there? If there was something more, she wasn't sure she wanted to know. The discovery about her grandfather and the impending task of telling her father the truth was already overwhelming. What if there were an even bigger secret lurking beneath the surface?

She was here to build up the courage to tell her parents she didn't want to take over the bakery, not dig up more heartbreak. Her heart quickened its pace, and her palms grew clammy with the rising tide of anxiety.

"I found an old article about the house from 1964. The oldest house recorded on Loch Duich has been in the MacDonald family for—" He stopped reading abruptly. "Bloody hell, phone died. I forgot how much losing power sucks," he said tipsily as he set his phone down on the coffee table with a thud.

Nora sat stunned into silence for a long while, staring at the flickering flames in the fireplace. She grabbed the whisky and took a rather large swig, sending her into a fit of coughing.

"You all right?" Alistair asked, but it wasn't the coughing that prompted the question. It was the fact that she had gone silent for so long that had him guessing.

She was trying her best to quell what felt like a rising panic attack, as if her body were so full of energy that it didn't know what to do. The weather seemed to rise up to meet her panic. The wind picked up and the branches of the tree next to the deck began thrashing against the cottage walls. The snow was now coming down so heavily that it nearly blocked out the setting sun.

Attempting to anchor herself, she focused on the burn of whisky making its way down to her belly, but this time it wasn't helping subdue the feeling. Nora closed her eyes, attempting a grounding technique a therapist had taught her years ago: trace your thumb over each fingertip, counting forward and then backward. However, instead of finding solace in the repetitive task, the energy within her surged even more, tightening its grip. The sensation escalated, her lungs constricting, and she couldn't shake the notion that without her rib cage holding it back, her heart might have pounded its way out of her chest.

"Nora," Alistair said, taking her hands in his. "Breathe. It's just a panic attack."

She looked up at him. How did he know what was going on?

"I think I'm going to pass out," she said through short, shallow breaths.

"No, you're not. Just keep your eyes on me."

Her breathing turned into short, quick bursts, and the sounds in the room began to ebb and flow. Panic etched across her face, her eyes widening with fear.

Alistair's eyes reflected back her own panic. He was trying his best to calm her, but as the situation escalated, she could tell he didn't know what to do.

Just when she thought her heart might implode from the panic, he swiftly leaned forward and kissed her. As their lips met, the energy building within her broke free, escaping into their kiss.

The kiss deepened, tongues intertwining in a dance, mirroring the intensity of the energy within her. Panic no longer coursed through her body. It had been replaced with primal desire. She leaned into him, feeling a sense of control over this newfound force. His hands moved up to cup her face as the kiss intensified. He ran his fingers through her hair, down her back, pulling her closer. In response, her kisses grew hungry, and a different kind of energy began to build within her—a spark of longing, a sensation she hadn't experienced in a long time.

Chapter Thirty-Two
BLASTED BOARD

Nora fell deeper into their kiss as the heat of their passion filled the room. She ran her fingers through his thick wavy hair, pulling him in closer. Her lips burned with each sweep of his, and she could taste the slight hint of whisky still clinging to them. A feeling deep within her began to rise to the surface, surging through her like a storm about to break land. With a swift motion, she swung her right leg over his lap, now straddling him. Alistair, responding in kind, grasped her hips and drew her closer, and the heat between them grew. As she gazed into his deep emerald eyes illuminated by the flickering candlelight, the flames mirrored the passion that consumed them both.

The tension within her continued to build as she slid her hands up under his shirt and ran them across his muscular build, intensifying the passion between them. Alistair, breathless, broke away from their kiss and asked, "Are you okay now?"

Nora looked at him, the desire evident in his eyes, eager to rekindle the fire he had momentarily interrupted. "I'm fine— scratch that, I'm great," she said, diving back into his lips.

He responded to her kiss but pulled away once more, concern etched on his face. "We've had a lot to drink tonight. Are you sure you want to do this?" he asked, looking deep into her eyes.

"Yes, yes to everything," she affirmed, meeting his gaze with unwavering desire. "But let's move it somewhere a little more comfortable," Nora proposed, standing up and making her way to the bottom of the stairs. Alistair followed suit, quickly ascending, and pulled her into another passionate kiss at the bedroom doorway. Though the room was cold, the heat they generated shielded them from the chill. As they stumbled into the dark room, entwined in kisses and discarded clothing, Alistair's toe caught on a loose floorboard.

"Aw, fuck!" he yelled out in pain, dropping to his knees and almost taking Nora down with him.

"Are you okay?" Nora gasped as she stumbled toward the nightstand, searching for the flashlight she had left there earlier. Flicking it on, she pointed the beam down at the floor, revealing Alistair seated cross-legged, holding his foot, which had a sizable gash across the big toe.

"Oh, my God, that's a lot of blood," she exclaimed, the effects of the alcohol making her head spin. It took all her strength to steady herself.

"I think I saw a first-aid kit in the closet downstairs. Just a second," she said, rushing down and leaving him alone in the dark room with his injured foot. She returned a minute later with a small box and opened it, pulling out alcohol pads and a few large Band-Aids.

"Thank God for the whisky in me," he said, holding his foot up and tilting his head toward the ceiling in pain.

"Okay, I need to clean it up, then I can bandage it. You ready?" Nora said, pulling out one of the alcohol pads and some gauze to soak up the extra blood. He nodded.

"Hold this," she instructed, handing the flashlight to him.

He shined the light down, revealing a gash that ran clear across the tip of his toe.

"Shit, that burns," Alistair muttered as she wiped away the blood that was still freely flowing.

"Oh, God, do you think it needs stitches?" Nora asked as the cut continued to bleed.

"No, it'll be okay. Let me see that gauze. It should slow the bleeding if I hold it there for a minute," he reassured her, taking hold of the gauze and wrapping it around his toe.

Her head was starting to ache, and the whiskey, combined with the smell of blood, had turned her stomach. After a few minutes, Alistair pulled the gauze away, and Nora wrapped two bandages around his toe.

"Well, this was not the way I saw this night going," he joked as he stood up, swaying. He tried to get his balance, which was tricky standing on his heel, along with being a little drunk. *Maybe he shouldn't go down the stairs*, Nora thought as she watched him try to right himself with little success. That would mean either sharing a bed with him tonight or her sleeping on the sofa. At this point, they would not likely be rekindling anything.

"Why don't I sleep downstairs tonight? You take the bed. You shouldn't walk down on that foot," Nora suggested.

"Absolutely not. I am not taking your bed. I'm fine. See?" he said, limping over to the door.

"Fine, but I am helping you down the stairs." She knew better than to try to argue with him, so she walked over and slipped her body under his arm as a makeshift crutch.

It was slow going and by the time they had made it down to the sofa, Alistair was in quite a lot of pain.

"Are you sure you're okay?" Nora asked, seeing the pain reflected in his eyes. "Is there anything I can get you?"

"No, I just need to try and sleep this off," he said, lying down and pulling the blanket off the back of the couch to cover himself. He closed his eyes, wincing a little as he propped his foot up onto a pillow.

"Well, if you need anything, just give me a yell," Nora offered, walking back toward the stairs. She turned around and said goodnight, but he said nothing back, and a wave of unease fell over her.

When she got back to her room, the events of the night played through her mind as she slipped into bed. The evening had started off so well and had ended so badly. The fact that he hadn't even said goodnight to her left her feeling awkward. She tried not to overthink the situation; her mind was foggy with alcohol, and she knew that nothing good came of perseverating. But she couldn't stop her mind from going to dark places. Was he sobering up and regretting what they had started?

The suffocating uncertainty of self-doubt was weighing heavily on her chest when Sam broke into her thoughts. Why was it that every time she got close to someone, the universe seemed to find a way of stopping things in their tracks? No, that wasn't quite fair to blame the universe when she had been the one who had messed things up with Sam. Their first year of dating had been wonderful, but everything went downhill after he asked her to marry him. His proposal had caught her completely off guard, and she had said yes even though she knew she wasn't ready for marriage. She should have just told him, but instead, she had dragged things out, coming up with a million reasons why she couldn't set a date. After a full year of her excuses, Sam began pulling away, growing more distant by the day, and their relationship grew strained. Determined to salvage their relationship, Nora decided to surprise him one weekend, armed with a box of his favorite pastries, a bottle of wine, and the news that she had finally picked a date.

He wasn't home, so she waited, excitement coursing through her as she rehearsed for the hundredth time the lines she wanted to say. As the hours passed, however, her excitement turned to apprehension when he never returned. She had fallen asleep on his couch only to awaken to the sound of the door opening the next morning. He stumbled in, looking disheveled and reeking of liquor and cheap perfume. Caught off guard by her presence in his living room, he hastily ran his hands through his hair and attempted to straighten his appearance. But it was futile; Nora could see right through his facade, noticing the cream-colored foundation on his shirt and the missing button on his pants. He stood speechless as she stared back at him, the truth hanging heavy in the air.

Nora rose to her feet, clutching the box of pastries tightly, and silently exited the apartment. It marked the final chapter of their relationship and the last time she would see him. He attempted to reach out once afterward, leaving a lengthy voicemail about how he should have ended things sooner and that his proposal had been a spontaneous mistake. He said that she needed to find herself before committing to marriage, and he needed a partner with a clear vision for the future—something Nora couldn't provide. His words stung, for they held a painful truth. She had vowed not to enter another relationship until she had a clear understanding of her own aspirations in life and so far, they still eluded her.

She blamed herself for his cheating, but when it came right down to it, she knew better. She had dragged her feet because deep down she knew what kind of man he really was; she just didn't want to see it. If she were honest with herself, she had known he wasn't *The One* when they first met. From the moment their relationship had started, it was bound to end in heartache.

As she sat drunk and wallowing in the past, something to her left caught her attention, startling her into almost falling out of bed. Coming from the stack of books on the nightstand was a ghostly blue glow.

Chapter Thirty-Three
PORRIDGE AND HONEY

The faint blue glow emanated from the pages of the little red book. Nora rubbed at her eyes and then pointed the flashlight at it. Nothing unusual. No blue glow. Just a book. The whiskey and her mind were playing tricks on her. Once she had looked at it, however, she couldn't resist its pull, and she picked it up, figuring it would be a good distraction from her depressing train of thought. Using the flashlight, Nora turned to the page where she had left off and started to read.

As I lay there on the cold, unforgiving floor, my mind raced with why James seemed to despise me. As hard as I tried, I could not come up with even the slightest reason. We did not know one another, and my gran had been nothing but kind and helpful to his family. Nevertheless, he lay there with his back to me, his mood chilling the room more than it already was. I willed my mind to slow for I needed all my strength and energy for the ride ahead tomorrow. I finally drifted off to sleep, my mind still churning with worry as I entered the realm of dreams.

The snow fell, veiling the landscape in a thick white haze as we journeyed on horseback up a steep ridgeline toward a hilltop overlooking the valley and a frozen loch below. A perfect circle marred the ice's surface, and within it a horse struggled desperately against the icy grip of the lake's frigid waters. Within a moment I was off the hillside and on the lake with the drowning horse.

Lying on the ice, I stretched my body out to grasp the reins, but my efforts were futile. I watched helplessly, tears streaming down my cheeks, freezing in the bitter air, as the horse succumbed to its watery fate, disappearing into the dark abyss below. As it sank out of sight into the frigid waters, an eerie sound pierced the silent valley—a haunting echo warning of impending danger.

A child, seemingly unaffected by the treacherous conditions, walked across the frozen lake toward the gaping hole left by the horse. Fear gripped me as the child drew nearer, my heart racing. I closed my eyes, seeking solace in the darkness, only to feel a chilling hand seize my shoulder. With a startled cry, I jolted awake, the echo of my own voice mingling with Addie's urgent calls from a distance.

"Cora, dear. It's just a dream," she said in a gentle tone as she helped me to my feet. Once I was upright, she patted my shoulder, then headed back toward the kitchen, leaving me standing in the middle of the room. I rubbed the sleep from my eyes and looked around, finding James sitting on a chair near the fire, acting as if he didn't even notice my presence.

"James, James, come sit next to me. Mama made my favorite this morning," little Alice exclaimed as she ran into the room and tugged on James's hand, urging him to join her in the small kitchen. He glanced at me before getting up and following her into the other room. I trailed behind him, trying to keep my distance.

An uneasy feeling clung to me as the drowsy remnants of the dream lingered along with the daunting task that lay ahead of us. I feared that our inability to get along would slow the process of getting the items needed for Gran's potion, and we were already short on time after yesterday's slow carriage ride.

The aroma of warm porridge and eggs filled the kitchen as I stepped in and took my seat at the worn wooden table.

"Mama is preparing porridge with cream and honey for us," Alice announced with a tiny squeal of delight. James smiled down at her, rubbing his tummy as if eagerly anticipating the meal. Alice giggled and fidgeted while waiting for her breakfast. Witnessing their sweet interaction, I found my heart softening toward him. He was gentle and sweet with her, and it seemed that he had the makings of being a good father someday. Such musings, however, were not fitting for someone of my station to linger on.

"Do you need any help, Addie?" I inquired, hoping she might give me a task to keep my mind busy.

"Could you please slice the bread there?" she asked, pointing to a fresh crusty loaf on a small table in the corner of the kitchen. As I began to slice the bread, Malcolm entered, tracking in a heap of snow from his boots.

"Aye, the storm has not decided to leave us yet. I'm afraid you won't be going anywhere in that carriage," Malcolm remarked, shaking off the snow from his hat.

I glanced at James, my concern evident. "We must go," I insisted.

"If you go, it will have to be on horseback, and even that will be quite dangerous in these conditions," Malcolm explained.

James exchanged glances with me before turning back to Malcolm.

"It's urgent that we continue on. Can you lend the footman a horse to take Ms. Douglas back to the castle? I will go from here on horseback the rest of the way.

"Of course, but I must tell you that riding in a storm such as this is very dangerous, James," Malcolm warned.

"I am not going back to the castle. I will ride with you. Besides, I know my way around a horse," I insisted. If he had his way I would be back in the castle before noon, and I couldn't let that happen.

"If you can't keep up, then I will leave you behind," James snapped.

"James," Malcolm admonished, clearly surprised at his tone toward me.

"If my father hadn't insisted I take her, I could have been on my way back by now. Girls are not strong nor brave enough to take journeys such as this," James spat.

"But I'm a girl, and you tell me all the time that I am braver than all the knights at the castle," little Alice said, breaking into the conversation.

James looked down at her, his hard face softening. He put his arm around her and pulled her into him, then kissed her head. "You are that brave, but most girls aren't. That's what makes you so special," he whispered gently in her ear.

"If Cora is not brave, shouldn't you be brave for her?" she whispered back. His face grew somber, and he looked at me, sorrow in his eyes, as if the innocent words of a little girl had made him think about his behavior.

"If you go, then you must stick to the roads. In weather like this, no going off on trails to cut time," Malcolm said.

"I understand. We will take heed of your words and travel carefully."

Malcolm took his seat at the table as Addie brought over a steaming pot, serving generous portions of porridge into each bowl. Cream and honey were set in the center of the table, and little Alice eagerly reached for the honey, but Addie intervened, playfully scolding her.

"I don't think so, lassie. You would have more honey than porridge if we let you put that on yourself," Addie teased.

I smiled at their interaction, feeling a warmth spread through me. I looked forward to the possibility of sharing that kind of loving banter with my own children someday.

"I see she inherited your love for all things sweet," James joked, looking at Malcolm and taking a mouthful of porridge.

"Aye," he said, adding a bit more honey to his bowl.

James took the honey from Malcolm, added some to his own porridge, then handed it to me with a slight nod and what looked like the beginning of a smile. It was the most kindness he had offered me since we met.

"Thank you, my lord," I said, smiling while adding honey to my bowl.

After breakfast, James and I gathered our belongings and bundled ourselves up for the cold. We expressed our gratitude to Malcolm and Addie, and James gave Alice a warm hug, lifting her up into the air, and she showered him with delighted giggles. She beamed until he gently set her down and kissed the top of her head.

"Take these," Malcolm said, handing us two thick wool blankets and a pair of riding gloves for me. "Just in case the weather holds."

James nodded his thanks, and we stepped out into the frigid air, snow swirling around us in thick flurries. James headed to the barn and returned a few minutes later with two tall black stallions, saddled up and ready to ride.

"Do you really know how to ride?" James questioned me.

"Yes, I'm well-versed," I replied, sticking my foot into the stirrup and swinging myself onto the horse's back. A look of surprise crossed his face as he mounted his own horse. Sitting upright, I waited for him to ride up next to me, the snow falling even heavier now. My anxiety built as I looked at the road ahead, thick with snow. If the storm didn't let up soon, we might not make it back in time for the potion to work, and Gran's fate would be sealed.

James drove his heels into the sides of the horse, sending it forward into the dense snowy haze, and I followed. Together we rode off, our tracks quickly disappearing into the storm's embrace as we ventured toward Letterfearn, on a journey that would change us both forever.

Chapter Thirty-Four

THE UNFORTUNATE
TRAVELER

The ride was slow and arduous as we battled against the biting wind and swirling snow on our journey toward Letterfearn. I feared the extreme weather would prevent us from returning within three days' time. Even with the riding gloves Malcolm provided, the bitter cold numbed my fingers within the first hour. I was tempted to stop and don Gran's mittens, but time was of the essence. I did my best to warm my frozen fingers one at a time as we rode, tucking them under my arms during brief pauses in our steady progress, though these moments were few and far between amidst the thick blanket of snow covering the trail.

Although the tension between us had eased somewhat in the presence of little Alice, James's cold demeanor returned as we rode away from the Turners' home. I couldn't bear the thought of enduring the long journey ahead in silence. The wind died down as I rode up beside him and said, "My lord, I want to thank you," hoping that showing my gratitude might help soften him.

"You should be thanking my father, not me," he bit back.

I was determined not to let his harsh words get under my skin. If we were going to save Gran, we would have to work together, which we couldn't do if he was determined to fight me the entire way. Bickering would only slow the journey. I needed to be the bigger person and help ease the tension.

"Yes, but you are out here braving this storm with me, not your father."

This caught his attention, and he looked at me for the first time, his eyes full of curiosity.

"Despite the cold, it's quite beautiful," I continued, hoping I had cracked his armor.

He said nothing, but I saw a change in his face as if the hard mask he had been wearing was dropping, and the gentle face I had seen in him with Alice was peeking out.

"Are you attending university, my lord?" I inquired, hoping to find a conversation he might engage in. He hesitated, seemingly unsure if he wanted to converse with me.

Eventually, he spoke, his tone still carrying a hint of smugness with it. "Yes, I attend the University of Edinburgh."

"I am from Edinburgh myself. My father was a professor of literature at the university," I revealed, prompting a glint of interest in his eyes.

"Oh really, what was his name?" he asked skeptically, his voice rising against the wind.

"William Douglas. Did you know him?" I questioned, suddenly aware that this might be just the thing to lighten him up. A flicker of hope sparked, and as if the weather had decided to help me, the wind slowed, and the snow fell more softly.

"I did. He taught me in my first year. I'm sorry to hear of his passing," he replied, his tone softening slightly. He paused, as if unsure to continue.

"He was one of my favorite professors. Unfortunately, I was compelled to switch to more diplomatic studies the next year and didn't have the privilege of taking his classes again before he passed. He was a wonderful teacher."

"Thank you. That he was. He taught me many things, one being a great appreciation for books and the craft of writing. I'm actually an avid reader, but my mother made me promise not to indulge in any reading during this trip," I shared, remembering what his mother had said about him always having his nose in a book. Maybe this would be where we found common ground.

"And why is that?" he inquired, genuinely curious.

Just then, the thick layer of clouds began to break apart, and small patches of blue sky peeked through. The snow had slowed to nothing more than light flurries, and the horses picked up their pace as we moved closer toward Letterfearn.

"Well, I am here on official family business. All my attention was to be put toward finding a proper suitor at the ball," I explained.

"Of course," he spat, his tone sharp and full of anger once again. His face hardened into a deep scowl. Confused, I looked at him.

"Of course, what?" I asked.

"Just as I suspected, this is another of my father's ploys to get me to find a wife and settle down," he said, his face turning into a deep scowl.

"Is that why you have been so cold toward me, because you thought this was some love match your father had set up? Did you not see my gran? She is gravely ill and in need of a tincture. That is our mission, and no plot has been concocted for us to be wed. My mother has been trying to marry me off since my father died, and believe me, I have not been the most willing of daughters to fulfill that obligation. I have absolutely no desire to be anyone's wife, let alone yours," I snapped back. This was no time for pretenses or misunderstandings; we needed to be on the same page, get the items for the spell, and be back to the castle within the next two days.

We rode on in silence as he digested my words. The sky darkened once again, and with the absence of the sudden bursts of sun, the world around us grew colder.

"I'm sorry for my rude behavior. I had thought you to be just another woman my father had sent for me to court. He has been desperately trying to find me a bride. The ball was more about that than celebrating the season. I thought this was just another way for him to force my hand: make me escort a beautiful woman for three days and hope I fall in love with her."

My face grew hot at the mention of him thinking me beautiful, but I said nothing, thankful the cold weather had already turned my cheeks the hue of ripe apples.

"What he doesn't understand is that I want to be free and travel, like he did before he met Mother. I still have a few good years before I gain the title of Duke and need to take a wife, and I want to spend those years exploring the world. I can marry later," he continued.

"You and I seemingly have more in common than I thought, but I'm not of noble birth. Why would you think your father would try to set you up with me?" I asked.

"My father thinks very highly of your gran, so I just thought he approved of you despite your social standing."

"That would be highly unlikely."

An uncomfortable silence fell between us as we crested the ridgeline that overlooked the moors below. The snow had begun falling again, and my back and legs were sore and weary from the ride.

Unfamiliar with the area, I asked, "How much farther?" as he slowed his horse.

"There is much more to the journey; we won't arrive until after night-fall," he said, looking toward the sun's position in the sky. "Once we descend the ridge, we can stop for a rest and something to eat."

We rode in silence the rest of the ride down the steep ridge, paying close attention to our horses' hooves and steering them away from the edge as we descended. Once we made it to the bottom, James dismounted and tied his horse to a small fir tree next to a cluster of rocks. The ground was only lightly covered with a scant dusting of snow.

"I think there is enough wood for a small fire," James said as he gathered small sticks from the ground. I dismounted and began helping, happy to be on my own two feet again.

After a few minutes we had gathered enough wood, and he set to lighting the fire. James struck his flint and steel several times, but the wind was relentless and nothing caught. Watching his fruitless attempts, I silently pleaded for the wind to cease just long enough for the twigs to ignite. As if the wind heard my call, it died down, and the fire crackled to life.

James opened his pack and pulled out a loaf of bread and a cheese wrapped in cloth. My stomach moaned out in hunger as it had been hours since we left Malcolm's, and with the cold and the riding, I had built up an appetite. He handed me a large chunk of bread and then went about cutting hunks out of the cheese with a small knife.

As we sat quietly eating, my mind wandered to Gran, and I ached inside to know if her condition had worsened or if she was even still alive. The thought turned my stomach, and I stopped eating. I stared mindlessly into the flickering flames as my thoughts wandered to places I wished they would not go.

"You say you are an avid reader. What is your favorite book?" James asked, breaking my trance.

Pulling myself back to the present, I looked at him and said, "I much enjoyed the play *Doctor Faustus* by Christopher Marlowe, but I believe my favorite book is *The Unfortunate Traveller* by Thomas Nashe."

"Aye, Nashe. Jack Wilton is one of the best rogue protagonists of all time."

"You know it, my lord?" I asked, surprised.

"Of course. His humor is like no other! Nashe's jests are timeless. His sharp mockery—it's like he's jesting at the very fabric of society."

"'Tis the kind of storytelling that leaves an impression. A journey filled with misfortune and yet, strangely captivating. I love how he takes risks with his storytelling. I hope to be able to write as well as him someday," I confessed. I did not know why I was opening up to him and telling him thoughts I had not told anyone.

"You wish to be a writer?" James asked, intrigue filling his words.

"I do, my lord, but women are not permitted to be authors. Plus, my mother would never allow it. My father, however, always encouraged me to write, so I continue to do so, even if only for myself."

"I find that honorable. One should always follow their passion. Damn what society has to say. Why should a woman not be allowed to write? What about Margaret Cavendish, Duchess of Newcastle? She has been printed."

"True, and her poetry is beautiful, but she is a duchess, and I am but a woman of modest means and not of noble birth."

"What about writing under a male pseudonym and hiring a man to send it to a printer?" he suggested, a mischievous smile playing across his face that I had not seen until now.

"That's an idea," I laughed.

"A good one. And if that doesn't work, maybe you should start your own printing house. Then you could print whomever you choose, men and women alike."

I smiled. Now that he knew I was not vying for his hand in marriage, his demeanor had completely changed. He was kind and charming, and I could now see the reason the Turners loved him so much.

"Thank you for taking this journey to help my grandmother, my lord," I expressed, pulling my cape tightly closed, trying to keep my heat in. With the lack of sun and the storm brewing again, the air had quickly grown colder.

"Please call me James. There is no need for formalities here. And I should be thanking you for the escape. If I weren't on this journey, I'm sure my father would have been selecting one of the women from the ball for me to promenade around the grounds," he replied.

"Likewise, please call me Cora," I told him before asking the question lingering in my mind. "James, what is it that you aspire to do?" I inquired, feeling a bit odd addressing him by his first name and not Lord Campbell.

"I am being groomed to take over my father's position. Being his only son, the duty falls upon me," he stated in a stark and matter-of-fact tone.

"Yes, but what is it that you dream of doing?" I pressed.

He looked at me, and for the first time, our eyes truly met. Time seemed to stand still, the bitter cold and darkening sky faded, and the green hue of his eyes and the spark within them were all I could see.

He paused a moment before he answered. "I would like to be an academic. I enjoy reading of times past and writing about them."

"I think that suits you, and I do believe my father would approve," I said with a smile.

James smiled and nodded, and we locked eyes for a long moment before he turned away and began packing his bag.

"We best be going on our way. Not much more daylight left, and we still have far to travel," James said as he looked out to the west where the sun had begun to set.

We mounted the horses as the snow fell softly, my belly full, my body warmed, and my mind filled with James's words as we rode toward the setting sun.

Chapter Thirty-Five

THE EYES OF GOD
ARE WATCHING

Twilight blanketed the land in its thin dusty veil as we rode up the winding path toward the well in Letterfearn. The horses' hooves crunched the frozen leaves that had long ago fallen, kicking up the musty scent of the forest floor. The snow was scant, but the ground was frozen and small patches of ice marked the trail like a dotted line for us to follow. The path meandered alongside a half-frozen brook and up a sloping hillside where the sun was making its final descent, painting the edges of the mountains in a thin layer of gold.

"It's just up ahead. I can see St. Mary's Chapel," James said as they crested the top of the hill.

A humble stone chapel stood silhouetted in the fading light. As we rode closer, I could just make out the impression in the earth where the well sat. With dusk upon us, gathering the water clearly would need to be delayed until morning when the light was more favorable. The spell instructed precisely how it had to be collected, with not a single drop to be spilled. In the dim twilight, the task would prove nearly impossible.

"Not a moment too soon. The sun is almost set," James said, jumping down and tying his horse to a post in front of the chapel. I followed with my bag slung over my shoulder, then fastened my horse to the post alongside her mate.

"The well must be over there," I said, pointing to the spot near the front of the church where the earth caved in on itself. It was too dark to make out much more than a divot in the ground where it sat.

"Yes, shall we collect the water now?" he asked, stepping forward.

"No, let us gather it in the morning. I am too weary from our travels and need to rest," I said, not wishing to disclose the true reason for postponing the task. Nonetheless, fatigue indeed weighed heavily upon me after our journey.

"If we are lucky, the chapel will be open for the people's pilgrimages to the well," he said, walking toward the small stone building. It was modest in size with a thatched roof, plain wooden door, and four small windows on the side facing the well. James walked to the door and turned the iron latch with a loud click. The large hinges let out a groan of protest as the door swung open.

"We are fortunate indeed. We can rest here for the night," he said, stepping into a large open room. Apart from a modest altar and a few simple benches, the room was eerily vacant in the dim light.

"I will fetch the blankets. You find a suitable spot for us to sleep," James instructed before leaving the building. I hesitated, then made my way toward the altar, keenly aware of the book of spells hidden inside my bag. As I neared the small cross resting on the pulpit, an uneasy feeling spread through me. Surely this must be a sin, I thought as my gaze fixed on the symbol of the church as I slowly walked past. The weight of my bag felt heavier with each step as my mother's words rang in my mind. *In the eyes of the Lord, unholy deeds are not left unpunished.*

Was bringing a book of spells into the house of the Lord an unholy deed? I pondered.

Though in her youth my mother had been quietly taught the old ways by Gran, she embraced Protestantism wholeheartedly after marrying my father, so I was raised in the house of the Lord. Unlike my mother, I never felt at home in the church. *I feel the divine presence most strongly in nature, not in the confines of these four walls*, I thought as I scanned the room.

To the right of the altar, a small alcove offered just enough space for our makeshift beds. Though the flagstone floor appeared far from comfortable, enduring a night on its cold surface seemed a small sacrifice if it meant saving Gran. Just as I was about to set my bag on the floor, James returned with the blankets.

"I think this is the best place to bed down," I told him, tapping my foot on the floor. "However, it's going to be hard and cold."

"I have an idea," he offered as he walked over to the nearest bench and slid it up next to the one behind it. "Maybe we don't have to sleep on the cold floor," he said with a smile.

I smiled back, realizing it was the perfect setup for a small bed, much better than the stone floor. "I'm not sure this is a very holy thing to do," I remarked as I slid the next two benches together.

"I think God will be just fine with us rearranging things a bit for the night," James said with a slight laugh.

After making our beds, James walked over to the last bench in the chapel, pulled out a candle from his bag, and lit it. The small flame cast a warm glow and large dancing shadows across the sloping ceiling as he retrieved the cheese and bread from earlier as well as two pieces of dried beef that he then set on the bench.

"Here," he said, handing me a section of the beef atop the bread.

"Thank you," I said gratefully as I took a bite. After a long day of traveling, it tasted divine, possibly the best thing I had ever eaten.

"You say you're a writer, but what do you write? Are you a poet like the Duchess, or a playwright like Shakespeare? Perhaps a storyteller like Nashe?" he asked, slicing off a bit of cheese and handing it to me.

"Truthfully, I have not written anything as grand as those you speak of, but I hope to one day write a book such as Nashe's. However, it is all but a dream."

"If your true passion lies in the pages of a book, that is what you must do, regardless of what society tells you," he said, taking a bite of bread.

I sighed. "I wish it were that simple, James, but women are not afforded that kind of freedom," I told him as I picked at my food, the conversation souring my stomach.

"Well, if for no one else, I will read your books," he said, with a sweetness in his tone that warmed me from the inside out. No man had ever talked to me as an equal, and it caught me off guard. I smiled, filling my mouth with food as I did not know how to respond to his kind words.

We ate the rest of our dinner in shared silence, brought on this time by contentment, not annoyance.

"You take this one," James said, standing up and pointing to the two benches farthest from the door. "It's less drafty here."

His kindness was in such sharp contrast to how he had first treated me when he thought me to be courting him. I was left wondering if I had been as cruel to the other men the night of the ball. Like James, I was a good person compelled to do something that didn't feel right. Humans are seemingly just like animals in that way — if cornered, they strike out.

Moving a small wooden box between the two makeshift beds, James set the candle upon it. I lay down on my bed and watched the flame's warm light reflecting off the cold fieldstone walls. My heart fluttered momentarily as James lay down, his face half lit with candlelight. He looked handsome with the dark shadows cutting across his sharp jawline. I had seen a different side of him today, a soft, caring, intelligent side, and now that I had a glimpse of the true man he was, my heart and my mind were in battle. This was not the time to be drawn to a man. Gran's life was in my hands, and I needed to keep my wits about me.

As hard as I tried to push it down, the feeling within me returned relentlessly. I realized what the feeling was—butterflies. In my mind, Gran's words echoed: Allow the butterflies in your stomach to be your guide. Should you feel them stir, focus on that sensation and heed its message. Let your intuition be your compass.

I looked at James as he lay down on his bed, his chest rising and falling with each slow breath. I was close enough to smell the rich aroma of pine and cinnamon mixed with woodsmoke clinging to him. To be alone in the same room with a man was scandalous enough, but even more so in the house of the Lord.

As if he could feel my eyes tracing the edge of his body, he rolled over and looked at me. Our eyes locked and time stopped once more. I was lost in the forest of his eyes as the flame's reflection danced within them. I lay still as stone, fearing that if I moved, I might break the spell we were both under. He moved forward into the empty space between our beds, close enough that I could feel his warmth, and then his lips parted.

Chapter Thirty-Six

WATER INTO ICE

My heart quickened, and I closed my eyes, thinking he was about to kiss me, but instead, he leaned in and blew out the candle flickering on the small box between us. Thanking the heavens he could not see the embarrassment reddening my cheeks in the darkness, I rolled over and feigned sleep.

I awoke the next morning just as the first rays of morning light were breaking the edge of the horizon, casting a soft glow through the chapel's windows. James remained asleep on his bench as I rose quietly, taking care not to disturb him. With my bag in hand, I headed toward the door, eager to collect the water from the well while he slept. I needed to read the spell's instructions carefully once again to ensure I didn't miss any steps. Keeping my footsteps light, I made my way over to the door. Turning the old iron handle, I pulled the door open slowly to avoid the creaking of the old hinges and then made my escape into the cold morning air.

The world outside lay under a sheer veil of fine snow, muting the colors below into a ghostly pale version of their once vibrant hues. I left a trail of footprints over to the spot where the earth broke away, revealing the healing waters of the well. As I approached, I noticed a small evergreen beside it, festooned with pieces of fabric, tied to its branches. It resembled the duke's grand tree decorated for the ball, but these were not decorations — they were offerings to the well, tokens of gratitude for its healing powers. The tree's boughs bore the weight of countless offerings, a testament to the many who had sought solace and healing in its presence over the years.

As I came upon the break in the earth where the spring emerged, the sun began bathing the frozen land with its warming touch, peeling back its frosty veil. As I peered into the small pool before me, I caught sight of shimmering reflections below — coins and other metal offerings glinting beneath the surface. It was yet another way for people to pay thanks to the spirit that guarded the well. Standing in the churchyard of St. Mary's, I realized that this act of leaving offerings was an ancient pagan ritual, preserved and honored even within the confines of the church grounds.

Placing my bag on a large rock, I stole a quick glance back at the chapel before pulling out Gran's book. It was wrapped in a wool shawl that should have been draped over my shoulders under my fur cape, but I had used it to conceal the book of spells during our travels instead. I hastily unwrapped it and opened it to the page I had marked with a crow feather.

"With a copper bowl gather water from the well but do not overfill it nor spill a drop. If you do so, you must wait a day's time to try again, or the spell will not take. Draw the symbol of the Ansuz rune beside the well and repeat these words three times, 'Wisdom from this water's well, counteract, reverse this spell,' " I read aloud.

Carefully, I wrapped the book back into the shawl and tucked it away into my bag, then retrieved the copper bowl and small glass bottle. I stepped toward the well, then knelt down by its pooling waters. In the thin dusting of snow next to the well, I scrolled a slanted F, the rune of Ansuz, with the tip of my finger. Pulling forth the color of the rich soil below, the rune stood out in contrast to the frozen ground around it.

The edges of the water clung heavy with ice, but the center was full of clear flowing water. Looking above me at the strips of fabric blowing in the light wintry breeze, I pulled up my wool skirt and ripped a small strip of my petticoat off, tying it to a smaller branch that had not received an offering.

I leaned forward with the small copper bowl and whispered, "Wisdom from this water's well, counteract, reverse this spell" three times into the wind before scooping the water from the center of the well. I had successfully managed to not overfill the bowl and grabbed for the bottle resting in my lap. Holding the bottle out, I held my breath as I slowly poured the water from the bowl into the bottle. I had almost completed the task when a rabbit hopped out from the underbrush of the tree, startling me. In that split second, my hand moved, and the last drops of water poured from the cup and fell toward the ground. I watched in dismay as the drops fell, my heart sinking with them. In that moment, fear jolted something awake within me, and the temperature plummeted as if death itself had entered the room, freezing the drops of water in mid-air. Without a second's hesitation, I lunged forward, extending the bottle just in time to catch the ice droplets as they fell into the open neck of the bottle. Then, as suddenly as the bitter chill had come, it fled. I quickly capped the bottle and tucked it safely away in my bag. Stunned, I stepped back, almost tripping over my bag. Had I done that? Had I turned the drops to ice in that moment of panic? Did I have powers such as Gran?

"You should have woken me," a voice rang out, making me jump.

I turned to see James standing at the head of the well. Panicking, I quickly wiped away the rune symbol into a blur of snow and dirt. Had he seen what had just happened? Would he think me a witch? I glanced down at my feet, relieved to see that the book still lay hidden away in my bag.

"I did not want to wake you," I managed to say.

"I see you have collected the water."

"Yes, I woke early and wanted to collect it so we could be on our way as soon as possible," I said, still trying to gauge his tone. I could not tell if his eyes were still tightened by sleep, or if he was glaring at me with suspicion.

"Let us eat, then. I will gather what's in the chapel, and we shall depart. If we ride now, we might be able to make it to Loch Ness before dark," he said in a reassuring tone, a small smile gracing his face as he turned and walked back toward the chapel.

I let out the long breath I had been holding. I was quite sure he had not seen the water turn into ice mid-air. Relief washed over me as I grabbed my bag and followed him.

After eating a quick meal of bread and nuts, we mounted the horses and left St. Mary's. The morning light graced the tops of the trees, casting long shadows across the path as we made our way back up the ridge. It was warmer in the sun's presence while we rode, the frost burning away where its beams touched. With little snow in the area, we were able to ride faster than we had on the way to Letterfearn.

Despite the sun, a storm was beginning to brew in my mind as I thought of how the water had turned to ice. Did I possess powers like Gran's? Was I a witch? The very notion seemed absurd. I had never exhibited any unusual abilities before. Perhaps it was simply a freak burst of cold, but deep down, I had felt the fear coursing through me like an icy fire raging from my core to the tips of my fingers. In that moment of dread, the water had frozen solid, allowing me to catch the ice droplets before they fell to the ground. The whole inexplicable moment had been eerie, with the ice droplets descending gently as if time had slowed down. I was at a loss for what to make of it, and the uncertainty chilled me to the bone.

I noticed the sky filling with a thick layer of clouds, and within moments, a storm appeared to be brewing. *Was the weather mimicking my moods,* I wondered. Was I somehow influencing the weather as well? The notion seemed preposterous, yet my mind entertained the wild possibility.

"Have you ever been to a play?" James asked, cutting into the silence of the morning's ride, which I was grateful for as my thoughts had taken a dark turn.

"Yes, once, but it was more of a stage interlude. Even though my father was a Protestant, he never agreed that the theater was for sinners. He was an educated man and appreciated what the playwrights had to offer, even the silly ones. Had she known he had taken me, my mother would have had his head."

"Where did you see it?" he asked, giving me a mischievous smile, already knowing where these kinds of plays took place.

"The Black Bull Tavern."

"Aye, I saw *The Bouncing Knight* there last year. My father would be none too pleased to find that his son had attended such foolery," he laughed.

"Really? That's the same one that Father and I attended!"

"Maybe we sat next to each other and didn't even know it," he joked, but something inside me reveled at the idea of such a chance meeting, like the kind written about in books.

"It was quite absurd, wasn't it?" he asked with a chuckle.

"Yes, it was. I wish I had been able to see Shakespeare's real Henry IV on the actual stage. It must have been grand," I mused as the sun broke free of the clouds for a long moment, lightening up the world around us.

He nodded in agreement as we rode down the sloping hill into the glen below. The wind blew from the west carrying with it the scent of woodsmoke. A small cottage sat snugly at the base of a large mountain, reminding me of Fernbeg, Gran's cottage in Oban. I instinctively touched my bag, feeling for the bottle that held the water from the well. We needed to gather the rowanberries and make our way back to the castle by morning, or it would be too late, and the spell would not work. A sickness washed over me as I thought about Gran, and I prayed that she was still fighting and had not succumbed to death's icy touch.

Chapter Thirty-Seven

WALK OF SHAME

Between the whisky and the reading, Nora was struggling to keep her eyes open. Before she could even turn the page to find out what happened next, her eyes closed, and she drifted off to sleep and into the dream realm.

Shrouded in darkness, the room was illuminated only by a faint moonbeam trickling in through a distant window. Shadows danced across the walls, casting everything in a monochromatic haze. Ragged breathing echoed through the cold air from the far corner, where the outline of a bed lurked in the shadows. The chill in the house was far too cold for anyone to live in comfortably. Nora walked over to the wall and ran her hand along its surface until her fingers found a light switch covered in a thin layer of frost. She flipped it on, but no light shone in the darkness.

She rubbed her arms in an attempt to dispel the chill that was slowly working its way into her bones. Making her way to the bed nestled in the back corner of the room, she followed the sounds of ragged breathing cutting through the frozen silence of the house. The bed, like everything else, was cloaked in a delicate layer of frost. Even the blankets were touched by an otherworldly cold, adorned with tiny crystals. The covers slowly rose and fell with each labored breath. She walked to the head of the bed and could make out a tuft of snow-white hair emerging from beneath the blankets, but the features of the person remained hidden in shadow.

The house was too cold, and whoever was in that bed was old and unwell. Turning, Nora found herself standing in front of the fireplace, arranging a few small pieces of kindling to start a fire. Running her hand along the mantle, she found a box of matches, but whenever she struck one, it shattered like ice in her hands. She tried again and again, but each match met the same fate. After the last match crumbled in her hands, she walked toward the window where a chair sat draped with a blanket. Pulling the blanket from the chair, she noticed movement outside the window.

Peering into the murky darkness, Nora saw the full moon illuminating the icy waters of the loch in a soft light. The waters began to churn and move as a creature resembling a large serpent with scales the color of storm clouds emerged from its center. Broad-headed with green eyes reflecting the moonlight, the creature appeared ancient and majestic. Its long neck extended well above the surface of the water, while its back bobbed up and down. It frolicked, diving in and out with a playful yet graceful motion. The mesmerizing scene held Nora's attention until the voice of a woman behind her snapped her out of the enchantment.

"In the shadowed depths where mysteries still dwell, may the whispers of Bridanach guide you well. For with her wisdom, there lies a gift, to save the souls who are adrift."

When Nora turned around, no one was there, yet the voice had sounded mere feet away from her. She turned back toward the loch, but its waters were still. Not even a ripple washed across its surface. Turning around, Nora was in the bedroom again, but this time the bed was empty and lay neatly made. She turned toward the windows overlooking the loch to find she was now in an old stone ruin, the freezing cold air seeping its way into the cracks and openings. Nothing but a pile of smoldering ash lay where a fire once burned within the dilapidated old stone walls. Ducking under pine boughs, Nora walked into the snowy land-scape that sat atop a hill overlooking a long loch. The sun was rising, and a feeling of fear raced through her that she couldn't explain. Looking around frantically, she found herself alone and began to panic. She closed her eyes, hoping to dispel the fear.

Nora jolted awake in bed, the little red book resting on her chest and the chilly embrace of the bedroom's bitter cold air sur-rounding her. The weird dream lingered in her thoughts as she rubbed the sleep away from her eyes. Compared to most dreams she had, this one had been remarkably visceral and real, more like a memory than a dream. She felt like she hadn't slept at all.

The electricity must have still been out because without the furnace, the fireplace downstairs was not enough to heat the upper level of the house. She huddled under the blankets, reluctant to go downstairs and face Alistair, especially after the awkward end to the previous night's events. Still, she needed to check on him to make sure his foot was okay. She let out a groan and watched her breath form wispy clouds in the frigid air.

Nora regretted having drunk so much whisky, as her head pounded in protest, a harsh reminder of her poor decision. She had no idea how to navigate the aftermath of her failed encounter with Alistair last night. She had to admit she was a bit disappointed.

She liked him and had wanted to spend the night wrapped in his arms. It wasn't like it could lead to anything. They were from different countries, after all, and she would soon be heading back to Vermont.

Unlike a singular misguided episode in college, there was no sneaking out and avoiding the situation this time. The thought of facing Alistair was anything but appealing and prompted Nora to linger in bed a bit longer. Rolling over, she lay on her side, gazing around the room. Her eyes landed on the floorboard that had ended her steamy moment with Alistair, and she couldn't help but scowl at it. That turned-up old board had dashed any possibility of waking up next to him. Then a flicker of clarity crept in — perhaps it had spared her from the huge mistake of sleeping with a man who was just drunk and had no particular interest in her otherwise.

As her mind wandered, the gentle rays of the rising sun bathed the room in a golden glow. In that soft morning light, Nora saw something beneath the lifted floorboard. A glint of white caught her eye, a hidden piece of paper, perhaps? Throwing off the blankets, Nora hastily grabbed her old UVM sweatshirt from the chair and pulled it over the clothes she had slept in as the brisk air sent shivers through her body. With a deep breath, she walked over to the board, anticipation building as she prepared to uncover the mystery hidden beneath.

Chapter Thirty-Eight

THE HIDDEN TRUTH

Nora knelt down and tried to lift the floorboard with her fingers, but it stubbornly refused to move. Undeterred, she got up, rummaged through her bag, and eventually settled on her hairbrush as a makeshift lever. Sliding the brush handle beneath the board, she coaxed it upward just enough to slip her hand underneath and pry it the rest of the way. Hidden under the board lay an old Clark's shoebox in a thick layer of dust and cobwebs, its exterior marked by the stains of time and speckled with mold. Nora carefully retrieved it and set it on the floor.

A jolt of excitement pulsed through her as she imagined what might be inside the box. Money or jewels or perhaps old forgotten love letters? Just before she lifted the lid, the thought struck her that maybe she should wait and open it with Alistair. It could be just what she needed to break the lingering tension and awkwardness from the previous night. Resisting the urge to open the box, Nora set it aside and made her way to the dresser where she changed into fresh clothes, tidied her hair, and applied a touch of makeup. She wanted to look put together, not like the hot mess from the prior night.

Descending the stairs with the box tucked under her arm, Nora found the lower floor deserted. Then she heard the noises coming from the bathroom that made it obvious the whisky was making an unwelcome reappearance. Opting to hold off on revealing the box until Alistair was feeling better, Nora busied herself in the kitchen. She decided that breakfast and a cup of tea would be the best remedy for his hangover, and it might help ease the embarrassment from last night. Plus, she could use a bit of the hangover remedy herself.

By the time Alistair emerged from the bathroom, Nora had whipped up grilled breakfast sandwiches of bacon, eggs, and cheese, and had boiled a pot of water for tea.

"Oh, God, what is that smell?" he said, wrinkling his nose as he came limping over to the island and sat down. He looked a bit pale, and his hair was sticking up at odd angles, but Nora thought he was still quite cute. However cute she thought him to be, it didn't ease the tension in the room between them, which was thick enough to cut with a knife. Nora's stomach churned as she looked away from him, pretending to be busy cooking. "Only my dad's famous bacon, egg, and grilled cheese breakfast sandwich. The best cure for a hangover is extra greasy food, you know," she responded, trying to cut the tension with a light joke while keeping her eyes anywhere but on him.

"Well, it seems that you Yanks have something in common with us over here then. However, I'm not sure this is going to beat a Scottish breakfast," he said in his customary snarky tone. Nora turned around and forced a smile, handing him a plate with the sandwich on it along with a cup of strong English breakfast tea.

Now it was Alistair's turn to regard the food with skepticism. She watched him look at it, his face still pale and his eyes bloodshot.

"Try it. I promise it will help," Nora encouraged, nudging his plate gently.

"Okay, but for your sake, I hope it doesn't come back up because I barely made it to the bathroom this morning."

He took a tentative bite, chewing slowly.

"Not bad, but it can't beat my mum's full Scottish breakfast," he said after nearly polishing off the whole thing.

"How's your toe?" she asked, mustering the courage to bring up the previous night.

"Sore," he replied, taking a prolonged sip of tea and deliberately avoiding eye contact.

Nora swallowed hard. She could sense the discomfort in his gaze, realizing from his expression that he was grappling with regret over last night. The air around them hung heavy with unease, and a wave of embarrassment washed over her, as she turned away, hoping to shield her wounded pride from him.

"What's this?" Alistair asked, his curiosity interrupted her attempt to compose herself.

Taking a deep breath, she turned to face him again, just as he pulled the shoebox closer. "Oh, funny story. You know that floorboard that cut your toe? This morning I saw something in the crack and pulled up the board. Lying underneath, in a cluster of cobwebs and dust, was this box."

"What's in it?" he asked.

"I don't know. Thought we could open it together," she

replied. As soon as the words left her mouth, regret washed over her—what was she thinking? "Together" sounded desperate.

To her surprise, Alistair met her eyes and smiled, momentarily easing the tension. Nora couldn't help but look at his lips as they curled up, remembering the way they had felt against her the night before. A warmth crawled up her chest and into her face, turning her cheeks a light shade of pink as the memory lingered.

"Go ahead, open it," Alistair urged, snapping her out of it as he pushed the box toward her. Nora walked over, took a seat on the stool beside him, and carefully removed the box's lid. Inside the old, worn cardboard box lay a stack of letters.

"What is it?" he asked, peering into the box curiously.

"Letters. Lots and lots of very old letters."

"No way. Must be the old owners of the house stashed them away."

Nora picked one up and inspected it. Addressed to Marjorie MacDonald, it was postmarked 14/12/1943. Nora's heart raced at the name. Marjorie had been mentioned on the back of the photograph of her grandmother sitting on the stone wall, the one labeled *New Year's trip to Marjorie's*. She was a MacDonald and must have been one of Colin's relatives. Eagerly, she pulled the aged paper from its shell and began reading aloud.

> *Dear Marjorie,*
>
> *I hope this letter finds you well and enjoying the small delights of the season. I wish I could be home with you to spend the holidays instead of being cooped up here in this stuffy old hospital. The only thing that is getting me through these long, arduous days is an American nurse named Edith. She is very kind and has been reading to me from Cora's book, as I am still not able to read from the*

blasted concussion I sustained after being shot. Forgive me for keeping this letter short as my mate Tim is writing it for me. It's hard to do much of anything academic these days but with each passing hour I am growing stronger.

I thank my lucky stars for your foresight and urging me to take the book with me when I left for the war since this little red book has saved my life in more ways than you will ever know. Please send me any information you have gathered while I have been away, and I will do my best to cipher whatever else I can.

Do have an extra mince pie for me and a mulled cider on Christmas Day. I promise that once I regain my health, I will make the journey back home to see you. Until then, my dear sister, stay safe and use what you have been given to do so.

With love, Colin

Chapter Thirty-Nine
A BOX FULL OF CONFUSION

Nora's pulse quickened as she reread the line for the third time: "She is very kind and has been reading to me from Cora's book." *Could it be the same book?* she thought. How had she ended up with the very same book as Colin? She had found it at the mysterious little bookstore, snugly wedged between the bookshelf and the wall.

Marjorie was Colin's sister. That meant the cottage had been her great-aunt's. What on earth was going on here? Betty Short-bridge was right. Fate had certainly played its hand of cards, in more ways than one.

Nora's eyes fixed on Alistair, and she quickly noticed a mix-ture of surprise and disbelief across his face. "Wait, I might be confused, but is this saying that the woman who used to live in this cottage was the sister of the man you think is your biological grandfather?"

"It looks that way. How crazy is that?"

"It's mental. Talk about coincidences. The fact that you ended up renting this place without knowing that has got to be more than a one-in-a-million chance."

An unease sat heavy in her gut. There was something more to this, something beyond chance. She could sense it like a subtle whisper in the wind. "It's strange. It's almost as if..." She trailed off, glancing at the old books and the mysterious atmosphere of the cottage.

Alistair raised an eyebrow. "Almost as if what?"

As if something wanted me here, she thought before dismissing the idea. "Never mind. Let's read another letter and see if it unravels any more of this mystery." She picked the next letter out of the box as the feeling of something otherworldly lingered in the air.

"Answers and possibly more surprises as well," Alistair said, flipping through the stack of letters in the old shoebox. "There has to be a dozen in here."

"I'm not sure I'm ready for any more surprises just yet. I already have to figure out how to tell my father about this one," she said, pointing down at the name MacDonald on the letter she held in her hands.

Alistair looked thoughtful. "If you wouldn't mind, I could help you read through them?" His eyes met hers, pulling her in, as if she had looked into them a thousand times. Nora sensed this was his way of making amends for the previous night. She smiled and nodded, silently accepting his offer.

"We better make some more tea if we are going to conquer that stack," he said, getting up and limping over to the stove.

"Are you feeling better?" Nora asked, noticing the color returning to his cheeks.

He met her gaze and smiled. "Okay, you win. That greasy breakfast grilled cheese thingy hit the spot, and I am feeling a bit better."

"I'm not going to say I told ya so," she joked, turning back to the letter in her hands. When she glanced up at him, their eyes locked as a thick silence fell over the room. The longing she felt deep within her core each time their eyes met returned, but it was more than just lust, though that did admittedly play a part. Rather, it was something much deeper. She had never experienced this kind of feeling with Sam. Come to think of it, Sam had never kissed her as passionately as Alistair had last night. Just thinking about their kiss made her long for a repeat.

As if Alistair had read her thoughts, he said, "Hey, I want to apologize for last night. I had a lot to drink and tried to stop your panic attack and—"

"I get it. Don't worry. I didn't think it was anything serious anyway. Just a drunken bit of passion," Nora interrupted him. His eyes held a mix of regret and gratitude, and he smiled.

"I'm not apologizing for kissing you. I am apologizing for not saying good night after the whole toe thing. I felt like a complete asshole all night afterward. It wasn't anything to do with you. It was more me feeling like an idiot for messing up what we had going," Alistair explained.

Nora was stunned; she had assumed he was regretting their almost-tryst, not that he hadn't said good night to her. She wasn't used to this type of openness from a guy, especially not a guy like him. He just kept surprising her.

"It's fine, really, but can I ask how you knew kissing me would stop my panic attack?" Nora inquired, genuinely curious.

"Not sure. Somehow I just knew it would help," Alistair replied, his tone uncertain yet sincere.

"Well, I'm glad you did it because it worked," Nora said with a smile. They shared an understanding that went beyond words, and the tension between them finally began to fade.

Alistair had prepared two piping cups of hot tea, but Nora came around and carried them over to their seats. She pulled her chair closer to him so he could rest his injured foot on the bottom rung before they delved back into the box of letters.

"We should sort them by date," Alistair suggested, taking the first letter they had read and placing it on the kitchen island.

"That's not a bad idea," Nora agreed.

She grabbed the stack of letters from the box and arranged them in a line in front of them. Within a few minutes, they had them sorted chronologically. The first letter was postmarked 04/12/1943, preceding the one they had already read. In total, thirteen letters sat before them, with the last one appearing to be a formal communication from the War Office. That one was not going to be an easy letter to read, Nora anticipated.

She pulled the first one in the line from its envelope, the smell of old paper and stale cigarettes clinging to it. She unfolded the paper, the once crisp ink having dulled to a dusty blue that had soaked into the fibers, making certain words a bit harder to read.

"*Dear Marjorie,*" Nora began. "*After enduring nearly a month in an Italian field hospital, I finally find myself back on Scottish soil at the Craigleith Military Hospital in Edinburgh.*

"*Yesterday marked a small victory as I attempted to bear weight on my wounded leg without assistance for the first time—progress, indeed, through the support of crutches* remains my constant companion. Regrettably, my ability to get around is still limited, and I am largely confined to the hospital bed.

"Boredom is consuming me and with this pesky concussion, I won't be able to read for quite some time. My mate Tim is penning this letter for me, as I cannot write at the moment. However, I still carry our family's book with me and plan to continue reading it as soon as I am able. I am on the mend, getting decent care, and aiming to be back home before the new year.

"With Love, Colin."

Nora sat quietly for a moment. He mentioned his family's book—was he referring to the same little red book that sat on her nightstand? Was it a treasured heirloom passed down through generations, or perhaps a written account by another member of his family? Questions flooded her mind, leaving her uncertain if she would ever uncover the answers to all of them. She looked out the window, her mind racing as the wind whipped around the deck in a mini gale, peppering the windows with a smattering of snow.

Alistair picked up the next letter. The penmanship was different on this one, not the messy hand of the first few letters but a neat scrolling script. Colin must have taken over writing the letters from his mate Tim. It was postmarked 25/12/1943. Alistair began reading aloud, pulling Nora from her thoughts.

"Dear Marjorie,

Merry Christmas! I trust this letter finds you cozy by the old stone fireplace, enjoying a generous helping of mince pie. Thank you for your recent letter. Hearing from you always lifts my spirits, and the information about Mary's note was helpful. I am pleased to report that I am now back

~ 295 ~

on my own two feet without any assistance, and I am able to write my own letters.

I must admit to you that I have fallen quite hard for Edith, and I believe she fancies me just as much. We have grown close over the past few weeks as she has cared for me. You know how they say love can mend the deepest wounds. In my case, I am inclined to believe it, as my leg is almost completely healed. She is the sunshine on even the cloudiest of days, Marjorie. I believe you will adore her as much as I do, and I can't wait to introduce you soon.

Tomorrow, I am to be discharged from the hospital—a Christmas miracle, indeed! Edith is being transferred to a London hospital come the start of the new year and has been granted a week off. We have decided to use this time to journey up north to visit you. It will be a joyous reunion, I am certain.

We shall be with you in a mere few days, my dear sister. Until then, stay well, and know that you are always in my thoughts.

With Love,

Colin

PS Edith finished reading the book to me this past week, and I've been attempting to decipher the curse. It's challenging to determine if it was transcribed exactly as spoken. Even a small change in a word could mean we may never unravel how to reverse it. Nonetheless, I'm working diligently on it. We will discuss it further when I arrive home."

Chapter Forty

LETTERS

"Curse?" Nora said, looking at Alistair, who had folded the letter and was slipping it back into the worn envelope.

"Yeah, weird. Maybe the hit to his head knocked a few marbles loose?" he suggested, placing the letter back on the small stack.

"You're probably right. It does seem a bit unhinged," Nora said, looking down at the pile and then up toward the bedroom where the book sat. Unhinged perhaps, but impossible? She wasn't sure of anything now. So many strange and unbelievable things had happened to her in the past four days that a curse didn't seem all that far-fetched.

"The trip he talks about must be the one from the photos," Alistair surmised.

Nora stood and walked into the living room, retrieved the photo album from the coffee table, and came back with it tucked under her arm.

"I have a feeling this might just follow the timeline of the letters," Nora said, flipping to the picture she had recreated on the Royal Mile. She peeled the clear plastic away from the photo and turned it around, revealing a date on the back—*December 26, 1943.*

"They were celebrating," she said under her breath, smiling.

"What?"

"This picture has always felt special; now I know why. They were celebrating Colin's discharge from the hospital."

She looked down at it with new eyes and saw her grand-mother's excitement. She imagined how she must have felt in the moment. They were about to spend a week together for the first time. Amidst the war's daily deaths and losses, this celebration must have felt like the highest of highs. The man she had cared for and fallen in love with was finally well enough to leave the hospital.

As Alistair opened the next letter, Nora flipped through the old photographs, seeing each one in a new light. After the picture on the Royal Mile, a few images of the Scottish landscape fol-lowed, places they had stopped on the way to Letterfearn, Nora assumed.

"I know that place. It's close to Glencoe. And that car is an MG TB. Bloody brilliant car. Worth a fortune these days," Alistair said, pointing to the photo of a long glen with an old-fashioned car parked on the side of the road in the distance.

"You don't strike me as a car guy."

"Got it from my grandad. He was into vintage cars. Took me

to shows when I was younger. He loved the MG T-series," he said with a boyish smile.

Nora couldn't help but smile back at his cute little outburst of car facts. She turned the page to find the picture of her gram sitting on the stone wall and the one of the loch with the cottage in the background. On the next page was a picture of her grandmother sitting at an old kitchen table next to a woman who looked to be a few years older than her. They had wide smiles on their faces and cups of tea in their hands. Nora stared at it. There was something familiar, but she could not quite place it, that was until she noticed the windows in the background. It was the cottage! Though it looked somewhat different from the way it looked now, the windows were exactly the same.

"Look, this must be Marjorie, and they're here in the cottage before it was renovated," Nora said, sliding the photo album over to Alistair. He looked down at it and smiled. "I think you're right. Look at the windows."

The album page held three more photos. One showed a heart drawn into the snow under a tree with what looked like clusters of berries hanging from it. Then there was a picture of the same old-style car parked on a road overlooking a beautiful valley to its left. The last photo stopped Nora in her tracks. Although she had seen it before, she hadn't paid much attention to it. An old headstone with trees growing up around it sat in the center of the photo. Lichen and moss had worked their way down onto its face, covering the birth and death dates, but the name carved into the stone read clearly: "Cora Darrow."

Nora's heart came to a sudden standstill. Nora's heart suddenly stood still. Could this be the same Cora from the book? No, her last name had been Douglas—unless Darrow was her married name. If that were true, then she hadn't ended up with James, as he was a Campbell. She looked over to Alistair to say something but realized she hadn't mentioned anything about the book to him yet. He was engrossed in the next letter as she slipped the photo out from the page and turned it over. There on the back was *Colin's 3x great-grandmother.*

Not only had Cora been real, but she was Colin's great-grandmother, which meant she was also her great-grandmother. Nora felt like she was falling down a rabbit hole; the more she dug, the deeper she plunged into a bottomless pit of questions.

"Getting chilly in here," Alistair said, breaking her train of thought. "I wonder if they will ever get the power back on?" He walked over and added the last three logs onto the fire. "I'm going to get some more wood while the snow's let up."

"Let me get the wood. You really should be resting your foot," Nora said, beginning to stand.

"No, I'm fine, really. It's just a cut. Believe me, I've had worse and can manage just fine. Plus, it's already starting to feel better," he said as he walked over to the door, trying hard not to limp. He put on his boots and jacket, then exited the cottage. Nora glanced back down at the photo and then toward the bedroom. She needed to finish reading the book. There were only a few chapters left, and her interest was fully piqued now that she knew Cora was real and a relative of hers. Colin's reference to the book having some kind of curse on it had her intrigued. Maybe that was why the book seemed to mimic incidents in real life; it was cursed.

She walked up the stairs into the frigid cold of the unheated bedroom. The temperature felt as if it had dropped ten degrees since morning. She quickly took the little red book and her neglected notebook off the nightstand and headed back down to the kitchen.

She grabbed a pen along with the photo album and the next few letters and went over to the sofa. There was so much to keep track of, she had to start taking notes.

The next letter was postmarked 02/01/1944.

Dear Marjorie,

I hope this letter finds you in good spirits and enjoying the new radio I brought you during our recent visit. It was so good to see you, even if only for a short while. Edith adored you and can't wait to come back for a visit in the spring. She sends her love along with this letter.

After leaving Letterfearn on Thursday, we arrived at Flora's a little past 8 p.m. You were absolutely right; the library at Fernbeg is a treasure trove of fairy lore. I could have spent an entire month reading and still not finished half of it. However, I did uncover a few interesting things.

Remember how Mother used to tell us that knowing a fairy's true name gives you power over them and can break their enchantments? Well, it seems to be true as I came across that very piece of wisdom in one of Flora's spell books. The challenge, of course, is that it's been centuries, and discovering the exact fairy is quite a daunting task.

Another intriguing find is that some fairies are bound by tasks. If you complete the task they've set, they are obligated to release you from any enchantment they hold over you. The difficulty here is that so much time has passed, and unraveling these tasks may prove impossible. I also found that rowan can be used as protection against fairies. It's unfortunate that Cora didn't have her bag with the berries on her at the time, as it could have saved us a load of trouble. However, I am afraid I didn't find much that we didn't already know.

On a side note, I can't help but wish for reconciliation between you and Flora. The estrangement between you two has lasted too long. It's time to let go of the resentment over the matter of the cottage. Mother's decision to give the cottage to Flora was guided by family lore, and it wasn't Flora's doing. She misses you, Marjorie, and I believe it would do both of you good to mend fences.

With Love, Colin

Nora looked down at the little red book sitting on the coffee table. What were Marjorie and Colin trying to figure out about fairy curses, and what did it have to do with Cora? She bent forward and retrieved the book, anticipation filling her as she opened it to where she had left off.

Chapter Forty-One
LOCH NESS

After riding for nearly half a day, we passed the Turners' home, heading northwest toward Loch Ness. The weather had calmed once again, and the snow had ceased. The farther north we went, however, the deeper the snow had gathered, halting our faster pace. I did not mind the ride being a bit slower as it made it easier to converse with James. I rode up next to him, my horse falling into sync with his.

"Do you have plans for the coming new year?" I asked.

"I had planned to travel to France. Your father spoke fondly of it as a place of inspiration for not only the arts but also scientific exploration. I had hoped to see Jean Racine's The Thebaid at the Hôtel de Bourgogne," he said.

"Hoped to? Do you not plan to still go?"

"My father has other plans for me. I am to pick a bride and marry by the new year. After that he plans to groom me in a career in diplomacy," he told me, defeat spreading across his face.

"Have you told him you want to travel?"

"Yes, but he does not approve. He is a kind yet stubborn man who has no bend. Being born of noble birth is a curse. Count yourself lucky."

"If by 'lucky' you mean forced to marry a man I do not love and spend the rest of my life in servitude to him, I am bound to the same ill fate as you. No say over my own life, just a poppet to be sold off like cattle," I said.

As I spoke those words, a storm began to form within me. I hadn't thought much of my mission in coming to Gran's since she fell ill, but my duty to marry well for my family still awaited me upon my return. I looked to the sky, wondering if my inner turmoil would manifest in the clouds above our heads. The storm within me recoiled as James smiled and said, "I suppose we are one and the same then."

As we rode on, he continued, "If you could follow your dream and become a writer, would you stay in Edinburgh?"

"No, I would love to find a little cottage like my gran's in Oban. I would write fanciful tales while looking over a loch and make pies for every meal. Raise sheep in the spring and spin their wool into yarn that I could knit in the winter by the fireplace," I told him as my mind wandered off into my daydreams. "I much prefer the country over the city," I concluded.

"I think that is a fine dream. Do you mind if I share it with you?" he asked, giving me a smile that sent waves of heat racing up my chilled body and set the butterflies dancing in my stomach once again.

"You may," I smiled back.

"What of children? Do you not dream of little feet running through the tall grass of your glen and chasing after your sheep?" The question caught me off guard as I had not thought much of being a mother until recently, after meeting little Alice.

"Yes, someday I hope to be a mother. And you?" I asked.

"Yes, I hope to have lots of little ones to chase after."

A spark ignited in his eyes as he spoke, and I thought back to how he was with little Alice. He would make a fine husband someday to a fortunate woman and a loving father to his children. Yet, I reminded myself that my blood was not of noble descent, quelling any fantasies I might entertain. We carried on our journey in silence as the wind picked up, making it hard to hear one another. The progress was slower than we had anticipated as the snow began to fall once again. Our horses were having a hard time keeping pace. James slowed as we reached a high point on the road, the relentless snowfall obscuring our surroundings.

"I estimate we are an hour south of the loch, but with this heavy snowfall, it's difficult to be certain," he remarked, his voice barely audible over the howling wind. Unfamiliar with the landscape, I could offer little assistance in finding crucial landmarks as we continued our journey. James stopped several times to ensure we remained on the proper route, the road disappearing beneath a thick blanket of snow, making it challenging to discern our path.

"The loch is just ahead at the end of this forest!" James's voice cut through the wind.

We pressed on, but the forest grew denser, the snowfall reducing visibility to mere feet ahead. I trailed behind James, the narrow path forcing us into single file as the forest closed in around us.

Suddenly my horse's ears perked up, sensing something amiss. A feeling of unease settled upon me, and I scanned the forest for any sign of danger. Nothing met my eyes, but an ominous feeling of being watched lingered with me. Glancing behind once again, I found nothing, but as I faced forward, my horse reared up, letting out a thunderous whinny and slamming its front hooves onto the snow-covered ground.

James turned at the sound of the commotion, his eyes widening in alarm. With swift reflexes, he spun his horse around, attempting to reach me before disaster struck, but I was already slipping from the saddle, my grip on the reins the only thing keeping me tethered. My heart pounded in my ears, drowning out the sounds around me. James shouted something, his expression filled with concern, but his words were lost on me. The horse reared again, sending me tumbling to the ground. Pain shot through me as my leg collided with a rock hidden beneath the snow.

I cried out in agony, the sound piercing the icy air. Startled by my scream, the horse bolted, fleeing back the way we had come. James reached me just as my horse galloped off into the swirling snow. Grave concern washed over James's face.

"No!" I called out, my voice filled with anguish as the horse vanished from sight.

"Cora!" James yelled, swiftly dismounting his horse and rushing to my side, extending a hand to help me back up onto my feet.

"I think my leg might be injured," I replied shakily, taking his hand and attempting to stand. The pain in my ankle was unbearable, and I couldn't put any pressure on it.

"I don't think I can walk," I admitted, wincing as I lifted my foot off the ground.

"Let me have a look," he said, dropping down to his knees and lifting my skirt, gently unlacing my boot to inspect my ankle. "Your ankle is already beginning to swell. It may be broken. Let me carry you over to the horse."

James carefully laced my boot loosely and then effortlessly scooped me up, carrying me as if I weighed little more than a feather. He brought me to the horse, and with a bit of effort, I managed to throw my good leg up and over, pulling myself upright. I bit my bottom lip as the pain shot through me while James mounted the horse.

"You best hold on to me. This terrain is about to become steep," James advised.

I took in a deep breath before wrapping my arms around him. I could feel the warmth spreading through my body as I embraced him, pulling myself close. I breathed in his scent and felt his breath quicken at my touch. A familiar ache deepened in my belly as something primal stirred within me, rising to the surface and easing the discomfort in my leg.

Once I had secured myself around him, he nudged the horse, and we began trotting up the last bit of the trail before the clearing. As we entered back into the open sky, the snow began letting up, and the loch was visible in the distance.

"Will the horse fare well?" I inquired, glancing over my shoulder toward the woods where it had bolted. My concern for the creature's safety in this weather grew with each passing moment.

"That horse has traveled this path before. It should find its way back to Malcolm's without trouble," James reassured me.

My ankle throbbed with each movement of the horse as we drew nearer to the loch, each jolt sending a sharp pain up my leg. The thrill I had felt at being near James swiftly diminished, overtaken by the growing dread that my injured leg might prevent me from gathering the rowanberries. I scanned the landscape for the tree, silently praying its branches would still have berries on them as any that might have fallen to the ground would have long been buried by the snow. Darkness was now descending rapidly, and even with the snow letting up, visibility was becoming increasingly difficult, and I strained my eyes to see into the distance. As we approached Loch Ness, James slowed his pace and came to a stop near the water's edge.

"Strange, the loch looks to be completely frozen over. The Cailleach must be nearby," he said, turning back and giving me a playful smile. "Do you see the tree yet?"

I looked around at the scattering of trees along the loch's shoreline but did not see the rowan tree I was seeking. "Not yet."

James gave me a nod and continued along the water's edge, moving north. Though I must have read the spell a hundred times, I wished to be certain I collected the berries correctly, yet I could not bring forth the book in James's presence. I loosened one arm from around his waist and felt my bag, checking to make sure the book was still there. Relieved to feel its corners, I wrapped my arm back around him and at the same time caught something out of the corner of my eye. Off to our left, just a short distance up the trail, was a small tree with snow covering its branches, but there was no mistaking the little red berries that hid beneath it, turning the snow a soft pink.

Chapter Forty-Two
THE RUIN

We rode slowly over to the rowan tree. Even from feet away, I felt an energy pulsing outward from it, radiating with a palpable magic. There was a small patch of berries nestled within a few branches from the bottom, and I could have sworn a blue halo of light surrounded them as we drew closer.

"James, can you ride up next to the tree, close enough for me to pick the cluster of berries there?"

He nodded and guided the horse as close to the tree as possible, but I was too small, and with my injured leg, I wasn't stable enough on the horse's back to pick them.

"I can't reach them," I said, frustration filling my every word.

"I can," he said, leaning forward and removing his gloves. I quickly thought back to the spell, trying to remember what it had said about how to gather them. I knew I had to keep them from the light once they had been picked, but there was something else. I watched as he leaned forward toward the branch, arm fully outstretched, when it dawned on me.

"Wait, no!" I yelled, stopping him just as he was about to pick the cluster from the branch. "You must not touch them with your hands."

He stopped, pulled his hand back, and retrieved his gloves. After putting them on, he carefully plucked the cluster of berries, being careful not to drop any as he went. I opened my pack and retrieved a small earthenware jar, into which he carefully placed the berries. A wave of relief washed over me, knowing we had obtained the last ingredient to bring Gran out of her spell-induced sleep. As soon as I secured the berries in my bag, the storm began to show its fury once more, the snow coming down in thick flurries.

"I believe we should seek shelter. The night is swiftly approaching, and considering the storm and your leg, it seems unwise to venture back," he said, guiding the horse northward.

"Are you certain? We risk freezing in this weather," I replied, attempting to make my voice heard over the howling wind.

"Malcolm and I have traversed this path countless times on our hunting expeditions. A little farther ahead lies the ancient ruin of Drum-na-Drochit. The remnants of the settlement should afford us suitable shelter for the night."

As the sun dipped behind the mountains, casting the world into twilight, we stumbled upon the ancient stone ruin. Nestled into the hillside, its weathered exterior covered in moss and dirt told a story of centuries forgotten. A natural overhang tucked into the earth on one end resembled a bear den. The front section lacked a roof and was filled with snow while the back end remained sheltered and untouched. James dismounted, tied the horse to a small tree, and walked over to inspect the ruin.

"You wait here; I'll be right back," he instructed, striding toward a cluster of pine trees. I watched as he skillfully cut boughs, gathering them into a bundle. He arranged them against the opening on the sheltered side of the ruin, creating a makeshift barrier against the wind. Retrieving a hand axe from his bag, he set to work chopping firewood from a dead tree nearby. Each swing of the axe echoed through the quiet landscape as he gathered enough wood to last through the night. With an armful of logs, he disappeared behind the pine boughs, reemerging several times until a sufficient stack lay ready for the fire.

With the sun nearly vanished beyond the horizon, the cold tightened its grip on the land. James assisted me off the horse by slipping his hands around my waist and carrying me into the ancient ruin. I blushed at his touch, the pain in my ankle subsiding once more, only to be replaced by a fervent warmth spreading deep within me.

The inside proved larger than I had imagined, and he gently set me down on a short stone wall. Fetching the blankets, he returned to wrap them snugly around me. To the left, he kindled a fire, utilizing an opening for the smoke to escape. Kneeling beside the fire, he poked at the flames that were devouring the small branches and logs, coaxing more warmth into our shelter.

"How is your ankle?" he inquired, settling down beside me.

"It aches, but I'll be fine," I reassured him.

"Did you catch sight of what spooked the horse?"

"No, I turned around, but there was nothing visible," I replied.

"It's not the first time a horse has been spooked coming through that forest. Malcolm told me once of a man who was traveling through during a summer storm. He decided to take shelter in the forest, but once he dismounted, his horse became frightened and took off. Stranded, the man waited for the rain to slow before walking toward the loch when he came across a beautiful woman in his path." James paused for effect, then carried on in a tone one uses for fanciful tales. "Her eyes were as mysterious as the loch itself. She smiled gently at the man and whispered, 'Your horse sensed the ancient magic lingering in these woods, for I am the guardian of secrets beneath the waters. What is it that you wish for the most?' "

"Riches, of course," the man answered.

"With a mischievous smile, she offered the man a gleaming silver coin, promising it would bring him luck beyond measure. Grateful, the man accepted the gift, only to realize too late that the coin bore a curse. From that day forth, he found himself bound to the shores of Loch Ness, forever seeking treasure. Malcolm believes the woman was a fairy, but Addie says she was a witch," James finished, standing to add another piece of wood to the fire.

"The poor fellow. What do you suppose it could have been?"

"I'm not entirely sure, but it reminds me of the stories my nan would tell me about kelpies."

"You don't believe it was fairy magic or witchery?" I asked, treading carefully into dangerous waters as I sought to understand his opinions on the matter.

"It's possible, but I tend to lean on the side of more fantastical beasts," he joked, trying to lighten the mood.

The story of witches and fairies set my nerves on edge, and I glanced nervously at my bag hiding the spellbook within it. What if he found it in my belongings? Would he see me as some sort of evil creature, like the woman in the story? I glanced down at my hands resting quietly in my lap, the very hands that had turned water into ice. I looked back up at James, realizing the vast chasm between us lay not only in our social standings but in these matters as well. As much as I longed to confide in him, to share every part of my story, I feared his reaction. If he were to discover the magic within me, he might condemn me to the gallows. The weight of sadness burned its way up my throat with the realization that my newfound gift felt more like a curse. Trying to regain my composure, I mindlessly leaned on my hurt leg, wincing as I moved. James caught sight of it and walked over, concern etched on his face.

"You're in pain," he spoke softly, lifting my leg and placing it upon his knee as he sat beside me. His touch was gentle, and his hand lingered. With only inches between us, our eyes locked, and we held each other's gaze. The firelight accentuated his sharp jawline and the rugged shadow of stubble that had grown over the past several days. My heart began beating rapidly in my chest, and I could feel my cheeks turn a bright hue of red as my thoughts began to wander.

"I'll be fine," I sputtered, reassuring him once again, but this time he paid no mind.

"It's alright not to be. I sense your pain," he said, leaning closer and delicately tucking a loose strand of hair behind my ear. Unable to break away from his eyes, I leaned forward as he pulled me closer. All my fears and worries melted away at his touch.

His lips met mine tenderly, and I fully surrendered to the kiss. As we kissed, the fire surged, igniting a passion more ancient than the ruins we found ourselves within. Warm and tender, his lips left a trail of fire as they followed the contours of my neck, sending a delightful shiver cascading down my spine.

As our lips parted, we hesitated, fully aware of the indiscretion we were about to commit. Yet, caught up in the fervor of the moment, we chose not to care. We fell back into each other's arms, yielding to our desire and letting the moment lead us.

His hand, which had been resting firmly on my hip, moved upward, tracing the curves of my body until it reached my neck. Never having been with a man before, a nervous anticipation coursed through me at his touch. I bit my bottom lip as he untied my cape, letting it drop to the ancient earth floor. His fingers traced the line of my collarbone and then moved down to the string of my bodice, which he slowly unlaced. I was on fire with a passion that burned within me. The nervousness I had felt moments before quickly turned into a longing that felt beyond my control.

His kisses continued their descent down my neck and onto my chest, kindling an ache deep in my belly. My hands, timid at first, moved up to his chest, growing more confident as the fire within me grew. I found myself unbuttoning his shirt, as a wave of yearning surged through me, mingling with the scent of desire that hung heavy in the air. My hands trembled as they met his skin and I traced the lines of his chest, feeling his warmth beneath my fingertips. His breathing became heavy at my touch as we explored each other's bodies. He pulled me closer, kissing me deeply, his hands unpinning my long auburn locks and sending them cascading onto my shoulders.

In a flurry of passion, our bodies intertwined, and a spark of magic ignited within me, awakening something ancient. His deep green eyes locked on mine as our bodies joined as one.

"You are everything and more, Cora," he whispered softly into my ear.

In that moment, our hearts beat together in a symphony of desire and our souls danced. Our passion intensified until we reached a crescendo, and my body was flooded with what I could only describe as pure magic. I could have stayed lost in his embrace forever. In that moment the boundaries that defined our stations had no claim over us, and we gave in to what we truly desired — each other.

After we lay entwined, the cold slowly seeped back in. The firelight flickered off the old gray stone walls, casting shadows across our faces. Despite the dim light, I could see the passion fading from James's eyes as reality began to set in, just as the cold returned. We were both keenly aware that this fleeting moment of passion would be the entirety of what we could ever share together. Our worlds were destined to remain apart, as he belonged to the nobility, and I was a woman with no significant standing. Nonetheless, in that brief moment, we were equals, our love being the only thing of true standing.

Chapter Forty-Three

SHIVERS

Alistair walked back in with an arm full of wood, startling Nora out of her reading. Her face was flushed from the steamy scene she'd just been engrossed in, and she quickly shut the book, hoping he wouldn't notice. She watched him walk over to the fireplace, his rugged appearance with an arm full of logs igniting a fire within her, sparked by the spicy scene in the book. At that moment she longed for a do-over of last night, but as he turned around, the look in his eyes quelled her hormones and set her nerves on edge instead.

"We might have a bit of a problem if the power doesn't come back on soon," he said, setting the logs down and stacking them in the wood ring by the fire.

"What kind of problem?" she asked, his concerned tone bringing her quickly back down to reality.

"A 'last of the firewood' kind of problem."

"We should probably call the rental company to see if they can bring some over," Nora suggested, getting up and walking over to the stove to make another cup of tea.

"We should check on Betty to make sure she has everything she needs and isn't low on wood as well."

"Good idea."

Nora set the kettle down, walked over to grab her coat off the peg board, and slipped her boots on. When she opened the door, a sharp gust of cold wind burst into the cottage, blowing her hair back. She grabbed her hat out of her pocket and yanked it down over her ears. Alistair followed behind her as she walked out into the cold wintry air. The snow was still coming down in thick flurries, but the cold was now much more bitter. *The winds must be bringing the arctic air down from the north*, she thought.

"God, it's freezing," Nora said, zipping her jacket up to her chin.

"At least the snow has just about stopped," Alistair said, looking out toward the loch.

Just before they got to the stairs, Nora saw something scurrying off to her right. She stopped just as the scruffy little dog came bounding down the sloping hill toward them. As soon as he caught sight of them, he slowed and then stopped.

"Hey, little guy. Where have you been?" Nora asked as the dog sniffed the air in her direction. She slowly crouched down to get on the dog's level, trying not to scare it. The dog came closer until it was only feet away.

"It's okay," she said as he stepped forward and sniffed her mitten, eyeing her hesitantly.

"You're a good boy," she said, and the little dog's tail began to wag. Cautiously he took another step closer, and Nora was able to pet him. He was too friendly to be a stray, but he had no collar. She removed her mitten and ran her hand over the soft fur of his ears. He looked up at her with his mismatched eyes, and she felt something deep within her stir. As if the dog sensed the shift within her as well, he stepped closer.

"You have a way with animals," Alistair said, watching the interaction.

Within a few moments, the dog was sitting at Nora's feet as if she were his owner.

"What are we going to do with him? He has no collar, but he must be someone's pet. We can't just leave him out in this kind of cold. He'll freeze to death," Nora said, giving him a scratch behind his ears.

"Let's see if he will follow us. We can't leave him in the cottage alone; he might destroy the place." The dog looked up at him and let out a small low growl then turned toward Nora and wagged his tail again. "Or should I say follow you," he said, eyeing the dog skeptically.

Nora agreed and stood up. Alistair walked up the stairs, and Nora followed with the little black dog at her heels. When they got to Betty's cottage, Alistair knocked, but no one answered. He glanced up at the chimney, and Nora's eyes followed. No smoke billowed from its top. Nora walked to the window to the right of the door.

"Betty," he called out with another knock, but still nothing. "Can you see anyone?" he asked Nora as she cupped her hands to the window and looked in.

"No. Maybe she got a ride out of here already."

"Not likely in this weather."

A cold shudder swept through Nora, and the dog let out a low growl as if danger was lurking somewhere inside.

"I'm going in. Something's not right," Alistair said, punching in the number and opening the door. As they entered Betty's cottage, goosebumps ran up her arms and neck, not just from the biting cold inside but from the eerie silence broken only by the faint creaks of the floorboards beneath their feet. It was too quiet, and a growing sense of unease took hold in Betty's absence. Alistair was right. Something was very wrong.

Chapter Forty-Four

RAGGED BREATH

The cabin was dimly lit, and the air was so cold it didn't feel much different from the outside. Alistair's footsteps echoed against the wooden floorboards as he made his way to the fireplace, its darkened interior a stark contrast to the flickering warmth it usually provided. With a hesitant touch, he tested the icy stones, his breath forming a misty cloud in the frigid air.

Nora felt her anxiety rise as she looked around, and a creeping sense of dread set in. They should have insisted that Betty stay with them last night, or at the very least, they should have come by sooner to check on her. What if she had frozen to death in the middle of the night? The thought turned her stomach as her anxiety tightened around it.

"The stones are cold. She must have gone the entire night without a fire. I don't understand. When I left yesterday afternoon, she had more than enough wood to last the night," he explained, looking down at the empty hearth. "I'm gonna get some wood," Alistair said, standing back up and limping as swiftly as he could out the door.

"Betty? Are you here?" Nora called out, her voice sounding sharp as it echoed off the frozen walls. Her worry doubled as the air hung silent. She walked over to the windows that faced the loch and pulled the curtains open, springing dust free and letting in the early afternoon light. The little dog stayed close by her side, emitting a low growl that intensified the unsettling atmosphere weighing down the air.

She made her way swiftly through the cabin when she heard a sound that stopped her dead in her tracks. It was the haunting noise from her dream: long drawn-out ragged breaths that seemed to cut through the thick cold air. She realized it wasn't just the ragged breathing that echoed her dream, but the whole cabin seemed to emulate what she had dreamt. She quickly followed the sound, each step seeming to echo louder in the cabin's stillness. The breathing grew heavier as worry fueled her steps until she found herself standing in the doorway of the bedroom. A small window above the bed illuminated the front of the room, casting the bed and everything below it in shadow. Betty's figure was buried below the blankets, and she walked over, unsure of what she might find.

"Betty? Are you okay? It's freezing in here," Nora said, her heart beating wildly with unease. Betty remained silent and unresponsive. Nora bent down and gently pulled the blanket away from her face, which looked as snow white as her hair.

"Betty?" she said again, trying to wake her.

Betty's eyes were closed, and if it weren't for the ragged breathing and tiny puffs of white clouds above her nose, Nora might have thought her dead. She reached out and placed a hand on her shoulder, expecting her to be cold to the touch, but it was the opposite—Betty was burning up. With her age and the time she had spent outside in the cold yesterday, enduring the unheated cabin must have been more than her body could handle, and she had fallen ill.

"Betty, can you hear me?" Nora asked, concern filling each word. The little dog jumped on the bed and curled himself up next to her as if to provide warmth. A deep wave of concern washed over Nora; they needed to call for help. Betty needed a doctor. She quickly left the room and walked over to the corded phone in the hallway to call 999 but there was no dial tone.

"Shit," she muttered to herself, hanging up the phone just as she heard Alistair return.

She walked back into the main living area and found Alistair bent over a pile of frozen logs, attempting futilely to light the kindling. This was another unsettling echo of her dream from last night. Like a shadowy shroud, an eerie sensation settled over Nora as she swallowed hard, watching him.

"Blasted thing," he said, striking the last match in the box with no luck.

Out of the corner of her eye, Nora noticed a box of cigarettes and another box of matches sitting on the oak kitchen table and walked over to them.

"Alistair, something is wrong with Betty," she said. He was kneeling in front of the fireplace with his hands on his hips, looking down in defeat. He turned and looked up at her, concern in his eyes. "Oh, God, is she dead?" he asked, standing up quickly.

"No, but I tried waking her up, and nothing. She feels like she has a high fever. I think we need to call someone," Nora told him, walking over and striking a match. It petered out before it hit the kindling in the fireplace, and she tried again. The logs were too wet to light, and they would be lucky to get a fire going. Nora thought about Betty lying cold and sick in the other room. They couldn't wait until the logs dried out; they needed a fire now! A wave of anxiety flashed through her, and she stretched out her hand and touched the cold stone of the fireplace, as if by instinct. A warmth burned through her as if her blood had turned to fire itself. She felt it move down into her hand and into the tips of her fingers. She grabbed a match and struck it again, but this time, the kindling instantly caught fire as if a blow torch had hit it, not a single match.

"How did you do that?" Alistair asked, looking down at the fire raging in the hearth with wide eyes.

"I don't know," Nora said, surprising herself and looking down at her hands.

"She only has enough wood here to heat this place for the night. We need to call the lettings agency," he said, turning his gaze back to Nora.

"I already tried to call 999, but the phone here isn't working. What are we going to do?" Nora asked.

"Shit, I was worried something like that might happen. She was outside for God knows how long yesterday. I should have checked on her again last night," he trailed off, walking toward the bedroom.

Guilt flooded Nora. Alistair hadn't come back to check on Betty because of Nora's panic attack and the impromptu kiss that led to their almost one-night stand. She followed him down the hallway, regret and shame sitting heavy on her mind. As they stepped into the room, the dog let out a protective growl aimed at Alistair but calmed down as soon as Nora entered the room behind him.

"Betty? Betty, can you hear me?" Alistair asked with genuine concern as he sat next to her and felt her forehead. She began to stir, her white hair moving on the edge of the blanket. She opened her eyes slowly and looked around, confused.

"Adam, is that you?" she asked.

"No, it's Alistair and Nora from the cottage next door. How are you feeling?"

"The waters rose! I tried to get away from them, but they came into the cabin through the cracks in the doors and windows. The water was so cold, too cold," she muttered as she tried to sit herself up. Alistair turned and looked at Nora, concern etching hard lines into his face.

"You have a fever. We're going to get you some help," Nora said, trying to reassure Betty as well as herself that things would be okay. Betty pulled herself up and looked at Nora. Her frail eyes, creased with age in the corners, looked deeply into Nora's as if searching for something.

"I'll be fine, dear. Bridanach told me so. She is watching out for me. She is the one who pulled the waters back out to the loch."

Nora's heart began to pound in her chest, each beat echoing with the realisation that she had indeed dreamt of this very moment. How had Betty known about the name Bridanach? Was it part of some Welsh or Scottish folklore? If so, why would she bring it up now?

"What is Bridanach?" Nora asked Alistair.

He shrugged. "No idea."

"Oh, my dear, you know, it's the water spirit from the loch. The one you saw yesterday," Betty said.

"Is that what they are called in Wales?"

Betty let out a weak laugh that sent her into a fit of coughing. When it finally subsided, she looked at Nora and said, "No, it's her name," and pointed toward the loch.

It was then that Betty noticed the little dog lying next to her on the bed. She looked down and smiled. "You're a clever little one, aren't you?" she said to the puppy with a sly smile briefly spreading across her lips.

Alistair pulled Nora aside while Betty was paying attention to the dog.

"The fever is making her delusional; we need to get her to a hospital right away. You stay here, and I'll make the calls. Can you make her some tea and see if you can find any extra blankets?"

After Alistair left the room, Nora knew exactly where to find the extra blanket and walked over to the chair near the window that faced the loch. Sure enough, a wool blanket rested on the back of the overstuffed armchair, just as it did in her dream. She picked it up and slung it over her shoulders as she walked back into the kitchen.

She filled the old metal teapot with water, placed it on the stovetop, and lit the gas eye with the lighter. The blue flame danced around the bottom of the kettle as she waited for the water to boil. Her thoughts wandered back to lighting the fire. How had it caught so quickly? Maybe she was wrong, and the logs weren't as wet as she thought. As much as she tried to rationalize it, she knew something strange had happened in that moment because it felt as if the flame had come supernaturally from her own body, not the match.

Then there was her dream. Everything in the dream was identical to what had just happened in the past few minutes. Her head was spinning. Was she tapping into some kind of psychic power? How she wished for the simple days when her biggest problem was telling her parents she wanted to go back to school and not take over the bakery. Now her life seemed to be filled with unexplainable supernatural events she had no idea how to comprehend. The sudden whistle of the kettle jarred Nora back to reality.

A box of tea sat on the counter, and Nora grabbed a mug from a set of hooks on the kitchen wall. She shivered as she poured the steaming hot water into the mug. The cabin's frigid air was working its way through her jacket. She let the mug warm her fingers briefly before she delivered it to Betty, who was still happily stroking the dog's scruffy coat.

"Drink this. It will warm you up," Nora said, handing Betty the cup of hot tea. She took the blanket from her shoulders and threw it over top of the other blankets on the bed.

"I saw this little guy the first day I arrived here," Betty told Nora as she blew on the tea. "He came out from under the old boathouse down by the water and ran up to the trash cans looking for food. He's no more than a pup, maybe six months old, I would guess."

"A stray, you think?"

"Most definitely. I tried to give him food, but he was shy and ran off. He seems like a different dog now. Very strange," Betty said, taking a tentative sip and looking at the dog. Whatever delirium she had been suffering seemed to be fading.

"He ran off when I first saw him, too, but not before he gave Alistair a piece of his mind," Nora said, thinking about the moment and giggling.

"Are you going to keep him? He seems rather attached to you," Betty observed.

"I can't. I'll be headed back to America in just a few days."

"Maybe you can get that fellow of yours to take him. I do, however, think he needs a proper name," Betty said, the tea bringing some color back into her cheeks. Nora's cheeks also blossomed with a bit of color at the mention of Betty thinking Alistair was her fellow.

"Hmm, what do you think about Lochland? Seeing how he came from the boathouse," Nora suggested.

"I love it, and it suits him."

The dog wagged his tail, causing the bed to shake and Betty to nearly spill her tea.

"It's so cold in here, I fear my lungs may be frozen," she said with a shiver and a cough. The color that had sprung back into her cheeks was fading, and her face began looking ashen once again. She handed Nora the mug and laid her head on the pillow.

"Are you hungry, Betty? It must have been a while since you last ate?" Nora asked.

"I'm fine just now. I think I'll take a nap. I am still feeling a bit out of sorts."

"Okay, you rest up. I am going to heat up some more tea and make you something to eat for later when you get up." Betty's eyes closed, and Nora left the room. The dog jumped down from the bed and followed her out into the kitchen.

"You hungry, little guy?"

The dog wagged his tail and came to sit at her feet. Nora rummaged through the cupboard and found a can of soup for Betty, along with a box of cornflakes and a tin of canned chicken for the dog. She grabbed a bowl from the counter, mixed the cornflakes and chicken together, then set it down for the dog before starting to heat up the soup for Betty.

Lochland dove into the bowl of food, devouring it quickly. She had never seen a dog eat so fast. Within a minute the bowl had been licked clean.

"I guess you were hungry," she said, reaching down and scratching behind his soft ears.

Just as she was tossing the empty tin into the trash can, Alistair returned, bringing in a cold gust of air, along with a worried look on his face.

Chapter Forty-Five

SNOWED IN

Shutting the door behind him, Alistair kicked off his boots, worry creasing his brow.

"What did they say?" Nora asked anxiously.

"Bad news. Because of the heavy winds and the cold temperatures, a ten-foot snowdrift is blocking the road to the loch. Medical services can't get here, and neither can the lettings agency to deliver more wood. They said it might be two days before they can get a machine up here to move it all."

"What do we do?" Nora asked, panic rising in her throat.

"First off, we need to get this place heated and move Betty onto the sofa. I am going to get this fire really cranking, and you search for some paracetamol. We need to try to get her fever down."

Nora went to look for the medicine. She figured that all

the rentals had the same medical kit. Theirs had aspirin, which Alistair had taken for his hangover.

After a brief search, she found the medic kit in the mirrored cabinet in the bathroom. Inside, she found aspirin but no other medicine. The aspirin would work for now, but it wouldn't last long, and soon they would need more if her fever persisted.

"Found some aspirin," Nora said, coming back to see that Alistair had gotten the fire blazing. "There are only two pills left, and they won't last more than a few hours. I wonder if the people in the other three cottages might have more?"

"Well, we won't get a chance to ask them because the letting agency mentioned that everyone else left early because of the storm. Didn't want to get stuck here. Smart."

"Well, at least we can take their wood."

He lifted a log with the iron poker, setting its edge on another and then looked at Nora.

"I already checked. This is all I found," he said, pointing to five logs resting in the round ring next to the fireplace. "There was a wood delivery scheduled for today but because of the roads, they can't get here, and without power, the oil furnaces in the cabins won't work."

"What are we going to do? If the roads are blocked, the power won't be back on, either. We're going to freeze to death," Nora said in a panic.

"No, we aren't. We'll give Betty the medicine and make sure this fire stays going, and then we'll go find some wood. There is a small wooded area behind the cottage."

"You're kidding, right? There's two feet of snow out there. It's going to be impossible."

"I thought you were from Vermont?" he said with a raise of his eyebrow. "You are way more used to this kind of snow than me. We don't normally get battered like this."

Nora rolled her eyes at him as she poured the soup into a bowl and then walked into the bedroom with the food and medicine. She sat on Betty's bedside and touched her shoulder gently.

"Betty, I have something for that fever and some soup to warm you up. I need you to sit up to take it," Nora said softly.

Betty opened her eyes slowly and propped herself up, taking the two tiny white pills and washing them down with the cold tea. Nora pulled the small nightstand closer to the bed and placed the bowl of soup on it.

"Try to eat a bit of soup. I'm going to make you a bed on the sofa next to the fire."

"No, with all these blankets and a fire going, I'll be fine," Betty said, sitting up and sipping on soup.

"I'm not sure that's a good idea. This room will take a while to warm up, and Alistair and I need to go out and search for some firewood."

"Don't you worry. I'll be just fine. Plus, that sofa is as hard as a rock," Betty protested.

"Are you sure?"

"Yes, now go," Betty said, waving her hand in a shooing motion.

Nora pulled the blankets up around Betty. "We'll be back soon," she said as she stepped out of the bedroom. Alistair was by the fire that was now raging in the stone hearth, quickly dispersing the chill in the room.

"She doesn't want to come out to the sofa. Said it's hard as a rock. She is eating, and the color is back in her cheeks," Nora announced as she came to stand next to him.

"As long as the fire burns steadily, it should warm the back area fairly quickly. The cabin isn't very large, and this fireplace should be able to warm the entire place without any trouble," Alistair reassured her.

"As long as you think it will stay burning until we get back."

"It will be hours before this even dies down a little. It's fully stocked. You ready?" he asked, walking away from the fire and opening the door.

Nora followed Alistair into the bitter winter air, Lochland close behind her. They ventured toward the sloping mountain, thick with pine trees and laced with danger.

Chapter Forty-Six

EYES OF EARTH AND SKY

Gathering an axe and a wood sled from the cottage, Nora and Alistair strolled away from the loch and toward the woodland, Lochland following close behind. As Nora looked up the long sloping hill toward the dark patch of thick evergreens, a sinking feeling that gave way to a pang of anxiety washed over her. The snow had begun falling heavily again, and Nora wondered for a brief moment if she, too, was controlling the weather, like Cora had in the book. The unsettling thought was followed by a burst of biting cold wind that swept up the valley toward them, solidifying the idea in her mind. The small field behind the cabins came into view, and amidst the snow, they encountered an elderly woman, hunched over examining something in her hands.

"What's that woman doing out here in this cold?" Nora asked Alistair under her breath.

"No idea. She must be from one of the neighboring properties. We should make sure she is okay," he said, confusion creasing his brow.

The woman was wrapped in a wool cape the color of freshly tilled earth, her gray hair peeking out from beneath a green knit cap. She was plucking withered frozen flowers from the ground, shaking off the snow, then placing them in a wicker basket hanging from her arm.

Alistair gave Nora a skeptical look as they approached. *Why be out in this kind of weather collecting dead flowers?* Nora wondered as she watched her diligently fill her basket.

"Hello," Alistair greeted as they approached.

"Hello, fine day for a foraging," the old woman replied, looking up from her task.

"Aye," Alistair responded, his tone lacking conviction. "Are you okay?" he inquired.

"Yes, of course. There is no better time to collect these than after the first heavy snow of the year. They become naturally preserved, and the cold has sent all the bugs off to other places to find warmth and shelter," she said, dusting off the snow from a large flower head.

At first, the idea seemed crazy to Nora, but then she remembered some of the weird things her grandmother used to do, like collecting rainwater in a bucket to wash her hair. She said it was an old beauty trick her mother taught her. Even though they seemed strange today, those kinds of things had been common practice back in the day. Maybe this was the case here as well. Some of the old ways that had been passed down were still alive and thriving within this old woman.

"This storm doesn't seem to be abating. Maybe you should head back before it gets any worse," Alistair suggested, gently hinting she should head home.

"Oh, nae bother, I'll be fine. I've been out in much worse than this," the old woman remarked, plucking another cluster from the ground. Breaking off a few flower heads, she approached Nora. "Later, for tea. You may need it," she said before returning to her duties. The woman's white curly hair hung low over her forehead, obscuring her eyes, yet Nora caught a glimpse of what she thought was one bright blue and one brown, but the woman looked away too quickly for a closer inspection. She wondered if her mind was playing tricks on her. She had never seen anyone with two different colored eyes, and now in the past five days, she had come across two people and a dog with the very same condition. *Very odd*, she thought.

"Thank you. Do you live around here?" Nora asked, politely taking the flowers and tucking them into the oversized pocket of her jacket. Alistair shot her a quizzical look.

"Aye, for a very, very long time."

"You don't happen to know who this dog belongs to, do you?" Nora said, looking down at Lochland.

"Yes, I do," she said, pausing for a long moment, then continued. "You, I believe." She looked at Nora with her mismatched eyes.

Nora smiled and nodded. That wasn't the answer she had been hoping for.

"You have a good day and get yourself back home safely," Alistair said, moving past the old woman, who had resumed her foraging, paying them no mind.

"Well, that was a bit strange," he remarked once they were out of earshot.

"Yes, very," Nora agreed, glancing back at the woman. There was something oddly familiar about her; a sense of déjà vu nagged at the corners of Nora's mind, as if they had crossed paths before, but that couldn't be possible.

The path grew steeper as they ascended the sloping hill toward the looming mountain ahead. Nora had to carry Lochland a few times through the deeper drifts. The snow slowed their progress, each step a struggle against the relentless winds that hit them from all sides. As the snowfall intensified, obscuring their view of the mountain's peak, they reached the towering pine trees that marked the edge of the forest. Alistair halted, scanning their surroundings for a suitable spot to gather firewood.

"I see a fallen tree over this way. Why don't you gather as many small sticks as you can for kindling?" he called out, his voice barely audible over the howling wind that swept along the ridgeline.

Nora entered the wooded area where the trees' canopy had shielded the ground from heavy snowfall. Lochland sniffed around the base of a tree, chasing a squirrel that had just scurried away. Bending down, she picked up a large stick and broke it into smaller sections, carried the pieces back, and deposited them in the sled. As she ventured farther into the thicket, she heard the echoing sounds of Alistair's axe cutting wood to her left and Lockland's rustling in pursuit of the squirrel to her right.

Despite the biting cold seeping through her mittens and jeans, Nora pressed on, gathering as many sticks as she could find. With each trip back to the sled, she felt a warmth spreading through her body, yet she remained cold from the biting winds.

Just as she dropped off another load of sticks, Alistair appeared, carving a path through the snow with a pile of logs in his arms. Nora's heart skipped at the sight of him, his cheeks flushed with exertion and a glint of sweat on his forehead. He placed the wood into the sled before wiping his brow and turning to her.

"I have about three more armfuls to bring back. I see you've had success as well," he said, pointing at the large cluster of sticks she had stacked up in the sled.

"There's more if you think we need it," Nora replied.

"It definitely won't hurt. Gather what you can. We might have to make a couple of trips up here. Let's stack whatever we can't fit in the sled under this pine. It should keep it somewhat dry until we can come back later," Alistair suggested before pulling his hat back on and heading back up the path to resume chopping wood.

Nora ventured back onto the small path she had made when Lockland came running up to her with a stick in his mouth, dropping it at her feet. She smiled and picked it up, giving it a good toss into the woods. He turned tail and sprinted after it, coming back a moment later to drop it at her feet again.

"I see you like to fetch," she said with a smile, giving the stick a harder throw deeper into the woods. A minute later, he came running back through the thick underbrush and dropped the stick at her feet again.

"Okay, but this is the last time," she said, throwing the stick as hard as she could. Lochland dashed out of sight into the undergrowth. Nora waited, but he didn't return. A worried ache grew in her belly, and she followed his footprints into the dense patch of woods.

There was no point in calling his name since he wouldn't know it yet, so she continued to follow his tracks instead. She traveled farther into the thicket, making sure to keep her bearings as this part of the forest was much denser than the rest. Stuart's warning about people straying and becoming lost kept her on high alert.

Ducking and moving aside small saplings, she continued forward in the direction he had gone. Rustling in the trees ahead caught her attention, and she followed the sound, along with his prints until she discovered Lochland sitting with a branch in his mouth. But it wasn't the stick she had thrown him; this one was full of berries.

"What are you doing, silly dog?" she said, and he looked up at her with his mysterious eyes of blue and brown. He leaped toward her and dropped the stick adorned with late fall berries at her feet. Nora smiled. "That's not the stick I threw. Where did you get this?" she said, picking up the small branch.

Curious to find where he had gotten the stick, she followed the little dog's trail deeper into the woods until it stopped. When she looked up, she saw a tree laden with dried clusters of reddish berries, hanging like frozen jewels in the frosty air.

She recognized the tree as the same one from the photo album. She walked over, pulled off a cluster of berries, inspected them closely, and tucked them into her pocket. She wasn't sure why she did it, but something deep within was guiding her.

Suddenly the wind picked up and whistled through the trees. There was something odd about the sound, almost musical. She stood still and listened intently in the direction of the wind. She caught the sound of a melody in the air—a soft, beautiful voice. Was it the woman on the hillside singing, her song echoing up the mountainside? No, the voice was coming from deeper in the forest, in the opposite direction. *Who would be up here in this kind of weather?* she thought. Then she remembered why Alistair and she were here in the first place and thought maybe someone else was up here also looking for wood.

"Hello?" she called out, listening for a reply, but none came. Just the sweet notes of the song upon the wind was all she could hear. She strained her ears to listen, to make out the words float-ing in the frosty breeze. Lochland let out a low growl, interrupting the song and hindering her ability to discern the words.

"Lochland, shh," Nora whispered as the haunting song car-ried back to her on the wind. Lochland began barking fearfully, as if he were warning her of impending danger. Then the forest took on an eerie unnatural darkness. A sense of foreboding washed over her. Something felt wrong. She strained to listen once more, but this time the wind had calmed, and the forest had fallen silent. No rustling leaves, no birds, no woodland creatures—just an unsettling stillness.

Lochland remained on high alert, and then she heard it again—the sweet lullaby carried by the wind, but this time it sounded broken and jumbled, and the hairs on the back of her neck rose. When she turned to head back to the clearing, she was disoriented and unsure of the right direction. The thick falling snow had all but covered her footprints.

Her heart raced, and panic bubbled up as a primal fear set-tled deep within her belly. Somehow she instinctively knew that whoever or whatever was singing was not to be trifled with. Trying to quell her rising anxiety, she broke into a run, her feet drag-ging in the deepening snow, desperate to escape the wooded area. Lochland kept pace, the wind carrying the distorted song once more. Devoid of its former sweetness, the tune sounded sharp and shrill, almost ghostly. Glancing over her shoulder, Nora felt a darkness approaching, though nothing was there. As she turned, her foot caught in the hidden roots of a tree, and she fell hard to the ground, her ankle twisting at an odd angle.

Nora screamed in pain, but her sharp cry seemed swallowed by the vastness of the woods. Lochland, alarmed by her distress, turned and ran to her side. Frightened and desperate to escape,

Nora attempted to stand, but her injured ankle gave way, and she collapsed back to the icy snow. Lochland whimpered before letting out a loud bark and darting off into the thicket, leaving her alone and vulnerable in the biting cold.

Chapter Forty-Seven

SONG ON THE WIND

Nora surveyed her surroundings, the gravity of her situation sinking in. The heavy snowfall had buried her tracks, making it nearly impossible for Alistair to trace her path. She had no idea how deep she had wandered into the woods, and with dusk approaching, the likelihood of him finding her was growing slimmer by the minute.

The icy unforgiving air seemed to pierce through her layers of clothing, and she zipped her jacket all the way up as she sat on the frozen ground. She looked back over her shoulder as the song seemed to be drawing closer. Within moments, the melody became so close she was able to make out a few stray words, but they were sharper and more shrill than before.

"Alistair," she called out, stricken with panic. She listened for a reply but none came. The only sound was the song, now cutting vigorously through the wind.

"Alistair!" she yelled again as she jammed her fingers into her ears to block out the awful melody.

Once serene in its wintry beauty, her surroundings now felt ominous and threatening, especially with the haunting realization that Cora had injured her leg in a similar fashion. Nora hadn't finished reading the chapter and had no idea what might lay ahead. Colin had believed the book to be cursed—what if she had cursed herself by reading it? Each shallow breath she took struggled to fill her lungs, leaving her gasping for air as panic tightened around her chest. A disorienting dizziness swept over her, making the world tilt at odd angles. The energy within her surged, pulsing inside her like violent waves in a stormy sea. She opened her mouth to scream for Alistair again but couldn't find her voice. Nothing but puffy gasps escaped from her lips.

Nora's panic had taken a different form this time. Unlike the crushing weight of the outside world she had experienced the night before, this felt like an intense energy that surged within her, as if she were about to combust.

Instinctually she pulled her hands free of the mittens and wiggled her fingers through the snow to touch the frozen ground below. As her fingertips met the frigid earth, she felt the energy within her race down her arms and into her hands, escaping into the cold forest floor. A sudden rumble radiated from below, followed by a thunderous crack that reverberated through the frozen landscape. The snow that clung to the branches of the trees above came raining down in large clumps, along with loose branches, pinecones, and acorns.

The world hung still; her heart returned to a normal pace, and her breathing slowed to a steady rhythm. The song was gone, replaced with a gentle wind blowing among the trees. The fear that had gripped her just moments ago seemed to have vanished into the ground through the tips of her fingers.

Just then, Lochland came bounding up the snowy path, Alistair in tow. Concern tightening his face, Alistair rushed toward her, his limp giving way as he moved faster. Relief washed over her at the sight of him.

"What the hell was that?" she heard him say before he arrived in front of her. His eyes darted around, trying to figure out what had just happened.

Nora, wide-eyed, met his gaze but remained silent. Had she somehow caused the earth to quake? Had she channeled all her pain and panic into the ground?

"Are you okay? What happened?" he asked as he crouched beside her.

"I was running and tripped. I hurt my ankle pretty bad. I'm not sure I can walk on it," Nora replied.

"Running from what?"

Nora was unsure of what to tell him, what had she been running from? She didn't know herself.

"The weird singing in the woods. Didn't you hear it?" she asked.

"No. The only thing I heard was the loud crack from the ground. Must have been the frost shifting or something. You must have heard it?"

"Yes, but it wasn't the crack that scared me, it was the creepy melody, like a distorted children's song," she told him.

"Probably just the wind in the trees. It can sound musical at times. Let me look," he said, pulling up her pant leg and examining her ankle. "It looks okay, no bruising or swelling yet. Does this hurt?" He lifted her foot and began to rotate it.

"Ouch!" she cried out as he moved it to the right.

"Can you put any pressure on it at all?" Alistair asked, standing back up and extending his hand to help her give it a try. She took his hand and was surprised to find that the fear of whatever had been lurking in the woods had been dispelled by his touch. She felt safe with him. Hopping up onto her good leg, she slowly put pressure on the injured one.

"God, no. I can't," she said, pulling her foot away from the ground and trying to balance while holding onto him. The pain radiated up her ankle into her leg, leaving a dull throbbing ache.

"Okay, I am going to take the wood down and come back to get you. Is that okay?" he asked, his eyes reflecting concern. Nora looked back over her shoulder toward the woods where the mysterious music had come from, shuddering at the thought of being left alone in the creepy forest.

"I think I can make it over to the clearing with your help," she insisted, not wanting to be left in the woods, even for a short length of time.

"If you think you can make it. If not, I'll be right back with the sled to pull you," he said as Lochland gave her hand a comforting lick.

"I think this one can take care of you while I'm gone," Alistair remarked, looking down at Lochland. "I heard you scream, but if it hadn't been for this little guy, it would have taken me a lot longer to find you." He extended his hand for the dog to sniff. Lochland, in turn, stretched his neck out and sniffed his gloved hand, then stepped closer, allowing Alistair to pet him for the first time. He smiled down at the dog, obviously happy that he was finally warming up to him.

"He's a good boy," Nora agreed, smiling at the two getting along.

Alistair assisted Nora to the clearing at the top of the hill. The sky was painted in a mix of pinks and oranges that echoed back in the water of the loch below.

"Oh, my God, it's gorgeous," she exclaimed, marveling at the picturesque view of the loch nestled into the valley.

"Then it will be the perfect place for you to wait for me," Alistair said, guiding her to a large rock on the edge of the hillside. "I'm going to get this wood down to the cottage and will be right back to get you."

"Okay," Nora said.

He nodded and then headed down the sloping hill back to the cottage. She watched him as he walked down the path, the weight of the wood-laden sled pulling ahead of him with each step. Lochland sat attentively next to her, the snow falling softly as the daylight began to dim. Despite the beauty she looked out upon, part of her was still on high alert. Whatever had been singing in the forest surely was still there, only yards away. The thought sent a shiver down her spine as she watched Alistair turn into a tiny speck at the bottom of the long sloping hill.

A sharp sound of a stick breaking to her left made her jump, and she turned quickly toward it. As she craned her head toward the edge of the forest, fear quickened her heart once again. A large stag stepped into the clearing from the woods. Nora froze, and Lochland, catching sight of the majestic creature, sprinted toward it.

"Lochland, no!" Nora called out to the dog, fearful he might get hurt by the massive deer. Oddly, the animal did not turn and run. Instead, it simply stood still as the little dog approached, wagging his tail. The stag bent down and ran its snout over the top of Lochland's head in a friendly greeting. Nora watched the unexpected interaction in complete awe.

The stag's eyes seemed strangely human-like. Nora thought back to the book on Highland folklore, to the chapter about the

Cailleach. Didn't it say the Cailleach sometimes changed into a hare or a stag? She believed anything was possible at this point, especially with the odd way the deer was acting. It lifted its head, locking eyes with Nora; something familiar in its gaze held her attention. Bits and pieces of memories came rushing back, but none of it made sense to Nora, as they were not hers. She saw an icy lake, a ship on a stormy ocean, and lastly, a frozen river. The images flickered in her mind like an old black-and-white film, giving her quick glances at the winter scenes and leaving her with a pit deep within her stomach.

The stag bowed toward her, lifted its head, and sprinted back into the forest, leaving Nora and Lochland atop the hill, looking over the valley below, alone once again.

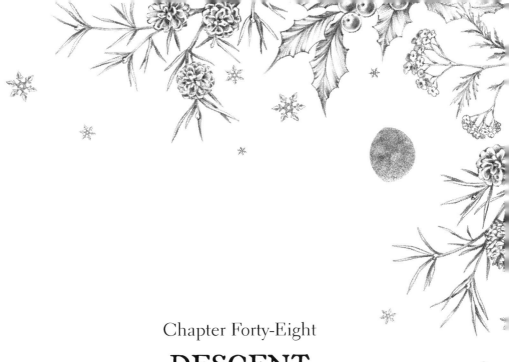

Chapter Forty-Eight
DESCENT

As Nora awaited Alistair's return, her mind raced with all the strange events that had unfolded since she arrived in Scotland. She had left her comfortable, predictable home in Vermont less than a week ago, but it felt more like a lifetime. Something had shifted within her, though she couldn't quite grasp what it was. She knew it was there, stirring just beneath the surface, tantalizingly out of reach.

She thought back to the letter Colin had written Marjorie about the book and the curse attached to it. The further she read, the more unusual things became. The real-life events that paralleled the book could have been dismissed as coincidences at first, but then there was the dream, the fire, the odd flashes of memory, and the earthquake, which made her question everything.

She glanced back over her shoulder toward the forest. Had she actually caused the ground to shake, or was that merely another peculiar coincidence? She couldn't ignore that all these bizarre occurrences began after she bought that book; perhaps it really was cursed.

As the sun dipped below the mountain behind her, cloaking the world in the first layer of twilight, the cold grew more intense. The chill from the setting sun pierced through her clothing, prompting Nora to pull her arms in close, trying to conserve warmth. Lochland felt the biting air as well and jumped onto her lap, curling up to help keep them both warm.

After a little more than a half hour, Alistair returned. Lochland emitted a low growl as he approached pulling two empty sleds behind him. "Hey now, I thought we were friends," he joked with the dog. "How's your ankle?" he asked, slightly winded, as he stopped beside Nora.

She attempted to rotate her foot, but the movement caused her to wince. "I'm afraid it's not much better."

"No worries. I will get you down this hill one way or another. One of the other cabins had another sled. We'll use this one to get you down the hill and the other for extra wood. A few more big pieces and we'll have enough for our cottage and Betty's cabin until morning," Alistair explained, his breath visible in the chilly air.

He made his way back to the pine tree to load the extra wood into the second sled. The sky grew darker, and another layer of twilight descended swiftly, leaving Nora with an unsettling feeling. She glanced over her shoulder into the woods, a deep unease settling heavily within her. Whatever lay hidden within those trees stirred a deep sense of foreboding within her.

"Okay, wood is strapped and loaded. Let's pray it makes it

without going off course," Alistair announced as he positioned the sled on the edge of the hill, setting it in the path he had cleared with the previous load of wood. Teetering the sled on the brink, he gave it a gentle push and held his breath until it slid perfectly to the field just above the cottage, slowing gently to a stop.

"Now our turn," he said, pulling their sled to the edge of the hill. With care, he helped Nora off the rock and into the sled, ensuring her injured foot stayed clear of the sled's edge. Settling in behind her, he encircled her with his arms. Nora's heart raced at their closeness, a familiar sensation from the night he kissed her, but now she sensed something deeper, a connection that was more than mere passion, evoking a rapid heartbeat calling out for something forgotten.

"Grab hold of the strings," he instructed, drawing her back from her thoughts.

"I know how to do this, from Vermont. Remember?" she quipped, taking hold of the strings. Alistair smiled and then maneuvered his leg out of the sled, kicking into the snow to propel them forward toward the edge.

As they perched at the edge, ready to descend, Nora felt a rush of excitement and fear, mirroring how she felt currently in her life. When the sled finally tipped over the edge and began its descent, Alistair held her tightly, sheltering her as they raced down the mountain, Lochland bounding behind them. The wispy snow kicked back in their faces, the wind reddening their cheeks and noses. As they sped down the hill, Nora giggled and caught a wide smile on Alistair's face when she glanced back at him. She felt like a child—carefree and present. She wished she could bottle up that feeling and take sips whenever life became challenging.

As they slowed down and came to a stop near the bottom of the field, Lochland caught up and ran circles around them, as if pleading to do it again. Alistair stood and walked to the front of the sled, grabbing the rope. "My lady," he said, bowing before pulling her toward the cottage.

"Faster, my gallant steed! Your lady's toes are in need of warmth and her belly food," she joked in a bad English accent.

He turned, raising his eyebrows and gave her a playful smirk. As if they had known each other far longer than the few days they had spent in the cottage, a newfound familiarity intermingled between them. Nora had tried to avoid him at first, but now she felt drawn to him and found herself enjoying his company. She felt a sense of trust with him and yearned to share all the strange events that had unfolded since she acquired the little red book. Yet, she feared he might think her mad, and she wasn't ready to take that chance just yet.

By the time Alistair had helped her into the cottage, twilight had given way to the night's embrace. He assisted her to the sofa and then retrieved the candles from the kitchen island.

"I'm gonna stack the firewood under the eaves in the back, then head over to check on Betty," he said, lighting the candles and placing them on the coffee table in front of her. "Do you need anything before I go?"

"No, I'm fine, but you might want to grab the flashlight on my nightstand," she suggested.

"Aye," he acknowledged.

Nora watched him ascend the stairs and return with the flashlight before heading out into the chilly night air. Once he was gone, she turned her focus back to the little red book resting before her. A sense of dread fell over her. This thing seemed more predictable than her daily horoscope. If the book truly was cursed and linked her to Cora somehow, she needed to know what came next, to finish it so she might understand the curse better and what it entailed.

Picking up the little red book, Nora strained to make out the words in the candlelight. She felt certain that what lay ahead in the story wouldn't be as happy and joyous as the previous chapter. Nora hesitated, wondering what that could mean for her own future.

Chapter Forty-Nine

ICY ILLUSIONS

The following morning greeted me with the biting cold of winter, seeping into my bones. Sitting up, I found myself alone within the ancient stone walls of the ruin, the fire reduced to mere smoldering embers. Wrapping the blanket tightly around my shoulders, I gingerly rose, my injured ankle protesting with every movement. I limped my way to the doorway, pushing aside the pine boughs to behold the world beyond, bathed in the soft amber glow of the rising sun.

The horse stood tethered to the post, but James was absent. A surge of panic gripped me, prompting me to step out into the deep snow that had accumulated overnight. I found a solitary set of footprints leading away from the loch to a thicket of trees atop a small hill overlooking the ruin. James was nowhere in sight. I turned back toward the ruin, the chill of the snow creeping into my boots, numbing my toes.

Determined to ward off the cold, I gathered the last remnants of kindling beneath the pine boughs and placed them atop the pile of smoldering embers, but the logs did not catch fire. I bent down, and as if by instinct, grabbed the end of one of the branches. I felt an energy surge from my core down my arm to the tips of my fingers. A sudden burst of light flashed, and the flames flickered back to life. It seemed my powers went beyond controlling the weather, I mused to myself as I hovered over the flames, allowing their warmth to thaw my chilled hands and feet. The comforting embrace of the fire sparked memories of my night spent with James, warming me from within even as the frigid winter cold still held me in its grip.

I blushed at the memory of our bodies entwined, reliving the sheer delight of moments we had shared. The magic of the night had woven our souls together, filling my heart to the brim with love so profound it threatened to overwhelm me. I was lost in reverie; James's return interrupted my thoughts when he entered the ruin, a rabbit in hand.

"Breakfast," he declared, a warm smile gracing his features.

"How?" I inquired, genuinely surprised at his successful catch.

"Malcolm and I used to hunt these parts, remember?" he explained, showcasing his skills as he skinned and dressed the rabbit. Fashioning a stand with two sticks, he roasted the rabbit over the fire. As he worked silently, there was an ease between us, as if we had always been and knew we would always be together.

"Thank you for tending the fire while I was gone. I was trying to conserve what little wood we had left for cooking," he said gratefully, flashing me a smile. A small opening in the wall of the ruin overlooked the loch, an old window, perhaps, fallen in and destroyed by time. I walked over and looked out. A low mist hovered just above the water's edge.

"Strange thing to see this time of year, the mist," James said, following my gaze out the small opening. The mist, made more otherworldly by the patchy morning light, reminded me of a story Gran used to tell me.

"Did your gran ever tell you stories about creatures that roamed the waters of lochs like this?" I asked James as I looked out toward the frozen water.

"I hate to admit it, but I was a scared child, so my mother forbade stories at bedtime because I would refuse to go to bed if I got even a tiny bit frightened. But of course, I know most of them now. I bet your gran had some grand stories of creatures to tell," he said, an endearing boyish grin stretching across his face.

"Yes, Gran is quite a good storyteller. Probably a good thing she wasn't your gran because you would have never slept again," I teased. "The loch this morning reminds me of a tale she told me years ago about a kelpie that came out of the misty waters and could shapeshift, turning into a beautiful woman or a prized deer, luring men and children to their deaths in the waters of the loch. She said the most malevolent ones picked lochs far away from villages and along paths that travelers often used," I told him, giving myself a bit of a shiver at the idea.

"Yes, Malcolm has told me similar tales. Do you believe in such things?" he asked as he cut off a piece of rabbit and fashioned it on a stick for me.

I sat for a long moment, thinking. I had never been sure I believed in such things but now that I myself had powers, all those tales became more of a possibility. I could not share this with him, however, as he might think me a witch or some kind of evil creature. The thought of keeping this secret from James pulled at my conscience and soured my mood.

"I think most tales start in truth," I told him as I took a bite of the rabbit. He smiled and nodded, looking out onto the frosty mist lingering on the loch below.

After we finished our breakfast, James packed our belongings and helped me onto the horse. As we rode up the path, I glanced back at the old stone ruin fondly, cherishing the memories it now held within its ancient walls.

The ride down the sloping hillside was slow, and James was quiet.

He hadn't spoken a word since we left the ruin, and a pit began to form in the base of my belly. Had I said or done something wrong? I played over the events of the morning in my head. Had it been the story of the kelpie? Had I said something that led him to be suspicious of me? What changed? Perhaps he regretted the passion we had shared, the reality of the gap in our social standing taking its place?

James suddenly slowed the horse to a stop and jumped down from its back.

"Is everything okay?" I asked as he turned to face me. James walked over and took my hand in his, bestowing a gentle kiss upon it. Startled by his sudden change in demeanor, I said, "What are you doing? I thought you were cross with me?"

He smiled. "Cora Douglas, I could never be cross with you. I'm sorry for my silence. Something has been weighing heavily on my mind since this morning."

"What?" I inquired, looking down at him from atop the horse, nervousness tightening my core.

"I care not for my father's wishes or societal constraints. I love you and want to be the man who herds your sheep and fathers your children. I want to buy a printing press and publish every book or poem you write. Society's judgments be damned," he declared, kissing my hand once more.

"James, what are you suggesting?" I inquired, taken aback by his sudden proposal.

"For you to be my wife. My father insists on my choosing a bride, and I choose you."

I sat there stunned, not knowing what to say or how to feel about this quick proposal even though I wanted to say yes more than anything.

"James, I am a woman of no standing; your father would disown you if you were to marry someone like me. I am not fit to be a duchess. I have not a noble name or a dowry to speak of," I said, my words tinged with sadness.

He pulled me down from the horse and held me in his arms, kissing me so passionately that I felt if I died at that moment, I would die the happiest I had ever been. "I care not for titles or wealth; I would gladly renounce it all for you, Cora," he whispered to me between kisses. I fell into his embrace, and if we had not been traveling in the depths of winter, love would have bloomed once more there on the hill overlooking Loch Ness.

I pulled away breathlessly, and he cupped my face in his hands.

"Yes, a million times yes," I said. He drew me back into a kiss, then lifted me, spinning me around in the cold, wintry air before setting me back atop the horse.

"Now, let us return this to your gran, and I shall share the news with my father," he declared, jumping onto the horse and guiding us back onto the path. The path led us toward the edge of the loch before weaving back into the thicket of the forest where I had lost my horse the prior day. As we neared the loch, James slowed the horse and came to a complete halt once again.

"Do you see that?" he said, pointing to a small figure on the thin ice covering the loch. I squinted against the brightness of the snow and the emerging sun. Once my eyes adjusted, I saw what he was pointing at — a small girl, no more than Alice's age, standing as if frozen on the ice. A jolt of fear raced through me as the dream I had at the Turners came rushing back.

"It's a child. She'll drown if she falls through," I said, not taking my eyes off the little one.

James called out to her, "It's not safe out there! Come back to shore."

The girl remained motionless. "Come back to shore," he called out again, louder this time, yet the girl did not hear him.

James looked at me, determination in his eyes. "We can't just ride on. We need to get her off that ice," he said, jumping down from the horse and tying it to a small sapling near the loch's edge. I nodded and watched as he took a slow, careful step out onto the ice, testing its strength.

"James, do you think it wise to go out there?" I called to him as a crack sounded out from the pressure of his foot.

"I'll be fine. We need to get her back toward the shore before the ice gives way. It's very thin. I will try to safely coax her back," James reassured me. As I watched him progress slowly to the girl, a sinking feeling came over me. Something was not right. Where had this child come from? There were no crofts in sight. Then, striking me like a bolt of lightning, the story Gran had told me of the kelpie came rushing back.

"James, no!" I screamed just as he reached the child. He turned back and looked at me, but it was too late. The child vanished at the very moment the ice gave way below his feet, and he plummeted into the depths of the frigid waters of Loch Ness. The fear in his eyes was the last thing I saw as he disappeared into its darkness.

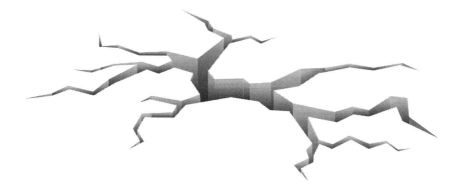

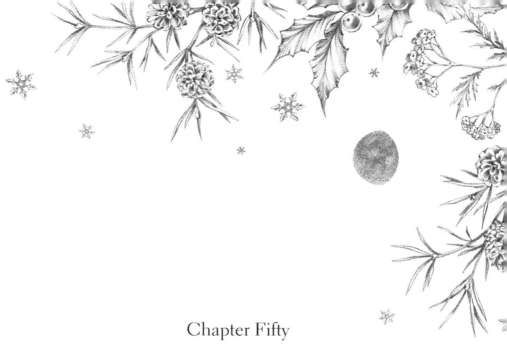

Chapter Fifty

SONG OF THE FAE

"No!" I screamed out, my voice echoing off the ice. I leaned forward and quickly untied the horse. With my hurt leg, there was no way I could walk out to where James had fallen through. But if I managed to get the horse to a safe point on the ice, I could dismount and crawl the rest of the way.

Without hesitation, I urged the horse toward the spot where James had gone beneath the ice. Wary of the icy surface, the horse pulled back, but I laid my hand on its neck and whispered words of comfort into its ear. It cautiously approached the hole where James had disappeared. Once we were closer yet still far enough back where the horse's weight would not break through, I dismounted, slipped off my bag, and crawled over the icy surface. I plunged my arms into the freezing water in a desperate attempt to find him.

"James!" I screamed, but the only response was my own voice echoing off the loch's frozen waters. The sting of a thousand needles pierced my skin before it succumbed to the numbing cold, but I pressed on in my frantic attempt to find James. Driving my arms deeper, my hands brushed against something warm and smooth. I tried to grasp it, but it proved too large for my hands to encircle. Startled, I withdrew my arms and moved away from the hole.

It was then that I saw it — the creature emerging from the depths. Its smooth scales glimmered in the sunlight like tiny green gems as its giant head broke the surface. It was not a kelpie but some other mystical creature of old, reminiscent of a dragon. I held back a scream as it surfaced, and there atop its large body was James. The horse, catching sight of the monstrous creature, bolted off the ice and down the trail toward the woodland, leaving me stranded.

Fear held me tightly in its grip as the creature perched in the water, delivering James to me. As the creature guided his body over to me on the ice, I grabbed him, pulling him close. Turning, the enormous creature looked at me one last time before disappearing back under the water.

I quickly pulled James away from the icy hole, only to find my worst fear realized. He was not breathing. His skin was gray, and his lips were a pale shade of blue. I screamed his name, pounding on his chest for him to wake, but he did not stir. I laid my head on his chest, hoping that I might hear the beating of his gentle heart, but it was as silent as a cold winter night. Tears streamed down my face as I sat there feeling utterly helpless, wishing that Gran were there to guide me. It was then I remembered her book resting in the satchel and I reached for it on the ice beside me. I flipped page after page until I found the spell I had been searching for: "Bringing one back from death's grip." I read the incantation aloud, "As death holds its grip fast, bring one back with this spell I cast. From behind the veil back to this realm, guide this vessel from its helm. From the darkness back to the light, aid this battle and win the fight."

Nothing happened. My eyes skimmed over the spell again, unable to understand what I was doing wrong. I knew I had magic within my blood, but I had no idea how to harness and use it to do my bidding. I repeated the verse again, pouring every ounce of energy I had into the words, but still his body lay cold next to me. Tears spilled from my eyes as I held him, his cold skin in harsh contrast against mine.

Just as I was about to recite the spell again, I was interrupted by music on the wind—a haunting melody that initially sounded like a lullaby. It grew louder, and I looked around, but there was no one in sight.

"Show yourself!" I yelled into the wind.

Just as quickly as the song had sounded, a woman appeared from nowhere, standing only feet from me. Young and beautiful, she wore clothing unsuited for the cold weather, a long flowing dress made of fine silk. Her long blonde hair was braided, with flowers woven through the cascading plait. I did not know if she was a goddess of old, a witch, or one of the Fae that wandered the land, and in that moment I did not care.

"Poor child, tell me of your woes?" she asked as if she did not see the body of my dead lover before me.

"My love has drowned in the loch. We had just found each other, and now I have lost him," I cried, tears streaming down my face and landing softly on the icy snow below me.

"Do not cry, child, for I can reunite you with him. All I need from you is that bracelet upon your wrist," she said in a voice as soft as silk.

I looked down at the shiny silver of Gran's bracelet peeking out from the cuff of my sleeve. Without hesitation, I pulled it from my wrist and handed it to the woman. Her smile widened as she took it, tucking it into a pocket of her dress. Bending down, she laid her hand on James's chest and looked over at me. "He loved you very deeply. I see many, many happy times you two will spend together," she said, smiling at me as if he were not lying there dead at her feet.

"Do you wish for your love to continue?" she asked, her gray eyes looking deep within me as if to find the answer without waiting for my reply.

"Yes," I said between my sobs.

She bent down, taking my hand in hers, and with her other, she grabbed James's cold, lifeless one. She closed her eyes, and I followed suit, and then she began to sing.

"In shadows of frost, love entwined,
A dance of souls, through time confined.
In each dance, a mirrored hue,
Yet frosty waters claim their due.
To shatter chains, to cease the waltz,
A secret dance when the moon proves false.
Seek within the heart's deep well,
A selfless step where shadows dwell.
When icy whispers bid you near,
A sacrifice, the path will clear.
Beneath the gaze of stars untold,
A choice to make, a tale unfolds.
Through whispered echoes, twenty-seven times four,
Forever love will bind once more."

The haunting melody lingered in the frigid air, a spectral echo of the mysterious woman's presence. I kept my eyes shut for a moment longer, praying that James would be alive and well once her ethereal song had woven the thread of life back to him. I pictured him waking up, as if from a long slumber, happy to see me and ready to continue on our journey back to the castle.

I opened my eyes and stared down at James, holding my breath as I waited for his eyes to flicker back to life, for his chest to rise and fall once again. The moments stretched on, and nothing happened. He lay cold and lifeless in my arms still.

"Why isn't he waking up?" I asked, looking up to where the woman had stood. But she was gone, and nothing but the wintry landscape stretched before me and James, still in death's grip. The reality of the situation crashed back with an unforgiving force, and I let go of the breath I was holding. James was untouched by the enchantment she had placed upon him.

The north wind, relentless and unforgiving, bit into my skin as if mocking the fleeting promise of our reunion. James lay still, his lifeless form stark against the white snow. I drew in another shaky breath, attempting to steady myself, as my world broke into pieces around me. The winds blew even fiercer now, carrying away the remnants of our shared dreams and leaving me utterly alone with nothing more than winter's harsh touch for comfort.

Chapter Fifty-One

FROZEN TEARS

As I cradled James's lifeless body upon my lap, I gently ran my hands through his hair, and silent tears flowed down my cheeks, landing on my dress, marking it with my sorrow. It dawned on me as I looked down upon my love: the woman who had offered her aid in exchange for the bracelet was a fairy, a trickster, who had played me for a fool. I feared I had made a treacherous bargain. In that desperate moment, I would have bartered anything to save James, even striking a deal with a fairy.

Gran's warnings echoed in my mind — tales of the cunning fae, who were skilled in weaving illusions and ensnaring desperate hearts. My new-found love for James and the future we envisioned together had clouded my judgment. The possibility that she might hold the key to his return drove me to make a bargain in haste.

With the landscape as the solitary witness to the tragic scene, I sat alone on the ice and began to sob uncontrollably. I had lost my love; his life vanished like a wisp of frost-kissed air. With my hurt ankle and no horse, I was likely to lose Gran, as well as myself. Even if Gran were still alive at this point, there was little chance I would be able to make it back in time for the potion to work. With little hope to fuel me, I lay freezing beside my love in the valley where we had pledged our love to one another. It would be a fitting end to our story, like Shakespeare's Romeo and Juliet.

In the numbing cold, my skirts froze to the ice, and my fingers grew numb. I clung to James, praying that the magic might still take effect. Maybe the spell the fairy had woven with her song just needed time. So, I waited, perched above the water of Loch Ness.

As I began to succumb to the encroaching cold, my senses dulled, and the sounds around me began to fade away. I felt like I was drifting off into a dream. Just as my eyes grew too heavy to keep open, the distant sound of hooves upon the frozen ground broke through the biting wind. At first, I thought it might be a figment of my imagination, a desperate attempt at manifesting help within the chilling silence that lay around me. The sound drew nearer, however, and I strained my ears.

Through the haze of sorrow and numbness, a shadowy figure emerged on horseback. Hooves crunched against the icy ground, creating a rhythmic melody that clashed with the mournful whispers of the north wind. As the silhouette drew closer, I faintly recognized the familiar form of the rider. The horse halted at the shoreline, its breath visible in the frigid air. The rider, his features obscured by a hood, dismounted and cautiously approached me on the ice.

"What has happened?" I heard a deep low voice say. The voice was familiar, but I was having a hard time placing it as the cold had caused my thinking to slow. I looked up to see the man remove his thick woolen hood and reveal himself. Standing there, shock spreading across his face, was Malcolm. I tried to speak but I had lost my voice to the cold that had nearly consumed me. I tried to sit up, but my body ached with protest.

"Whoa there. Take it slow, lassie," he said in a gentle voice as he bent down, scooped me up in his arms, and walked me back to his horse, which stood on the edge of the loch tied next to another, the horse that had been frightened in the woods the day prior.

Atop the horse's back, I teetered side to side, my frozen limbs not working properly to hold me steady. I watched with tear-stained eyes as Malcolm scooped up James's body and walked it back to the other horse. He laid him atop it and secured his body with ropes. Tears continued to fall from my eyes as if they were bottomless wells.

Malcolm mounted the horse upon which I sat, holding me securely with one arm as he steered us back toward his house. As I looked back at the horse carrying James's body, I caught sight of Malcolm's face. His stark eyes were full of pain, the pain of one who has lost a child, and the ache within me grew. In the aftermath of the storm, the journey back passed swiftly, the winds now a mere whisper against the quiet backdrop of our shared sorrow.

Upon our arrival in the late afternoon, Malcolm, his face marked with grief, aided me in dismounting the horse and guided me into the warmth of his home. Positioning me near the crackling fire, he handed me my bag and walked into the other room. In a grief-induced trance, I sat staring into the fire — a stark reminder of the warmth now extinguished in my life. I could hear the muted conversations between Malcolm and Addie in the adjacent kitchen.

"I found them in the middle of the loch. James was already gone, and Cora was half dead herself from the cold. Poor thing, eyes were near swollen shut from all the tears she had shed."

"No, not James!" I heard Addie cry out, her sobs filling the room. "How?" she asked once she had composed herself.

"It appears he fell through the ice on Loch Ness and drowned. However, I know not the particulars, for Cora has yet to speak a word,"

Malcolm replied. Just then little Alice came running in from the other room, curious to know what her parents were whispering about.

"Is James back, Mama?" little Alice asked, and the room fell silent.

"Oh, sweetheart, I'm sorry, no. Why don't you find your doll," her mother suggested.

"Put a kettle on. Once she is warmed up, she will need some tea and something to eat. Maybe then she will tell us what happened. I am not going to bring James's body back to the duke until I know," I heard him say just as little Alice came into the room to sit next to me by the fire, her doll held tightly in her tiny hands.

"Hello, there. Is James back?" she questioned me.

I swallowed hard, trying to push down another wave of tears that were threatening to spill forth.

"No, Alice. He is not," I said, my voice finally coming back to me even though it was hoarse and broken.

"Do you want to play dolls?" she asked, unperturbed by my disheveled appearance and the sorrow in my eyes.

"Maybe in a bit," I told her with a weak smile.

I sat there until the feeling in my feet and hands began to return, only to find a new kind of numbness starting to set in. My heart, so broken that each beat felt like shattered glass within my chest, now was dull and lacked much feeling at all. In that moment, I feared it might never feel the same again as I watched little Alice play.

"Cora, would you like some tea and bread?" Addie asked from the kitchen.

I got to my feet, my ankle still swollen and sore, yet the physical pain paled in comparison to what I was feeling in my heart. I limped my way to the old oak table and sat down. Addie brought over a cup of tea and a large slice of bread with a thick piece of cheese to the side. I sipped the tea, feeling the warmth chase down my throat into my belly, yet it did nothing to warm me. The chill of James's death still held me within its grip.

Malcolm came and sat at the table, poured himself a large cup of tea, and then asked me the question I was dreading. "Can you tell us what happened, love?"

I stared down into my cup of tea for a long time, trying to find the words. He may not believe my fanciful tale, yet I had to tell him. I sat quietly for a moment before I found my voice.

"We were on our way back after collecting what we needed for Gran. James rode down by the loch on the trail near its shoreline. Just before heading into the forest, we saw a child on the thin ice in the middle of the loch. He refused to leave her and jumped off the horse, venturing out onto the ice toward her," I said, my voice ragged and steeped in sadness. "Just as he reached her, she vanished, and he fell through the ice. I tried to get out to him, but I had injured my leg the day before, and I didn't make it to him in time. I managed to pull his body from the water but could not save him," I told them, tears running down my cheeks. I had decided to leave out the parts about the kelpie and the deal I had struck with the fairy as I had no idea how they might react to such a story.

"What happened to the girl?" Addie asked, her motherly concern deepening the lines on her forehead.

"I don't know. It was strange. She vanished just as he reached her, or maybe fell into the ice with James," I replied.

Malcolm looked at Addie with distress in his eyes, then turned to me. "There are kelpies in that loch, you know? I warned James many times while we hunted near there, but that boy only believed them to be tales told to scare children." I remained silent, but we shared an understanding of what had actually happened on the loch.

"Now, the duke will want to know what a hero his son was in his death, so we will tell him that he jumped in after the girl but sadly was unable to save her and himself. No need to mention the idea of kelpies to the duke, as this will all come as a shock to him as it is," Malcolm said, taking a sip from his cup of tea. "I know there was some urgency to your trip with James in getting medicine for your gran. I will take you back along with James's body as soon as you feel up to riding again."

"Malcolm, might I inquire as to why you came to the loch today?" I asked, my voice laden with sorrow.

"Last night, one of the horses returned, and I knew at once that something must have occurred. When the storm abated this morning, I resolved to bring the horse and seek you out, to ensure all was well. I am glad I did, or I fear that you might have met the same ill fate as James. I just wish I had come sooner," Malcolm explained, his voice heavy with regret.

I wished that Malcolm had not come, as I would have happily died with James on the loch, letting death's cold embrace strip me of my pain. Yet my life was not the one that hung in the balance; Gran needed me, and so for her, I pushed on.

Chapter Fifty-Two
CURSED LIVES

Upon my return to the castle, a whirlwind of events ensued. The news of James's untimely death swept through the corridors like wildfire, casting a veil of sorrow over the entire estate. I knew the moment when the dreadful news reached the duke and his lady, for the heart-wrenching cries of the duchess reverberated through the sturdy stone walls, echoing the anguish that seized us all.

I had little time to offer my condolences to the duke and duchess, for I needed to make it to Gran's chambers with the ingredients for the spell before it was too late. If I could not save her, the trip and James's death would have all been for naught. The grief thick in the air had all but consumed me, but I pushed on with the remedy tucked safely in my bag.

I limped into the room to find Gran lying motionless on the bed, and for a moment I thought the worst. Her skin was paler than before, and her eyes looked sunken and dark. Her chest rose and fell in raspy quick bursts, which despite the strain, was music to my ears. She somehow looked smaller than when I had left her. So much had changed in those three days that it seemed almost a lifetime ago. I wasted no time and quietly closed the door and took the book from my satchel, hiding it within the bed linens as I pulled the berries and water from my pack.

With trembling hands, I heated the water over the crackling flames of the hearth, adding the rowanberries, along with the original spell's ingredients, which I took from the small pouch I had hidden in my bag. I let them steep as I recited the ancient incantation: "Healing waters of the well, aid in helping break this spell. To wake thy from a forceful sleep, berries of rowan I do steep. To counteract a spell gone wrong, I call upon the Goddess's Song."

The final words of the incantation hung heavy in the air, their significance weighing upon my troubled mind. Memories of the fairy's twisted song echoed like a broken melody. A wave of nausea washed over me as I recalled the frightened look in James's eyes before he plunged into the icy waters and the desperate moments following his death.

I poured the mixture into a pewter cup, its heat radiating through the metal and searing my hands, jolting me from my despairing thoughts. The aroma of the rowanberries wafted through the room. Its bitter earthy scent filled the air, carrying with it the essence of magic. I completed the ritual, repeating the words of the spell as instructed twice more, before allowing the brew to cool. According to the book, the potion was to be applied to the forehead and wrists of the afflicted. Once awakened from their enchanted slumber, they were to consume the rest of the tea.

Once the tea had cooled to a tolerable temperature, I dipped a cloth into it and carefully applied the mixture to Gran's forehead and wrists. Then, with bated breath, I waited.

"This shall make you better," I whispered softly, reassuring both of us.

The minutes stretched into an agonizing wait, and doubt began to creep in. Gran remained still, her slumber unbroken. What if the spell had failed? Had I come back only moments too late? Did I lack the magic necessary to save Gran's life, just as I had failed to save James's? Maybe magic did not flow through my veins as strongly as it did Gran's. The spells in the book may not work for someone untrained such as myself. I had just discovered the power within me but had no idea how to wield it.

I was on the verge of losing all hope when Gran began to stir. Initially, just her fingers moved gently along the bed linens; then her eyes began to flutter under her lids. Within a moment, they slowly opened, and I breathed a sigh of relief.

"Gran, are you well?" I asked, taking her hand in mine and giving it a gentle squeeze.

She looked at me and then down at the cup in my hands, motioning for me to give it to her. I assisted her in sitting up and then passed her the cup. Gran blew weakly on the tea before taking a long, deliberate sip, followed by another. Not a word escaped her lips until she had drunk the entire cup, the dullness in her eyes gradually fading with each sip.

"Rowan?" she said, confused.

"Gran, the spell you cast to help you sleep after the ball went awry, and you did not wake. It's been three days now," I told her.

She looked at me, recognition dawning on her in spite of the haziness clouding her eyes, the kind that comes from being very ill. The spell had roused her from her sleep but had not pulled her from the illness she had been battling. The joy of seeing Gran awake was quickly extinguished as I realized that it had awoken her but not cured her.

"Ah, you possess the gift," she said, a smile gracing her lips. "I pondered which of my grandchildren the Goddess would bestow it upon, and it seems it is you, my dear Cora. I am truly glad it is so. There is much you must learn now."

Then she noticed the sorrow in my eyes, and her joy also faded. "What is it, my child?"

Biting back the tears, I took a deep breath before I spoke. "After you fell ill, I discovered your spellbook and a counter-spell for the one you had performed. I persuaded the duke that I knew of an ancient remedy of yours that might aid you, but I required time to gather the ingredients myself. He insisted that his son accompany me. Thus, Lord and I journeyed to Letterfearn, to Tobar Mhoire, and then on to Loch Ness to procure the necessary ingredients for the spell to aid you."

"You need not continue," Gran said. "On the very day he was born, just after I had saved his life, I had a vision. He was grown and deeply in love with a beautiful woman. Though you were not yet born, I knew it was you, for you bear a striking resemblance to your mother in her youth. That is why I informed your mother of the ball. I knew she would insist upon your attendance, and that you and James would meet. Do not concern yourself with your status, for it shall matter not. I saw you two happily together," she said, a weak smile spreading across her aged face.

I looked at her, tears welling in my eyes, then spilling down my cheeks. Her expression changed, and she knew. "No, it cannot be. This is not what I foresaw. I have never had a prediction go awry. What has happened?" she asked, her eyes growing misty with tears.

"On our return from Loch Ness, he glimpsed something on the ice—a child. As he approached, the ice gave way and the child vanished. The tale you told of the kelpie in the lake surged back to me and I knew it was no ordinary child. I tried to save him, but I was too late."

"Did they recover his body?" she asked, a glint of hope shining in her eyes.

"Yes. I attempted to save him with a spell from the book, but it proved ineffective," I replied, feeling a pang of shame.

"What spell did you use?"

"To bring one back from death's grip."

"And it did not work?" she asked, confusion furrowing her brow.

"No, it did not."

"Did you repeat the incantation thrice while over his body?" she inquired.

I pondered the question. Had I spoken it three times? No, the fairy had appeared before I could utter the incantation for the third and final time. A wave of dread washed over me as I realized the truth: the magic must have attracted the fairy, who had intervened before I could complete the spell and save him. How could I have been so negligent? Why had I not recognized it in that moment?

"I did not. Before I could speak it for the final time, a song interrupted me, and then a woman appeared, vowing she would bring him back to me."

Gran's eyes widened as concern carved lines into her pale face. "Cora, tell me you did not strike a bargain with a fairy," she said, fear palpable in her every word.

"I wasn't thinking clearly. I only wished to save him," I wept, tears streaming down my cheeks.

"What were her exact words? The precise terms of the bargain," Gran insisted, her tone forceful.

I cast my mind back, struggling to recall the exact terms of the bargain, word for word.

"She wanted the bracelet you gave me and told me she saw many happy times ahead of us. Then she asked me if I wished for our love to continue. I, of course, said yes and gave her the bracelet, desperate to save him."

"Oh, my child, I fear you have ensnared yourself in a fairy's curse. Fairies fulfill their bargains, but not always as one might hope. Their fulfillment is often bound to the precise nature of their queries. She did not ask if you wished him to live again; she asked if you wished for your love to continue, which is quite different. Did she sing afterward?"

I felt stricken at how naive I had been. In my grief, I had not been thinking rationally.

"Yes," I said, looking down, trying to hide my shame for falling for such trickery.

"And the song, do you remember it?" she asked with a cough. Her face was growing pale again, and the hazy look in her eyes was slowly returning. "I don't have much time, my love," she said.

I thought back to that awful moment. Pulling at the recesses of my mind, I tried to hum the melody. As I did, the words came spilling forth. A lullaby on the wind, a song that promised happiness and love, yet it now played like a nightmarish death waltz in my mind.

"In shadows of frost, love entwined,
A dance of souls, through time confined.
In each dance, a mirrored hue,
Yet frosty waters claim their due.
To shatter chains, to cease the waltz,
A secret dance when the moon proves false.
Seek within the heart's deep well,
A selfless step where shadows dwell.
When icy whispers bid you near,
A sacrifice, the path will clear.
Beneath the gaze of stars untold,
A choice to make, a tale unfolds.
Through whispered echoes, twenty-seven times four,
Forever love will bind once more."

"Good. You must write it down at once. Do not forget or alter a single word, for it is the sole means of breaking the fairy's curse. You will need to decipher the riddle to understand the nature of the curse and how to lift it. Do it now, in the book," she instructed, pointing to the book of spells before she settled back against the pillow. She appeared to weaken with each passing moment, her breaths becoming short and ragged once more.

I seized the book and walked over to a small desk in the corner of the room, where I found an inkwell and a pen. Locating an empty page, I began transcribing the words of the fairy's song one by one. When I had finished, I closed the book and turned my gaze back to Gran.

"How long have you been unwell?" I asked, watching her visibly fading before me.

"For some time now, but the sickness has taken hold quicker than I thought. That is why the sleep spell did not work properly; my life force is too weak. I fear I'm not much longer for this world." She coughed again, this time her hand coming away with a scarlet stain upon it.

"No, grant the spell more time. You must teach me of my powers and how to wield them; I need you," I said, a tear slipping down my cheek.

"My dove, the spell will not save me. It is my time to go."

"I cannot bear to lose you as well. You are the only one who truly understands me, who can guide me. I love you, Gran. You cannot leave me." The words spilled from me like a rushing river.

"Cora, all must meet their time," she said gently. "I shall impart as much as I can before the spell fades, but you must be strong and learn these things for yourself once I am gone. Come closer," she urged, patting the bed. I moved to her side and sat down.

"Long ago, when I was but a young lass, I had a courageous friend named Freya. We encountered a perilous woman who took the life of Freya's beloved and then had her hanged as a witch. Yet, before Freya met her end, she cast a spell upon herself to be reincarnated until she could vanquish the evil the woman had unleashed upon the world. I vowed to care for her home, Fernbeg, until her return, and that all my descendants would do the same. You, my dear child, are the next in line to safeguard the cottage until she comes back, and you shall pass this duty to your own child, and so forth, until our line ceases or Freya can defeat the darkness. I know this may be daunting. Your mother wished for me to withhold such knowledge until I was certain you possessed the gift," she explained.

I sat there stunned. Mother had kept Gran from telling me about magic all these years. "That book you hold is one of many in the library at Fernbeg, and as I will not be here to teach you, you must turn to them for guidance. You have the spark within you; nourish it and grow the flame," she said, smiling though I could see the pain returning to her eyes. Her lips were turning back to the pale shade of blue they had been, and I could now see it was not the spell that had caused it but whatever sickness she was fighting.

She began coughing, and the fit seemed to last an age until it slowed and then stopped. She rested her head again, closing her eyes for a moment before speaking. "I have a task for you. In the cottage, there is a letter upon my desk. You may read it, then place it in the pocket of the green cape found in the trunk at the foot of my bed. Return the cape to the chest, and do not open it again. Do you understand? This is of great importance."

"Yes, Gran," I said as her breathing grew labored, and her eyes began to glaze over. I took hold of her hand as she looked up at me and whispered her final words. "Remember, my dear child, though I may depart from this world, I shall live on through you and the magic that you possess." With that, a deep silence fell over the room, the only sound being my own breath as hers had ceased. It was then the duke entered the room, his eyes as full of grief as my own, and together, we sat in silent mourning.

As I sit here, penning down the events of that tragic day, I can't help but feel the weight of the years that have passed. Four decades have come and gone since I lost the two people I loved most in the world. Their memories are forever etched into my soul. As I sit at the old oak table in Fernbeg's kitchen, I write this account with the intention of passing it down to my daughter and her daughter someday, ensuring the tale of their kin stays alive. As I reflect, my mind falls back to the fairy bargain I struck, which still haunts me.

Despite years of trying, I've been unable to decipher the spell the fairy cast upon me all those years ago. I've often wondered if our love continued on through the life of our daughter, Ailig, that maybe she was part of the riddle. The night we spent in the ruin, when we shared our love, led to her conception. I've cherished watching her grow, playing amidst the sheep in the fields surrounding our cottage. James was not alive to witness these beautiful moments, and his absence echoed through the years. Even though the duke and duchess were never able to properly claim Ailig as their granddaughter, they were generous, loving, and kind to us always, visiting us whenever time allowed and making sure we were never in need of anything.

As I approach the twilight of my life, a sense of unease grips me. I'm visited nightly by dreams of the fairy's haunting melody, its ethereal song calling out to me in a way I cannot ignore. I fear that the story may not be over, that there are still secrets hidden within the depths of that bargain, waiting to be revealed.

I sign this letter as Cora Darrow, taking back my birthright of the Darrow name and passing it down to my daughter, so that it may live on as Gran intended.

Chapter Fifty-Three
LOVE IS A CURSE

Nora set the book aside and digested what she had just read. The pain and sorrow of the book threatened to consume her. Tears welled in her eyes and spilled down her cheeks; an ache deep within her sprang to the surface. She knew the sadness that came along with losing a beloved grandmother, but she had never known a love like Cora and James's. She couldn't imagine losing both a soulmate and a beloved grandmother in a single day.

Her love for Sam wasn't the kind of love typically depicted in stories like this. If she were completely honest, their relationship had been more of a long-term fling than something built on unwavering love for each other. If she had truly loved him, she wouldn't have dragged her feet when he had asked her to marry him. She realized Sam's infidelity had been a blessing in disguise; she had been saved from marrying a man she didn't truly love, leaving space for someone she could.

A lightness came over her for the first time in two years. She was actually happy their relationship had ended the way it did. Sam was a necessary part of her past—he had taught her exactly what she didn't want in a husband. That was a gift in itself.

Maybe this trip was just what she needed to let him go. Even though she still didn't know what she wanted to do with her life, at least now she was free from the burden of Sam.

Her thoughts wandered back to the heartache Cora had suffered. Now she understood what Colin was talking about. It had been Cora who was cursed, not the book. But why was Nora's life mirroring the events she'd read about? More than mere coincidences, the recent events had her mind spinning with a whirlwind of questions that she might never find answers to.

The feeling of untamed energy came flooding back and bounced around inside her, causing her heart to flutter like a caged bird. She opened her notebook and wrote down the fairy's song from the book. It reminded her of the poems she often wrote, but as she penned it down, it felt broken, cryptic, and altogether wrong.

Suddenly the wind picked up, and a loud thwack on one of the windows facing the lake caused Nora to jump and drop the book onto the floor. A branch from the young oak tree near the deck had caught the wind, thrashing it into the window with force. The book lay splayed on the floor, resembling a fallen bird, with the last page sticking straight up like a solitary feather. When Nora picked it up, she noticed something on the backside of the last page.

Excitement surged through her; how had she not noticed this before? At first, she thought it was a note from Colin, but the handwriting was not the same. The note was written in a fancy script with ornate flourishing letters, reminiscent of a woman's hand. Though the ink was faded, the note was still legible. Not waiting a minute longer, Nora rested herself against the cushions of the sofa and began to read.

It has been one hundred and fifty-eight years since that fateful day when I first lost James, and once again, I find myself engulfed in the grip of loss. One hundred and fifty-eight years later, and I finally understand how the fairy curse was meant to unfold. Our love continued as our souls became entrapped in an endless loop of love and loss, destined to find each other and then lose one another over and over through reincarnation. Had it not been for a ritual at Hogmanay, I might never have understood. It unlocked memories from my past life, and once I awoke from my vision, I remembered it all.

I had my original handwritten copy printed into this book, hoping that the enchantments within it would not be lost to time. I write this account in the back, hoping that my future self will read it and continue the quest to break the curse. As you may have noticed, I had the printer leave this blank page at the back of the book so that anyone who might read it and work out parts of the curse has a place to record them, a place to keep them safe and together with the other clues.

I've deciphered one section of the code: "Through whispered echoes, twenty-seven times four, forever love will bind once more." The curse was cast upon me as Cora in 1667, and I was reborn Marion in 1775, separated by one hundred and eight years—twenty-seven times four is one hundred and eight. If my calculations are correct, my next life will begin in 1883. It appears that in every family descending from the Darrow line, a baby girl is born every one hundred and eight years, ensuring this dreaded curse continues. James, on the other hand, does not seem to be bound to any specific lineage like I am. Trapped in this cycle, his soul finds any vessel it can to fulfill its tragic destiny.

Today, on my fiftieth birthday, it has been thirty years since I lost Peter, the reincarnation of James, out at sea. I know that water plays a role in the curse, but I have yet to uncover much more than that. If my future self is reading this, I pray that you have found a way to break us free from this torment. May the Goddess guide you on your journey, and may you finally bring an end to the cycle of love and loss that has plagued us for centuries.

Nora's mind wandered back to the strange visions she had experienced on the mountain as the stag entered the clearing. She had seen a ship tossed about on a stormy sea. Could it have been a psychic vision of these events? She closed the book and set it in her lap, shaking her head. No, she wasn't a psychic. She could barely navigate her own life, let alone unravel the mysteries of someone who had died centuries ago. This whole thing was starting to mess with her head.

As the questions swirled in her mind, one thing became clear: she had to discover more about the truth behind this curse, no matter where it led her.

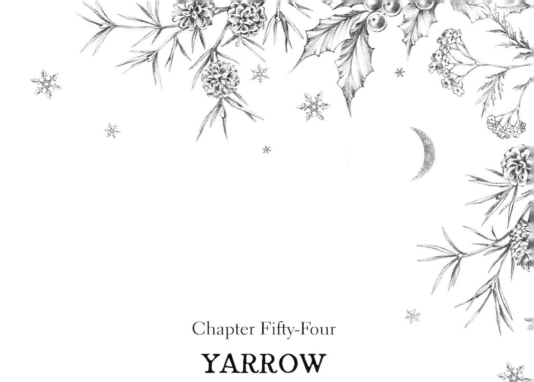

Chapter Fifty-Four

YARROW

Nora set the book down, her mind spinning with confusion. Had Colin been attempting to decipher the curse that Cora had unknowingly fallen under all those years ago, believing that he and Edith were the reincarnations of Cora and James? She picked up the next letter from the pile and began reading, eager to discover if her theory was correct and if Marjorie and Colin had found a way to break the curse.

> *19/1/1944*
>
> *Dear Marjorie,*
>
> *I hope this letter finds you well and starting off the new year in good spirits. Last week, I received long-awaited orders directing me to a facility in England where I will be working in an office filling out paperwork. It's not a very*

exciting job, but it is what I can do to counter the German forces after being wounded in battle. However, there is quite a bit of downtime in which I am able to work on decoding Cora's curse.

Even though I'm closer to Edith here in England, I'm still quite far away from London and not able to see her. I miss her terribly. The ache of her absence weighs heavy on my heart. I understand all those songs about love in a very different way now that I have experienced it myself. I yearn for the day when this bloody war is but a memory and we can return to the simple pleasures of our normal lives.

I received a letter from her this week, reassuring me of her safety, though the hospital where she serves is nearing full capacity with wounded men returning from the battle-field. I cant say I miss the days when I stood shoulder to shoulder with my comrades, slogging through the rugged hills and muddy fields of Italy, but it was a bit more exciting than filing paperwork.

I'll write whenever I can. Until then, remember the words from my last letter and think about reconnecting with Flora.

With love, Colin

Nora realized this must have been when he was sent to Bletchley Park to work with the codebreaker. He couldn't disclose his location or the nature of his covert work to Marjorie or Gram, a fact that must have weighed heavily on him. She imagined the difficulties of his dual responsibilities—codebreaking for the British government and trying to break the curse—and what a strain they must have put on him.

Pulling the next letter from its yellowed envelope, Nora could smell the aged cigarette smoke that still clung to the woven paper, fully immersing her in times past.

27/1/1944

Dear Marjorie,

As I write this letter, I can't help but feel overwhelmed by homesickness. It's been over two weeks since I arrived at this facility, and the days seem to blend together as we work tirelessly. With the war at full tilt, we have been overrun with paperwork. The long hours and lack of fresh air or sunlight are taking their toll. Despite the challenges, I've managed to make some influential friends here and called in a favor. We've uncovered a fascinating revelation about our family's history that I think you will find interesting.

According to the last page of handwritten text in the book, Cora was reincarnated in 1775 and believed she would be reborn again in 1883. With the help of my friend, we traced our family's lineage back to that year and discovered something remarkable. There were only two Darrow women who gave birth in 1883: our mother and a cousin named Millie.

It turns out that Awen, Aunt Millie's daughter, was the one we were looking for. Unlike Mother's first child, who sadly died at birth, Awen survived. But her life took a tragic turn when she turned twenty. Her fiancé, Charles, drowned in 1903 during a holiday trip to Wales. Overwhelmed with grief, Awen took her own life. To think that the curse may have claimed another victim is heartbreaking, and this time, Awen was unaware of its existence.

This discovery has shed light on another aspect of the curse. The verse "In shadows of frost, love entwined, a *dance of souls, through time confined" suggests that the love between Cora and her beloved always blossoms at the onset of winter.*

I'm still piecing together the rest of the puzzle, but I'm hopeful that we're making progress. With any luck, I'll be able to unravel the curse completely, and we can move on with our lives without breaking our promise to Mother.

Until next time, dear sister.

With love, Colin

PS Thank you for the idea of giving Edith a sweetheart brooch. I found a wonderful silversmith in Edinburgh who crafted me a brooch with a dove surrounded by a Celtic knot and a thistle. I gifted it to her the day she left for London, and she adored it.

After finishing the letter, Nora realized she had the sweetheart brooch that Colin spoke of. She had pinned it to her scarf the day before she left for Scotland. It was one of her gram's favorites, a cherished item Nora knew she couldn't part with as her parents sorted through her belongings in the sugar shack after she passed. It broke Nora's heart to think of her gram keeping so many things to remind her of Colin throughout the years. She wished her ankle wasn't hurt so she could retrieve the brooch from the peg board by the door and inspect it now that she understood its significance, but she would have to wait until Alistair came back. Instead, she grabbed her notebook and pen off the table and began to write.

Scribbling down notes eagerly, Nora delved deeper into the letters. The correspondence mainly revolved around Colin's long days spent working with a man named Kurt, whom he didn't get along with, and his longing to be back with Edith. Nora realized what a true hero he was, hiding his identity behind the facade of a mundane paper pusher, while in reality, he was breaking codes and saving countless lives. One particular letter stood out, detailing Edith's special clearance to visit him. Colin's excitement at seeing her again was palpable, and he proudly shared news of her promotion to work alongside a surgeon in London. The passion with which he spoke of Edith stirred a bittersweet emotion within Nora, feeling the echoes of their love upon the paper despite knowing that their story didn't end well.

She was on the verge of opening the second-to-last letter when a flicker of blue from the corner of her eye caught her attention. Turning to face the bookshelf, she noticed a faint blue glow emanating from the third row from the top, nestled between two books.

Scooting herself down to the other end of the sofa, she tried to stand, but her ankle was still too sore to bear any weight. That wasn't going to stop her, however, so she propped herself up on the armrest and hopped on her good leg a few feet over to the wall of books. Wedged between a large green book about natural medicine and a 1982 world atlas was a thin leather-bound book that emitted a faint blue glow. Doing a balancing act, she was able to grab the edge of the book and pull it down from the shelf above her head. Tucking it under her arm, she turned to hop her way back to the sofa when the door opened, and Lochland came bursting into the house, Alistair following closely behind.

"Whoa, boy, easy there," she said as she hopped a few more steps and then made a dive for the couch, landing softly on its middle.

"Nora, what are you doing? That ankle isn't going to get better pulling those kinds of stunts," Alistair scolded as he stripped off his jacket and removed his boots.

"How's Betty?" she asked, setting the book on the table in front of her. She would have to wait to open it now. Lochland sat at her feet, and she began to stroke his soft ears.

"A bit better now there's heat in the cabin. I tried to convince her to come back here and stay the night so that we could keep an eye on her, but she is stubborn as an old goat. She won the fight, but I told her I would be back over to check on her later tonight."

"Well, if she won the argument, she must be feeling better."

"I heated up another can of soup for her, but we need to figure out something that we can give her to help with the fever. The medicine is wearing off, and it's only a matter of time before the fever comes back."

"Maybe there is some extra aspirin in the medic kit in the hall?"

"I've already checked. Nothing left there other than bandages and a few antiseptic wipes," he said, walking over to the chair next to the fire and warming his hands. Deciding Alistair had the right idea, Lochland made his way over to the rug in front of the hearth and laid down.

Nora looked back at the bookshelf. *There was a book next to the one I just removed that might help*, she thought.

"I have an idea. See that large book on the third shelf up? It has a green spine," Nora said, pointing at the bookcase. He stood and pulled the large book from its dusty place on the shelf.

"Bring it over here," Nora said, patting the cushion beside her.

Alistair sat next to her and handed her the large book. "*Nature's Apothecary*," he read off its cover as she flipped it to the back and began looking through the index.

"How can you read in this light?" he asked as he picked up one of the candles and held it up so that the flickering light cast down across the page. Her finger traced down the paper until it landed on the word "Fever" and the corresponding page number 108. She flipped to it and began reading the passage aloud to Alistair.

"When it comes to naturally healing a fever, several plants immediately come to mind, such as willow bark. However, there are lesser-known herbs that are equally beneficial in reducing fever. Elderflower (*Sambucus nigra*), with its delicate blooms, carries potent anti-inflammatory and diaphoretic properties. Another noteworthy herb is yarrow (*Achillea millefolium*), known for its astringent and fever-reducing attributes, making it a steadfast companion in the journey to alleviate an unwanted fever." Under the passage were drawings of the two herbs. Nora's eyes widened as she stared down at the drawing of the yarrow.

"Alistair, can you hand me my jacket?" she asked.

He reached over and pulled it from the chair and handed it to her. She reached into her pocket gently and pulled the head of the large dried-up flower the old woman on the hillside had given her on their way to collect wood.

"Oh, my God, how did she know?" Nora said, turning the flower in her hands and then laying it next to its twin drawn in the book.

"Who?" Alistair questioned.

"The old woman on the hillside picking the dead flowers when we went to collect wood. She handed it to me and said I might be needing this later. How did she know? So weird."

"That is strange, but maybe she figured you might get sick after being out in that storm."

Perhaps, but Nora felt deep down that something more supernatural was at play, and it was about time they figured out what it was.

Chapter Fifty-Five

THE GIBBERISH NOTEBOOK

Nora skimmed the page until she came to a section with instructions on how to process the yarrow into a tea that would help reduce a fever.

"Looks like we have just the thing to get Betty's fever down, thanks to that old woman," she said, handing Alistair the flower.

"Are you sure this is going to work? These flowers bloom in the summer here. It's been dead for a while."

"The book says it needs to be dried before making tea anyway. I'd say it's dry enough," she said with a chuckle. Alistair shrugged and flashed his dashing grin before rising with the flower in one hand and the candle in the other, making his way into the kitchen. Setting the candle on the island, he ignited the stove and placed the kettle on top.

Nora watched as he rummaged through the cupboard in search of a mug. The flickering candlelight accentuated his sharp features, emphasizing his jawline and cheekbones. He was grippingly handsome, and memories of their kiss resurfaced. Heat spread through her as the events of last night replayed in her mind. She wondered if she might have another chance to kiss him like that again or if that moment had passed.

She found it hard to believe that the man standing before her was the same one she had bumped into at the market. He seemed like an entirely different person now. She supposed everyone had their bad weeks, and she had apparently met him during one of his. His gruff exterior had gradually faded, revealing someone charming and humorous underneath, someone she genuinely liked, someone she might be falling for. What would be the point though? Even if they did have a connection, she was returning to Vermont in only a few days.

"How long does it say to steep the flowers?" he asked as he poured the boiling water over the flower heads and snapped her out of her thoughts.

"Dried flower heads should be steeped for ten to fifteen minutes," Nora read from the book.

"Perfect, we have a bit of time to check something out in your gran's picture album."

He walked back over to the sofa, picked up the album from the coffee table, and then sat beside Nora. "I need to see something," he said, flipping through the album until he reached the last few pages. "Look." He pointed at a photo of the loch from the vantage point behind the cottage where they had gathered wood.

"It's the hillside," Nora said, looking down at the photo. Even after all these years, the landscape still looked almost identical. The idea that she was here in the same place her grandmother had been and experienced the same views and surroundings sent a warmth through her, making Nora feel close to her once again.

Alistair pointed to a photo of a small cottage white as snow, tucked at the base of a large mountain overlooking a loch. "I wonder where this place is?" he asked.

Nora peeled back the yellowing film that held the pictures in place and removed the photo, turning it over to read the inscription on the back. Her grandmother was nothing if not thorough when it came to marking dates and places on each of the photos. This photo had a date of 12/31/1943 scrolled along with the words *Fernbeg Cottage, Oban, Flora.*

This must have been the cottage at the center of the rift between Marjorie and Flora, Colin's other sister, the disagreement of which he had mentioned in the last letters. The very same cottage that Cora's grandmother had lived in and passed down to her.

"Aye, Oban. Great Scotch," he said with a wink.

"I think we have both had enough Scotch for a few days," Nora said, flashing him a sly grin as she remembered the taste of it on his lips.

As she turned the photo back over, her eyes fixed on the image. The idea that she was related to the real people and places in the little red book still left her head spinning. Now that she had confirmed the connection to her ancestors, she felt a growing desire to confide everything to Alistair, but the challenge was how to tell him that her grandfather had been on a quest to break a family curse. Alistair seemed open-minded, and she thought that he would be interested in the odd mystery she was unfolding about her family. But there was always a chance that all this weird shit might scare him. But she decided to take the risk.

Just as she was about to tell him, he stood up and walked toward the door.

"I'm going to take the tea over to Betty and stock up her fire so it lasts her through the night. Be back in a bit. No pulling any stunts while I'm gone," he said, shooting her his infectious smile. He pulled on his coat and boots, then walked back into the kitchen to get the mug before heading out the door.

"Okay. Tell Betty I hope it makes her feel better."

He smiled, nodded, then left, disappearing into the darkness.

Nora turned her attention to the book she had pulled from the shelf just before Alistair had returned. She was eager to see what was in it and why it seemed to glow. Asking Alistair if he saw it glow had been tempting, but she hesitated, not wanting him to think her any stranger than he already might. Adding this to the growing list of oddities wasn't something she was ready to do just yet.

Even now she could see a faint hue of blue on its edges, just like the aura she had seen around the little red book the night before. She rubbed her eyes, wondering if it was the candlelight playing tricks on her.

In the dim light, the shadows danced around her as she picked up the black leather book. Upon closer inspection, the outside was not black but a very dark shade of brown. She turned it over in her hands, and on the front was a set of embossed initials—C.M. A nervous anticipation rose up from her core as she flipped it open.

Colin's familiar handwriting filled page after page with numerical equations and cryptic symbols, remnants of Colin's codebreaking endeavors during the war. Nora didn't understand any of it; it was essentially gibberish to her, but she felt a sense of connection to her grandfather as she traced the elegant curves of his scrolling cursive.

As she drew closer to the back of the book, she came upon a section titled "Cora," underlined at the top. The fairy song was written in black ink, and he had crossed out words in red and circled others in blue. A tangled web of lines, words, and tiny notations filled the margins of the page. The next page, however, had writing she could finally understand:

After Tom was able to gather the records of Awen's death, I began looking at this in a different way. I believe it's written half literally and half metaphorically. For example, "In shadows of Frost, love entwined, A dance of souls, through time confined" is half metaphor and half reality. Cora's soul, in whatever body it inhabits, will always fall in love with James's soul at the onset of winter, and it is always sudden and short-lived.

"To shatter chains, to cease the waltz, A secret dance when the moon proves false." This line has something to do with breaking the curse, but I still haven't figured it out. I hesitate to move forward until I do.

Nora turned to the next page where there were more nonsensical scribbles with words and dates. She could tell it was still about Cora and the curse, but her grandfather's mind worked in a way that hers did not, and she saw nothing but puzzling words and phrases that did not join anywhere.

She looked back at the stack of letters, thinking that if Colin had figured it out, he would have written to Marjorie about it. The next letter in the stack, however, did not match Colin's handwriting, but Nora knew right away whose handwriting it was—her gram's.

Nora quickly picked up the letter and pulled it from the envelope with a sense of anticipation. Unfolding the paper and smoothing it onto her lap, she was met by the faint scent of roses, a fragrance that had always lingered around her grandmother and had embedded itself in the memories of Nora's childhood.

02/10/1944

Dearest Marjorie,

I do hope this letter finds you well and keeping warm in this dreadful cold snap. I'm not sure if the Highlands have gotten the cold we are experiencing in London right now, but each time I leave the hospital, I am almost a popsicle by the time I arrive back at my flat. Dreadful weather. I do hope with the end of this winter also comes the end of this war. I have been working long hours with a surgeon named Donald Cameron. He is a complete drill sergeant to everyone who works under him, but I think he fancies me, so I have it a bit better than the others. The poor guy doesn't have a chance as I am madly in love with your brother.

I was so excited when I got clearance to visit Colin last weekend. However, a weekend was far too short and left me missing him even more. I wish we were not stationed so far from one another. I have to keep reminding myself that it is only temporary, and when this war ends, we will be able to be together.

I wanted to send this letter to tell you that I have decided to stay in Scotland when I am relieved in July. I haven't told my family yet, but there is nowhere in the world I would rather be than here with Colin. I can't wait to start our life off together once this blasted war is over. I was hoping that maybe you wouldn't mind if I came up and stayed with you until Colin was relieved in August. If I am imposing, I can always stay with Flora, but to tell you the truth, the cottage, Fernbeg, kind of gave me the heebie-jeebies.

I can't wait to picnic in the moors and swim in the waters of Loch Duich this summer like we talked of at Christmas. Until then, I will think of you, my dear friend, and send letters when I can.

Keep yourself warm,
Love from yours truly,
Edith

Nora reread the letter twice more, each time she stopped at the line "I have been working long hours under a surgeon named Donald Cameron." The man Nora had known as her grandfather her whole life had been working with her grandmother while Colin and she were together. How had she ended up with him instead of Colin? Had Donald come between them? Her interest was piqued even more now, and she intensely wanted to find out what had ended their love story.

Chapter Fifty-Six

LOVE AND MOONBEAMS

Nora looked down at the dwindling stack of letters. There were two left: one final letter from Colin and the dreaded letter that she assumed was a death notice.

Just as she picked up Colin's final correspondence, her stomach let out a loud groan, and Lochland's ears rose up. He let out a low growl and looked about the room in search of the noise.

"It's okay, boy, just my stomach," Nora laughed.

A moment later, Alistair came trudging in, prompting a long, loud string of barks from Lochland.

"Whoa, there, boy, just me," he said, holding both hands up as if he were being robbed.

"How'd it go?"

"Good. I waited to see if the tea was going to help, and she seemed to be doing better by the time I left. I made her a toasted cheese sandwich, then stocked the fireplace again. I tried one last time to get her to come back with me, but she pretty much told me to bugger off," he said with a chuckle.

"I'm surprised she said no to that invitation," Nora teased.

"Very funny," he laughed. "She should be good until morning. Then I will go back and check on her," he said as he stripped off his jacket and boots and walked into the kitchen.

"I am starving. You?" he asked as he rooted around the place.

"Same. My stomach was making enough noise a minute ago that Lochland growled at it," she said with a giggle.

Alistair found two cans of tomato soup in one of the cupboards and heated them up. He served out two large bowls, each with a thick slice of bread with butter, and brought them into the living room, setting them on the old coffee table in front of Nora. The rich aroma of the creamy tomatoes reminded her of home. Homemade tomato soup was her mother's go-to dinner on cold winter evenings. The smell gave her a twinge of homesickness, but the idea of going back to her old life felt strange. So much had happened since she had arrived in Scotland, yet she still had no clue what she wanted to do with her life. She felt like she may never find purpose, her true passion. Maybe she just didn't have one, or maybe she was just one of those people destined to work a normal 9-to-5 job and be content with that.

"Do you think they will have the roads cleared by tomorrow?" Nora asked, taking a slow tentative sip of the soup, which was nowhere near as good as her mother's homemade version.

"I hope so, but it really depends on how many places along the way need to be cleared of snow drifts."

"My flight back is two days from now. I'm worried I might not make it back to Edinburgh in time," she confessed. The homesickness quickly faded, replaced with the desire to be snowed in a bit longer with Alistair. She still didn't know how she would go about telling her dad about his true father, and then there was the conversation she needed to have with her parents about the bakery. Nor was she ready to leave Alistair. Her mind was awash with a hundred different scenarios of what might happen if she stayed longer, even though she figured it would probably just end in heartache.

"It might be a close one, that's for sure. What do you need to be back for?" he asked, blowing on a spoonful of soup. Nora's mind drew a blank for a moment as if she couldn't think of a good reason to rush back.

"It's the busiest time of the year at the bakery, and my parents are counting on me to help them. I can't just leave them hanging. What about you? You must have something you need to be back for as well?"

"I need to convince my boss not to fire me, but that might be a long shot if Tom actually told him I said, 'fuck off,' " he said with a sideways smirk.

"Bosses don't typically like to be told that," Nora joked.

"Do you have travel insurance? You might just want to reschedule your flight," he suggested, taking a bite of the bread.

"No, it was an old flight voucher and I didn't buy travel insurance."

"Ouch. Well, out of pocket it is then if you can't make it."

Booking a new flight could end up costing her thousands of dollars. The thought made Nora's stomach turn. She didn't make a lot of money working at the bakery and had already used a significant portion of her savings for this trip. Her recent car accident complicated matters further as the insurance company provided scant compensation due to her car's age. The predicament left her without enough money to buy a replacement car unless she dipped into her savings, which was minimal now.

"Did you find anything else interesting in the letters?" he asked as he stood up and placed his bowl into the sink. As Nora chewed through her last bite of bread, she thought about how she wanted to tell Alistair about the book. It was all a bit confusing even to her, and she was a little worried that he might think she was nuts.

"Yeah, something kinda crazy, actually," she said, realizing he had given her a perfect segue.

"Really, what?"

"This is going to be hard to believe," she told him, taking a deep breath before going on. "When I first arrived here, I had wanted to recreate the photo of my gram on the Royal Mile with the book and wine bottle. I went into a bookstore in search of a little red book to use for the photo. I happened to see this one wedged between the wall and the bookshelf in the store and fished it out," Nora said, showing Alistair the book as he sat down next to her. "I began reading it and knew there was something strange about it. At first, I thought the book was predicting events that were happening to me, but then I began to realize it was pulling me in, egging me on to keep reading. I know that sounds crazy, but I promise that's not even the half of it," Nora said, handing over the book.

"Those letters that Colin wrote to Marjorie were about this very book and a curse inside it. I think it might even be the same book that he had carried into the war that ended up saving him. Look here." She pointed down at the indent in the cover and turned the page to show him the darkened spot that was on nearly every page but the last few.

Alistair stared down at the book for a long moment, saying nothing. Nora's stomach twisted as the silence drew out. Did he think she was crazy? Her mind whirled with self-doubt, and she wished she hadn't brought it up.

"There is no way a bullet hit this. There would be a hole," he said, finally breaking the momentary silence. Nora breathed a sigh of relief. Yes, he may be doubting the idea, but he wasn't acting like she was a complete nut job.

"That's what I thought too, but I swear it's the same book."

"It's definitely weird that you just happened to pick up the book that your grandfather had been reading, but it must be another copy," he challenged.

"It's not. I know it's the only one in existence because it was originally a handwritten account from one of my ancestors, which a family member had printed into a book so that it could stand the test of time. I have no idea how it ended up in that shop since it seemed to be an important family heirloom passed down from generation to generation," Nora told him.

Alistair inspected the book more closely now, opening it and looking for the publishing information just as she had done the first time she opened it.

"What's it about?" he asked, intrigued.

"It's sort of a tragic romance. Girl meets boy, they fall in love, he dies, and she becomes cursed by a fairy."

"Aye, it's a fairy story? Those never turn out well. How do the letters tie into the book?" Alistair asked, inching closer to her as he set the book back down on the coffee table. She could see his interest had been piqued.

When he sat back, they were so close their legs were touching, and Nora felt a flush come over her. Heat rose from her belly and spread through her like wildfire. All of a sudden, the only thing she could think about was how close they had come to a night of passion.

"Well?" he asked, looking at her with raised eyebrows.

She had been so caught up thinking about the romantic possibilities, and the blasted board that had stopped it all, that she had forgotten what he had even asked her.

"The letters and book. How do they fit together?" he reminded her.

"Colin was trying to decode the fairy curse in the book. I'm not sure yet if he cracked it. One more letter to go to find out," she said, pointing at the letter sitting on top of the photo album.

"Do you want to read it together?" he asked, picking it up.

"Sure."

Alistair pulled it from the envelope and began to read aloud.

26/2/1944

Dear Marjorie,

Writing with good news on two fronts today. Firstly, I've gone and bought a ring. Next weekend, I'm off to surprise Edith in London, where I plan to ask her to marry me. She makes me believe in myself and sees me in a way no one else ever has. That is how I know she is the one. I figure you'll be pleased with the notion, knowing how well you two hit it off during our visit.

Edith and I have been talking about settling down in Letterfearn after the war. I heard that Jim Corliss, Davie's lad, is considering selling the farm. Wouldn't it be grand if we could call that place home? You know how taken I am with Edith, which drives me even more to finally put an end to this curse for good.

Alistair stopped reading.

"Are you okay?" he asked as tears slid down her cheeks and landed softly on her lap.

"It makes me so sad to hear how much they loved each other and to know that for all these years, she had kept him a secret. It must have been so hard to do. I think I understand now why she used the photo album as bedtime stories. It was her way of telling me about him, to keep him alive," Nora said, tears still falling freely.

"That's the kind of love we all dream about having someday, if we are lucky," he said, leaning in and gently wiping a tear away from her cheek with his thumb. "I'm not sure I will ever get that lucky. Love like that doesn't seem to run in my family. My parents are pretty good proof of that," he confessed to her, his tone turning somber.

"I don't think that's true. You'll find it someday," she said, touching his hand that still rested on her cheek. They locked eyes and held each other's gaze for a long moment before Nora leaned forward and kissed him.

This kiss felt different from their first drunken one. She fell deeper into it, and he responded in turn. She ran her fingers through his wavy hair, savoring the silky texture that seemed to ripple through her hands like a summer breeze, pulling him in closer. The letter slipped from his hand and landed softly on the floor as he slid his hand down the slope of her back, his touch gentle yet firm. His fingertips lingered on the curves of her hips, and he pulled her in closer. As their lips met again, she breathed in his scent, reminiscent of a crisp autumn day, igniting a longing that reached beyond the physical.

As their lips lingered, a charged tension filled the air, electric and palpable. The room seemed to pulse with anticipation as his hands traced the contours of her skin. Like a whispered promise, his touch kindled a fervent desire within her once more. They were both hungry to resume what they had started the night before, but this time it felt true, not driven by whisky and desperation. Things seemed to be falling seamlessly into place.

She explored the grooves of his chest and shoulders with her hands, each touch adding fuel to her growing fire. The ache deep in her belly intensified as she pulled his shirt up over his head, briefly breaking their kiss. He mirrored her actions and removed her shirt with one swift motion.

As their lips reunited this time, a familiar thrum of energy pulsed within her. Usually, it signaled an impending panic attack, but this time she channeled it, pulling it into her core. She felt a sense of control, a mastery over the energy that had once threatened to overwhelm her.

Seizing the power coursing through her, she guided him on top of her as they fell back onto the sofa. A flurry of clothing scattered the floor like fallen leaves as they became entangled in each other's embrace. Their bodies moved in harmony, illuminated by the flickering candlelight and warmed by the crackling fire, as if they had been transported back in time.

The dancing shadows cast by the candlelight painted a shadowy picture of their love across the windows overlooking the loch. The moonlight reflected in the water below, sending sparkling moonbeams to join the blue glow enveloping them as they approached the precipice of their lovemaking. Reaching their peak, the glow turned to a dark hue of purple that wrapped around them like a wreath, then gradually faded, without either of them being the wiser.

Falling into each other's arms, they lay in the afterglow, listening to the rhythmic symphony of their heartbeats until sleep gently claimed them, cradled by the blue aura that encircled them and the moonbeams that bathed the room in a soft gentle light.

Chapter Fifty-Seven

AFTERGLOW

The soft wisps of morning light broke through the large windows facing the loch and bathed the floor in its warm embrace. Still wrapped in each other's arms, Alistair and Nora were awoken by the pitter-patter of tiny paws bounding around them. Nora giggled as Lochland licked her nose.

"Alright, boy, enough. That's my job," Alistair said, pulling Nora toward him for a kiss, which she halted, covering her mouth.

"Morning breath, sorry," she said with a smile as she stood up, slowly putting pressure on her bad ankle, which surprisingly felt better. Wrapping the blanket around herself, she left Alistair completely exposed on the sofa.

"Your ankle, is it better?" he asked as she made her way into the kitchen.

"Yes, still hurts a bit with full pressure, but I think it will be okay," she said as she put on the kettle. Stealing a glance at him while he got dressed, a flush spread across her cheeks, turning them the shade of ripe strawberries as she remembered how the contours of his body felt against hers. Despite her efforts, a smile refused to be suppressed at the corners of her lips.

Last night had been nothing short of magical, as if they were two pieces of a puzzle that had finally found their perfect match. The connection she had felt with Alistair surpassed anything she had experienced with other men, even Sam.

"Tea?" Nora offered, watching Alistair as he slipped on his shirt and a sunbeam bathed him in a warm glow. The storm seemed to be clearing, with bright patches of blue sky beginning to show. The parting clouds should have been a welcome sight, but the reality that they wouldn't be snowed in much longer hit Nora like a brick wall.

"Always," he replied, making his way toward her. With his rugged five o'clock shadow, he exuded a newfound charm that she found irresistible. She preferred this more unkempt look to his previously clean-cut appearance. She felt happier than she had in years, which made the thought of them going their separate ways even harder, but she couldn't think about that right now. She needed to enjoy every ounce of the moment.

Approaching her from behind, he wrapped his hands around her hips, pulling her close and planting a kiss on her neck. She spun around, shooting him a playful glare, followed by a mischievous grin.

"I know, I know. Morning breath," he chuckled, raising his hands in surrender before settling onto one of the stools by the island. Nora poured two cups of tea and joined him.

"If they clear the roads, you'll leave tomorrow?" he inquired.

"I need to head back to the city if we can manage to get out of here, that is," she replied, realizing the idea had also been plaguing his mind this morning.

"What are you going to tell your parents?"

Nora paused, blowing gently on her tea. She was at a crossroads, uncertain of what path to take here. Though she missed the bakery and her parents, returning to her old way of life simply didn't feel like her destiny.

"I honestly don't know," Nora admitted, taking a long sip from her mug.

"You said you don't want to take over the bakery, but what do you want to do instead? I'm sure if your parents know what you're passionate about, they will support you."

"I'm not sure I'm passionate about anything," she admitted as a sorrowful expression fell across her face.

"That's definitely not true."

"What do you mean?" she asked, looking up from her mug.

"I see a whole lot of passion when you are writing away in that notebook of yours. I might have taken a peek inside the other day. Your poems are witty and beautiful," Alistair said, giving her hand a comforting squeeze.

"You read my poems?" she said, pulling her hands away quickly, angry at the fact he was snooping in her things.

"I know it was a stupid thing to do, but I was hoping to understand you a bit better. Here was this beautiful woman so unsure of herself, and I wanted to understand why."

Nora's shoulders softened, and she looked up at his sincere eyes. He thought she was beautiful and wanted to understand her? Even before they had warmed up to each other? Had he felt that same initial pull that she had?

"You really think my poems are good? I only write them for

fun or to help me calm down when my mind is feeling lost. It's my way of processing my emotions, I guess," she admitted.

"Yes. Not to mention, your other writing is quite good. Ever considered being a journalist?" he teased.

Nora had never considered writing as anything other than a pastime, but the more she thought about it, the more Alistair was right. She did find passion in it; writing always brought her comfort and a kind of joy that she couldn't find elsewhere. Could she make a go of writing in some way? Alistair had seen something in her that she hadn't seen in herself. Colin's words echoed in her mind: *She makes me believe in myself and sees me in a way no one else ever has; that is how I know she is the one.* The idea made her heart flip-flop in her chest.

"What about you? Do you want to go back to the magazine?" she asked, shifting the attention back to him.

He paused for a moment before responding. "You know what? I honestly don't know, either," he admitted with a chuckle.

"We're just two lost souls," Nora said as she rose from her seat, reaching for a piece of bread from the bag. She tore it into tiny pieces and added them to a bowl along with half a banana, setting it down on the floor for Lochland. The dog bounded over, sniffing at the food before eagerly devouring it.

"Wow, he was hungry. We better get him some dog food as soon as we get out of here, poor thing," Nora remarked, bending down to scratch behind Lochland's ears. "Speaking of, what are we going to do with him? I can't take him back to America," she added, looking at Alistair with pleading eyes.

"I don't know. I'm not sure I have time for a dog," Alistair confessed, looking down at Lochland. The dog licked his hand, and Alistair stroked his head, causing the dog's tail to wag furiously.

"You're kidding, right? Look at you two. You're meant for each other," Nora insisted, hoping to persuade him. She couldn't bear the thought of Lochland ending up in a shelter somewhere. Alistair looked down at the dog, a soft smile tugging at the corners of his mouth, and Nora knew she had made her point.

"Well, this little guy probably needs to go out, and I should check on Betty. Her fire has probably burned down by now. You should stay off that ankle even though it's feeling better. When I get back, how about we make some food and ravage that bookcase again," Alistair said, raising his eyebrows suggestively.

Nora laughed as he stood up, walked over to the door, and pulled his jacket off the peg board revealing her scarf underneath.

"Alistair, can you hand me my scarf?" she asked as he put on his jacket. She had forgotten about the brooch until now and wanted to inspect it.

"Sure," he said, walking it over to her. "You cold?"

"No, yesterday when I was reading one of the letters, Colin mentioned giving my gram a brooch, and I realized I had it pinned on my scarf," Nora said, turning the scarf over in her hands until she found it. "He called it a sweetheart brooch," she said, showing him the silver dove.

"Yes, they were common back during the war. Soldiers gave them to their girlfriends as a kind of promise. I wrote a piece on it a few years back for a Normandy remembrance article. Birds were a common symbol used to signify their return," he told her as he took a closer look at the brooch. "This one is beautiful, and he chose a dove, which was considered special."

"Why is that?" Nora asked.

"Doves are known to mate for life. Even after their mate dies, they stay loyal and never take on another mate. Colin picking that dove really showed his devotion to your gram," Alistair told her with a sweet smile lifting the corner of his lips.

"I'm glad I kept it. It almost ended up in the Goodwill box after she passed, but I couldn't let it go."

"Maybe you could feel the echoes of their love coming from it, and that made you keep it," he said.

"Maybe."

They locked eyes for a long moment, and Nora knew she was falling for him hard. By the way he was looking back at her, she suspected he was feeling the same thing. *Why did love always seem to come at the most inopportune times?* she thought.

"I better go check on Betty," he said, breaking the connection as if struck by the same thought and walking toward the door.

"Come on, boy," he called to Lochland, who came running eagerly. "We'll be back soon." He shut the door behind him, leaving Nora alone with her thoughts, and the last letter. The one she knew held the final chapter of Colin and Edith's love story and perhaps, the answers to the questions she had been searching for.

Chapter Fifty-Eight
A MOTHER'S LOVE

After Alistair left, she glanced at the pile of her clothing lying on the floor next to the sofa. The heat of the previous night rushed back, and she felt a blush creeping over her at the memories. She dropped the blanket, got dressed, and grabbed the last letter. Yet, she couldn't bring herself to read it, knowing it was Colin's death notice. So, Nora decided to read it later; she wasn't sure if she was ready for that yet. Instead, she grabbed her notebook and began writing while everything was still fresh in her mind. She started a timeline, documenting everything she knew in chronological order, starting with her gram enlisting to be a medic nurse. She hoped that, along with the photos and letters, her timeline would give her father a better idea of the chain of events.

She picked up the photo album and looked through it as she studied her notes, making sure she hadn't missed anything. Every image in the album held a different meaning to her now. They had once been photos of her gram's adventures in Scotland, but she could see now that it was Edith's personal love story. Instead of a written account, Nora had these images to remember the love Edith and Colin shared. Just as she was about to turn to the last page, Alistair and Lochland came back.

"It's a shame your ankle is hurt because it's perfect sledding snow," Alistair said as he kicked his boots off. Lochland ran over to Nora and jumped up on the sofa beside her, his wet paws leaving a trail of paw prints that Alistair followed.

"Whatcha doing?" he asked as she set her pen down and petted Lochland.

"Trying to write everything down to give to my dad. I figured a timeline would help him understand things better. I was just looking back over the album to see if there was anything I missed," she told him.

Alistair scooted Lochland aside and sat next to Nora, wrapping his arm around her.

"How is Betty today?" Nora asked, leaning into him.

"Much better. She asked about you, wanting to know if there was anything she could do for your hurt ankle. I told her you were fine and that I had things under control, and you know what she said?"

Nora giggled at his animated tone.

"She said it was highly unlikely that a man would have anything under control unless a woman was there telling him what to do. Can you believe that? She is one feisty old bird," he laughed.

Nora laughed along with him. "That she is," she joked back.

"What do you want to do today?" he asked.

"I like your idea from earlier. I think that bookshelf is calling my name. What do you think, want to snuggle up and read?"

He raised his eyebrow. "Nora Cameron, you might be my dream girl," he said, getting up and holding his hand out to her. They walked over to the bookcase and pulled down a stack each, depositing them on the coffee table.

"Let's make a tray of some snacks first," Nora suggested.

Alistair made tea while Nora prepared a plate full of cheese, crackers, nuts, and the last of the fruit.

They spent most of the afternoon reading, breaking here and there to tell each other about what they had read, along with a few heavy make-out sessions. Being with Alistair felt easy, without needing to talk or figure out something exciting to do. Just being together was enough for Nora. The idea that tomorrow they would be going their separate ways once the roads were clear made her sick to her stomach. Could they make this work? Long-distance relationships were hard just being a few states away; how much harder would being separated by an ocean be? Would Alistair even want that? She couldn't muster the courage to ask. She looked at him engrossed in a book titled *Nautical Invasions*, and her heart sank at the idea of having to leave him. This must have been how her gram felt when she was sent to London and had to leave Colin back in Scotland.

As the late afternoon set in and the sky grew too dark to read comfortably, they set their books aside and sat quietly in each other's arms for a long while, both avoiding the elephant in the room: their departure.

"How do you think your dad is going to take the news about his birth father?" Alistair asked, looking down at her open notebook.

"I honestly don't have a clue. My dad is a pretty chill guy, but this is life-changing news. I just hope it's not too much for him at his age," Nora said.

"That's not going to be an easy conversation, but at least you have the photos and letters to help show him that it was a true love story."

Alistair picked up the album and began flipping through the pages until he got to the end. He quickly flipped it back to the front and looked at the inside cover, then turned back to the last page as if he were inspecting it.

"What is it?" Nora asked.

"Does this look like someone changed the back of the cover?" Alistair said, turning it from front to back again, scrutinizing it closely.

Nora saw that he was right. Someone had glued a piece of paper over the back cover. She wedged her finger under the edge and lifted the corner. Slowly peeling back the aged layer, she saw the edge of a photograph along with a white-lined sheet.

Nora stopped and looked at Alistair. "Holy shit," she said as she slowly removed the photograph.

There, in black and white, was a picture of her grandmother, smiling at the camera. Colin was behind her, his arms wrapped around her waist as he kissed her cheek. Nora's heart swelled at the sight of it. She turned it over; no date was written on the back, just the words *my love* scrolled in her grandmother's neat handwriting.

Nora carefully removed the paper next and unfolded it slowly. It was a letter, hidden away for years, yellowed and fading. The writing was blurred in spots, as if tears had fallen on it. Nora held her breath for a moment.

Seeing her hesitate, Alistair asked, "Do you want me to read it to you?"

She shook her head and focused on the words penned on the page.

To my sweet child,

I write this to you in hopes that someday you will discover it and learn the truth of your parentage. I found out I was pregnant with you only a few short weeks after your father died. Though bittersweet, it pains me that you will never know his love. His name was Colin MacDonald, and he was the kindest and most loving man I had ever met. We shared a bond that was unbreakable, even after his death. You are the proof of that abiding love.

You are due to come into the world any day now, and I cannot wait to meet you, to see if you have your father's eyes and his smile. Because he and I were not married, you, my sweet child, even though conceived in pure love, are born out of wedlock. My father, being a religious man, would have cast me away if I came home unwed with a child. So, I have accepted a proposal from a surgeon I have been working under. He has offered to marry me and give us a stable life, but only on the condition that I never tell anyone, not even you, of your parentage.

I feel as though I have no other choice but to agree. I am writing you this letter so that someday you might discover it, hidden here in my memories, and know who your true father really was—a courageous man.

I do not know what the future holds for us, but I promise you that I will love you with every ounce of my being, and I will do all that I can to continue on and carry Colin with us, even if only in my heart.

With all the love I have to give,

Your mother,

Edith

Nora finished reading and handed the letter to Alistair, contemplating her grandmother's words, though they had been meant for her father, not for her. Why hadn't she told him after Donald's passing? Why maintain her silence even then? Perhaps she felt that since he had honored his promise to give her and Colin's son a good life, she needed to uphold her end of the bargain as well.

Alistair looked up after reading the letter and handed it back to her.

"That's some heavy shit. You okay?" he asked, pulling her into a hug.

"It's hard to read. She seemed so broken."

"At least now you have proof to hand your dad instead of this puzzle of photos and letters for him to piece together."

Nora folded the letter and tucked it back into the photo album behind the picture of them together. Then she closed it and set it on the coffee table next to her notebook.

Lochland jumped up onto her lap and began licking the tears from her cheeks. "Aww, thanks, boy," she said, giving the dog a big hug.

He jumped back down and began running circles around the sofa.

"I think he needs to go out," Alistair said, getting up and walking over to the kitchen. Nora followed, still limping slightly on her injured leg.

"Why don't I take him out?" Nora suggested.

Alistair looked down at her leg. "I don't think that's a good idea. The path is slippery, and I don't want you hurting your ankle again. We will be right back," he told her as he slung on his jacket and walked out the door with Lochland at his heels. The room fell into a heavy silence in their absence, broken only by the crackle of the fire. Nora's gaze fixed on the coffee table, where the photo album and Colin's codebook lay side by side—silent witnesses to a past she thought she had nearly unraveled. Each item, a fragment of her grandparents' legacy, held the last whispers of secrets they both held onto. Despite her progress, she knew there was more concealed within the codebook about the curse. Determined to uncover the remaining secrets, she felt a growing urgency to decipher the hidden truths before she had to leave Scotland and head back to America.

Chapter Fifty-Nine

DREADFUL LETTER

Nora limped over to the fireplace and added the last of the logs to the bed of embers. She poured another cup of tea, returned to the living room, and grabbed Colin's codebook. She wanted to see if anything else might help explain the full story of her ancestors and the curse that had plagued Cora.

The majority of the remaining pages were filled with war codes—numbers interwoven with letters in vertical lines—none of which she remotely understood. She flipped through it, looking for anything Cora-related, when a page containing drawings of the moon caught her attention. She began to decipher what he had written.

At the bottom was a line from the fairy song: "To shatter chains, to cease the waltz, a secret dance when the moon proves false." The word "false" was circled in red, and a line connected it to a drawing of a black moon with the word "eclipse" under it. Then he had underlined the words "shattered chains and cease the waltz" with a connecting line that read: "conditions that one must be present to break the spell." Another line went back up to the drawing of the moon, creating a loop. Nora took out her notebook and began to write down his notes in the order she thought made sense to her. She realized he had figured out another part of the curse.

"Conditions that one must be present to break the spell, a full moon eclipse," she read aloud. A smile graced her lips; this little codebook gave her a sense of connection to Colin, her grandfather whom she had never met.

Turning to the next page, she eagerly anticipated what else he had decoded, but it was blank, as was the next page, and the one after that. This was the final entry in his journal. Nora looked down at the letter from the War Office, now resting alone on the coffee table. She knew there was no getting around it now; she needed to read that letter and find out what happened to Colin. She needed to know how he died. She slowly picked it up, hesitating for a moment before opening it.

> 6/3/1944
>
> Dear Ms. Marjorie MacDonald,
>
> It is with great sadness and a heavy heart that I write to inform you of the tragic loss of your brother, Corporal Colin MacDonald. On March 4, 1944, during a bombing incident in London, he lost his life while on leave.
>
> Corporal MacDonald was an invaluable member of our unit, known for his exceptional skills on the battlefield and his eagerness to help continue the fight even after being wounded. His dedication and contributions played a

crucial role in our efforts, and he was held in high regard by all who had the privilege of serving alongside him.

We understand that no words can truly ease the pain of such a loss, and we extend our deepest condolences to you and your family during this incredibly difficult time. Corporal MacDonald's sacrifice will forever be remembered, and his bravery and commitment to duty will remain etched in our hearts.

Please know that the entire military community mourns with you. We are here to offer support and assistance in any way we can. His personal belongings will be sent to you along with any personal effects that were recovered.

May you find strength in the cherished memories of your brother and in the knowledge that his service and sacrifice have left an indelible mark on our nation.

With sincere condolences,
Patrick Lane
Military chaplain

Nora swallowed hard, pushing down the grief that threatened to overwhelm her. Reading the letter, she knew it was a death notice, but the emotional impact hit her harder than she expected. Nora felt as if she had come to know Colin through his letters over the past few days. It pained her deeply that he had worked with the group that had made such a significant impact on winning the war by breaking the Enigma codes, yet even in his passing, he was never acknowledged for his contribution. Marjorie and Gram remained unaware of his true heroism until years later.

She wondered if he had gone to London to propose to her grandmother, and Nora wondered if he had ever gotten a chance to do so before he died. Her heart ached for her gram; to have lost the love of her life in such a tragic and sudden way must have been devastating.

Then it struck her—it was a tragic love story, like in the book. Maybe he was the reincarnation of James, and her grandmother that of Cora? Maybe that was why he had been trying so hard to figure it out. But the years didn't add up. It hadn't been long enough for them to have been the reincarnations.

She had mixed feelings about the little red book. On one hand, it was the story of her family lineage, and on the other, a death note. She looked back at Colin's notebook and opened it to the page about the fairy curse. Skimming back over his notes, she realized there was no way he could have been the reincarnation of James. Even though he had fallen in love with Edith in the winter, Colin was Cora's descendant, not her gram's.

Nora reached forward to grab the little red book off the coffee table, wanting to reread the note in the back when she caught sight of a letter on the floor. Alistair must have dropped it when she kissed him last night. Picking it up, she realized he hadn't read the whole thing, only just the beginning of it. She smoothed it out on her lap and began to read the rest of the letter.

> *I have figured out yet another part of the fairy's song.*
>
> *"In each dance, a mirrored hue, yet frosty waters claim their due." The first part of this is a metaphor implying each new life they inhabit, their fate is mirrored. The end of the verse is literal, as their love ultimately meets a tragic end in water.*
>
> *"To shatter chains, to cease the waltz, a secret dance when the moon proves false."*
>
> *I've been dwelling on these lines, and it's becoming*

clear to me. The spell can only be broken during a lunar eclipse. "Seek within the heart's deep well, a selfless step where shadows dwell." A selfless act during the eclipse, that's the key.

"When icy whispers bid you near, a sacrifice, the path will clear."

The icy whispers, the waters that ended James's life — it's pointing toward a sacrifice. Perhaps when the reincarnation of James is drawn near the water, Cora's reincarnation must intervene, and perform the selfless act. It's not crystal clear yet.

I'm hopeful, Marjorie. This is progress, closer than anyone has come to unlocking the curse. If we succeed, then we don't need to end the curse by not having children. I have not burdened Edith with any of this as I am so close to ending it. I understand why Mother made us promise not to have kids, as one of our grandchildren would be afflicted with the curse, but asking us to put our lives on hold was unfair. I think she harbored guilt over not doing that herself. I will do everything in my power to try to solve this so that you and Flora may have children someday, and so might Edith and I. Think what a grand time we all would have with little ones running around.

I plan to propose to Edith next weekend in London, and by the time I return, I aim to have the entire mystery unraveled. We'll finally break this curse that has haunted our family for centuries. Until we speak again, my dear sister.

With much love, Colin

Nora's heart sank as a cold sweat washed over her. Colin had not figured out the curse, as he died only a few days after he wrote the letter. Marjorie and Flora had not had children, making good on their promise to their mother to end the curse by not carrying on the bloodline. Which meant they hadn't known Edith was pregnant. She had kept it a secret, marrying the doctor quickly, covering up the pregnancy.

Nora reread the letter, stopping at the line *I understand why Mother made us promise not to have kids, as one of our grandchildren would be afflicted with the curse*. Then something hit Nora like a freight train when she realized what it all meant. She grabbed the little red book and flipped to the last handwritten page.

"The curse was cast upon me as Cora in 1667, and I was reborn in 1775, separated by one hundred and eight years—twenty-seven times four is one hundred and eight," Nora read aloud. Nora's mind raced as she grabbed her notebook and pen, feverishly adding up the numbers. "1883 plus 108 is 1991. No. No, it can't be!" she gasped, her voice trembling with disbelief. How had she not seen this before? How had she not put two and two together?

Born in 1991, Nora was the sole descendant of Cora's bloodline born during that year, as her father marked the end of the lineage. A tightness gripped her chest, and a familiar energy radiated from her core, filling her like an overflowing chalice. Panic set in, her breath coming in short bursts as the room began to spin around her. The last image she saw before the world turned dark and caved in on her was her hands pulsing with the same blue glow as the books.

Chapter Sixty
ECHOES

She awoke to the sensation of frost biting at her legs and feet as she found herself sitting on the cold, unforgiving ground. Her gaze fell upon James, cradled in her lap, his face pale and his lips tinged with blue. An ache in her chest pierced through her, unlike anything she had ever experienced, and she cried out in agony. She tried desperately to draw him closer, to bridge the unfathomable distance that now separated them. No matter how tightly she held him, all she could feel was the cold emptiness that surrounded her. She closed her eyes, seeking comfort in the darkness, hoping to ease the sting of her tears.

When she finally dared to open her eyes, she found herself standing on the cold sands of a rocky shoreline. Before her stretched a fierce sea, turbulent waves lashing at the shore, relentlessly pulling chunks of land back with each receding wave. The sky above was thick with cloud cover as dark as coal. A mix of rain and ice pelted her from the harsh gales, forcing her to shield her eyes as she peered out toward the horizon where the sky met the sea. Far off in the distance, a ship emerged. At first, her heart swelled with joy at the sight, knowing her love, Peter was aboard. It had been a month since their last meeting, and their reunion was just miles away.

As the ship drew closer, however, the storm intensified, causing the sea to become more wild. Initially filled with hope, her heart began to race furiously as she watched the ship thrash violently amidst the towering waves. She held her breath as it tipped back and forth. Then with the sweep of one giant wave, the ship capsized.

Amidst the brutal storm, she stood helplessly on the shore as the vessel carrying her love sank to the depths of the ocean floor. Tears stung her eyes, but she refused to look away, clinging onto a sliver of hope that someone may have survived. Yet, deep down, she knew no one could endure the icy waters of the Atlantic in such a tempest. She felt the moment his life ended as her heart ceased to beat momentarily. When it started again, the world around her felt different—darker and filled with an emptiness bearing the weight of a thousand worlds. Resting her head in her hands, she sobbed for what seemed like an eternity, her hands turning to ice and her feet growing numb with cold.

When she pulled her hands away, she found herself standing on a beautiful stone bridge overlooking a frozen river. Soft snowflakes fell gently from the sky, and rays of sunlight pierced through the thick layer of clouds, casting a serene wintry glow over the landscape. By her side stood Charles, a handsome man, his fingers intertwined with hers as they gazed out at the breathtaking scenery before them. The river flowed through the valley, flanked by majestic snow-capped mountains on either side. Although there was little snow on the ground, a thin layer of ice covered the river's surface, concealing its icy depths.

Charles drew her in for a kiss, and she felt a surge of joy swell within her. In his embrace, she felt whole, at peace. As he pulled away, a smile illuminated his beautiful chestnut eyes, reminiscent of her favorite time of year—late autumn. She smiled back when a sudden gust of wind sent her bonnet flying into the air. Without hesitation, Charles lunged forward to catch it, not realizing how close he was to the low wall of the bridge.

She watched in horror as his foot caught on one of the uneven stones that made up the bridge. He stumbled, losing his footing, and fell over the bridge's low side into the icy river below. Rushing to the edge, she peered down, but there was only a gaping hole where he had broken through. Climbing down the steep embankment, she searched frantically for any sign of him, but the hole revealed only a raging river below. At that moment, the realization struck—he was gone. As she fell to her knees, grief consumed her.

Then she saw it—her bonnet, resting on the frozen riverbank. In a fit of despair, she tore at it, trying to rip it into pieces as she screamed into the void, unleashing her pain. Her eyes remained fixed on the dark hole in the pristine ice, knowing that he was lost to her forever.

Suddenly, the scene morphed, and she found herself sitting on the edge of Loch Duich with the cottage behind her. Twilight had settled in, casting a serene hue across the landscape. Tracks led down toward the water on the other side of the staircase by the cabins, drawing her gaze. Following them with her eyes, she spotted the silhouette of a man standing at the water's edge, his gaze fixed on the center of the loch. As he turned, revealing his sharp jawline, she recognized him immediately. She called out to him, but her voice was lost in the wind, barely audible even to herself.

As the sky began to darken further, a sense of urgency gripped her, moving her down to the water. Carefully navigating the icy slope, she made her way to the shore's edge and stepped out onto the frozen surface. The cold seeped through her thin shoes, chilling her feet. Peering down she noticed movement beneath the ice, something large stirring below, yet it did not scare her but instead gave her a sense of peace.

Then a voice called out her name on the wind—"Cora," "Marion," "Awen"—or was it "Nora"? She realized it was her soul being summoned by the voice of an old woman, raspy and brittle, whispering urgently, yet she strained to make out the words. Stepping farther out onto the ice, she strained her ears, longing to hear the secrets being carried by the wind. As the ice beneath her began to crack, she pressed on, determined to hear the old woman's message. Just as she felt she was on the verge of understanding, the world shifted, and another sound pierced the cold air.

"Nora! Nora, please," she heard the voice call. She touched her cheek, which was wet despite the fact she had not gone into the water. She heard the pleading voice again.

"Nora, please come back. Come back to me." She spun around, but there was no one there. She closed her eyes to focus on the voice.

"Please," she heard the voice say again, and this time she recognized it as Alistair, and he sounded distraught. As she opened her eyes, Nora found herself lying on the sofa in front of the large windows of the cottage's living room, alone.

Chapter Sixty-One

ICY WHISPERS

Nora sat bolt upright, her heart pounding feverishly in her chest as the heartache and pain of her past lives flooded her consciousness. She felt as if she were being torn into tiny pieces from the inside out. Tears slid down her cheeks and landed like heavy rain on the little red book resting in her lap. The realization that she was the reincarnation of Cora had sparked a torrent of memories from previous lives, rushing in with unforgiving force.

She remembered writing the story as Cora, and having it printed into a book as Marion. Her mother had given it to her as a gift on her eighteenth birthday as Awen, but she never even opened it. If she had, she might have saved herself the anguish and stayed far away from love. Now she held it as Nora, and it was too late for that notion since she had already fallen in love with

Alistair. Even though she had tried to fight it, she now realized it was beyond her control. Alistair was James's reincarnation, and she was destined to love him, just as she had in every lifetime.

Suddenly she realized Alistair wasn't in the cottage. A sinking feeling came over her, and she felt as if she had just been violently pulled down by an undertow. Her breath caught in her throat as she stood up quickly and limped to the windows overlooking the loch. The once sunny day had turned to a cloudy twilight, and thick snow was falling yet again.

Even though it was nearly dark, she could make out his silhouette down near the water's edge on the other side of the cabins. He was yelling, and her eyes followed the direction of his gaze to see Lochland out in the center of the loch, standing on a patch of ice so thin it looked like a black hole.

The tragic deaths of all her loves played out in her mind like a movie on fast-forward, Alistair's looping at the end. Her heart leapt up into her throat, and she darted toward the door. She could already see that Alistair had begun to venture out onto the ice. She slipped on her boots and tried to sprint out the door, but her ankle slowed her down. She got to the stairs and yelled, "Alistair, no! Don't go on the ice!" but the storm had intensified, and the fierce wind carried away her words. There was no way she was going to get to him in time before he ventured out too far.

Then she heard the fairy's song drifting through the air, a haunting lullaby that filled her with an unsettling sense of dread. It was the same song she had heard in the forest. It was then she realized that the fairy had been lurking in the shadows, patiently waiting to claim its due.

"No!" she cried out into the deafening wind, the words eaten up by the air around her.

The wind blew harder as she made her way to the loch as

fast as she could, the song coming along with her, more broken and sinister this time. Nora instinctually lifted her right hand into the air and pulled it back in one long sweeping motion. Abiding by her command, the wind turned direction, and the song faded off into the distance. As her memories returned, so did a deep-seated knowledge of magic, rekindling her understanding of how to wield its power.

She watched with dread as Alistair stepped farther out onto the ice. Fear gripped her, and all her lives came together as one. All the love and loss and pain channeled into one wave of energy. She looked up into the dusty night sky just as the clouds broke free, and the moon broke through, in an eclipse state.

"When icy whispers bid you near, a sacrifice, the path will clear. Beneath the gaze of stars untold, a choice to make, a tale unfolds," she said aloud. "A sacrifice of self. It was the literal meaning, just like Colin had thought."

In that moment, the last bit fell into place. She was the one. She had to be the sacrifice in order to end this and save Alistair.

Biting through the pain of her injured ankle, she ran as fast as she could through the thick snow. Instead of heading toward where Alistair stood on the loch, she veered toward the water's edge closest to her and darted out onto the thin ice.

She made it halfway into the middle of the loch when she heard the first crack, loud and echoing off the edges of the mountains that surrounded her. She heard her name called on the wind and spun to see Alistair out on the loch to her right, his arms waving frantically above his head in a stopping motion. They were separated by the thin layer of ice where Lochland had been. She noticed that Lochland was now by his side as he turned back to the shoreline and raced around the edge of the loch to where she had gone.

She didn't stop. Instead she walked closer to an open patch of water in the center. Another crack reverberated from the ice, and she felt it shift below her, like the ground had done up on the mountain when she had channeled her energy into it.

She smiled, knowing what she needed to do, and bent forward, placing both palms flat on the surface of the ice. She pulled from deep within herself, focusing all the energy she had once thought to be fear and anxiety. However, it had been her power all along—the magic of the Darrow women trying to break to the surface. She pulled it from her core and pushed it down through her hands out onto the frozen water. The ice below her hands lit with a blue glow as the thunderous crack rang out into the night air. In the blink of an eye, she was gone, consumed by the dark icy waters of the loch.

Chapter Sixty-Two

ECLIPSE

The last thing Nora heard was Alistair's frantic call as her body broke through the ice, plunging into the frigid embrace of the loch. At first, the water's touch felt like a thousand needles piercing her skin, but soon a fire-like warmth coursed through her veins. Despite the instinct to fight, the water held her in its grasp, refusing to release her to the surface. Just before disappearing into the murky depths, she looked at the eclipse, the absence of the moon's soft glow providing a strange kind of comfort. With each passing moment, her mind drifted to the faces of those she had loved and lost, and finally to Alistair. Determined to break the curse that had shackled her and James's souls to a constant loop of love and loss for centuries, she made a decision, and with one last breath, she welcomed the water into her lungs, knowing that her act of selflessness would bring an end to their eternal torment and set their souls free at last.

As she drew in the water, an icy fire seemed to consume her body, and the once faint blue glow surrounding her became all-encompassing. The energy she had stored within, since the intimate night with Alistair, broke free from her core, flooding every inch of her being until it could no longer be contained. The light erupted, illuminating the entire loch. In that radiant glow, she saw the lake creature from her dreams just a few feet away, a silent sentinel ready to guide her into the next realm. A sense of peace washed over her as the creature glided beneath her to cradle her body on its massive back and usher her into the tranquil abyss of the spirit world.

******

Alistair rushed toward the hole in the ice where Nora had fallen through. Dropping onto his stomach, he crawled to the opening, his heart pounding with fear.

"Nora! Nora!" he called out, extending his hand into the icy water in a desperate attempt to grasp her, only to be met with emptiness. After several futile tries, he quickly removed his jacket and boots, preparing to dive in and rescue her. As he leaned forward, ready to plunge into the frigid waters, he felt a pull at his back. Startled, he turned to see Lochland biting onto his sweater.

"Let go, boy!" Alistair yelled, attempting to shake the dog loose. Lochland clung to him with the strength of a much larger dog, resisting Alistair's efforts to break free. Realizing time was running out, Alistair made a quick decision to jump into the water with the dog attached, hoping Lochland would let go once they submerged. Steeling himself for the freezing plunge, Alistair neared the hole when a woman's voice stopped him in his tracks. He looked back to see the old woman from the hillside, standing only feet away.

"She is already gone. You must let her go," she said as he turned back and faced the hole in the ice. As if her words were slowing his movements, Alistair paused to look down into the black hole in the ice. He knew the woman was right. She had been underwater for far longer than any human could withstand in temperatures like this. Tears filled his eyes, and Lochland let go of his sweater, dropping to the ice and sitting next to the old woman.

Alistair stood still as stone, his eyes fixated on the hole.

"Why? Why would she do this?" he asked, his voice cracking with sorrow. He knew she was prone to panic attacks, but he hadn't thought she was suicidal.

"There is always a reason," the old woman said as she stepped up next to him.

Just then a flash of something large swam just below the surface of the ice, and Alistair jumped back in fear. The woman, however, stepped forward and bent down. She began making circles in the water with the tip of her finger.

"Come forth, Bridanach," she called into the water.

The ice began to crack, sending long fissures shooting out from the hole and toward the shoreline. Alistair stepped back again, moving away from the breaking ice. Great chunks began to lift up out of the water as the large head of a lake creature emerged. It rose up to the height of the old woman and hovered in the water face-to-face with her. She spoke to it in some kind of ancient language, and then the creature descended into the water only to resurface moments later with Nora's body on its back. After gently gliding her over to the old woman on the ice, the creature descended back into the depths of the loch once again.

Nora's lifeless body lay there blue with death at the feet of the old woman. Alistair, in shock at what he had just witnessed, stayed frozen in place for a long moment until finally dropping to his knees at Nora's side. In a desperate attempt to save her, he began chest compressions, but as hard as he tried, her heart would not beat.

"No!" he cried out, tears streaming down his cheeks. "Why?" he asked.

"To save you and break the curse, she needed to die," the old woman said solemnly.

Lochland came to his side and lay next to Nora's lifeless body, whimpering.

"This makes no sense. Why would she have done something so rash? What if the curse was nothing more than a tall tale made up and passed down in her family?"

"Oh, but it wasn't. You will see, my dear," the old woman said, looking up toward the false moon. Alistair lifted Nora up and held her, his beating heart pressed against hers that lay still.

The silence that followed was deafening; the wind did not blow, nor did the thrushes sing their twilight ballads, as though they had all bowed their heads in silence for Nora's sacrifice. Then, as if night had decided to switch to day, the moon began to break free of the eclipse's darkness. The first moonbeams touched the mountain behind the house, cutting out the silhouettes of the trees and ridgeline, then made their way to the edge of the loch, illuminating the cottage and tiny cabins along the shore. Moonlight inched its way across the ice, closer and closer. As it washed over them, Alistair looked up at the old woman, who seemed much younger than before.

"You must let her go now," she said, walking up and touching his arm. "Let her go."

"I can't just leave her here on the ice. I need to bring her back to the shore," he said.

"Alistair, you must let her go." She looked at him, her face growing more youthful by the minute.

Alistair swallowed hard, not understanding anything that was happening and continued to hold Nora tightly to his chest. Nothing made sense in that moment. *This has to be a bad dream,* he thought. He closed his eyes, desperately hoping that when he opened them again, he would be curled up on the sofa in the cottage with Nora in his arms.

But when he opened them, he looked down at the lifeless body of the woman he loved. In that heartbreaking moment, he wished he had told her he loved her. She had won his heart from the moment she ran into him at the market. Even though he had been irritated at first, he hadn't been able to get her out of his mind the entire day. Then they somehow ended up on the same bus to Letterfearn. He couldn't ignore the pull he felt toward her, so much so that he had gone back to the cottage the first night of the storm, making up some story about everything in town being booked. The truth was, he hadn't really looked. He had wanted to go back to the cottage so he could get to know her.

"I love you," he whispered, still cradling her.

He began to rise with Nora in his arms when the woman struck her cane on the ice, sending a shocking sound bouncing off the mountains. Ice began to creep up and around Alistair's feet, freezing him to the spot where he stood, not allowing him to move her away from the loch.

"I know this is hard for you, but you must let her go," she said emphatically, her mismatched eyes sparkling in the moonlight.

He looked down at Nora's face, her features serene in death, and kissed her forehead. Then he looked at the old woman, who was no longer old but young and beautiful. At that very moment, he knew who this woman was; he had been told stories of her since he was a wee boy. She was the Cailleach, the winter witch, a guardian of death and birth; she signified the circle of life.

He kissed Nora's lips one last time, but there was nothing there except the cold touch of death. He laid her on the ice in front of him and then looked at the Cailleach. He hoped that she was as kind and peaceful as the stories had said and that she would use her powers to help. She gave him a gentle smile and then looked back to the sky.

The moon was almost fully visible once again, except for a tiny strip of darkness still clinging to its edge. As the final shadow fled, the moon became whole again, and its beams of soft white light bathed the loch once more.

The Cailleach stood in front of Nora's body, casting it in shadow as she bent down to put her hand on Nora's chest just above her heart. She whispered a song faintly into her ear, then stood up. Stepping aside, the Cailleach let the moonbeams bathe Nora's body in their soft healing light.

Chapter Sixty-Three
IN THE DEPTHS

Nora woke to total darkness. Startled, she looked around, trying to gauge where she was, but it was too dark. She strained her ears for anything, but there was nothing other than complete silence. After a few minutes, her eyes began to adjust, and the silhouette of a man emerged from the murky black abyss. As he drew closer, the night began to fade into a dusky twilight. Not until he was mere feet away could she make out his features. It was Colin.

"Nora," he said with a wide smile playing across his lips.

Stunned, Nora stared at him. Realizing she was sitting on the ground, she began to stand.

"Colin?" she asked as he reached his hand down to help her.

Just then she heard a voice cut through the shadows and echo down toward them.

"Take his hand," the voice said. It was her gram's voice.

Nora felt an overwhelming sense of déjà vu. Walking out from the thick cloud of twilight, Gram emerged looking as she had in the photo album—vibrant, young, and happy.

Nora took Colin's hand and stood up as her gram walked over and stood beside him.

"Gram," she said, stepping forward to hug her, but it was as if she wasn't standing on the same solid ground that they were. Though they seemed mere feet away, each step toward them only left Nora in the same spot she had been. Colin put his arm around Edith's shoulders and pulled her in tightly to him. They looked at Nora with beaming smiles, pride showing in their eyes.

This had to be the afterlife, but why was she not able to be with them, to hug them? Was she just in a coma and not dead? Had she been wrong about the sacrifice? Had she failed to break the curse?

"I don't understand. Where am I?" she asked as shadows ebbed and flowed around her.

"You're in what we like to call the waiting room. A place you go after you die until it's decided where you will go next, but don't worry, you won't be here long," Gram said, still smiling at her.

"You've been here before, remember?" Colin said, looking over his shoulder at something she could not see.

"When?" Nora asked, confused.

"The night of the car accident. Most people don't return from this point, back to the living world. But you're not most people. You're a Darrow, and magic runs in your veins," Colin told her.

Nora thought back to the night of the accident. "I died that night?" she questioned.

He nodded. "Then you used your magic to bring yourself back to life."

She wasn't sure if it had been her magic. *It was more likely the curse had worked its "magic" to make sure that I played my part in the 108-year cycle*, she thought. But now that she was dead, a feeling of hope washed over her. If she were right about the last part of the fairy song, her sacrifice had broken the curse.

At that moment, a dark beam of green light encircled her, like a lasso hovering just around her middle. Her hands began to glow with a bright blue light. Taking a deep breath, she reached out and touched the green thread of light surrounding her. As her fingers grazed its edge, it quickly split and disappeared like a rubber band being cut. A lightness came over her, and she knew deep within that she was now free from the curse that had held her captive for centuries.

She looked at her grandparents. Colin was surrounded by a blue halo of light that she now recognized as magic. She understood now that the glow she had seen on the night of the car accident and over the past week had been her magic lighting the way, helping her, guiding her. The realization filled her with a sense of peace, as if the pieces of the long-lost puzzle were finally falling into place.

Colin beamed at her and said, "You did good, lassie."

Nora stepped forward to go to them and leave this in-between place when she heard a song breaking through the darkness. This time, however, it was not that of the fairy but a song much older, a melody of life, death, and rebirth. She didn't understand how she knew this since it was in a language she did not recognize or understand. She turned back toward the darkness, to face the direction from which the song came. It called her, beckoning her to follow. She looked back at her grandparents.

"Go, follow the song," Colin said.

"Where will it take me?" she asked, worry filling her words.

"To where you are meant to be," he said.

"Goodbye, my dove, until we meet again," her grandmother called out to her as she grew farther and farther away without either of them moving.

Soon Nora found herself alone again when a dove appeared. It hovered before her, then flew into the darkness toward the sweet melody, guiding her forward.

******

Alistair stood, frozen in place as the moon's glow lit the devastating scene before him. His eyes welled with tears, and as he brushed them away with his sleeve, he caught movement out of the corner of his eye. Looking down, he saw Nora's arm move slightly, and then her leg. He looked up to question the Cailleach, but she was gone, like a whisper in the wind.

He gazed down at his feet, relief washing over him as he realized they were no longer encased in ice, and he was free to move. Wasting no time, he stepped forward and knelt beside Nora. Gently cradling her head in his hands, he watched as her eyes fluttered beneath their lids, and her chest began to rise and fall with her returning breath. Tears of joy welled in his eyes.

Nora's eyes slowly opened, and she looked up, dazed. Alistair's heart swelled with a mixture of relief and love as she met his gaze. Without hesitation, he pulled her into an embrace and kissed the top of her head.

"Oh, thank God," he muttered as he felt the warmth of her body radiating toward him.

"Alistair," she said. Taking his face in her hands, she pulled him into a kiss, tears sliding down her cheeks.

"Are you okay?" he asked, reluctantly pulling away.

"Yes, I feel fine," she said as she looked down at her wet clothing and touched her right leg as if to make sure she was truly here in the physical realm. "I don't understand. I shouldn't be here. I figured out the fairy curse. Only an act of self-sacrifice under an eclipse could break it." Lochland jumped up and began licking her face before Alistair had a chance to answer.

"I'll explain it all later, and you can explain this whole fairy curse thing to me. But first, let's just get you inside and out of those wet clothes," he said, helping her to her feet.

They made their way slowly across the icy loch back to the cottage, their path lit by the moon. Just as they stepped foot on the shoreline, the lights in the cottage flickered on, along with the rest of the houses around the loch, peppering the shoreline like fireflies.

"Power's back," Nora said, smiling.

"Seems so," he said under his breath as he turned to look toward the center of the loch where they had just been. It was still, no water creature or Cailleach to be seen. Just ice and moon-beams.

Chapter Sixty-Four

THE FINAL LOOK

They spent the night wrapped in each other's arms, talking by the fire, neither of them wanting to let the other one go. Nora told Alistair the entire story of the curse from the beginning to the point they found themselves at now. Alistair had no recollection of any of his past lives, but after everything he had seen that night, he didn't question her even once. Instead, he relayed his own story of how the old woman from the hillside had been the Cailleach and that she had somehow brought Nora back to life with the help of a creature in the waters of the loch.

They finally fell asleep in the wee hours of the morning only to be awoken shortly thereafter by the bright beams of sunlight streaking in from the large windows. For a long while they stayed curled up in each other's arms, both silently thinking.

The power was back on, which meant the roads were probably cleared, and they could leave. No longer locked away in the little bubble the storm had created, they both realized real life would come crashing down in an unforgiving wave. The curse was now broken, and their souls were no longer tied together. Where did that leave them? Nora still felt a connection to Alistair, but now that their souls were unbound, did he still feel the same about her? She tried to push the negative thoughts aside and focus on the little time they had left together, but no matter how hard she tried, worry came sneaking back to the forefront of her mind.

"The roads must be cleared," Alistair said, ending the silence and saying what they both were thinking.

"Looks like we'll catch that bus back after all," Nora said, not at all sounding happy about it. "I'm not sure I'm ready to leave yet," she admitted.

He pulled her in and looked down at his watch.

"It's only eight; we still have a couple of hours," he told her, pulling her in a little closer, as if he also wasn't ready. She looked up and kissed him, a long deep passionate kiss, one that she didn't want him to forget.

"Are you sure you're okay?" he asked.

"Yeah, why?" she said, confused.

"Morning breath, remember?" he teased.

She laughed, then kissed him again. "If I can break a centuries-old curse, I can also break my own rules sometimes," she joked back.

Alistair got up to put the kettle on and pop some bread in the toaster.

Nora walked over and sat at the island, watching him pace the kitchen.

"Are you okay?" she asked, echoing his own question.

"I'm just thinking about everything. It's a lot to take in."

"It is. It's going to be strange going back to my life in Vermont after everything," she confessed.

"I get that. I feel like last week was a lifetime ago."

For Nora, it felt like lifetimes and lifetimes ago. Even though she had regained all the memories of her past lives, they were slowly fading. She couldn't remember what James's face looked like anymore, or Peter's or Charles's. They had all faded into one: Alistair's face.

They spent the rest of the morning packing while talking about everything that had happened. Nora called Stuart, the all-in-one driver, for a lift back to the bus station. Alistair had found a bus back to Edinburgh at noon and booked them both tickets online.

Before Stuart arrived, she and Alistair walked over to check on Betty. She was out on the walkway when they arrived with her bag resting next to her.

"You leaving, Betty?" Alistair asked as they approached her.

"Yes, a car should be here any minute to pick me up. I am itching to get back home after all of this," she told them.

"How are you feeling?" Nora inquired as she leaned against the railing of the walkway.

"As good as new," she said, and she looked it. She had seemingly made a full recovery from her mysterious illness overnight. "I want to thank you both for everything you did for me. I'm not sure what would have happened if you two hadn't been here."

"Of course. We're just happy you're feeling better," Alistair said as a black car pulled up into the turnaround near the cabins.

"That's me," Betty said.

Alistair picked up her bags and walked them to the car. Before Betty got in, she turned and said, "See, you two make a cute couple," then winked and got into the backseat and shut the door.

Alistair put his arm around Nora, and they waved goodbye as she drove off down the road. They turned and walked back down the stairs toward the cabin when Alistair said, "I think she might be right."

"About what?"

"Us being a cute couple," he said with a smile.

"Yeah, it's too bad the storm didn't hold out a few more days so we could have explored that further," she joked, but in all seriousness, she had wished it were true. Everything had happened so fast that they hadn't had time to talk about what was next. And it was too late now. They would be headed to the bus station in the next few minutes, on their way back to their prospective lives. They entered the cottage for the last time, taking the final sweep of the place before Stuart arrived.

"You know, this place is actually your birthright. If you can prove you are Marjorie's last living relative, you might be able to get ownership over it," Alistair told her as he zipped up his bag and sat it next to the door.

"I don't know; I'm not sure I belong here," she said, taking the stack of letters out of the shoebox and placing them in her bag on top of the little red book, the photo album, and her grandfather's code journal. "I think it's time to make a fresh start of my own," she told him, as she looked around the cottage one last time.

She walked over to the bookcase and pulled down the copy of *The Unfortunate Traveller*. She dusted off its jacket, tucked it under her arm, then pulled down *Nature's Apothecary* next. Walking back, she placed both books in her bag.

Alistair raised his eyebrows at her. "Technically, these are my books, seeing how they were Marjorie's," she said with a sly smile.

Alistair smiled back as she zipped up her bag and headed

toward the door where he was pulling on his jacket. "Lochland, come, boy," he called to the dog who was sleeping lazily on the sofa curled up in a little black ball. Lochland perked his ears up at the sound of his newfound name and jumped down, springing over to Alistair's side.

"See? What did I tell you?" Nora said, smiling at the two.

"Ya, ya," he retorted, giving the dog a good scratch behind his ears and smiling down at him. "You all set?" he asked, picking up their bags and opening the door.

"I think so."

Nora stood for a moment after Alistair and Lochland walked out and took in the cottage one last time. Taking a deep breath, she closed her eyes, saving the image to her memory. When she opened them, she could have sworn she saw an outline of a woman standing near the windows, but she blinked, and she was gone. She smiled and said softly under her breath, "It's over, thanks to those letters you hid. Thank you." She wondered if Marjorie had known all along that she would visit here and would be the one to find the letters. The Darrow women were known for their second sight, after all. A moment later the sun broke through the thick cloud cover, and the room lit up with the mid-morning sun as if Marjorie were smiling down at her, answering her question.

Nora scanned the cottage one last time before she turned and walked out the door, closing it gently behind her.

Chapter Sixty-Five

GOODBYE

After a long, nauseating bus ride through the winding High-lands, they arrived in Edinburgh in the late afternoon. As they stepped out into the bus station, reality came crashing down around them in the form of shouts, train whistles, and a barrage of unwelcome smells that assaulted their noses. After spending the week in the country with no power, the city overwhelmed their senses. Not accustomed to city life, Lochland cowered at Alistair's feet as people pushed past them in a hurry to their next destinations.

"I have to run if I am going to catch my flight. I only have an hour and a half to get there and check in," Nora said, a sadness filling her words as she spoke them.

"Yeah, I think I need to drop this guy off at my flat and then go grovel for my job back," Alistair said.

Nora nodded, trying to find the right words to say to him. Their souls were now free, and with that freedom came a choice — to go find love elsewhere, to be free, to be themselves without the other. She loved him and wanted to be with him, but with that love came the memory of so much pain and suffering. They shared a love transcended through time, deeper than most people would ever experience, but now they both had a choice, and she was unsure whether Alistair would choose to be with her or if she truly wanted to be with him.

They had very much been unfortunate travelers, like the book, moving in and out of this earth for hundreds of years, and now that journey had come to an end. She was free yet even more confused than before. She had no clue what the next step was, but she knew she had the strength to walk that path alone if she had to.

"I'll catch up with you later then. Send you an email or something," she said, immediately regretting the words for sounding so cliched, cold, and not at all how she felt.

"Sounds good, Nora. Be seeing you," he said as he stepped forward and pulled her into an awkward embrace. She breathed in his scent one last time and then broke away from him before her emotions broke free. She bent down and pulled Lochland into a big hug, kissing the top of his head. "Be a good boy, Lochland, and keep this guy in line," she said to the dog as she ruffled his ears and stood back up.

Alistair dropped his bag and quickly stepped forward, pulling her into a kiss that surprised her. She melted into him, rising to her tiptoes as if she couldn't get enough of him. He pulled her in closer, and she dropped her bag and ran her fingers through his silky hair, not wanting to let go. The sounds of the city faded, and for a moment it was just them. Nora felt her magic surge inside her and then the sun broke free of the clouds, lighting up the tiny snowflakes that fell around them, like sparks of magic. The sounds of the city returned, and the sun slipped back behind the bank of clouds as he broke their kiss and pulled away. Alistair wrapped the MacDonald tartan scarf around her neck and lifted the sweetheart brooch up to look at it one final time.

"Will you come back to visit us?" he asked, looking down at Lochland, who was staring up at them with his big brown eyes. She tried to speak, but the words caught in her throat, coming out in a broken burst tinged with sadness. "Of course I will."

She wanted to tell him she loved him, that she didn't want to leave him, but she also knew she needed to have some space from him, to make sure it wasn't just the remnants of the curse and their past loves influencing her. And she knew he needed that as well.

He smiled and let the brooch fall through his fingers and back onto her chest, then leaned forward, quickly kissing her one last time.

"I really hope you do, Nora," he said with forced optimism in his voice.

She smiled at him and grabbed her bag off the sidewalk. Leaving him felt like it might break her, but she had to return to Vermont. She had come here to find herself, to figure out what she wanted to do with her life, and she did. Still, she didn't feel any better about her life's trajectory. She felt even more lost than before.

Smiling at him one final time, she waved, then turned and walked down the street. She didn't dare look back at him for fear that if she did, she might not ever be able to leave. Instead, she walked on, tears falling and streaking her cheeks.

Dusk had fallen, and all the Christmas lights in the city were on and filling the world around her with a joyful glow. She had almost forgotten it was Christmastime. As she walked through the festive cheer, it did not light up her heart the way it used to; instead, she felt emptier than ever. She decided to keep her eyes on her feet and press forward, and that is exactly what she did until she disembarked off the plane in Boston International and got onto the bus back to Vermont.

Chapter Sixty-Six

HOME

Nora arrived back at her apartment early that morning and in a daze. She had told her parents she wouldn't be in until later in the day, giving herself a bit of breathing space before their barrage of questions about the trip. She knew she was ready to talk about the bakery, but she was still trying to sort out how to break the news to her father about Colin.

She set her luggage by the kitchen table and mindlessly pulled a Tupperware container out of the fridge with a note attached that read *Welcome Home! Love, Mom.* She peeked inside to find her mom's homemade mac-n-cheese, complete with Ritz cracker topping, and stuck it into the microwave. As she waited for her food to heat up, she turned on the TV and sat down on the couch.

She found herself falling right back into her old routine as if nothing had changed. Scrolling mindlessly through rom-com movies, she only stopped when she heard the beep of the microwave. Getting up to grab the food and a fork, she then headed back to the couch.

Taking a fork full of cheesy macaroni and shoving it in her mouth, she stopped for a moment and looked down at what she had just eaten. Her mind had been so consumed with thoughts of all she had been through in the past week that she hadn't realized it was jalapeño mac-n-cheese until her tongue started burning.

Setting the container of food on the coffee table, she rested back against the large cushions and stared at the pinewood ceiling. What the hell was she doing? She looked around at the place she had once thought of as home, but now it felt stark and empty. Nothing felt right. Everything was misaligned, as if she had walked back into someone else's life, not her own. She looked back at the TV, and her heart sank at the movie onscreen in front of her: *Christmas in Scotland*. She swallowed hard, trying to push down the emotions that were threatening to spill forth, but Alistair's smile kept playing in her head on repeat like a broken record.

A month ago, she thought the worst thing she would have to face was telling her parents about not wanting to take over the bakery. That now felt trivial. She had wanted to do a bit of soul-searching, but it wasn't her own soul she had been searching for — it was Alistair's. It had been his all along. She felt like her life had been in a holding pattern because it had been. It was holding out for him. Suddenly she knew exactly what she wanted to do with her life.

She walked to the table, picked up her cell phone, and called her parents. To keep moving forward to where she wanted to be, she had to have the hard conversations. In order to do that, she needed to tell her parents face-to-face about the bakery and Colin. Within a few minutes, they were on her doorstep, eager to see their only daughter and to know how her trip had gone.

"How was the trip, pumpkin?" her dad asked as he kicked off his boots and pulled her into a big hug.

"It was good."

"I see you found dinner?" her mother said, looking at the Tupperware container sitting on the coffee table.

"I have something I need to talk about," she said, coming right out with it and catching her parents off guard with her serious tone.

"Oh, God, did something bad happen to you over there?" her mother asked, scanning her up and down for visible marks.

"Of course not," she said, pulling out a chair and sitting down. Her parents followed suit, eagerly waiting for what she was about to tell them.

"What would you guys say if I told you I didn't want to take over the bakery?" she asked and then held her breath.

The room fell silent, and her parents shared a look. To Nora's surprise, her mother was the first to speak. "I would say you know best where your own dreams lie."

Nora sat completely stunned. She had prepared herself for an all-out fight to the death with her mother over not carrying on the family business.

"Really? I thought you would be upset," Nora said.

"Of course not. Yes, we love the bakery and want to see it continue on, but we love you more and want what is best for you," her father said.

"I know over the years I put pressure on you to run the family business, but I only did it out of love. You seemed so lost, and I thought if you had the bakery to take over, you would have some sense of purpose. If I had known it wasn't what you wanted, I would have never pushed it on you," her mother said.

"But what will you do if I don't take it over?" Nora asked. The question had been plaguing her since she had decided to tell them.

"We have another couple of years left in us to run the place. Maybe we can find someone who will buy it and keep it as a bakery," her father said.

"Now, the big question is, what do you plan to do?" her mother asked.

Nora fell silent for a long while, and her mother reached over and placed her hand on Nora's. The small gesture surprised her and gave her the strength to carry on.

"I want to be a writer. The University of Edinburgh has a good program that I might want to attend," she told them, holding her breath for their response.

Her father smiled. "See, Gram always knew what was best. She knew going to Scotland was just want you needed, even all those years ago."

Nora smiled at him and then looked over at her bag resting on the other end of the table. She got up and pulled her bag over to where she was sitting. Unzipping it, she pulled out the stack of letters and the photo album.

"There's something else I wanted to tell you," she said, handing her father the stack of letters. "Gram kept a secret that I think you should know about. I discovered it when I was in Scotland."

Her father looked down at the stack of letters and opened one. His eyes darted back and forth as he read. When he finished, he set it down and looked up at Nora.

"I don't understand. Who are these people? It sounds like this guy Colin was in some kind of relationship with Gram," he questioned.

"He was. They were madly in love with each other until the

day he died, eight months before you were born," Nora said, waiting for the words to sink in. Nervousness rose within her.

"Are you trying to tell me this Colin guy is my father? There is no way. Mom met my dad when he was stationed at the military hospital."

"Yes, that is true, but she was already pregnant with Colin's child, you. Grandad liked her and knew she was pregnant, so he offered to marry her only if she agreed never to tell anyone you weren't his son. Not even you," Nora explained as gently as possible. She could see the hurt and confusion in his eyes as he glanced back at the letters.

"Are you sure about this, Nora?" her mother questioned, placing her hand on her husband's shoulder.

"I'm sure. It's all there. You'll have to look at the photos, read the dates on the back, and then read the letters. I made you a timeline and stuck it in the album along with a letter I found hidden in the back," she told him, trying to gauge his reaction. "I'm sorry, Dad. I didn't know if I should even tell you, but I thought you had the right to know. Nothing good comes of secrets being hidden in the past."

He was quiet for a long time as he took in what Nora had just revealed. His eyes glazed over, and for a moment she thought he might cry. He finally looked up from the stack of old yellowed letters and said, "I'm glad you told me. You know, I think she tried to tell me in her own way throughout the years. Always hinting at things my father liked or was good at, things that didn't fit him at all. Now it makes so much sense. She had been talking about my birth father, not Grandad."

"I think she wanted to honor her promise but also leave us breadcrumbs so that someday we might discover the truth on our own," Nora said as she stood and walked around the table, pulling her father into a big hug. "Colin seemed like a really great guy. I think if you do a bit of research, you are going to be surprised at what a war hero he was," Nora said as she let go.

"How did you figure this out?" her mother asked.

"A friend. A journalist for a magazine called *Tartan and This-tle*," she said. Just the thought of Alistair left her with a pit in her stomach, and she had to push down the longing she felt to be with him.

"A friend?" her mother questioned. "This friend wouldn't happen to be a handsome Scotsman, would it? And maybe the reason you want to go back to school over there?" her mother teased.

Nora just smiled, and her mother raised her well-manicured eyebrows. "I see. Well, I think it was about time," she said, giving Nora a knowing smile.

"When do you plan to go back? Next fall when classes start?" her father asked, picking up the pile of letters and tucking them inside the photo album.

Nora looked over at her bag and then toward the door. "Would you be mad if I said now?" she laughed.

"Now?" her parents said in unison.

"What if I promise to come back for New Year's?"

"But it's Christmas, and you know how busy—" her mother began but stopped herself. "Alright, but we get you until your birthday if you come for New Year's," her mother bargained.

"Deal," Nora said.

Her father stood, tucking the photo album under his arm, and pulled her into a warm bear hug. "I'm gonna miss you, pumpkin, and thank you for this," he said, gesturing to the album and then kissing the top of her head before heading for the door.

"I'm proud of you. I know it wasn't easy to let go and move

forward, but I am so happy that you finally did it, honey. Go find your dream. Your father and I will always be here whenever you need us," her mother said, pulling her into a long embrace.

Nora couldn't believe how well the conversation had gone with her parents. Why had she been so stressed over it all these months? Her dad taking to the idea of Colin being his father went much better than she had anticipated as well. Her worries had built up in her mind so much they had become monsters under the bed, but in the end, there was truly nothing to be afraid of.

As they left, a sense of knowing came over Nora—a knowledge of what she wanted and the assurance that she would be okay, even if her future wasn't planned out. She had too many lifetimes of planned outcomes, and for once, she was happy not knowing what came next.

With that, she grabbed her bags and walked out the door toward where her heart was calling her. Scotland.

EPIL⁰GUE

A year had passed since Nora's initial trip to Scotland, and she and Alistair were celebrating by meeting the realtor at Mercat Cross monument to be shown a possible location for their business venture.

When Nora returned to Scotland, she showed up on Alistair's doorstep after bribing a secretary at *Tartan and Thistle* for his address. When she arrived, he was sitting on the front step looking down at his phone with a look of defeat on his face and Lochland at his feet.

Lochland spotted her first, letting out a loud string of barks and pulling so hard that the leash broke free from Alistair's grip. He turned to scold the dog when he saw her. A wide smile spread across his face as he got up and ran to her. Picking her up, he spun her around in the air while kissing her, like a scene out of a television movie.

"No matter what lifetime we are in, I will always choose you, even without the curse holding us together," she told him, breaking free of their kiss.

"I love you, Nora Cameron. I couldn't stand to be another day without you. I was literally just looking at tickets to Vermont," he said, flashing her the screen of his phone. She smiled and kissed him again as Lochland jumped around them, his leash binding them together.

After an afternoon of lovemaking, he told her he had been fired from the magazine and that no amount of groveling was going to make his boss take him back. In the tangle of bed sheets, surrounded with afternoon beams of light coming into the windows of his tiny flat, they came up with the idea of opening their own print house. It had been their dream as Cora and James. Now that the curse was broken, they could make the dream a reality.

The plans had started as pillow talk almost a year ago, and after a lot of hard work and planning, they were ready to look at a place the realtor said was a hidden gem. Nora had finally been able to put her business degree to good use and now they were on the verge of making their dreams come true.

"She's late," Alistair said, looking down at his watch.

"No, she's not," Nora said, pointing up at the large clock on the building adjacent to them. "Calm down. You're making me nervous," she told him as he paced back and forth in front of her.

"I'm just really excited to see this place. To score a shop space on the Royal Mile is unheard of."

Nora walked over and stopped him from pacing by pulling him into a kiss. His body relaxed at her touch. Wet, cold rain started to fall, and Alastair pulled his collar up on his jacket.

"Bloody rain," he said, looking up at the dark sky.

Nora grabbed his hand and looked up. The rain quickly turned to white fluffy snowflakes that floated down around them.

"Better?" she asked with a smile.

"I'm not sure I will ever get used to that," he said, grinning widely. "I love you, my magical little lass." He beamed, squeezing her hand.

"I love you too," she said, looking up into his bright green eyes.

Just then she heard their names. "Nora, Alistair? Thanks for meeting me here," a tall, well-dressed woman said as she strolled up to them.

"Caroline, how are you?" Nora greeted her.

"I know you must think this is a bit odd, meeting here instead of the listing address. There is a good explanation, though. It doesn't have an address," she said with a laugh.

"What do you mean? It must have an address," Alistair said.

"It really doesn't. Somehow the city never gave it one, and it's between 108 and 109. Here, let me show you," she said as she walked ahead of them, her high-heeled boots tapping away at the cobblestone street.

Nora and Alistair followed until they came to a place that Nora recognized as the wine and spirits shop where she had purchased the wine for the recreation of Gram's photo. As they walked down the street a bit farther, Nora felt an electric pulse of energy surge through her. Her magic was on edge.

Suddenly Caroline stopped and turned toward a thin building that sat snugly between the larger shops to the side of it. A teal door with large paned windows on each side faced them. Nora's heart caught in her throat. The bookstore!

"Weird. I have walked this street a hundred times, and I've never seen this place," Alistair said.

"Let's go in, and I can show you around," Caroline told them, unlocking the door and turning the large brass knob. The interior was dark with the only light coming from the windows, but Nora knew right away it was the same place where she had found the book a year ago. Caroline flipped on the overhead tin lights, and they filled the room with a warm glow.

"Supposedly, it was a bookstore in the forties, but it has been abandoned for at least forty years," Caroline said, picking up a book off a small table near the window. "Looks like there are a few remnants still here," she said, wiping the dust off her hands along the side of her jacket.

How could it have been abandoned since the sixties when she had just been in here a year ago? The shop was now just a large empty room with a counter in the back and the beautiful art deco iron staircase spinning its way to the second floor. Even though the books and shelves were gone, she could still feel their echoes in the air around her.

"There is no way this place is in our budget," Alistair said, walking over to the staircase and running his hand on the banister.

"My client said she would like to see it being used again, so she's letting it go cheap as chips."

"What kind of steal?" Alistair asked.

"The kind if you guys weren't my friends, I would buy it and sell it for a lot of money. She only wants fifty thousand pounds for it."

"No way. You're joking. Caroline, that shit isn't funny," Alistair said.

"I'm deadly serious. I couldn't believe it myself. She is quite old and doesn't have any children. I think she just wants to see it end up in the hands of someone who will take good care of it. When I told her what you wanted to do with it, she seemed thrilled and told me the price."

Nora picked up the book that Caroline had set down when she first came in.

"She doesn't happen to have one blue eye and one brown eye, does she?" Nora asked.

"Yes, how did you know?" Caroline said, stunned.

"Just a wild guess," Nora said, looking over at Alistair and holding up the book *The Unfortunate Traveller* by Thomas Nashe.

Alistair smiled at her from across the room. The Cailleach had been helping them and guiding them all this time and even now was watching out for them. The thought made Nora's heart skip a beat.

"Please tell me you guys are going to take it?" Caroline said.

"Just so happens that is exactly what we have in our savings," Alistair told her, walking over to Nora.

"I have the paperwork right here if you want to sign the agreement."

Caroline handed them a pen, and they took turns signing the paper on the old countertop where stacks of books had once been. The ring on Nora's finger caught the light as she signed her name, sending a spray of prism light across the paper as if magic sealed the deal.

"We will have an official closing in a few weeks. Congratulations! I will give you a few minutes," Caroline said, walking out the door.

"Can you believe this?" Alistair said, picking Nora up and spinning her around, sending dust flying up from the floor and raining down around them.

"Literally nothing surprises me anymore," she joked, leaning down and kissing him.

"What are we going to call our printing press?" he asked.

"I'm not sure. What do you think?" she replied as they walked toward the door.

Alistair looked back over his shoulder and said, "What about Darrow and Campbell?"

Nora smiled. "It's perfect."

Printed in Great Britain
by Amazon

82f55b00-a3d5-4e9d-ae2d-bb69fcac7787R01